PRAISE FOR

Lovers at the Chameleon Club, Paris 1932
by Francine Prose

"So dazzlingly does Francine Prose re-create this seamy chapter of mid-century Paris that it's tempting to think of her as not a novelist but an editor who corralled all these people into a raucous work of history. . . . *C'est magnifique!*"
—*Washington Post*

"Sexy, illicit . . . the best stories come to us many times over, repeated until even their true parts bear the qualities of fiction. They're also the ones we can't possibly know all of. This powerful, perceptive book offers these truths, and—even better—a great story to shroud them."
—*Philadelphia Inquirer*

"The breadth, nerve, and intricacy of Francine Prose's big new novel should surprise even her most regular readers. A bona fide page-turner."
—*New York Times*

"A tour de force. . . . The result is fresh, layered, and nuanced. It's historical fiction done right and one of the finest accomplishments of this accomplished author. . . . The novel dazzles. With sure, intelligent narrative and elegant detail, Prose has crafted a story that honors its characters and a pivotal time in history."
—*Miami Herald*

"[E]xcellent novel. . . . With a deft and frequently scathing touch, Prose sends up nearly every literary type imaginable and then some."
—*San Francisco Chronicle*

"Prose exuberantly conjures up the romance of that unstable era . . . filled with felicitous imagery and sparkling period details."
—*Wall Street Journal*

"A master of the craft delivers a riveting period piece that probes the origins of evil."
—*O, The Oprah Magazine*

"Prose's novel pulses with the heartbeat of real life, brimming with colorful characters as artists (including, notably, Pablo Picasso), petty forgers, Nazis, and resistance fighters meet on the page. . . . It is a testament to Prose's considerable talent that she's able to execute such an ambitious work so flawlessly." —*Shelf Awareness*

"Prose does an impressive job crafting a plot in which each version of the story takes on its own dimensions and echoes—and the biggest question may be just which one of those narrators is the most outrageously unreliable." —*Tampa Bay Times*

"Engrossing. . . . The narrative twists and turns, circles back to add depth to previous scenes, at other times casts doubt on the reliability of a narrator, and occasionally calls into question the entire endeavor of historical fiction." —*Elle*

"*Lovers at the Chameleon Club* is a teeming social portrait, told through several peculiar voices—Lou's is not one of them—and made real by astonishingly authentic details. . . . Prose is versatile and fluid." —*Asheville Citizen-Time*s

"Many surefooted novelists have tried to embody Paris in its boozy, gender-bending, art-and-outrage pre-occupation golden age of the twenties and thirties before, but the ever-exceptional Prose succeeds in making the city alive by supplying it with a dissonant, avant-garde chorus of voices. " —*Interview*

"An ingenious excursion into the Parisian demimonde." —Maureen Corrigan, NPR.org

"The novel skillfully portrays the headiness of Parisian cafés, where artists and writers came together to talk and cadge free drinks, and the terror of the Nazi occupation. . . . Prose deftly demonstrates with a wink the self-seeking nature of memory and the way we portray our past." —*Publishers Weekly*

"Francine Prose, in a testament to her talents, has managed to create a wartime saga that is both original and epic." —*Daily Beast*

Lovers at the Chameleon Club, Paris 1932

A NOVEL

Francine Prose

HARPER ● PERENNIAL

NEW YORK ● LONDON ● TORONTO ● SYDNEY ● NEW DELHI ● AUCKLAND

Lovers

at the

Chameleon

Club,

Paris

1932

HARPER ● PERENNIAL

A hardcover edition of this book was published in 2014 by Harper-Collins Publishers.

P.S.™ is a trademark of HarperCollins Publishers.

HarperCollins books may be purchased for educational, business, or sales promotional use. For information please e-mail the Special Markets Department at SPsales@harpercollins.com.

FIRST HARPER PERENNIAL EDITION PUBLISHED 2015.

Designed by Fritz Metsch

The Library of Congress has catalogued the hardcover edition as follows:

Prose, Francine
  Lovers at the Chameleon Club, Paris 1932 : a novel / Francine Prose.
    pages cm
  Summary: "A richly imagined and stunningly inventive story of love, art, and betrayal in Paris of the 20's, 30's, and 40's"— Provided by publisher.
  ISBN 978-0-06-171378-1 (hardback) —ISBN 978-0-06-171380-4 (paperback) —ISBN 978-0-06-219913-3 (ebook) 1. Paris (France)—Social life and customs—20th century—Fiction. 2. World War, 1939–1945—France—Paris—Fiction. I. Title.
  PS3566.R68L68 2014
  813'.54—dc23
                                    2013048443
ISBN 978-0-06-171380-4 (pbk.)

15 16 17 18 19 ov/rrd 10 9 8 7 6 5 4 3 2 1

For Howie

Between the wolf in the tall grass and the wolf in the tall story there is a shimmering go-between.

—VLADIMIR NABOKOV

Part One

Paris
May 14, 1924

Dear parents,
Last night I visited a club in Montparnasse where the men dress as women and the women as men. Papa would have loved it. And Mama's face would have crinkled in that special smile she has for Papa's passion for everything French.

The place is called the Chameleon Club. It's a few steps down from the street. You need a password to get in. The password is: *Police! Open up!* The customers find it amusing.

A bar, a stage, a dance floor, leather banquettes, tables around the edges. A typical Paris nightclub, except for the clientele. But here's the most surprising thing: the owner is Hungarian. She calls herself Yvonne. She's tall and blond and dresses in red and has a weakness for sailors. She sings in that husky voice Papa adores, subdued and choked with tears. When she sang I heard Papa's phonograph, muffled and locked in his study.

Yvonne's song was about a woman whose sailor boyfriend has drowned at sea. I'd never heard a sadder song, not even from the gypsies. Yvonne sang with her eyes closed, one hand raking her hair. In her other hand, pressed to her forehead, she held an unlit cigarette.

She sang, I will never see him again. Never. Never again. A mournful arpeggio rippled from the out-of-tune piano while the tenor saxophone looped circles around the voice. The other musicians put down their instruments and sat back, watching Yvonne. It's over, she sang. All over.

I felt clammy and chilled to the bone, though the club was smoky and hot. I reached for my camera the way, as a boy, I used to reach for your hands. But I'd left it in my room. I was hoping to make a few friends before I asked to take pictures of bankers and diplomats whose wives might not know that their husbands go out dancing in high heels and dresses.

Even after a year in Paris, it took some getting used to. The hardest part was not staring. Or was I supposed to stare? Photographing these birds of paradise will be a challenge, don't you think?

I was trying to communicate—with nothing so obvious as a smile, but let's say a smile of the eyes—my admiration for the chic of women in tuxedos escorting women in evening gowns. As if these glorious peacocks cared what a penniless Hungarian artist thought of their fashion choices! Even Papa admits that the French have always had mixed feelings about anyone who hasn't lived in France since the Neanderthal Era, though here in Montparnasse they like anything exotic.

By the time Yvonne finished the second verse, everyone was in love with her. I completely forgot myself and wept along with the rest. The ocean knew where her sailor was. We have seen him, said the waves. He is sleeping with us. You will never kiss his lips or feel the weight of his body again.

Uncoiling from the knot into which the song had tied her, Yvonne stood and opened her arms. The audience exploded. She lit her cigarette, blew a long plume of smoke, and welcomed the crowd to her home, which she told them to think of as their home, a place where they could feel free to take off their trousers and spread their legs and relax. She said some other things in this vein, including some jokes that might have embarrassed Mama, though Papa would have taken them in the French good humor intended.

I felt that Yvonne was laughing at us for having been so sad, even though she'd made us sad with her song about the sailor. The crowd was mostly regulars. I could tell they knew what was coming.

The Chameleon's famous all-girl band struck up a jazzy fanfare, and a dozen men and women trotted onstage in skimpy sailor suits. What bizarre human pretzels they made, doing flips and backbends until their faces were staring forward from between their knees. Slithering over and under each other like a nest of snakes, they threw in plenty of crisp salutes and precision marching. A giantess in a navy officer's uniform lifted a tiny Asian girl in an orange kimono who sat cross-legged, like the Buddha, cupped in the giant's hands, and sang a lilting melody about first love and cherry blossoms.

When the show ended, the dancers strolled among us, their sailor hats upturned. I thought a million times about the sacrifices you are making. But didn't you raise me to believe that everyone should be paid for their labor? I dropped a few coins into the cap of a sailorette who gave me a saucy smile. When she turned and winked over her shoulder, I wondered if the sailorette might be a sailor.

The band was playing swing tunes. A few couples starting dancing. Men with men, women with women in monocles and mustaches. But if you're picturing something lewd, you couldn't be more wrong. They were as stiff as children at a grade-school dance. Leaning against the wall, Yvonne watched, smoking a cigarette.

Yvonne caught the eye of the headwaiter, a woman in black trousers and a butcher's apron: Fat Bernard, who also sings. Without a word being spoken, waiters swarmed the room. Soon they were practically sprinting with rattling trays of bottles and glasses. The sailors and sailorettes pitched in. The music got louder, the customers shouted to be heard.

Dancers drifted onto the floor. One couple did the tango, though the band was playing a foxtrot. Sweeter than sweet, crooned Fat Bernard in a syrupy tenor. Lovers kissed. An argument broke out when a dancer grabbed a brandy from a tray headed for someone's table.

I took advantage of the chaos to approach Yvonne. It was too noisy to talk. I pantomimed taking a picture. I shouted, I want to take your picture! At first she couldn't hear me, but her expression changed when she realized that I was speaking Hungarian.

You know how we love our language, how those Asiatic vowels whisk us back to the powdered heaven where our mama sang us to sleep. Ask us anything, in our mother tongue, and we will say yes. Yvonne stared, then told me to do something to myself that Mama shouldn't imagine.

Her refusal was doubly surprising. From my letters, you must have concluded that Parisians like having their pictures taken, especially French girls.

"Why not?" I yelled over the music. My voice squeaked like a boy's. Yvonne grabbed my elbow and dragged me over to a door she unlocked with a key that clanked from her spangled belt.

Don't worry. You can read on. I swear my only desire was to photograph Yvonne and her clientele. It was entirely about my art: the basis of your faith in me and your generous stipend, the tuition you are paying to what Papa calls the art school of life, which will soon decide if I have what it takes to be an artist.

Yvonne was right to say no. I would never have had the nerve to order a woman like that around for as long as it took to set up a shot in an "office" more like a courtesan's nest in Papa's Balzac novels. The cushions, the lacy garments tossed on the couch, the tangles of stockings and sandals exuded a flowery perfume, Yvonne's trademark gardenia.

She pointed at a table on which there was a terrarium. Its glass walls were beaded with moisture. Inside a miniature garden bloomed, complete with tiny topiary and classical Greek statues.

"Versailles!" I said. "What a coincidence! I photographed there last week."

Yvonne said, "Are you blind?"

Mama, Papa, you know better than anyone what a visual person I am, how I learned my colors before any child in our town, how I could always find the potato bugs in Mama's garden and was the first to spot Papa trudging home after a hard day of teaching. So you will understand how embarrassed I was by how long it took me to see the green chameleon standing perfectly still behind a thimble-size statue of Cupid shooting his bow and arrow.

This is why I have fallen so madly in love with this city! Despite the worries, despite my guilt for delaying Papa's retirement, despite the soul-destroying jobs, it still makes me dizzy with joy to see the word *Paris* in my handwriting at the top of this letter! Where else can one go to a cross-dressers' nightclub and meet a Hungarian chanteuse who keeps a lizard in the style of Marie Antoinette?

Yvonne scooped up the reptile and pressed it to her breast. The quivering chameleon gradually turned the scarlet of her dress.

She said, "Look how little Louis matches my heart."

Was this why Yvonne wore red? Was her club named after a lizard? I'd assumed it was a metaphor for her clients' changing skins. Could I write about this for the *Magyar Gazette*?

Yvonne said, "Louis is not my first. That was my Darius-the-Prince, my lizard killed by a jealous sailor. For Darius I created a tiny Persian garden." She sighed with what I hoped was grief for her departed pet and not impatience with a fool she wouldn't be bothering with, except for the chance to speak Hungarian.

She said, "One night I was working out front. My friend, a German admiral whose name you would know, let himself into my office and put my darling Darius on my paisley shawl. He died, exhausted by the strain of turning all those colors."

I looked at the shawl that Yvonne was careful to keep from touching her pet. There *are* no German admirals whose names I would know. Forgive my ignorance. How often has Papa said that a smart man never loses sight of what the military is doing?

Yvonne said, "My customers don't come here to get their pictures taken."

"I understand completely," I said. "Thank you and good night."

Our conversation had given me so much to think about, and I was so eager to start thinking about it that, on my way out, I barely saw the dancing couples. I noticed a man in a judge's wig dancing with a shirtless fellow with a striped necktie hanging down his back. I passed several bellhops of indeterminate gender and two men with corkscrew curls and bee-stung lips.

Don't worry, I thought. I'll be back. My camera will immortalize you in that delicious foxtrot. I grabbed a handful of business cards with the club's address and a sketch of a lizard.

I know your blood must run cold at the thought of supporting a son whose ambition is to photograph transvestites. How did he get that way? Where did he learn this? Certainly not in our town, where *art* means silhouettes of a peasant girl and boy kissing, in wooden clogs.

It had stopped raining, and I walked to save money and in the hope that exercise might help me sleep. The streets were strangely empty for such a beautiful spring night. The French have odd superstitions, like those tribes that lock up their daughters so the moon won't get them pregnant. The worn-thin soles of my shoes slapped against the cobblestones. There were more cats than one normally sees, except in the cemeteries. A huge black tom cat crossed my path. Don't bother knocking on wood. If *I* weren't superstitious, I would say I felt lucky.

Do you recall that Papa used to read me a story about a boy who wakes up to find that the Martians have kidnapped everyone but him? Were you aware that, night after night, I'd tiptoe to your door and stand there until I was sure you hadn't been stolen by spacemen? Did my insomnia start then, or had it already begun?

Entering the rue Delambre, I saw a guy flicking his cigarette lighter to help two friends picking a front-door lock. I considered turning around, but it seemed safer to keep walking. As I passed, one yelled at me, "My cousin forgot his key!"

If only I'd had my camera! Another joke. Ha-ha. Actually, I was wondering which of my friends I could pay to dress up like thieves and reenact the scene. I worked out the composition. I thought about locations. It was a welcome distraction from replaying my chat with Yvonne.

Eventually I spotted the sign outside my hotel, a milky flickering meant to discourage guests because every mouse hole is occupied by an artist who can't pay the rent, a situation in which I would be if not for your kindness. The night clerk was snoring in that alarming way of dying and snorting back to life. I woke him. There was a package for me. What a thrill to see my name in Mama's precious hand!

I tore open the parcel as I trudged up the stairs. Along with Papa's letter about the peasant woman dragging her sick pig into Uncle Ferenc's surgery until they explained that he only treats humans, I found a vial of yet another insomnia cure that Mama (against my advice) purchased from the chemist. Did I not write that I needed *socks*? Or did clairvoyant Mama know what I *really* needed?

Remember how you'd promise that my insomnia would disappear? That I would grow out of it, that everyone slept, sooner or later. That hasn't happened. The only difference is that I am no longer in my childhood room, lying in the dark, hating sleepers everywhere who take sleep for granted.

Paris is an insomniac's heaven. There is always something to photograph, something hidden in the shadows. One can see so much more in the darkness than in the light of day. How fortunate that my problem should have turned out to be a blessing, sending me out to take pictures in the velvet night. I know what you are thinking: if I'd stayed home, my insomnia would have gone away on its own.

Back in my room I turned on the "light" and crushed a gigantic water bug that rose to fight me on its hind legs. I opened the vial from Mama and, as directed, dripped four drops into a glass. Red roses bloomed in the water. I drank the potion, lay down, and tried not to think about my embarrassing chat with Yvonne. You can imagine how easy that was for your hypersensitive boy whose throat has been sore for a week.

I recalled Dr. Drumas, or was it Dr. Fiksor—anyway, one of those "experts" to whom you took me—advising me to calm my racing thoughts by giving myself a task. I decided to translate Yvonne's song from French into Hungarian. The vowels soothed me, and soon enough I imagined the scent of talcum, and it seemed to me I heard Mama singing me to sleep.

That's when I made the fatal mistake of trying to remember the tune. Not Mama's tune. Yvonne's. My eyes shot open, and I realized what my talk with Yvonne had meant. I'd failed to notice her lizard because I have no talent and will spend the rest of my life taking wedding and graduation portraits in our dusty, provincial town.

I decided to write you, to bring you, if only in spirit, into this mildew-ridden but otherwise delightful room. This letter is the only good thing to come out of another white night. I know I am spoiled to be young and free and in Paris and complaining because it's almost dawn and I am awake.

Don't worry, dear parents, I'll sleep. Yvonne's tune eludes me, but I plan to hypnotize myself with the arpeggio of waves against the shore. Your sailor is dead. Your sailor is dead. That should put me right out.

Don't forget to write. And if you get a chance, send socks. Silk, if possible. Black.

> Hug and kiss each other for me, your loving son,
> Gabor

From *The Devil Drives:*
The Life of Lou Villars

BY NATHALIE DUNOIS

Author's Preface: The Mystery of Evil

I FIRST HEARD the name of Louisianne Villars whispered when I was a girl, visiting my great-aunt Suzanne Dunois, the wife and later the widow of the photographer Gabor Tsenyi. I remember hearing Lou's name and feeling a chill, as if the winter wind had blown open the door of my great-aunt's enviable Paris apartment, an old-fashioned artist's studio with whitewashed walls, leaded windows, and a collection of modernist chairs that guests, especially children, were forbidden to sit on.

For many years, all I knew was that Lou Villars was the woman in a man's tuxedo in Gabor Tsenyi's photograph "Lovers at the Chameleon Club, Paris 1932." Doubtless my readers are familiar with the portrait of the lesbian couple, the pretty girl in the sparkly gown sitting beside her broad-shouldered lover with pomaded hair and a man's pinky ring on her finger. Both stare into the middle distance, with unfocused expressions, unreadable—or so I thought, until I began my labors on this book.

I'd never understood why Lou Villars's name had so lowered the temperature in the room until I attended a 1998 show of Tsenyi's work, at the Centre Pompidou, to which I'd traveled from Rouen, where I had been living and teaching for almost twenty years.

The wall text for "Lovers at the Chameleon Club" explained that the woman in the tuxedo was a French auto racer named Louisianne

Villars, who later spied for the Germans and collaborated with the Nazis. I shivered, just as I used to in my great-aunt's apartment. The chill lowered my defenses, and I caught a fever. A fever to understand. And so was planted the mutant seed that has grown into *The Devil Drives*, my message in a bottle.

Throughout this unexpectedly long and demanding project, it has been a source of profound exaltation and even deeper despair to immerse myself in the dramatic and terrible life of Lou Villars—a pioneer in the field of women's athletics, a woman who insisted on her right to live like a man, an international celebrity who knew everyone worth knowing, but who, because of the crimes of her later years, as well as her violent death, has completely vanished from the memory of the living. It has been a duty and a privilege to resurrect the spirit of a woman buried by a society determined that stories like hers go untold.

Even in the 1960s and 1970s, when young Frenchwomen like myself were exhuming every dead woman who ever picked up a paintbrush or conducted a science experiment or crossed a desert, everyone—even the female athletes entering the doors that Lou Villars kicked open for them decades before—even those women chose to let Lou remain forgotten in her unquiet, unmarked grave, possibly even a landfill.

The story of the writing of this book is a tale of unanswered doorbells and letters, of phone connections gone dead, of records mysteriously vanished from libraries and archives. And what other explanation can there be for these roadblocks and silences than our nation's sensitivity about its World War II record—its willful erasure of the shameful truth about our historic past?

How different this book would be if I'd had just one hour to sit down with Lou Villars and ask her, woman to woman, face-to-face: Who were you? What made you do what you did?

What I wouldn't give to speak with the people who knew her, to ask the living and the dead how one woman could have done so much harm: Gabor Tsenyi, whose art immortalized her; his patron, the baroness Lily de Rossignol, who hired Lou to race her family's cars; Eva "Yvonne" Nagy, who ran the famous Chameleon Club, where Lou got her start; Lionel Maine, the woman-hating blowhard American cult writer whom my feminist sisters have unsuccessfully tried to exorcise from the canon; the German auto racer Inge Wallser, who broke Lou's heart; Jean-Claude Bonnet, the infamous collaborator who destroyed so many innocent lives during the Occupation. Or for that matter my great-aunt, whose contact with Lou ranged from the friendly to the sadistic.

Having been denied that chance, having gotten no response to my requests for interviews, having encountered, time and again, the concerted efforts to remove Lou Villars from history and, one could say, *from the planet,* I have had to embroider a bit, fill in gaps, invent dialogue, make an occasional imaginative leap or informed guess about what my subject would have thought and felt.

I realize that this method is frowned upon in strict biographical circles. But by the conclusion of my research, and thanks to my education in literary and political theory, I have come to believe—and I hope my readers will agree—that I have partly answered the question of what drives, so to speak, a person like Lou Villars. Not that there ever was another person like Lou Villars. Without claiming too much for my little book, I will only say that I have tried to make my humble contribution to the literature on *the mystery of evil.*

How could someone, how could *anyone,* do what Lou Villars did? How did she sleep at night? Why would a French patriot who worshiped Joan of Arc tell the German army where the Maginot Line ended? And why, during the Occupation, would she work for the Gestapo?

Before I realized that my career would involve teaching the French classics to first-formers and correcting papers, I dreamed of becoming a philosopher, of spending my time contemplating (and perhaps solving) the great philosophical riddles. Though this has not been my destiny, I now find myself faced with a moral quandary worthy, in my opinion, of serious consideration:

Lou Villars did evil, unforgiveable things. So what does it say about the biographer, me, that researching and writing her life has given new meaning and purpose to my own less dramatic, less reprehensible existence?

Chapter One:
The Childhood and Early Education
of Lou Villars

SOON AFTER I began my research, I consulted several neurologists to ask if a relatively mild childhood head injury could affect a person's entire future. The doctors agreed to see me when I explained that I was a writer, a profession for which, in my experience, physicians feel an absurd respect. At first they seemed happy to chat, perhaps because, before this book took its toll, I was still young and reasonably attractive.

I'd begun to wonder if Lou had been permanently affected by a fall from a swing on which she had been playing with her older brother, Robert. I owe my knowledge of this incident to the late Dr. Frederic Pontuis, the Villars family physician, who kept a log of his house calls, and whose grandson Gilles was kind enough to share with me his grandfather's account of an emergency visit to the Villars home to tend the injured girl.

Later Lou would trace certain themes that ran through her life—her veneration for Joan of Arc, the insomnia, the spying—to this early mishap.

The neurologists I interviewed had never heard of Lou Villars, or pretended not to. And though her story was interesting, it took a while to tell, and I could see them getting restless by the time I got to the part about her racing career, her court case, and the Berlin Olympics. Inevitably they reminded me that they had patients to see.

Without hard scientific data to back up my theories, I will simply write what happened and trust my intelligent readers to draw their own conclusions.

It was a Sunday afternoon. Lou was ten years old. She and her brother Robert had gone out to play after lunch.

Henri Villars, Lou's father, had been a lieutenant colonel in the French army, a position from which he was removed (with a pension for life) for reasons that have gone unrecorded, perhaps due to the intercession of his fiancée's influential family. After his retirement from the military and his subsequent marriage to Clothilde Dupont, the daughter of local landowners, the couple, together with Henri's mother, moved to a country house, two hours northwest of Paris, where they lived, comfortably but not extravagantly, on Colonel Villars's pension and the annuity from Madame Villars's inheritance.

Their first son, Robert, was born in 1907, followed four years later by the arrival of a daughter, Louisianne, a name chosen by her patriotic father for its association with the French colony stolen by the Americans. Lou's birth disappointed Henri, who had hoped for a second son, especially because his older boy was already showing signs of a mental instability that today would likely be diagnosed as one of the more disabling and volatile forms of childhood autism.

Lou Villars always claimed that her struggle to dress in boys' clothes began as soon as she knew what clothes were. A governess was hired, the appropriately named Miss Frost, possibly the source of Lou's lifelong dislike of the British. From the start, Miss Frost made it clear that dressing Lou was not part of her job. That fell to the maids, who enjoyed a fight, even with a child.

On the Sunday Lou was injured, her parents, her grandmother, her governess, and her Uncle César were drinking coffee after lunch on the veranda while Lou and Robert played in the garden, on the swings. As Robert pushed Lou with all his might, the swing rose higher and higher. Another girl would have screamed from fear that it would fly all the way out and flip around, like Robert's yo-yo, which Lou planned to steal some night, leaving a doll in its place. Maybe Robert suspected this and was trying to kill her first. On the morning of Lou's most recent birthday, the gardener caught Robert sprinkling Lou's cake with the poison they used to kill pigeons.

Robert smelled of licorice. It had something to do with his illness. At night he shrieked like an owl. It wasn't a scream of pain or fear, so Lou was never frightened.

As she rose higher above the lawn, Lou thought it would be nice to fall and die, or else find out that her dream was real, that she could fly by flapping her arms like a bird. She was secretly building up her muscles by lifting the weights with which Robert exercised, under his nurse's supervision. She would kick Robert lightly as she flew over his head, then soar through the air until she touched down in a field where a crowd had gathered to applaud her landing.

The roar of the crowd turned out to be Robert's grunt as he gave the swing a powerful shove. Lou turned to watch him run away. Turning was a mistake. She fell, and slowly, slowly, the earth rose up to meet her. She expected darkness, but the world went black, flashed once, and stayed bright.

In the white magnesium glare she saw a woman, slightly buck-toothed but beautiful, cute as a baby rabbit. Her face was bruised, her head thrown back, she seemed to be howling in pain. The howling woman was no one she knew. But Lou recognized her from some-where, possibly from the future. She watched an owl swoop down a stone arcade. Then she saw a crowded stadium, then a room with many small tables, and a ladies' maid with a man's full beard setting out tablecloths.

When she opened her eyes again she was lying on the grass. Blood pooled in the creases of her palms. French blood, Papa would say.

She limped to the veranda and hid behind a hedge. Spying was always exciting, even though there was never anything to see, not counting the time she saw Uncle César back Miss Frost into a corner and dry his hands on her breasts. Lou thought breasts were disgust-ing, particularly Miss Frost's large, pillowy ones, so ill suited to her cold, ungenerous personality.

Mama and Papa, Grandma, Uncle César, and Miss Frost were sipping the last drops of demitasse under the pergola dripping with wisteria. Cake crumbs dusted the cloth. Robert wasn't allowed to eat cake. The doctors believed that sugar triggered his attacks.

During lunch, Grandma had remarked that her friend had just re-turned from the Olympics. A tiny American girl had taken the bronze medal in swimming.

Lou's parents had ladled up their sorrel soup. No one cared about sports except when the French teams won. Was there really a tiny American girl? Grandma made up stories. Maybe it was her way of saying that it was all right if the only thing Lou liked was playing rough games with her brother. It was sweet of Grandma, who was always gentle and kind, and who was sorry that Lou's parents despised her because she couldn't embroider or play the piano, and wanted to dress in trousers.

Now Lou edged closer to the patio, where the adults were discussing money, a conversation that excluded Miss Frost, who, as she often told Lou, was paid almost nothing. Raised in China, Miss Frost liked to talk about the brave British children whose eardrums were pierced with chopsticks during the Boxer Rebellion. Miss Frost read her *The Arabian Nights* and said the stories were evil, read her *Water Babies* and *Flower Fairies* and said those stories were good. It was through Miss Frost's eyes that Lou toured the trenches of the Ardennes, choked with the swollen corpses of boys who'd drowned in rivers of poison mustard. Miss Frost's little brother had been killed on the fields of Flanders. Miss Frost cried a great deal. She told Lou that no one had ever loved her, and no one ever would.

Was it not unprofessional to complain like this to a child? In all my years at the Lycée, I have never once broken down in the presence of a student, though certainly there have been moments when the stresses of my personal life compromised my ability to maintain a professional demeanor.

It took the grown-ups forever to notice Lou at the edge of the veranda. Lou was starting to feel sleepy. Her mother saw the blood on her dress before she saw the blood on her hands, her knees, and finally her face. As always, Lou had to brace herself against Mama's disappointment.

She could have said that Robert pushed her. But she would never betray her brother, not even under torture.

Grandma led Lou away, bandaged her wounds, and applied a tingly ointment that stopped her lip from bleeding. The doctor ordered Lou to remain awake for forty-eight hours. Her grandmother offered to stay up.

It was during this critical time that Lou first heard the story of Joan of Arc: how Saint Michael gave the shepherd girl her first suit of

armor, hammered and polished by the tears Christ shed for France—a
miracle that persuaded the generals to put her in charge of the army.
Lou's grandmother did voices; Lou especially liked the sheep bleat-
ing perfect French, begging Jeanne to kill them for meat to feed her
soldiers. Grandma told her how Jeanne was given the gift of tears, a
gift she never used until, in prison, she was forced to wear a dress that
her falling tears turned into armor; how the fire refused to burn her
until a sorcerer summoned the devils who stoked the flames of hell,
at which point Jeanne's heart turned into a dove that flew out of her
mouth and pecked out the eyes of the British judges.

Each time her grandmother finished, Lou made her begin again.
She loved hearing the saint call out for Jesus. It was thrilling and
hilarious to hear the blinded judges groping in the dark, yelling,
Help! Help! in English. The longer she and Grandma went without
sleep, the harder they cried when the saint was killed. Staying awake
seemed like a gift until, as so often happens with gifts, it became a
burden.

Soon after Lou's fall from the swing, she was sent to school in the
north. Her papa bought a red Hispano-Suiza sedan and learned to
drive for the trip.

Grandma sobbed as Lou and her father drove off. But everyone
else was brave. As Henri and Lou headed into the hot September
wind, the sunflowers turned to watch. Rows of plane trees rushed at
them, then changed their minds at the last moment. Papa pointed into
the distance, and a cathedral flew past, its spire pointed heavenward,
poking God so he wouldn't forget the tiny town huddled beneath it.

"Our beautiful country," her father said. "Our precious wounded
homeland."

Lou didn't ask what the wound was. She didn't want to spoil Papa's
good mood.

One can only speculate about whether Lou's career choice was a
response to Henri Villars having been such a terrible driver. Luckily
there were only a few cars on the road. Henri ran over a cat and once
nearly hit a child whose mother snatched it up just in time. All the way

to Brittany, Lou imagined her father suffering a fatal, no, a *near*-fatal heart attack that would require her to take the wheel and drive him to a doctor.

To Lou, the Convent of Saint Bridget seemed like a fairy-tale castle populated by princesses disguised in brown robes, as British nuns. Lou tensed when she heard their accents, but their encouraging voices were nothing like the jabs of speech with which Miss Frost inflicted information. But why was Papa, who loved everything French, sending her to an English school?

Sister Francis introduced herself as the sports instructor, then waited for them to recover from the shock of how tall she was. Ducking beneath the low stone arches, the nun led them through the cloisters and onto the playing fields. Lou saw girls dancing around a pole, holding ribbons that never got tangled. Older girls with curved sticks chased a wooden ball across a grassy lawn. Lou might as well have been watching them take lessons in levitation. The girls wore shirts and leather neckties under their V-necked sweaters.

When Sister Francis asked if Lou played sports, Lou nodded, then shot her father a warning look. He would never contradict her and anyway seemed distracted, resigning himself to God's decision to send him two strange children. Though it was also possible that he was thinking about his car.

When he left they kissed cheeks, and then, surprising the nuns and themselves, shook hands like two friendly fellows. Lou told him to drive carefully.

"I always do," Henri said.

Though Henri and Clothilde Villars failed Lou in every way in which parents can fail their children, we must give them credit for transcending their prejudices and sending Lou to a place where they thought she might be happy.

Life at school was better than it had been at home. Lou knew how little to ask for and more or less what was expected. Miss Frost had told her that convent girls slept naked on the stone floor, and that the night nuns wore one shoe to make it sound as if they were

approaching half as fast as they were, so the bad girls had only half
the time to stop whispering before the nuns kicked them and pulled
their hair. For a few nights Lou waited in fear, but nothing like that
happened. In any case she hadn't been whispering. She had no one to
whisper to.

Lou smiled and nodded even when she had no idea what was being
said. She did what her teachers told her. Obedience was a deliverance,
a privilege, and a relief. The uniforms were much better than the lace
frocks the maids at home insisted on, the maids who had so revoltingly
told her how babies were made in the process of explaining why she
couldn't dress like her brother. Sometimes Lou missed Robert. She
missed his scent of licorice, the roll of fat around his belly, the funny
way he tilted his head, as if he were listening to voices: the voices that
told him to kill her.

She complained because the other girls did, but there was nothing
she didn't like: washing her hair in icy water, the bread crusts abrading
her gums. The crisp impersonal sting of Sister Luke's cane said, You
are real. You exist. She loved the concept of mortification, which the
girls were warned against. It was the first time she'd heard it suggested
that the body mattered, that it wasn't merely the filthy birdcage of the
soul but the shining temple of the Holy Ghost. The priest at home
hadn't known about the body coming from God or had decided to
keep it secret.

Lou had spent her life so far being told not to run. But now Sister
Francis ordered her to hurry and join the girls sprinting around the
track. She'd run to escape from her brother but never to get ahead. As
she approached, the others sped up, their faces contorted with the fury
she would have felt for a new girl who came out of nowhere and won.

She had no friends, but she wasn't lonely. All night she lay in the
dark, listening to the fluttery breath of the living girls and the rattling
sighs of the dead ones. The snoring of the night nun was the all-clear
signal freeing her to slip out of bed.

There was plenty to see in the convent when everyone was asleep.
The leaves on the trees in the cloister garden spread like furry
splotches of ink. The moonlight found the dying Christ and striped

his bony knees across the chapel wall. Twice she saw Sister Luke knock on Sister Benedict's door, then wait, then knock harder, then go away in tears.

Miss Frost had promised to write her, but she sent only one curt note saying that Lou's parents had fired her without a cent of severance pay. The first winter Lou was away, Papa wrote that her grandma had died. In Mama's next letter she explained that they had put Robert in a place for boys like him, a hospital in Paris.

One night, she watched an owl fly down the arched arcade, chasing a mouse that skittered into a crack in the stone wall. As the owl hid in the cornice, she heard the squeaky prayers of the mouse. The owl swooped down and snatched up the mouse and flew away to behead it.

The door to Sister Francis's cell was open just wide enough for Lou to see a slice of her back as she mumbled over her prayer book.

The owl reappeared in the cloister, and Lou followed it, thinking of a holy card she'd gotten from Grandma and cherished until Robert threw it into the fire. On the card a trio of butterflies led two pretty blond children along a flowered path. The Good Shepherd walked behind them, looming over them like a giant trained bear. Lou and Robert were the children. The butterflies were owls. God wasn't gently guiding them but pushing them over a cliff.

The night nun found Lou in the cloister and took her to the Mother Superior's office. Lou dragged her feet like a prisoner en route to the guillotine. The headmistress didn't seem angry as she asked why Lou wasn't asleep. Lou replied that she'd been awake since she got to the convent.

It turned out that the headmistress was an insomniac, too. We are, she said, a special breed, chosen to keep watch for the comet that will destroy us. She said: the angels sing to us when no one else is listening. She said: the holiest saints lived their whole lives without sleep. She said: we alone remember the night before God ladled us out of the bubbling stew of chaos. She said: Adam only fell asleep once, and look what happened to him. She recommended meditating on the Last Supper, moving down the table from apostle to apostle, recalling every detail about each disciple. In this way, sleep will sneak up on you before you get to Judas, whose betrayal will wake you, and you will have to start over.

Lou thanked her and went to bed, knowing that it wouldn't help her sleep to imagine thirteen bearded men in robes eating lamb at a table. She pictured the owl, her father's car, the swing in her parents' garden, her mother's demitasse cups. The images cascaded and fell like a deck of cards. She concentrated on remembering her brother's licorice smell. Confusion made her sleepy, or else it was a sign that sleep had sneaked up and overtaken her before she knew it.

Anyway, she could sleep during class, doze off and dream about the hands on Sister Francis's stopwatch, dreams punctuated by the girlish squeal that the sports nun made when Lou ran the track faster than she had the day before. Lou was jolted awake by fear that she would be called on and mocked, though the teaching nuns never mocked her and she was hardly ever called on.

She would break yesterday's record and beat the teams from the other schools. Her teachers would be proud of her and allow her to stay. The other girls would respect her despite her low marks in class. She would see the admiring faces she recognized from her dreams of landing the airplane she piloted by flapping her arms. Girls would creep into her bed at night like they crawled into each other's.

The girls talked about their bodies. They made growing up into a race. When two nubbins popped out on her chest, Lou's first response was relief at not having been the last to get them. But once she had breasts she didn't want them. They grew and became unwieldy. She tore a bandage from a pillowcase and bound her breasts so they didn't bounce when she ran.

She was slow to start bleeding. She hated it when she did. The harder and longer she exercised, the less regularly it happened.

One day a ferocious Irish girl jumped Lou in the washroom and pushed her up against a wall. Lou was stocky and solid, but the Irish girl was twice her size. She had been one of the runners whom Lou outran, early on. Lou fought back, protecting herself, but she was distracted by the muscles squirming inside the arms that pinned her down. When the Irish girl lowered her head and butted Lou in the stomach, a peculiar melting sensation traveled up the length of her thighs, a warmth she hadn't felt since Robert nearly killed her, on the swing.

As the two girls grappled, a crowd of students gathered. How strange that Lou could be fighting for her life and still hear what they were saying: Was it true that Sister Francis had a penis? How would Lou know what Sister Francis had beneath her robe? Was this what these girls thought about, in this holy place?

As she ground her fist into the Irish girl's eye, the minutes slowed, and the screams of the girls recalled the giggles of Mama's maids explaining why she couldn't wear Robert's trousers. Lou used to enjoy fighting with Robert. It was like catching a fish in your hands, which she'd once seen him do.

Luckily, it was Sister Francis who broke up the fight. Sister Francis washed the Irish girl's face and sent her to her bed without supper, then wiped Lou's eyes with the handkerchief she kept tucked in the sleeve of her scratchy brown robe.

It was chilly. Late autumn. The corridor smelled of mold and rotting leaves.

The nun led her down a flight of stairs. She unlocked a door and turned on a lamp, illuminating a large room, bare except for several huge contraptions for extracting confessions under torture: metal racks and leather horses, pulleys and pedals and bars, a rope ladder strung against the wall, iron balls and wooden clubs. Sister Francis smiled like a wolf. Fear sizzled up and down Lou's spine until she understood what she was seeing.

From then on, in the afternoons, she ran the track, jumped hurdles, and practiced with the teams. Then she and Sister Francis went down to the makeshift *salon de sport* and, in the unheated basement gym, built Lou's strength and endurance. And so began one of the blessed, brief intervals in the life of Lou Villars when she could enjoy the gifts God gave her to compensate for what was denied her, and for what would be dangled in front of her and then cruelly taken away.

Dispatch to the *Magyar Gazette*

PARIS, AUGUST 23, 1925

A Hero in Chains

WITH HIS EYE patch and mane of ermine hair streaked with black, Prince Gyorgi Perenyi carries himself like a true Hungarian hero disguised in the rags of a prisoner of the French state.

Accused of masterminding a plot to flood the market with counterfeit francs, Perenyi is languishing in a Paris jail. In the worst miscarriage of justice since the Dreyfus affair, the authorities have charged him with trying to destabilize the French economy. But why would a man with the prince's resources and reputation stoop to such a scheme, even if his fortune has been decimated by the French under the hateful recent treaty that parceled out our homeland?

The prince insists he has nothing against the French, that his soul has been purified by love for his native land. In an exclusive interview he told this reporter, "When this misunderstanding is resolved, I will return to my castle to see the newborn cub fathered by the bear that was my childhood pet. For generations my family has been present for the birth of the bears, but I will not be so fortunate. I must accept my fate."

Making sure no guards are listening, he added, "I am an artist. The bank notes were my art. I intended to paper the walls of my mistress's bedroom. The pain of being an artist is worse than the pain of losing an eye in battle. I am one of the few who have suffered both and can compare them."

So my visit with this artist-patriot ended, and our hero returned to his cell with such composure and courage that one couldn't help seeing him as the latest in the line of heroic Hungarian martyrs.

Dear parents,

I'm enclosing my latest story for the *Magyar Gazette*, with my original ending. The cheapskate editors, paying me by the word, cut my piece at "native land" and refused to print (or pay for) the final paragraphs, my favorites. I admit I went overboard about the martyrs and the Dreyfus affair, about which our country is still divided. And the information about the mistress and the counterfeit bank notes is not precisely what they want in a Hungarian family paper.

Promise me that you will burn this letter as soon as you read it. But who else can I confide in?

I invented the story. The interview never took place, because the prince has been put under twenty-four-hour surveillance. He'd been caught smuggling out a fortune (in counterfeit francs) in a botched escape attempt.

I did attend the trial's final session. I got a good look at the man, who is exactly as I described. And I feel sure that he would have said the words I took the liberty of putting into his mouth. I am especially proud of the passages about the bear cubs and the wallpaper.

I suppose I am boasting, though underneath Mama's chuckle, I can hear her disapproval of any lie, however small. While Papa must be shaking his head at my pandering to the Francophobia that grips our homeland, a sentiment responsible for so much heartbreak for Papa, who wanted to be an artist in Paris but, in order to support Mama and me, was forced to teach the sons of the provincial bourgeoisie. How grateful I am to live out the dream that was denied him!

I have included the "interview" as an example of what I am doing to survive. I suppose I would be unhappier if this trash were closer to my art, if I were a writer, prostituting my talent, like my American friend Lionel Maine: the most honest, eloquent, passionately life-loving egomaniac I have ever met. Like me, he is in love with Paris, and Paris loves us both: the rare romantic triangle that inspires no rivalry or resentment. When he joins me in my nighttime rambles through the city, I feel that he is trying to put into words what I am trying to show in my photos. It makes me doubly grateful that my gift is for the visual image and not the written word as I crank out jingoist trash for the *Magyar Gazette*.

I hope you will not misinterpret this letter as a complaint about the generous allowance you continue to send. I feel nothing but love and gratitude as I kiss you,

Gabor

PS. To protect your privacy and mine, I have adopted a pen name: Tsenyi. That it means *genius* is an immodest little joke that may amuse our fellow Hungarians.

From *The Devil Drives:*
The Life of Lou Villars
BY NATHALIE DUNOIS

Chapter Two: A Stranger Arrives

ONE MORNING, A tall man with a cane arrived at the convent. The man had thin, fox-colored hair and a wispy, ragged beard. His gray eyes, behind wire-rimmed spectacles, were hooded but alert. Word spread that the visitor was Sister Francis's brother. The girls watched, as if at a magic show, as the stranger flipped a lever that turned his cane into a stool on a tripod with pointed legs. He stabbed his chair into the ground beside the hockey field and sat down.

Lou knew he was watching her. She made one goal after another until the other team quit and stalked off the field, inspiring Sister Francis's familiar lecture about sportsmanship being the love of Christ in practice. Then her brother caught her eye, and she said, "Class dismissed."

A short time later, Lou was working in the gym with Sister Francis, scrambling down the rope ladder when she looked over her shoulder and saw that the brother had set up his cane-stool and was sitting there, watching Lou. She began to tremble.

Sister Francis waved her over. "Mademoiselle Villars," she said. "This is my brother. Dr. Marcellus Hadrian Loomis."

Dr. Loomis shook Lou's hand and motioned for her to sit on the balance beam. He joined his hands in front of his chest, hunching his shoulders and interweaving his fingers so his elbows flapped against his sides as he spoke in slow, ungrammatical French.

"Officially, I am a doctor, but in fact I am a researcher. Years ago I heard a colleague say, in a public forum, that the female body was not designed to bear more weight than a baby or a frying pan. Never both at once. Our girls must be crated and packed away, like fragile porcelain teacups, until they are ready to marry and reproduce. But that didn't sound correct. I began to look into the subject, to conduct my own studies, and do you know what I learned?"

Lou shook her head no, as did Sister Francis, though the nun must have heard this before.

"Our madhouses are full of girls whose minds have been twisted and shattered by society's refusal to help their blood reach their brains. The TB wards are crowded with girls hemorrhaging to death for lack of exercise and fresh air. Our slums seethe with the physical slackness that leads to decadence and Bolshevism, all because of insufficient oxygen and physical training."

He thrust his folded newspaper at Lou, pointing to the front-page photo of a man in a helmet and goggles. "Do you recognize this man?"

"Monsieur Lindbergh," Lou said. He was a hero among the girls.

"Very good," said the doctor. "I am not a gambling man, but I'll bet that, when you were a child, you imagined you could fly."

Lou gripped the balance bar. What other secrets did he know?

He said, "If you are willing to work really hard, my sister and I can help you conquer gravity without leaving the ground. Are you willing to work hard?"

"Yes," Lou said. "I am." Finally, someone had asked.

Dr. Loomis moved into a cottage near the convent and attended every training session, race, and game. Sister Francis surrendered the stopwatch, and now he was the one who called out the times and told Lou how to move, how to breathe, where to put her knees and elbows. It was pleasant to discuss her body in that distanced way, as if she were a new machine they were perfecting. Dr. Loomis said that athletics were the hope of the future, along with speed, the automobile, and loyalty to one's country.

One afternoon, the literature nun was reading aloud from Racine when Lou was called out of class. She found Dr. Loomis and Sister Francis waiting for her in the Mother Superior's office. She assumed she'd done something wrong. But Sister Francis and her brother were telling the Mother Superior that Lou's achievements would reflect well on the school and attract talented students whose enlightened parents shared the convent's modern ideas about education. They'd come to persuade the headmistress that everything should be done to encourage and nurture Lou's gifts.

Lou's bed was moved beside the window, which Dr. Loomis insisted be kept open. When the others complained about the draft, she got a room of her own. Special shoes were ordered so her feet could grow. Her ankles got their own regimen of hot water baths and massages from Sister Francis. She ate food that was different from what the others ate: raw vegetables, whole grains, stewed fruit, but no meat and not the sweets that the girls enjoyed on birthdays. She didn't miss the puddings and cookies, especially when Dr. Loomis bought her blood oranges from Sicily in the dead of winter.

She spent hours on the stationary bicycle they called the Gymnasticon. Her calves and thighs became muscular and hard, and it seemed to Lou that an alien, stronger self was being born inside her. In the evenings she paced the corridors with a medical textbook balanced on her head. Once, when the book fell, the circulatory system tore loose and skittered across the pavement. Dr. Loomis said it was important to excel at a range of sports; each would develop a different set of reflexes and muscles. She was only mildly surprised when he produced a punching bag and announced that her training would now include the skills required to become a champion boxer. Flailing away at the bag, she thought dreamily of Robert.

They began to travel to distant parts of France, in steamy second-class compartments smelling of garlic sausage and soggy diapers. Lou took part in athletic contests and attended meetings of local women's sports clubs, groups of female athletes whose eyes blazed with the light of a holy mission and who admired Lou's talent and hard work. She kept in touch, by mail, with a discus thrower from the Auvergne, a high jumper from Provence.

One night she tiptoed through the convent and, lurking in the doorway of Sister Francis's room, spied on the nun and her brother. They were speaking English. The only words Lou understood were *Lou* and *the Olympics.*

Soon after, Lou was informed that they were going to Paris, with the Mother Superior's blessing and with the consent of her parents, who sent word that they wished Lou all the best.

From *Make Yourself New*

BY LIONEL MAINE

Reflections on Self-Pity, Paris, October 1928

AMONG THE DEMONS that taunt a writer before he can open a vein and write in his own blood are the devils that whisper: Are you brave enough to tell the truth? Crazy enough to reveal the magic secret that will lose its power if even one other person finds out?

Let's say you have discovered a cure for the garden-variety psychic ills that plague mankind: guilt, anxiety, envy, dread, and, above all, self-pity. And let's say the cure is: Paris. Let's say you put this discovery in a book that, by some miracle, is read by millions worldwide. And some fraction of its readers decide to do what you did: sell everything, cut every tie, move to Paris with nothing but a good pair of walking shoes and the will to survive on cigarette smoke, wine, sex, music, poetry, and moonlight on the Seine. Pretty soon you can't turn a corner without running into a crowd of Americans who have followed you here under the illusion that the City of Light is an asylum for Cincinnati neurotics.

But I am determined to write a new kind of book. And so, despite the likelihood that I am sealing my own doom, I will shout it in uppercase letters: MAKE YOURSELF NEW IN PARIS!

Self-pity makes it easy to write, thanks to the diabolic voice hissing in my ear: You can say whatever you want. No one will ever read it. You can write "Come to Paris and look me up and I'll lend you fifty francs" without fear of one person taking you up on your offer.

I was in a dark mood after I'd walked my girlfriend Suzanne home and kissed her good night at the door of the dump she shares with her widowed mother. My giant hard-on didn't help. In fact it tipped me forward into the rabbit hole of self-loathing, poverty, unemployment, the depths of being unpublished, balding, ten years older than my friends at an age when ten years makes a big difference, evicted from my hotel (again!) for nonpayment of rent. The shame of being thirty and not having a room to which I can bring the woman I love. Okay, thirty-four. By the time he was my age, Jesus had been dead for a year.

And yet, and yet . . . the truth is: I have never felt so alive! Why? Because I am in Paris! I could be back in Jersey City at the copy desk, calling the mayor's office to make sure that his youngest son is really nicknamed Jimmy Jim. And at the end of another hellish week, I could be handing over my teensy paycheck to Beedie and baby Walt.

Those poor slobs in my former office are the ones I should pity! Except that I am apparently so depraved that I can work up a cold sweat of grief for being a bastard who ditches his wife and kid and takes off for France. Poor me! Fortunately, Beedie has remarried a bootlegger too alcoholic to notice the pennies she skims off the grocery money and sends when my desperate pleas make her wonder how she's going to tell little Walt that Mommy let Daddy starve to death, in a foreign country.

If I believed in God, or in anything except my talent, my heart, and my cock, the first thing I would thank the deity for is my survival instinct. When gloom sets in, I know enough to start walking. I inhale the scent of a Paris night, rotten vegetables, horse manure, sewers, cigars, and flowers. The hot breath of Napoleon, the panic of Marie Antoinette, the faint breeze stirred by the guillotine blade dropping on Danton's neck. Lavishing my attention on every overbred pooch, I gladden its owner's soul with my admiration for Fifi or Rex, whose need has dragged its adoring slave into the luridly lovely night.

Tonight I passed two farm boys lying on top of a cart heaped with cabbages, under a streetlamp, both masturbating like crazy, not giving a damn who saw. What a city! Paradise! My hard-on had subsided, and it cleared my mind. How could I have wasted one instant of this stupendous night on anything but gratitude and pleasure?

As gravity pulled me through the alleys twisting down from Montmartre, every streetlight was the one at the end of the tunnel. So what if I'm a useless middle-aged bum? A phony and a poseur. Who cares if no one reads my work? I can write what I want and rip the ghastly wig off the beautiful bald head of truth!

At the bottom of the rue Blanche a group of sewer repairmen were sitting, smoking and belching on top of a smoking, belching machine. Would I like a swig of champagne? They were celebrating a birthday.

"*Bonsoir*," I said in my best French.

"Charlie Chapleen!" they said. "Hot dog!'

I asked if they'd be here tomorrow night. I said, "I have a photographer friend who would love to take your picture."

The birthday boy said, "Our sincere apologies. But that is unlikely. We will be wherever our fair city suffers a painful blockage."

In Paris even the sewers are maintained by poets! After a few gulps of champagne, I was feeling even better. I crossed the sparkling river, floated through St. Germain, then cut through the Luxembourg Gardens, which at that hour is usually empty, except for the usual perverts draped around the fence waiting for someone who wants to beat them or be beaten. But tonight the park was crawling with police. Some poor soul had been found dead on the tree-lined gravel path where spoiled French brats go for pony rides.

One cop mumbled that a clochard had died from exposure and starvation.

News like that means one thing to your average citizen, and quite another to a starving writer with no idea where he'll be sleeping. I had to be very careful not to see my own grim future in this unfortunate stranger's.

I also had to be careful not to get arrested. I'd had a few run-ins with the French police. The last time was when my friend Gabor, the crazy Hungarian genius photographer, bribed me and two other guys (with a decent Bordeaux) to dress in cheap suits and caps and pretend to be thieves picking a lock so he could take our picture. You can imagine how that played out, explaining that to the law, Gabor, in his awful paprika-spiced French and me spewing the raw unfiltered patois of Jersey City. By that point the cretinous gendarmes had naturally concluded that we were enemy spies sent to photograph top-secret installations.

We'd probably be on Devil's Island, breaking rocks right now, if not for the intervention of Gabor's friend the baroness Lily de Rossignol, who is not only rich and generous but also an aristocrat—or married to one, at least. I have yet to meet her. Why doesn't it surprise me that Gabor has kept us apart? When I finally set eyes on this saint of art, I'll tell her how grateful I am.

As I passed the dead man in the park, the memory of that incident prevented me from approaching the cops and announcing, "Officers, that corpse is family! *Mon semblable, mon frère!*" I knew how I would answer if they asked how we were related: I too have come to Paris to starve and collapse in the street, to say adieu to this alley of trees pointing straight at the God who, if he existed, would be deaf to my prayer. In the morning I too will be found, preferably by one of the pony-riding brats' more attractive nannies. And I will be buried in Paris, if not with Victor Hugo's pomp and circumstance, then at least tossed into a pauper's grave, like Mozart.

Luckily, Suzanne and I had run out of money before I'd drunk enough to say that to a cop. I was sufficiently sober to weigh a night in prison against a night on the floor of whichever friend I could persuade to open his door. Fortunately, I was in Paris, where according to Suzanne, a gray sky is a mackerel sky, where each falling leaf skips across the pavement with a sexy smoker's crackle. At least I wasn't in Jersey, drinking myself blind.

Who knows if the dead man wanted to live? I only know that I do. I will sell my blood to the hospital and rent my brain to ghouls. Future critics will trace my claw marks down the walls of the abyss. Did my dead "brother" in the park have strategies like mine? Did he have my inner resources, my will to scramble up from the depths?

I have my tricks. Gabor and I entertain ourselves with a game we call "free drinks on the dead poets." He and I walk into a café, preferably one named after a French philosopher or playwright. We fake a heated argument until at last I shout, "I don't care what you say! The best poets have always been French!" Soon our table is surrounded by literary jingoists to whom I preach about the greatness of the French poets, especially those who died young.

I could do the death of Rimbaud with half my cerebral cortex missing, but I put my whole heart into it, quoting *A Season in Hell*, daring someone to tell me that it isn't sheer brilliance, raving about the poor bastard's short life, the marathon walking, the affair with Verlaine. Though, depending on the crowd, I sometimes say the *friendship* with Verlaine. The Abyssinian voyage, the gun running, the cancer, the gangrene or whatever, the amputated leg.

That so many of my listeners already know the story tells you something about the French. How many barflies in Camden are equally well versed in the life of Walt Whitman? The French buy round after round to hear the American cowboy rave about their martyred poet-saint. The hotter Abyssinia sounds, the thirstier they get.

But even the looniest patriots have a limited interest in the madness of a teenage homosexual, however poetically gifted. The crowd returns to whatever they were doing before: gossiping, flirting, insulting each other. I forget what people do when they can pay for their own drinks. Meanwhile Gabor and I split what's left in the glasses that our new friends have left on our table.

That was how I met the beautiful, freckle-faced blonde with the ever-so-slightly rabbity teeth who turned out to be Suzanne. She stayed at our table after the others left. Sobbing her eyes out. I was afraid to ask what was wrong. I didn't want to hear about the Rimbaud-esque fiancé who died of the shaking chills in some fly-infested shithole in the Congo or the Suez.

Any male who pretends not to hate women's tears is a coward, a liar, a traitor to his sex. Trust me, ladies, we fear your tears more than your vaginas, which can't bite us unless we knock and ask to be admitted. Women's tears can drip on us and dissolve us like acid. More poisonous than venom, tears are the mustard gas in the trenches of the war of women against men.

Still, there was the undeniable fact of her beauty. She gave off that whiff of animal life that no man can resist, in this case a hint of the baby rabbit that might, with proper encouragement, become a dirty bunny in bed. I offered her the remnants of some stranger's beer. I mumbled in my fractured French, What was wrong? Could I help? She answered in flawless English.

She was crying for Rimbaud. That poor boy, the pain, the delirium, the loneliness, the death. She told my story back to me with twice as much feeling as I'd put in. With twice as much as I feel for myself at three o'clock in the morning! The lonely hospital ward in Marseille! The final hallucinations!

I said, "What final hallucinations?"

She said, "He imagined he was writing."

I said, "What's your name?"

With that, we introduced ourselves, which is usually the next step after the lady has had a good cry on your shoulder.

"Suzanne Dunois." She shook my hand.

"Lionel Maine," I said.

"Gabor Tsenyi," said my friend. I'd forgotten he was there. I gave him a look in the silent language that men have spoken since the first caveman muscled his pals out of the way and dragged the first cavewoman home to his lair. Mumbling some excuse, Gabor got up from the table and left.

Suzanne told me she'd lived with her mother since her father was killed in the war. She'd been a toddler, she hardly remembered him, yet even now the smoke of certain cigars could bring on floods of tears. I prayed that no one in the café was smoking that brand. She'd wanted to go to a university, but there was no money.

I complimented her English, and she told me she had an uncanny gift for learning foreign languages. She supported herself and her mother by teaching French at a school for foreigners and supplemented her salary by modeling at an art school. Somehow she and Mama got by, except when both the language and art schools forgot to pay her, which happened more often than I might think. She said my French was excellent, but I could use a few lessons.

Let me digress a moment to talk about beginnings. How much simpler life would be if we were wise enough to stop at the first blush of romance, the start of a business transaction or a casual friendship. If we knew enough to pause and think: this is as good as it gets. Everything will go downhill from this moment on. So once again our instincts are the opposite of what they should be, propelling us forward exactly when they should be holding us back.

In that first conversation, Suzanne revealed everything: her intensity, her empathy, the depths of her compassion. From the way she carried on, you would have thought Rimbaud was her dead brother. It is the rarest of qualities: to feel something—anything— for someone beside yourself. And in my experience it is rarer still to have empathy for people you don't know. Alone among her compatriots, Suzanne can imagine what it is like to suffer the tragedy of not being French. It makes her a popular teacher among the foreignborn. Had I not been blinded by desire, I might have seen that there would be moments when all that gushing sympathy could be a pain in the ass, that her impulsiveness and her strong emotions would conspire against me.

On our first date, I blew my last centimes on tickets to *The Passion of Joan of Arc*. That Dreyer's film was so popular says volumes about the demented French intellectuals' idea of entertainment. Night after night the theater was packed with people paying to watch a jury of thugs torment a beautiful girl who resembled one of the prettier butches from the Chameleon Club.

First we watched a newsreel about the signing of the Kellogg-Briand Pact. Rows of suits in top hats gathered around a long table. The brightest bulb in the ballroom was the photographer's flash. Another American genius had persuaded his fellow diplomats to sign a treaty making war illegal!

"Ha-ha," I said. "That's hilarious." Maybe a little too loud. Suzanne scowled. I remembered that her papa had died in the trenches.

"I love you," I whispered in her ear. A lemony perfume rose from her neck.

The French still want to believe in peace. I envy fanatics. But they scare me. So why was I sitting through a film about a heroine who chooses to be burned alive rather than even pretend to give up her goofy religious convictions? When she fainted in the torture chamber, the crowd stamped and shouted like spectators at a bullfight.

No matter. From the very first frame I recognized the hand of a master. Even so, a part of me—the male part—thought, Can't someone make her stop crying? The film would have lasted five minutes if she could have answered a simple question without her eyeballs jiggling in their sockets. When the judges asked Joan how old she was, and she counted nineteen on her fingers, Suzanne lost it. The guy in front of us turned around. She was projectile weeping all over the back of his neck. Clearly, I hadn't thought this through. We should have gone to see Buster Keaton. That Joan of Arc was a soldier in a war in which thousands were killed was something you might not have deduced from this film. There will always be wars, no matter how many treaties are signed.

I understand that you, my reader, should I have a reader, haven't stuck around all this time to hear me pontificate on the inevitability of war. You want to know how the date went, and . . . let's get to the point. Did I fuck her?

Lest anyone imagine that Suzanne's excessive emotionalism was a problem, let him also imagine what it's like to have sex (which we finally did, after a somewhat awkward courtship) with a woman who not only feels twice what a normal woman feels, but also every sensation that you are feeling too. It turned out she would try anything and had a few ideas of her own. I didn't ask where she'd got those ideas, or if she'd just figured them out. We went at it till the sheets were so wet that we wrung them out in the sink, then groped each other and, laughing, lost our balance and fell back on the bare mattress.

In bed, Suzanne was the greedy beast most men can only dream of. Out of bed she was the soul of patience, an angel of reassurance. She read and reread my work, she had total faith in my talent, she knew I'd be famous someday. So many fans would follow me here that we would have to leave Paris.

Reader, if you were beside me, you would hear me groan out loud, stabbed by the pain of remembering the time when Suzanne and I were in love. Belief can be very seductive if what the person believes in is you.

How could all that intensity not be as contagious as a yawn? And how could all that rawness confine itself to useful emotions? I turned into a jealous shithead. Was she sharing Mama's bed tonight? Where was she—really—when she claimed to be teaching? Whose hard luck story had moved her to take off her clothes? When she modeled at the art school, she started with her clothes off.

Until then, there had been plenty of women. Sometimes, after they left, it took me weeks to notice that they were gone. But now I'd come to Paris to become the lovesick, pussy-whipped ninny I'd thought existed only in the estrogen-poisoned brains of Marcel Proust and F. Scott Fitzgerald.

It wasn't entirely my fault. Suzanne's enormous appetite was not just sexual, but gastronomic. She couldn't go two hours without eating. A woman who hated being hungry so much should have thought a million times before taking up with a penniless, legally unemployable writer. But shouldn't a grown woman be able to skip an occasional meal? I'd noticed that when American women are in love they stop eating completely, a financial windfall for American men.

When Suzanne hadn't eaten, everything annoyed her. My talking, my not talking. My accent. My age. My desire for her. The harder she tried not to show it, the more she shrank from my touch. I despised myself for not having the money to buy her the freshest oysters, the crispiest fried potatoes, the silkiest underthings, the softest, most bug-free bed in Paris.

I know she would deny this. She'd say she got fed up with a monster of self-involvement like *moi*. Me, a monster? Self-involved? She was looking for excuses.

After our affair ended—a sad story I will tell in the following chapter—I was depressed for weeks. Then I put it behind me. But did I ever get over her? She came to symbolize everything I wanted and would never have. And so I conclude this chapter more or less where I began, having returned full circle to the subject of self-pity.

Special to the *Magyar Gazette*

The New Diana Thrills Paris

THE RAGE OF Paris this season is a seventeen-year-old girl who is giving the fastest Frenchman a run for his money. For the past week, a convent-school student known as Mademoiselle Lou has been thrilling crowds at the Vélodrome d'Hiver with her speed, strength and endurance.

From a distance, an ignorant stranger might mistake Mademoiselle Lou for a stocky, muscular fellow in a white blazer and flannel trousers. But on closer inspection, one sees the full red lips and dark curls that give this confident young woman's face the saucy sparkle of feminine beauty.

The audience cheers as she sprints the course, nimbly jumping the hurdles, heaves a javelin, then hops on a bike and streaks past the crowded bleachers. This record-breaking athlete is already being mentioned as a favorite to compete in some event (as yet unspecified) in the next Olympics. Meanwhile the whole city is buzzing about this creature whose very existence proves that the modern French woman has boldly snapped the chains that still imprison her sisters in the more old-fashioned, less progressive cultures.

May 15, 1928   .

Dear parents,

I cannot go on like this! My days in journalism are numbered! I must find another way of supplementing your stipend, another job that will let me have my nights free to wander the city, taking pictures. It's demoralizing enough to be demoted—or *pro*moted, according to my editors—to the sports pages. But when I actually find a subject worth writing an article about, they refuse to print it.

Last week I attended the event described above. This time I only made a few tiny improvements on the truth. That sparkle of saucy feminine beauty was my invention, as were the hurdles and the bike. And Paris is hardly abuzz about Mademoiselle Lou, though they *should* be buzzing about this young woman who, in our country, would prob-ably be exhibited as a circus freak.

I would never have heard of this girl if not for my friend Lionel. With typical directness—excuse the language, his, not mine—my American pal remarked that the sight of a big, healthy, muscular girl in pants, running and chucking a spear, made him feel like a happy bumblebee was buzzing in his trousers.

It was perfect for the sports page! Even my stingy editors agreed, though they only gave me two hundred words.

Lionel warned me to get to the Vélodrome late. The girl has a pro-moter, a pretentious Brit who lectures the crowd in abysmal French. There might have been more of a buzz if this guy weren't such a bore. This self-styled doctor sells health tonics and an exercise machine he calls the Gymnasticon.

I arrived late, but not late enough. In a long white coat, "Dr." Loomis stood behind a podium set up on the track. Let me try to give you the flavor of his French:

"The body she is cathedral. The arteries and veins is tentacles of female heart and blood he runs back and forth to the girl the woman the mother and then baby, bringing health. The stomach is chair of the soul, of compassion, the happy and pretty. The breathing, the moving house, the green fruits and natural juice will turn a cuttlefish into a giant. I myself was such tiny but thanks for my fitness liquid and the miraculous Gymnasticon I stretched beyond what doctors predicted my mother."

Did he really mean *cuttlefish*? What was he trying to say?

Two hundred words. No room for anything fancy. The fellow was wasting my time as he listed the requirements for health: sunshine, fresh air, exercise, a balanced vegetarian diet. Baths! Cold in winter, hot in summer, liberating the pores from its jailers, oil and dirt and dust. He pulled down charts of bodies flayed and sliced down the middle. On one a pretty woman smiled, unaware that the other half of her face was a grinning skull. He spoke a bit excessively about the female organs. Fortunately, only a few ladies had come to the performance—among them my friend, the baroness Lily de Rossignol.

Have I mentioned her, Mama and Papa? She is a former Hollywood star who came home to Paris and married a baron whose family manufactures luxury automobiles. A queen of high society who seems far younger than her age. Perhaps it's her adventurous spirit. She is one of those daring souls who will try anything once. How Papa would admire this patroness of the arts, this glamorous French eagle who has taken me under her wing!

Like the rest of the Vélodrome audience, I'd stopped pretending to listen. I looked around for Mademoiselle Lou, who had taken a seat beside a tall nun in a brown robe. I watched the girl rotate her head and ripple her muscular shoulders.

When (at last!) Dr. Loomis finished, he announced that Mademoiselle Lou would now attempt to beat the men's javelin record. The girl removed her blazer and, just as a man would, folded it neatly and placed it on her seat. Underneath her jacket she wore a long-sleeved white shirt and a black tie.

Do you remember when you took me to see Shakespeare's *The Tempest*? For months I was afraid to close my eyes lest a growling Hungarian Caliban murder me in my bed. As Mademoiselle Lou grabbed her knees and inhaled, I again saw that snarling beast emerging from its lair. Though maybe this is just prejudice, the panic of a male in the presence of a female who could flatten him in a fight.

Rolling her hips like a sailor, the girl strutted down the track. A few crude audience members shouted coarse remarks at the spectacle of a woman doing knee bends and jumping jacks. I thought of the Chameleon Club. The contortionist sailorettes did backbends in my mind.

Mademoiselle Lou ran for a short distance, then let the javelin fly. Good God, I said in Hungarian, and then, in French, *Mon Dieu*. How fast, how far, how confidently that young woman hurled the spear.

The nun who stood up was ten feet tall. Her habit flapped behind her. The measuring tape trailed at her hem. Why didn't I bring my camera?

She read the result. The men's record had been broken!

The girl's eyes were dull, her face dark red, she was panting and streaming sweat. When the applause subsided, Dr. Loomis announced that Mademoiselle Lou would answer a few questions.

The reporter from the right-wing paper asked how long her family had lived in France.

"Forever," she replied.

Another journalist asked if Mademoiselle Lou agreed with Dr. Loomis's theory that physical exercise would not compromise her future as a wife and mother.

She said, "My only future plan is to compete in the Olympics."

Dr. Loomis frowned. Had he hoped she'd say that his system was preparing her to bake a perfect Tarte Tatin while popping out a litter of French babies? Clearly, he didn't want us to think that his program encouraged the Amazonian tendencies so common now in Paris.

That ended the question period. Dr. Loomis announced that he would be selling his elixirs and offering free Gymnasticon demonstrations in the stadium lobby.

"That poor unhappy girl! Did you see her face?" the baroness asked me. "Please! Go down there and talk to her! Flirt with her! Do something!"

I climbed down the steps and ventured onto the track. Mademoiselle Lou was alone, momentarily forgotten. She sat in a chair with her head in her hands, her elbows on her knees. I tried to think of a question that might elicit some pungent quote that would move the story off the sports desk to the news section, or at least the culture pages. How do you think your achievements will change the life of the average Frenchwoman?

Perhaps if I'd asked that probing question my story would have been published, though I can't imagine how a different ending would have satisfied the small-minded editors who decided that my article made the reader think overly much about female plumbing. Maybe they sensed how their public would receive the suggestion that God had created woman to do something besides rolling out strudel dough. Maybe they would have printed the piece if Mademoiselle Lou were Hungarian instead of a potential threat to Hungarian *men* in the up-coming games.

I should have requested a private interview, but the girl looked so desolate that my cool journalistic instincts gave way to my warmer human ones. I fished around in my briefcase until I found what I wanted. Some higher force moved me to hand Mademoiselle Lou the business card of the Chameleon Club. She slipped it into her pocket just as the giant nun appeared and led her away.

The reason I have bothered you with the sad drama of my failure as a reporter is because I must ask you to send a little extra this month. There is something I have neglected to tell you, not from any wish to deceive you but to spare you unnecessary worry.

I don't know if I mentioned the photos I was taking of a notorious petty criminal named Big Albert and his gang. Until now they'd adopted me as if I were one of their own. I think they were flattered that I thought their faces were interesting, which, believe me, they are. They let me imagine I'd joined their outlaw family. But last night, when I returned from shooting what may be the most extraordinary nocturnal group portrait since Rembrandt's *The Night Watch*, I was shocked to discover that my wallet was missing.

This theft has plunged me into a fiscal crisis. So I must ask for enough money to survive on while I figure out how to end my shameful dependence on the *Magyar Gazette* and find a job more in keeping with my talents. Every penny is helpful, since—as you may have heard—the price of bread is rising to a level that is turning the average working man into an insomniac like myself!

Thank you again, with all my heart,
Gabor

From *Make Yourself New*
BY LIONEL MAINE

NO SOONER HAD we got to the hotel room than we took off all our clothes, no sooner had we twisted ourselves into an acrobatic position orchestrated by Suzanne, no sooner had I stopped wondering which filthy ex-boyfriend had taught her this, no sooner had my delirious cock silenced my chattering brain than we heard someone pounding on the door and shouting, "Police! Open up!"

I told the desk clerk to go fuck himself, but he kept yelling from the hall that the room was rented to a Hungarian. It was against the rules to loan out rooms on a short-term basis. The French have rules about everything. Nothing is too trivial or intimate to be regulated by the Napoleonic Code.

"Short-term?" I whispered to Suzanne. "Is he insulting my manhood?" Suzanne was unamused. The clerk would have gladly gone on knocking forever. It was a pleasant break from the reception desk and an outlet for the resentment produced by a lifetime of handing others the keys to ecstasy or despair. He'd been on the telephone when we sneaked past and let ourselves in with Gabor's key.

I was reasonably sure that, even in France, our presence was legal. But it didn't seem like the ideal moment to discuss tenants' rights. Suzanne rolled away from me and pressed her face into the pillow.

Knock knock.

"Just a minute," I said.

Suzanne cursed. Why was she blaming *me*? Obviously, the poor thing was as horny and frustrated as I was. What an enlightened culture! So unlike our own hypocritical country, where ladies are taught to lie back, close their eyes, and think of Calvin Coolidge. How refreshing to live in a place where it is taken for granted that coitus interruptus can leave a woman cranky. Though perhaps I should have thought less about French sexual attitudes and more about Suzanne, who had begun to yell at the clerk. With each new perversion she proposed for him and his mother, I fell more deeply in love.

Before I came to Paris, I thought I knew something about women. Hilarious, said Paris. You Americans know nothing. The women of Paris are a separate species. They compete to be the wildest. They work on their bad reputations. If Kiki has no pubic hair, she makes sure the whole world knows. There is a girl in Montparnasse, a blond tart who calls herself Arlette and is famous for the strawberry birthmark that covers half her ass.

Meanwhile I wander among them, a sexual Columbus, marveling at the customs of this exotic breed, these gorgeous moths who fling themselves at the flickering candle, determined to immolate themselves for love, to burst into flame before they end up pinned beneath a washing tub, a mother-in-law, and five squalling brats. They live for freedom, for dancing, good dinners and wine, for music and trips to the Riviera. They refuse to sell their bodies for a diamond ring but will gladly rent them to rich old men and talented young painters. Like geishas, they are artists: their art is how much they can drink, how many drugs and how many lovers of both sexes they can take, how quickly they strip naked at artists' balls and rip off their shirts on Bastille Day.

It's all in fun. Sex is different here. Brothels are licensed and safe! Bald ladies, fatsos, amputees? Sex in a bedroom decorated like an ocean-liner cabin, an igloo, the boudoir of a French king? The customer need only ask. Friends visit a whorehouse as casually as a group of clerks in Hoboken go out after work for a beer.

Without much hope, I reached for Suzanne. She pushed my hand away.

"I'm starving," she told the wallpaper. "And I'm sick of this room."

Twice that day, I'd caused a scene at the American Express. Why

were they pretending that my check hadn't come? Hadn't I written to
my ex-wife: Dear Beedie, I am in mortal danger! I've joked about starvation before, but this time I'm not kidding.

Once again, my survival instinct muscled down my panic, and my
sex-starved, protein-deficient brain lumbered into action. I remembered that Gabor was dining at the Café des Vosges with the baroness
Lily de Rossignol.

This afternoon, as Suzanne and I were grappling on his gritty
sheets, Gabor was (on my suggestion) escorting the baroness to see a
charming Sapphic creature hurling deadly weapons in the Vélodrome
d'Hiver. I knew they would enjoy it, partly because my Hungarian
friend was always on the lookout for sports-related stories and partly
because the baroness sounded like someone who would appreciate a
performance that involved an Amazon, a giant nun, and a snake-oil
salesman. I knew from my own experience that one could work up
quite an appetite watching the exertions and the intriguingly broad
behind of the sexually ambiguous, vaguely alarming female athlete.

Another brilliant idea of mine was telling Gabor where he and his
lovely patron should dine. If Suzanne and I just happened to stroll into
the Café des Vosges, and if we just happened to run into them, Gabor
might just mention that I was the one who told him about the athletic
demonstration. And the grateful baroness might just invite us to join
them.

What a schoolboy Gabor is! Sometimes I wonder which of us is
the naive American and which is the savvy European. He still seems
astonished when the baroness picks up a check. How can he not understand that she will pay for the food he eats, the wine he drinks, the
oxygen he breathes? She will promote his art, support him, and sleep
with him, but only on her terms. Either he is truly innocent or else
pretending because of some atavistic male vanity he'd be better off
without. Perhaps such women don't exist in his Hungarian backwater:
older, rich, not caring what it costs to stave off boredom. But for me to
tell Gabor would test the limits of our friendship. Two women could
easily discuss all that and more—another reason why a man must be
careful around women.

My plan had obvious risks. What if the baroness changed her mind about where she wanted to eat? What if I convinced the snooty maître d' that our friends were inside, and led Suzanne past all those glittering diamonds, past all those sparkly perfect teeth lightly marinated in champagne—and found Gabor and the baroness installed at a cozy table for two?

But the gods of Paris were smiling on us, or in any case consoling us for our ruined *amour.* I spotted Gabor from across the restaurant. A less loyal friend might have taken a sudden interest in the potted ferns. But Gabor grinned and beckoned us over.

In her sleek platinum bob and ermine coat, the baroness turned to watch us approach with the sleepy languor of a jungle cat. It was a relief to discover that she wasn't my type: too bossy, too spoiled, too arrogant, too close to my own age. But most men would have fucked her in a heartbeat, as Gabor could have, if he'd wanted. Only God, or another Hungarian, could fathom why he has been so excessively respectful toward his attractive patron.

Gabor hugged me and kissed Suzanne. Blushing, he introduced us. The baroness knew who I was and made a point of not caring who Suzanne was.

She said, "So you are the American writer we can thank for sending us to see that pitiful girl, her tedious British Svengali, and that utterly delectable, colossal cross-dressing nun?"

I said, "The nun was a female, I think."

"Oh, really?" said the baroness. "How long have you been in Paris?"

I said, "I want to thank you for getting us out of jail."

She looked at Gabor. "Jail? Why is this not ringing a bell? I really must quit drinking."

Gabor said, "When I took that photo of the three crooks breaking into the house . . . ? Lionel was one of the thieves . . . the one in the checkered cap . . . ?"

"Right," she said. "A *faint* bell. I own a print of that, don't I?"

"In fact you do," said Gabor.

The baroness ran one pearly fingernail down the length of his cheek. "Now I remember. And you"—she inspected me—"the *old* thief, am I right?"

After an awkward silence, Suzanne asked Gabor, "How *are* you?"

"Never better," the baroness told me, as if I were the one who'd asked *her*. She refocused the brute force of her attention on Gabor, who was looking apologetically at Suzanne, as if to say, Don't blame *me*. Suzanne smiled sweetly at him, as if to say, I don't.

Whom exactly did I have to fuck to make someone look at *me*? Should I lecture the baroness about good manners? Or whisper a warning against offending Suzanne, whose sense of justice was as fierce as her compassion, and who might be planning to make the baroness pay for her rudeness? Would our lives have been different if I'd grabbed Suzanne's hand and dragged her out of that den of the bloodsucking rich and found a deserted corner and had semirough sex with her against a wall?

Why did I do none of that? Because when Suzanne finally turned toward me, I saw the face of someone witnessing a miracle, and when I looked over my shoulder to see what the miracle was, I saw a waiter heading toward us with a giant platter of oysters.

From the (Unpublished) Memoirs
of Suzanne Dunois Tsenyi
To be destroyed on the occasion of its author's death

(1928)

ONCE A BOYFRIEND told me, "Suzanne, there are two kinds of people. People who lean toward you and people who lean away."

I said, "What about people who sit up straight?"

He said, "They haven't decided."

If I were like Lionel, I would write a book: *Obvious Lies, Bad Advice, and Wrong Information I've Gotten from Men.* A book? An encyclopedia! But in this case my friend was right. Gabor's baroness not only leaned away, she seemed to levitate above the table and peer down at us from a great height as we waited like naughty children until her ladyship said, "Join us."

For all I cared, she could have been looking at us through a telescope from Mars. There was a chance, a very good chance, that she was going to buy us dinner.

She asked Lionel, "Do you like oysters?"

Lionel said, "Suzanne loves oysters."

"I'll bet she does," she said.

Oysters was the magic word the waiters lip-read across the room. Or perhaps they'd already been ordered, and the telepathic waiters knew to bring more.

Lionel had told me about a club where women perform erotic acts with fluffy kittens and lambs. Disgusting! But I could perform with oysters. Too bad no one was watching me have sex with a dozen bivalves. Lionel, Gabor, and the baroness were too busy talking. Well, fine. More oysters for me. I slurped a few and waited politely, then finished off the platter. I was never one of those girls who require constant attention.

Another boyfriend used to tell me, Watch and learn, Suzanne. And though he only said it in bed, I took his advice to heart.

I watched the baroness order. More oysters, escargots stewed with butter and cream, a mushroom bisque, lamb steaks, *bloody*, please tell the chef, haricots verts, and mashed potatoes. Then cheese, a sherry cake, wild strawberries, and coffee.

She'd let the waiter choose the wine. Something expensive, red, and delicious. She asked Gabor and Lionel, "Will that be enough?" Before they could reply she said, "If not, we'll order more."

When the second round of oysters came, the baroness forbid the men to speak until they'd eaten. How much did it cost to earn the right to tell people what to do? After the empty platter went back and she'd grabbed the champagne bottle from the waiter so as to refill her own glass, she began to question Lionel about his writing. In other words, was he famous, or was she wasting her time and money buying him dinner?

Disappointed by Lionel's answers, she pouted at Gabor. Who was this American phony he'd swindled her into feeding? Three things kept me from jumping to Lionel's defense: First, the baroness hadn't actually said anything insulting. Second, I was still hungry. And third, I'd decided to leave him.

The baroness's disdain had no effect, or almost no effect, on my decision. I was tired of his jealousy, sick of his belief that the only permissible topic of conversation was his unrecognized genius. In all our time together, he had never once asked how Mama was, or how my day had gone. Of course, had I been in love with him, none of that would have mattered.

The baroness remarked that her husband's cousin had started a literary magazine called *Tomorrow*. Or *Today*. Or *Right Now*. Not *Yesterday*, she was sure of that. Who would call an avant-garde journal

Yesterday? When she sobered up and remembered, she would give the address to Gabor. Lionel should submit his work.

The desperation with which Lionel wanted to be published in this magazine whose name the baroness couldn't recall was painful to behold. I had long since lost my Catholic faith, but I still believed that I would be punished for my sins: crimes of heartlessness, mostly. The crime of not loving someone who loves you. The crime of making a man suffer. But I didn't love Lionel. There was nothing I could do. A quick ending was more merciful, a clean cut would heal faster.

He said, "On Sunday nights I sometimes read my work aloud at the Café Dôme."

The baroness said, "Oh, really? That must be wildly entertaining."

The look that passed between Gabor and me was like a conversation in which we tried to decide who would wade in and save Lionel from drowning. Which of us would convince her that this crude American was the real thing? I believed in his talent, and so, I knew, did Gabor. But my opinion was not the one that would persuade the baroness.

Looking at Gabor, I felt the first stirrings of that attraction, let's call it desire, that can spark up out of nowhere when a woman and man can communicate without words. I felt guilty that the subject of our silent exchange was the imperiled dignity of Gabor's friend and my soon-to-be-ex-lover. Why had I never noticed how beautiful Gabor's eyes were? Because he had never looked at me the way he was looking at me now.

Before Gabor could speak, the baroness said, "I felt so sorry for that poor girl in the Vélodrome, that unfortunate creature whose body they'd deformed so she could do tricks. Like one of those beggar children whose legs have been broken, or those dwarf Japanese trees. Imagine running and throwing a spear in that unflattering outfit."

Lionel said, "With a face like that, there's not much you can do."

It's over, I thought. I'm leaving him. I'm telling him tonight.

The baroness said, "There is always something a woman can do."

I said, "Maybe it was *her* idea. Maybe she wanted to break the record."

The baroness could not have seemed more startled if an oyster had addressed her from its shell.

"Why would a woman want *that*? Is your little friend a feminist?" she asked Lionel.

"Suzanne's a toughie," Lionel said. "Watch out."

"I too am a toughie," the baroness said.

"Hot!" warned the waiters, settling down ramekins at our places. I leaned into the tendrils of garlicky steam curling up from the ceramic.

"Eat," the baroness said. "Go ahead. I'll just finish this cigarette."

Parsleyed cream dripped from the snails I speared with my tiny trident. In a trance of pleasure, I forgot the others and scrubbed my dish with bread. Lionel too cleaned his plate. The baroness laughed, or semi-laughed, semi-amused by our ravenous hunger. Our empty dishes disappeared, and the lamb steaks arrived.

The baroness said, "*Bloody* means nothing anymore. *Bloody* means *incinerated*. Didn't I ask for them bloody? Are these rare enough for you?"

"Excellent." Lionel's mouth was full. I didn't want to look at his mouth.

While we ate, the baroness smoked and drank. Every time she tapped her cigarette, the ashtray was whisked away. When it was slow in returning, she made a trough for her ashes in the mashed potatoes she wouldn't let the waiters remove.

Buoyed by the delicious food, my spirits began to lift. Pretty soon I liked everyone. The waiters, the other diners, even Lionel and the baroness. Especially Gabor. How witty they were. Lionel told his joke about limiting himself to one glass of wine per night but making sure that his glass, his one glass, was never empty. Laughing, we toasted the punch line. Fill it, please!

Poor Lionel! When he looked back on tonight, would he wonder when exactly I decided that our love affair was over? Fortunately, it was Lionel's policy to look back as rarely as possible. What happened to Orpheus, Lionel said, was entirely the woman's fault. Same with Lot. Blame the wife. If Lionel had looked back, he'd still be in Jersey with Beedie and little Walt.

The baroness told a story about her husband and her brother-in-law, Didi and Armand. They were in business together, manufacturing automobiles. Her story began with a long list of famous names I'd never heard of. Duke A said something to Viscount B, who said something to Princess C and the German industrialist D. The upshot was that Didi and Armand hired the world's fastest auto racer to take their new sports car around the track and report any problems.

The driver agreed on one condition: that he test the car only at night, and that he have the track to himself with no one there to spot him. For a while the arrangement worked until one night a cop saw headlights circling the track, and not having been alerted, found the driver doing a hundred and twenty kilometers an hour, wearing only a helmet and a lady's black lace nightie.

"What happened?" Gabor asked.

"Nothing," said the baroness. "The driver delivered his report. It went to the engineers."

"In America he would have been executed," said Lionel.

"Hardly," the baroness said. "I spent years in Hollywood. You think there aren't perverts there? I knew a producer who could only achieve orgasm by having Asian virgins set off firecrackers on his chest. How does someone figure *that* out? Does he roll away from his wife one night and think, What would really make me happy is a Chinese schoolgirl blowing Catherine wheels off my nipples?"

The men laughed, a little nervously. Watch and learn, Suzanne.

Gabor and Lionel excused themselves and got up to go to the toilet, leaving me with the baroness. She leaned so far away from me, she was practically horizontal. Then she lit another cigarette and said, "If my brother-in-law were here, he would only speak to you—and not one word to the others."

"Doesn't he like men?"

"Armand likes men fine. He is married and very religious. In fact he belongs to Opus Dei. He was among its first members. A pioneer, one might say."

I was afraid to tell the baroness that I didn't know what Opus Dei was, though later I would learn from Gabor that it was an extreme right-wing Catholic sect with radical ideas about how the universe works and with practices that, one heard, included self-flagellation.

"Apparently," said the baroness, "this cult or coven or whatever it is has no problem with . . . never mind. I meant: the only reason Armand would talk to you is because you are French. Unlike our two friends, who are foreigners, in case you hadn't noticed. Armand is patriotic to an almost fanatical degree. Correction: a fanatical degree. In addition to his religious manias he is a founding member of the Order of the Legion of Joan of Arc. Though I don't believe that he agrees with the thugs who go around roughing up immigrants, Jews, Bolsheviks, and the rest."

The baroness looked at me, really looked at me, for the first time all evening. As if I'd evolved from a talking oyster into a fellow human in whom she was confiding, or whose opinion she wanted. The flicker of her shifting moods bathed her face in a flattering, honeyed light. I wanted to tell her something. I wanted to talk about my father's death and my mother's poor health. I can't imagine why I thought that she would be sympathetic.

"What about your husband?" I asked. "Does he share his brother's political views?"

"Ah, my husband. Didi is a different story completely."

The baroness flapped one hand at the waiter and told him he had forgotten the brandy. He returned with four snifters. He was sorry. The management was sorry. The Armagnac was on the house. Should he leave the gentlemen's glasses? The baroness waved him away.

Where were Gabor and Lionel? I finished my cake and brandy. As the baroness rooted around in her purse for more cigarettes, I switched my glass with Lionel's and drank his brandy too.

When the men came back they seemed disappointed that the baroness and I weren't talking. Had they imagined that any two women will become intimate friends the minute the boys leave the table? Our silence was infectious. Gabor drank his brandy. Lionel picked up his empty glass and looked at me but said nothing.

"What now?" the baroness asked. "You're the racy young crowd.

Wait. I have an idea. Gabor promised to take me to that cross-dressers club. What a perfect conclusion to our day at the Vélodrome!"

"It's Tuesday," said Gabor. "The Chameleon is closed tonight."

"Pity," the baroness said.

After another long silence I said, "I know about a party."

"*Whose* party?" Lionel asked.

None of your business, I thought. After tonight I would never again have to find a way to subtly communicate the fact that the friend I was going to visit was female or homosexual: not a sexual threat. Another boyfriend used to say, "Your lover's jealousy knows you better than you do." That statement will not be included in my encyclopedia of misinformation I've gotten from men.

"Ricardo and Paul," I said.

I'd met Ricardo and Paul at the language school where I taught and where they'd enrolled to improve their French. Ricardo was a medical student from an old Argentinean family. His lover Paul was a Malaysian sculptor who'd stowed away on a steamer from Singapore. Ricardo was tall, handsome, reserved, Paul an extroverted sprite. They were opposites in every way, but what they shared was a generosity of spirit: Ricardo gave freely of his money and time (already he diagnosed and treated half of Paris for free) while Paul lavished unlimited energy on their parties, and on changing his appearance—his hairstyle and outlandish costumes—to amuse their friends.

It was through them that I'd met the painters and poets who'd admitted me into their circle—mostly because I was pretty, I knew, but that was how it was. Beauty and money were the only keys with which women could open the door to that locked room. I'd gone to meet Paul and Ricardo in the Café Voltaire on the night I met Lionel, the night he'd spoken so movingly about Rimbaud. He should never have told me—later—that he only did it for the free drinks.

"You know this Ricardo?" the baroness asked Gabor.

"Slightly," Gabor said.

"Everyone goes there," I said. "Sometimes there are costumes. Sometimes Kiki and Man Ray get into a fight." Why was I talking them into this? Was I showing off? Or did I want to lure the baroness into my territory, where we would see who had more power?

Gabor said, "My papa is a passionate fan of Kiki's."

"Even in Hungary?" said the baroness. "How marvelous. Do you know her too?"

Gabor said, "I've seen her at parties. But only with her clothes on."

The baroness said, "I collect Man Ray's work. I have from the beginning."

Watching her, I could see the prospect of fun battling her reluctance to visit a kingdom where she wasn't yet the queen.

I said, "Picasso came to one of their parties, dressed as a toreador."

"Picasso?" That magic word trumped whatever doubts the baroness might have had.

No bill was presented. No money changed hands. The smiling maître d' hoped to see us again.

The baroness's red Delage sedan was waiting for us outside. She sat up front with the driver. Her cigarette smoke wafted out and back in through the windows. Wedged between the two men, I was conscious of their thighs against mine. Lionel pressed against me: forceful, possessive, hopeless. My contact with Gabor was more tentative but eloquent, nonetheless.

We pulled up in front of Paul's atelier, where we pushed our way through the partygoers overflowing onto the street. A turbaned genie guarded the door, his brawny arms folded. *Pussycat* was the password, as the whole city knew.

Tonight's guests had been instructed to dress as famous sculptures. Medieval kings and queens had arisen from their tombs. Several women had come as the *Venus de Milo*, powdered white, in white drapery, their arms pinned behind their backs. Two American boys were pretending to be cowboys à la Remington, riding the backs of two other boys wearing horses' heads. Sure enough, there was Kiki, in an extremely short toga. She kept on announcing that she was *The Dying Gaul*; then she'd lie on the floor and giggle until a man helped her up.

Paul and Ricardo had sprayed themselves silver and were nude but for loincloths made of peacock feathers. I kissed them and told them how marvelous they looked. The musicians were on break, so we could hear one another.

"And who are your feathered friends?" the baroness said, with a laugh.

When I introduced them, Paul said, "I believe I've met your husband."

Ricardo slapped the back of Paul's hand.

"I'm sure you have," said the baroness. "What sculpture are *you* supposed to be?"

Ricardo said, "In Buenos Aires there is a fountain on which there is a statue of two splashing lovebirds."

"I've been to Buenos Aires," the baroness said. "I don't remember a fountain like that. If I go back, will you tell me where to find it?"

"Next time," said Paul, "we will take you."

Gabor said, "I'd like to photograph you two in those costumes."

"Impossible," said Ricardo. "My family would disown me."

The baroness said, "Masks would do the trick. Not even your own mother will recognize you." She rested her hand on the small of Ricardo's back, just above his silver ass. "The four of us can have dinner. We will eat and drink well. Then Gabor can set up the shot. And we'll take it from there."

The band couldn't have chosen a better moment to start playing.

"They just performed for the German ambassador," Ricardo shouted in my ear.

I said, "I saw them last month at le Jazz Cool Club."

In fact it had been two months ago, the last time Lionel had money. I looked around for Lionel, but I couldn't see him.

"They're playing for us for free," said Paul.

"Oh, are they?" the baroness said. "In that case, we should show our appreciation." She grabbed Gabor's hand and led him onto the dance floor. I was surprised and saddened by how gracefully they moved together. Lionel danced terribly. The only time we'd gone dancing, he pretended it was funny to stumble and drag me across the room.

Ricardo nodded at Paul, who led me out among the dancing couples. Paul was quite a bit shorter than I, so at first it was awkward.

But after I'd had a few pulls from his brandy flask, the difference in our heights seemed amusing, as did the fact that my partner was not only silver but naked except for a few strategically placed feathers.

Someone cut in, another medical student who must have imagined that a Roman helmet and an armored breastplate would be irresistible to the ladies. It was infinitely resistible, but he too had cognac in a flask. By the time the song ended, I was grateful for the centurion's steadying hand on my back.

The music stopped. Ricardo and Paul tapped their flasks with spoons.

Ricardo said, "And now, my dear friends, it's time to play Living Statues."

The room darkened, and spotlights appeared, each trained on one of the low white pedestals spaced around the loft.

"Goddesses! Arise!" said Paul.

I began to shiver. A half-naked couple beside me hunched their shoulders and rubbed their arms. The female guests were excited and frightened by what they'd been asked to do. The men were excited, and also scared that none of the women would do it, and that the women's refusal would reflect on them. I noticed quite a few guests edging toward the exit, then stopping in the doorway to see what would happen. No one spoke or moved until a woman's bare arms rose over the heads of the crowd, and everyone stamped and cheered.

Not *any* woman. Kiki! She pulled off her toga and stepped naked onto the pedestal and into the cold white light. My eyes ached from staring at all that dazzling flesh. The spotlight raked the room until it found another girl shedding her clothes and climbing onto another column.

The next person to strip was a puckish blond boy. As he perched on his pedestal, everyone stared at his penis, the women curious, the men entranced, each comparing it with his own. Quivering, it rose slightly and curved to one side, as if retreating from our attention. Once more the mood shifted, and I sensed a tremor of violence. I must have drunk more than I thought, because I became convinced that it was my duty to save the poor boy from being devoured in a frenzied Dionysian rite.

The rush of blood in my ears said, Do it. It's just like modeling at the art school. But that was for money. That was work.

I'd stripped in public once before, on a suffocating Bastille Day. I'd only taken off my shirt, and the café was dark. I danced all night in the arms of the man who'd said, Watch and learn, Suzanne. Whom was he dancing with now? Was he saying that to her?

It was different to strip in a room full of friends, a place I would return to. As if anyone remembered which girls took off their dresses! I would never have considered it were I not so drunk and so aware that Gabor and the baroness were out there in the dark.

I raised my arms above my head. Someone whistled. The spotlight found me. Two men carried over a pedestal. I slipped off my dress and handed it to Ricardo, who had materialized beside me.

He said, "You don't have to do this."

Hands helped me up onto the column, which was wider than it looked. Still I had to keep my knees and feet together. The spotlight was very hot. Sweat trickled between my breasts. My nipples stood up, and I covered them with my hands. The crowd roared again and moved closer. I pretended that I was a plant growing toward the sun. I couldn't see into the blackness past the circle of light. As my eyes adjusted I spotted Gabor and the baroness. Her arm was draped over his shoulder. But he was staring at me.

Watch and learn, I thought. Now it was her turn. It was wrong to use my youth as a weapon. It was not a fair fight. I should have been grateful for the meal. But the baroness should have been nicer.

Once more the crowd applauded. Another girl was stripping. A few of the men kept staring at me, as if to maintain our connection. What if one of my students were here? Tomorrow, I could be conjugating the past subjunctive with a man who'd seen me naked.

I tottered. Hands reached up to help. I wanted the hands to be Gabor's. I thought I heard Lionel's voice. Ricardo gave me my dress. The cool silk splashed down my face like a shock of ice water. Ricardo hugged me, pressing me to his silver chest. His skin was moist and sticky. By the time I looked up, Gabor and the baroness were nowhere to be seen, and I slipped out of the party without telling Lionel that I was leaving.

From *The Devil Drives:*
The Life of Lou Villars

BY NATHALIE DUNOIS

Chapter Three: Sin City

WHEN LOU TRIED to imagine Paris, she pictured the fresco depicting hell in the church she'd attended as a child: images of the damned boiling in cauldrons, gnawing on their own flesh and the limbs of their fellow sinners. Why would Dr. Loomis and Sister Francis take her to a place that she'd spent every Sunday praying to avoid? Why couldn't they go on as they were, touring the provinces to compete in races and games, then returning to the convent? Lou was getting stronger, faster, more in control of her body, more adept at deciphering the messages it sent. She even enjoyed Dr. Loomis's lectures, which she'd heard so often that she could use the time to meditate on her mistakes and how to correct them.

Dr. Loomis complained about the drafty trains, the overcooked vegetables, the lumpy hotel beds. But for Lou, travel was an adventure. She was happy to go where she was told, to do as she was instructed, to make new friends wherever they went. She treasured her letter from a swimmer asking when Lou would visit Royan again. The previous month had brought a postcard from a runner in Limoges who'd broken the district record by imagining Lou waving her across the finish line.

Paris was a spider's web, a ribbon of flypaper over the stove, a bog of quicksand into which you could sink forever. Her parents said Robert was there, but they'd refused to say where. When Lou phoned to ask, they hung up and pretended the connection had gone dead. With Grandma gone and Miss Frost fired, there was no one who would tell her. For all Lou knew, he was sick and scared and desperate. She would find him when she got older and had the money and time.

She'd heard about Paris from Miss Frost, who'd lived there briefly after the war but was glad to escape the beggars with scorched faces, the amputee veterans who vaulted off the pavement on their stumps and lunged at you as you passed. Dr. Loomis promised that Lou would love the City of Light. But one had to be careful. It was a snake pit of sin, a breeding ground for every maggot and germ, every species of moral contagion.

On the way they stayed in Amiens. All day, Lou had the sense that the nun and her brother were keeping something from her. For the first time, Lou lost focus and gave the javelin a halfhearted throw. Dr. Loomis seemed not to notice. His lecture was half its usual length, and as a consequence they sold twice as much health tonic. All of which confirmed Lou's suspicion that their stop in Amiens was about something besides the javelin.

Dr. Loomis forbade Lou to eat dinner. Shortly after seven, he told Sister Francis to wait at the hotel and set off with Lou on a brisk walk through the seedier parts of town. When Lou asked where they were going, he said it would be a nice surprise and not to be afraid.

At last they reached an enormous shed that loomed up from the black shadows behind a depot for burned-out trains and trolleys. From a distance Lou heard the voices of men roaring with animal rage. Bright light and cigar smoke poured from the open door.

How easily one can imagine little Lou's trepidation! Picturing this disturbing event, I recall the time when a lover brought me to a boxing match, supposing—with characteristic obtuseness—that I might enjoy it. I remember thinking the men had come for the pleasure of losing their humanity in a crowd of wild beasts exhorting the fighters to beat each other senseless.

Such was the scene that confronted Lou, who'd been brought there to fight a professional twice her age.

What an eerie experience it was to find, in the dusty archive of *Le Journal d'Amiens*, a photo of Alfonso Vargas, taken around the time of his fight with Lou Villars. Vargas stares into the camera like a criminal posing for a mug shot; one eye is as white and smooth as an egg. His graying hair is severely parted in a style Lou often wore, though unlike Lou he sports a full mustache and is missing two front teeth. In the accompanying interview—printed alongside a story about the vagrant crisis in Amiens—Vargas talks about having been a champion before his career hit a rough patch and he wound up homeless. Nowhere is it mentioned that he'd come to Amiens to engage in bareknuckle combat with a seventeen-year-old girl.

Lou had fought a punching bag, but never a human being. She'd shadowboxed, done push-ups, sit-ups, run mountain roads uphill. Sister Francis had thrown a medicine ball at her midsection, but too gently to have much effect. Whom would Lou have sparred against? Her fellow students couldn't be trusted not to gossip.

Nothing had prepared her to find herself surrounded by men crying out for her blood.

Dr. Loomis said, "Vargas is blind in one eye. He can't judge distance. There is no way you can lose. Just don't murder the poor old guy."

The closer Lou got to Vargas, the less threatening he seemed. One eye was a milky ball rolling around in its socket.

The audience bristled and shrank back, clearing a space in the center. There wasn't a proper ring, ropes, or mat. A thin layer of straw thatched the dirt floor.

A bell rang, and the crowd shouted, Kill her! Knock the bitch's lights out! Vargas threw a punch that, when Lou twisted away, struck her shoulder too lightly to hurt but hard enough to enrage her. It was like being a child again, flailing away at Robert. How sweet it felt to hit and be hit, how caressing the contact. Vargas's fist shot out like a lizard's tongue and caught the side of Lou's jaw. Lou *could* have killed him. She wanted to. But she held back.

The point was not to hurt but to dance. What she really wanted was to pound the old man until someone made her stop. Now everyone was advising them on how best to murder each other. Some of the yelling was in Spanish. Lou didn't want to know what it meant. She knew it was about her. She focused on not letting Vargas get close. It was easy to keep out of range if she stayed on his blind side.

Then someone threw something at Vargas. An orange bounced off the back of his head and rolled across the ground. Maddened, he flung himself at Lou, a windmill powered by a lifetime of failure. She drew back her fist and socked him hard, in his good eye. She was so fascinated by the sight of blood welling up in his eyebrow, which filled and spilled over and filled with blood and spilled over again, that for a moment she forgot herself and just stood there, watching. Vargas dropped to the ground, where he rolled like a man on fire trying to put out the flames.

The crowd cheered itself hoarse, and a referee—where had he been until now?—raised Lou's hand above her head. Dr. Loomis appeared beside her, bending down to whisper in her ear.

"My champion," he said.

Back at the hotel, Sister Francis pressed an ice pack to Lou's chin. Lou always hated how the nun prayed over her cuts and bruises. Dear Jesus, let your loving kindness heal our little sister. It reminded her of how disgustingly the nun breathed when she concentrated on cutting Lou's hair. Despite her repulsion, Lou was grateful that Sister Francis cut it short, like a man's, without having to be asked.

All night Lou dreamed of Joan of Arc, rescued from the fire, burned but intact, her bobbed hair charred, her corpse sliced open from neck to groin, her innards spilling out, writhing like Saint Teresa welcoming the angel. Lou dreamed that she and her parents and Robert were driving through the countryside, and three men with rifles jumped out from behind a hay wagon and massacred them all. Lou woke and dozed off and dreamed of cobwebs shedding droplets of ice.

The next day, on the train, Dr. Loomis was in such a chipper mood that he entertained his sister, Lou, and himself with a monologue about the crimes of Paris. His breath smelled like mutton stew. The odor of lamb fat coated the story of how the twin Corsican maids chopped up their employers and made the children into sausage; of the wet nurse who sold plump Christian babies to a Turkish sultan; of the devil Jew Dreyfus who had plotted to bring down France.

At school the Parisian girls boasted that, at home, night was as bright as the day. But as the taxi took them from the train station past the houses where the grisly murders had occurred, Lou was alarmed by how dark it was: darker than the country, where at least there were stars. The walls were stained and furred with mold. Greasy puddles of cold rain shimmered over the drains. Shadows flickered in the doorways, and every window concealed a crime behind the lying facade of the lamps.

The Hotel Monaco was wallpapered with autographed photos of bare-chested prizefighters scowling at the camera over boxing gloves cocked like the paws of giant dogs. The foreign man who ran the hotel gave Lou a suspicious look, then smirked so only she could see when Dr. Loomis explained that they were staying here to breathe the air of Sport. The owner assumed he was lying, but the presence of the Nazarene nun made the truth hard to decipher.

In the hotel basement was a poorly lit, malodorous gym beneath which Lou could hear running water. On the train Dr. Loomis had told her about the Mad Butcher of the Sewers, who chained and tortured his victims under the city streets.

All the other guests were boxers. At night Lou heard them in their rooms rhythmically punching the walls. Lou's insomnia returned, but she enjoyed it less than she had when she'd listened to Grandma's stories and sneaked around the convent.

Lou had never minded sharing a double bed with Sister Francis. But now the nun's metronomic snoring kept her awake, and she lay rigid, trembling, longing to pinch Sister Francis's nostrils shut and stop the drone, the wheeze, the gulp, sounds punctuated by the boxers hitting the walls. Waves of homesickness washed over her. But how could she be homesick when she no longer had a home?

Just before dawn she drifted off, only to be woken by the grating birdsong of Sister Francis's good morning. They found Dr. Loomis in the hotel's steamy, airless breakfast room, where the proprietor's daughter lurched among the tables, slamming down trays of stale bread and coffee—or in Lou's case, a bitter tea brewed from raspberry leaves that Dr. Loomis provided. The doctor loudly held forth about how, in the waitress's native land, girls carried water jars on their heads, which encouraged regal posture, sufficient oxygenation, and excellent liver, lung, and kidney function.

Fortunately, no one was listening. Not the furious waitress, not the younger boxers drinking coffee and smoking, not the elderly fighters still reeling from the punch they never saw coming. No one heard Dr. Loomis's speech about his trip to Germany, where he'd watched peasant women chop wood, while their statuesque blond daughters attended naturist camps offering nude calisthenics. Had the guests been paying attention, someone might have taken offense at Dr. Loomis's claim that the physically fit German youth were far superior to the French, which might be a serious problem in the event of another war.

Lou feared she'd been brought to Paris for another boxing match. But as they walked to the taxi stand, she was so surprised to see her face on a poster advertising a series of athletic demonstrations at the Vélodrome d'Hiver that it took her a while to recognize the furious girl in a shirt and tie, and a man's short haircut.

She dozed off in the taxi. When she awoke, she thought she was still asleep, dreaming of a sultan's palace, spun with silver fretwork and crowned with minarets—an enchanted castle from *The Arabian Nights*. It was the first time that Lou Villars had been moved by beauty. How tragic, and how fitting, that the thing of beauty should have been the Vélodrome d'Hiver, now mainly known for its diabolic role in the German Occupation.

Instinctively, Lou crossed herself. She hoped that no one was looking. Dr. Loomis smiled and said that she was right to be moved to prayer. They were closer to God here than they would be in Notre Dame. When Sister Francis frowned, he laughed and repeated it louder.

Inside the vast arena, Lou looked up and for a moment was afraid the sky might come crashing through the thin membrane of glass. It was dizzying to contemplate the bleachers that rose in tiers, sickening to imagine them packed with people come to see her.

Lou didn't fill the stands. But the crowds were decent, and they grew steadily during her three-week engagement. The track owners made a small profit at a time when no bicycle races were scheduled and they would otherwise have lost money.

Each time Lou entered the stadium, she felt sick with nerves. It bothered her that Sister Francis always pretended that her javelin toss had broken the men's record. Didn't these "sophisticated" Parisians understand that no new record could be set in an amateur demonstration? They might as well have come to watch a woman sawed in half.

Lou was right. Looking back through the decades during which we have learned so much about the male gaze, we can state with assurance that not one male in Paris cared about setting records or about Dr. Loomis's lectures.

One afternoon Lou actually did break the men's javelin record. But success came at a price: she twisted her ankle in the run-up. Afterward, she sat on a bench by the track, trying to ignore the pain.

A stranger with curly dark hair and the pinwheel eyes of a madman came over and spoke to Lou in an incomprehensible foreign accent. He gave her a business card, which she put in her pocket. She thanked him. She would have said anything to make him go away.

By evening, the pain had intensified, but Lou hid it from Sister Francis and Dr. Loomis, whose energetic massages always made her injuries worse. She accepted the fact that pain would be part of her life. But after their celebratory dinner at a bistro near the hotel—salad, mutton, and a bottle of red wine for Dr. Loomis, parsley potatoes and chicken for Sister Francis, and for Lou a bowl of boiled kale and a sliced unripe pear—she stood up and heard herself yelp like a puppy whose tail has been stepped on.

Dr. Loomis made her sit down again and, right there in the restaurant, prodded her swollen ankle. He told her to come to his room at seven for therapeutic massage, then unceremoniously dropped her foot as he turned to ask his sister what ointments and medicines she'd brought.

At five to seven, Lou hobbled up four flights to the doctor's room, larger and nicer than the one she shared with Sister Francis. It even had a balcony overlooking the street. Dr. Loomis sat on the terrace, drawing in a sketchbook.

"Lie down on the bed, Louisianne. Let's take a look at that ankle. My little champion is in pain." His French, never good at the best of times, was halting, thick and furry.

No one but her Papa had ever called Lou by her full name, and it worked its magic, even though she would later say that from this point on, she—like my readers, I imagine—sensed what was coming next. Technically, she was an innocent, but Lou was a creature of instinct.

She eased herself onto the bed. Dr. Loomis set his drawing pad on the nightstand. She turned so she could see it. He'd been sketching a passerby.

Half a dozen sheets of paper were tacked to the wall by his pillow. On each one, a realistic head was attached to a body rendered in the style of his grisly anatomical charts. Half of each body was covered by skin, the other half flayed down to muscle.

Reeking of mutton and vinegar, Dr. Loomis kneaded her foot with his fingertips until the pain was nearly unendurable. Then he loosened his trousers and her trousers and lay down on top of her and tried to pry her legs apart.

His flesh was cold and damp with sweat. Many things became clear. Her uncle hadn't been drying his hands on Miss Frost's breasts. The boxers in the hotel weren't punching the walls.

When Dr. Loomis lifted his head to breathe, Lou punched him in the nose. He'd seen her fight Vargas. Did he think she would lie there and let him do what he wanted? Blood splattered out of his nostrils and onto her white flannel trousers. He swung and hit her eye. Snowflakes skittered across her visual field. She wriggled out from under him and jumped off the bed. Then, before he could move, she slammed his head into the wall. She could hear him yelling as she hobbled down the hall.

On the way to her room she passed a mirror. One eye was already swollen. She raised her arm to wipe her face, then decided to leave her tears as evidence. Evidence of what?

"What happened?" asked Sister Francis. But Lou could tell that she knew.

"Nothing," Lou replied. She would no sooner tell on Dr. Loomis than she'd told on Robert. Not telling was a point of pride. Sister Francis bandaged her ankle, praying. Lou felt warm liquid drip on her foot. Sister Francis was crying.

The nun said, "Pray for forgiveness, dear. God bless you and good night."

Lou waited till Sister Francis was snoring. She eased one foot onto the floor. Her ankle felt better already. Where could she go with no money? Reaching into her pocket, she found the card with the sketch of the lizard that she'd gotten from the stranger at the Vélodrome.

The hotel owner watched her go without mentioning the blood on her clothes. Lou waited in the doorway until her eyes adjusted to the darkness. A man stopped and eyed her up and down. She moved away from the door.

She liked the sound of her footsteps against the cobblestones. God healed her ankle just as he'd cured Saint Joan's soldiers. She walked and got lost and asked directions and walked and asked someone else. It was nine in the morning by the time she found the address on the card.

She knocked. A fat man in dark trousers, a white shirt, and an apron opened the door. The fat man was a woman.

The woman dressed as a man said, "I thought you were the wine merchant's boy. You're not the wine merchant's boy."

Once more there was blood on Lou's white clothes. Once more she stood in a doorway.

The fat person told her to wait. She returned with the most beautiful woman Lou had ever seen: blond and tall and dressed like a mermaid, but in red, with a spangled red tail. She held a red lizard pressed against her breast.

"Don't be afraid," the woman said. "Come in." Her voice was not a French voice, but throatier and less chirpy. The woman led her past a stage decorated like a ship and across a room in which a bearded man in a short black maid's dress and a frilly apron was flapping white cloths onto little round tables.

Yvonne

EVA'S PARENTS HAD a poultry farm near Lake Balaton. She was three when she held her first duckling. After that she tried to be present when the baby ducks were born. She sang to them in a honeyed voice. They thought she was their mother. Each morning a flock of ducklings followed her to school, and she absorbed their habit of instant and fierce attachment.

She imprinted on the first boy she kissed. She dreamed of him, despite or because of the fact that he dreamed of becoming a sailor. He ran away and was drowned on his first voyage out. The village blamed his bad luck on her. After that no mother would let her son go near her, though almost every boy tried to go around his mother's back.

She was apprenticed to a midwife in a distant town. Had they known about her boyfriend's death, they would never have let her touch a woman in labor or a newborn baby.

One night, when the midwife was away, Eva was summoned by a rich Parisian vacationing with his Hungarian wife, who had grown up nearby. Eva reached inside the woman, who had fainted, and delivered a healthy infant just as its mother awoke.

Like the magic fish in the fairy tale, the father told Eva she could have anything she wanted. She wanted her sailor boy not to be dead.

She said, I want my own flock of ducks.

He said, You can do better.

She said, I want my own poultry farm.

He said, You can reach higher.

She said, I want to travel.

He said, Where?

Not long before, she'd read a newspaper item about a nightclub singer who had been murdered in Paris. The dead girl had left an empty space that needed to be filled.

She said, I want to sing in Paris.

Nothing could be simpler, said the grateful millionaire. He owned property in every neighborhood. He would inform his office. They would find her a place of her own. A nightclub was a small price to pay for a healthy wife and child. Parisians loved new clubs. No one talked about anything but the latest hot spot. Had she sung professionally?

She nodded. She'd sung to the ducks.

In Paris she looked up a childhood friend named Gyorgy. It took her weeks to find him, partly because he'd become Georgette. Georgette said that Eva too must change her name.

In France she was Yvonne.

Georgette knew artists, fashion designers, musicians, gangsters, people with shadowy pasts and mysterious new fortunes. Very modern, very free, very fond of dressing as the opposite sex. They needed a place where they could relax and have fun.

Yvonne's club was an instant hit. Georgette gave Yvonne her first lizard, which not only provided the name for her club but also everything she needed: the transfixed love of a duckling, the sandpaper touch of a man. She enjoyed watching it turn colors. She liked to decorate its little home. She was sad when the first lizard died, but she found a replacement.

Yvonne's clientele worshiped her. Her staff called her Yvonne the Terrible, but it was a loving joke. The musicians admired her voice but thought she should pay them more. She wrote songs about the sailor boy whose face she could hardly remember. Word got out that she liked sailors, which narrowed the field of men with the nerve to approach her. Among her lovers were captains, admirals, stokers, even an occasional fisherman who found his way to the city. She'd always liked the taste and smell of salt on a man's skin.

But none of these men understood, or wanted to understand, how hard she worked, how early she woke each morning to add up the books and order the wine and charm the delivery men who cheated everyone but her. What man wanted to hear about the constant money worries? No one knew what it took to go onstage and shed years of troubles, gallons of whiskey, and packs of cigarettes, and travel back through age and time to reenter the mind of the girl whose sailor never returned.

Yvonne was thoughtful and discreet, alert for the scent of the predator. She warned her clients if she thought they were involved with the wrong person, but she respected their privacy and shut her eyes to a lot. Or pretended to shut her eyes. Nothing happened at the club without her knowledge. She protected her customers from voyeurs and unwelcome publicity. She'd turned away the Hungarian who wanted to take pictures, despite how much she'd enjoyed speaking her native language.

Who had time and energy for a husband and children? For a few hours a week, she could lock her office door, smoke a little opium, and play with Louis the Lizard. And yet she always found time to adopt and nurture the strays who found their way to the club after hearing that it was a refuge where you would be taken in and not asked any questions.

Most of the runaways were young. Yvonne put them to work doing odd jobs, taking coats, busing dishes. The cute ones dressed in sailor suits and escorted the dancers onstage. Every kid who knocked on her door imagined that he or she was the first. The first one who'd been born into the wrong body, the first to love the wrong person, the first to have been beaten up, the first to have washed up on the safe shore of Montparnasse. Yvonne liked basking in the warming sun of their admiration.

One day, Fat Bernard called Yvonne out to meet a chunky girl wearing bloodstained white flannel trousers.

Yvonne had seen her somewhere before. It took her a moment to recognize the young woman on the posters plastered around the city, announcing a sports exhibition at the Vélodrome d'Hiver. A record-breaking something or other, soon to be a competitor in the upcoming Olympics, the girl had glared out of the ugly sign, threatening passersby with a spear. Now one eye was purple and swollen shut. Some evil bastard somewhere was sleeping like a baby. Yvonne asked Fat Bernard to take her to the backstage shower.

When the girl reappeared in a robe and a terry cloth turban, Yvonne led her to the wardrobe.

"Thank you," the girl kept saying.

Yvonne showed her the racks of costumes, suits, and dresses. The girl looked to Yvonne for direction. Yvonne shrugged. Pick what you want.

The girl reached toward a man's tuxedo. Her fingertips bounced off it, as if recoiling from a hot stove.

"Go ahead," said Yvonne. "Try it on."

Paris
July 15, 1928

Dear parents,
Yesterday evening I went to the baroness's for dinner. She and I have shared pleasant evenings, meals, trips to plays, museums, concerts, nightclubs high and low. Yet never once has she invited me to her home, though I have heard, from others, about her parties.

I'd assumed I was banned because her husband Didi resents the time she spends with me and the small (by their standards) but generous (by ours) loans with which she has gotten me past some rough spots. Recently, I was pushed to the breaking point when an acquaintance, a terrible painter, described the fabulous meal he'd enjoyed at the baroness's table.

Late one night, after the baroness and I had had a few drinks at the Dingo, I asked her why she'd never invited me. Was her husband jealous? If so, I would understand. The baroness laughed. She and her husband didn't have that sort of marriage, and besides he never inquired what she did with her time—and his money. Then why had she hosted my untalented friend, and not me?

She sighed. "What is the difference between you and your friend?"

"I am a good artist, and he is a bad one?"

"That is not the point. The point is, he is French. The problem is my brother-in-law, Armand, my husband's business partner—"

"I know who Armand is," I said.

"He's always at these dinners. And he is something of a maniac about pure French blood or some such distasteful concept."

"So the problem is that I am Hungarian?"

The baroness rolled her eyes.

So it seemed like a triumph, like proof of the power of our friendship when I received a handwritten invitation to dinner at her home. Maybe her brother-in-law wouldn't be there. Maybe his views had softened. Who cared what he thought of Hungarians? I was determined to go.

My desire was not about social climbing but purely about art. If I want to photograph Paris, *all of Paris*, from its palaces to its hovels, I will have to breach that fortress known as high society.

On the day of the dinner, I kept hearing Papa's warning: never be early. To surprise one's hostess getting dressed is an unforgiveable act of aggression. How well I remember the calculations by which our family arrived at Grandma's Sunday lunches and the vice principal's holiday tea precisely twenty minutes late, along with all the other guests who showed up at the same moment.

I arrived twenty minutes after the appointed hour. On time, by the standards of our town. Rudely late in the sixteenth arrondissement, where the guests were already sipping champagne. Who would have guessed that French aristocrats are as punctual as Germans?

I should have asked the baroness what to wear. I was crazy to consult Lionel and to listen when he said that socialites love rubbing shoulders with filthy smelly artists. He said it gives the chronically bored a thrill to think that their home has been invaded by a dangerous lunatic. Why did I imagine that the poorest writer in Paris could tell me how to turn myself into the plaything of the rich?

I asked Lionel, "Are you sure? Her brother-in-law hates Hungarians."

Lionel said, "Armand de Rossignol won't even know you're there. He is addicted to opium, and those dinner tables are long. Your baroness will seat you as far away from him as possible."

I felt a vague unease as I tied a red scarf around my neck and pulled a gangster's cap down on my forehead. Late or not, I should have gone home and changed when the butler who answered the door asked to see my identification.

He stood close, prepared to tackle me, while I searched my pockets

and in the process knocked over a vase that didn't break but only—
only!—spewed water, lilies, and slime across the marble floor.

A servant appeared and fixed the problem with a nimble flick of the
mop, a sleight of hand that took long enough for him to hiss, "Ming
Dynasty, you ignorant fool."

I sidled into the conservatory scented with tropical flowers, rumbling with the bassos of men in evening dress, punctuated by the
sweet tremolos of women with arms too smooth to keep their spangled dresses from spilling off their shoulders.

When I entered, the conversation stopped. Everyone stared, or so
it seemed.

I saw the men patting their pockets and their wives clutching their
evening bags. It is how we Hungarians act when a Gypsy boards the
tram.

The baroness swanned out of the crowd, swooping down to save
me. How happy she was to see me and how lovely she looked. Her silk
dress fit her like a coating of lilac liquid gleaming with silver bugles.
If I'd brought my camera, I might have broken our unspoken agreement and insisted on taking her picture. She handed me a glass of
champagne, brushed cigarette ash off my jacket, and hooked her arm
through mine.

Shouldn't this have signaled that I wasn't threatening or contagious? Yet when the baroness introduced me, her guests' smiles flickered and died. My name meant nothing to them, but their names were
the names of wines, perfumes, and banks. Mr. Brandy, Miss Cologne,
Mrs. Laundry Soap, and quite a number of Mr. and Mrs. Luxury Automobiles.

A servant hit a silver triangle, turning the guests into obedient
zombies. They shuffled beside the servants who showed them to their
places at the candlelit table set with crystal, china, heavy silver, sprays
of peonies and camellias.

The baroness patted my arm and left. I had no choice but to annoy
everyone, leaning in to read the cards until I found my seat between
two women closer to your age than mine. You will understand what
kind of dinner it was when I tell you that the lady on my right was a

cousin of Prince Yusupov, the murderer of Rasputin, while on my left
was the duchess on whom Proust modeled a character whose name
Papa would recognize, if I could recall it.

The Russian looked like a close relation of the mad monk's assassin. Proust's ancient muse seemed marginally less disturbing. I introduced myself to her as a friend of the baroness's, a photographer and
a writer. She seemed to think we'd met before, and said something I
didn't catch. Apparently she believed I'd recommended a doctor for
her cats. The veterinarian had worked miracles. I told her she was welcome. What did I like to photograph? I said I'd just been shooting in
an opium den.

My dinner partner shrank away, rigid with discomfort. Too late,
I remembered that our hostess's brother-in-law is rumored to be an
addict. The woman was practically apoplectic to think that someone
might overhear me. I would be to blame if she was never invited again.

I gulped my wine, then turned back to the Russian. This time I
planned to say, Like your cousin, the prince, I am acquainted with
darkness. I would tell her about the nights I spend walking the streets,
befriending thieves and pickpockets, police, prostitutes, and pimps.
. . . Maybe I would leave out the prostitutes and pimps.

The Russian turned her back on me before I could begin. I looked
around. The baroness caught my eye and smiled. Why didn't she seat
me near her if she liked me so much?

At the other end of the table was her husband Didi, as relaxed as if
forty dinner guests were a few friends at his club. Even though he was
sitting down, I could tell that he was tall. Everything about him was
exquisitely neat and crisp: his suit, his hair, his glowing pink skin, his
perfectly clipped eyebrows. Every cell of his being seemed forceful
and decisive, except for his eyes, which were a watery and uncertain
blue. His nose and mouth looked as if they had been pinched like rubber and allowed to snap back, then pinched and shaped again.

Darlings, you know how I admire the French, as do you, Papa. Even
so, it struck me that such a nose exists nowhere except in the middle
of a French face: a nose that makes you imagine God compressing two
nostrils into the tightest space that will let its owner breathe. Nos-

trils that thin were bred to convey a message: superiority, privilege, culture, money. Though you may wonder how a pair of nostrils could communicate all that. Despising the French for their nostrils—I am as bigoted as they are!

But where was the infamous brother-in-law? Another man with similarly pinched nostrils sat across the table from me, half dozing. It could only have been Armand. The Hungarian-hater.

A squad of servers delivered a dish to each guest at the precise same instant. On my plate were three small fish surrounded by a ring of green grapes. I hunched over my plate like a buzzard. I had to drain my whole glass of wine to get the nerve to look up again. Once more, I glanced at the baroness; once more, she noticed and turned away from the man with whom she was chatting. She twinkled encouragement at me. Observe how the sunbathing aristocrat waves at the drowning immigrant!

When I looked to see how others were tackling the first course, I observed the women cutting their grapes in half with tiny knives and forks. Were their lips and teeth too delicate for fruits the size of marbles? If I bisected a grape, it would at least postpone the more challenging problem of the fish. The first grape I attempted to cut flew across the table, landed beside Armand de Rossignol's plate, and roused him from his trance. He scowled at the grape, then at me. Of course it wasn't just any grape. It was the grape of a Hungarian.

Loudly enough for the whole room to hear, he said, "Did you lose something, my friend? Or is this how they introduce themselves in your part of the world? Do they pick boiled peppers out of their greasy Gypsy goulash and fling it across the table to say, 'Hello, nice to meet you.' "

He glared at me, I glared back. Everyone was watching. A white-gloved waiter appeared with a silver bowl into which he dropped my renegade grape with unconcealed disgust.

Gripped by a mild spasm, Armand bucked forward and sank back in his chair. I saw something flash in the lapel of his tuxedo, the cross made of twisted, fiery stakes: the symbol of the Order of the Legion of Joan of Arc. The Order was founded by decorated war

veterans sworn to purge France of Jews, Bolsheviks, Freemasons—
and foreigners like us.

I addressed myself to the fish. Its spine crumbled beneath my fork.
Lethal shards sprung from the flesh. What school had my fellow guests
attended to learn marine anatomy so well that the feathery skeletons
came loose with a single tug of the knife? A thatch of bone splinters
bristled from the mangled carcass on my plate. Burrs stuck in the back
of my throat. I swallowed, then coughed and gagged. The guests turned
toward me, some sympathetic, some concerned, all annoyed by the possibility that I might choke to death at their convivial table.

"Drink some wine," someone commanded. Others concurred,
"Drink wine!"

By the time the waiters had filled one glass, and then another,
either the bones had dislodged themselves, or I no longer cared. I
watched the homicidal fish disappear along with the plates of pearlescent, picked-clean bones.

Someone grabbed my shoulders from behind. I jumped and cried
out, a gaffe that the ladies around me pretended not to notice. A waiter
was tying a bib on me, obviously because I couldn't eat without chok-
ing like a baby.

I was about to fight him off when, just in time, I noticed that the
other diners were also wearing bibs as they applauded yet another military parade of waiters hoisting silver platters heaped with giant lobsters.
Had this menu been planned to torment the landlocked Hungarian?
Where in all of Hungary could we have procured a crustacean that
size? Silver nutcrackers appeared, and the guests turned into surgeons,
wielding picks and instruments designed to separate every morsel from
its shell. Have you ever eaten lobster? Probably Papa has.

Like the rest, I began with the tail, a satisfying chunk that slipped
onto the plate on which I could carve and dip it into a tiny dish of
herbed mayonnaise. Soon I grew overconfident, or maybe the wine
made me careless. When I attacked the head, not so much from appetite as to find out what was inside, a pale green blob of something
resembling nasal mucus landed on the Russian woman's arm.

I hurried to mop it up with my napkin, but, having little experience with removing lobster brains from a relative of Rasputin's assassin, I made everything worse, slicking runny ectoplasm across her forearm and onto the tablecloth.

A corps of waiters was dispatched to clean up the mess, and as the diners fell silent to watch this impromptu entertainment, I felt compelled to say something.

"Speaking of lobsters . . . last week I attended an amusing event. The Undersea Ball at the Nautilus Club." An inner voice told me to shut up. But a rival voice disagreed: you could be the life of the party. Or *this* party. Anything I did or said would be like a transfusion that might resuscitate this corpse of a social occasion.

I said, "They hold it once a year. The men all go as sea creatures. A few sharks trawl the waters. But most of the club's clientele dress as shrimps and angelfish and octopuses. Or is it *octopi*?"

No one had an opinion on that. There was nothing to do but go on. "The belle of the ball was a singer in an elaborate lobster hat. More like a headdress, really. He sang the most original song, using different voices to tell the sad tale of a rich married woman who telephones her lover to ask why she hasn't seen him. The lover, who has tired of her, claims that his dog has been sick. The woman suggests he call her veterinarian. He says the veterinarian came. He says his dog has died. Hysterical, she calls the cemetery and buys a plot for little Fifi, until the lover is forced to admit he doesn't *have* a dog. He never did. In the last verse the woman understands that she has been lied to. It was touching to hear this song sung so well by a lobster."

I waited for laughter. Chuckles. Anything. The guests stared at their plates.

They thought I was the baroness's lover! Which made my story about the adulterous woman not merely tactless but insane.

Surely you have guessed by now: there was no Undersea Ball. I'd invented the story out of two elements, a veterinarian and a lobster. But what had possessed me to bite the hand that was feeding me? The baroness had turned pale. I sent her a look of contrition. Or semicontrition. I was sorry. But it wasn't my fault. She should never have asked me to dinner.

I lurched and nearly stumbled as I got up from the table. Servants surrounded me, giants expressly hired to load the overindulged into taxis.

I declined the taxi. I was drunk, but not too drunk to know I didn't have the fare. I walked home and fell on my bed.

This morning I was awoken by the receptionist ringing to announce that he was bringing a visitor upstairs. My mystery guest must have paid the lazy slob a fortune to dislodge him from his desk!

How dear and kind the baroness looked as she leaned over my bed, her eyes moist with affection, sympathy, even pity.

She said that she was sorry. It was all her fault. She'd planned to seat her brother-in-law as far from me as she could. But he'd fallen into a chair directly across the table. She couldn't very well move him. Would I ever forgive her? I told her that I was the one who needed to be forgiven.

She kissed me chastely on the forehead, then began to walk around, inspecting everything, heading toward the corner I use as my darkroom. My impulse was to hide the prints on which I was still working. She studied a photo of a clown kissing a trapeze artist at the Medrano circus.

She asked, "Why haven't I seen this one?"

She said we had our work cut out for us. My French could use improvement, as could my wardrobe and table manners. As soon as I was ready, we would discuss my future.

So, it seemed, I'd been pardoned. The baroness was still my friend. The memory of last night returned in all its horror. Was she planning to make me her lapdog, a clown for the entertainment of every rightwing bigot in Paris?

But before I could speak, she said, "First things first. Let my secretary know what photographic equipment you need, how much money you will require to do more work like this. I don't mean work like *this*. I mean new work, *the work you want to make*."

She blew a kiss in my direction and let the door slam on her way out. I sat up and rubbed my eyes. Had I dreamed her visit? Could a dream have spiced my room with her exotic perfume?

Dear parents, do you have any idea what this means for us—for you? No more scrimping to send me the pennies that have sustained me until the last few days of each month. No more humiliating negotiations with the *Magyar Gazette.* Now you can go back to saving for your retirement as I devote myself to my art and prepare to enter the world that may yet appreciate and applaud me.

Even before I got out of bed, before I began to think about what to ask from the baroness, I wanted to send you this invitation to accompany me on the shining road before us. And if you imagine I will write you less often, or love you less, or be any less grateful, then you have forgotten who I am.

Your adoring Gabor

From *Make Yourself New*

BY LIONEL MAINE

An Essay on *l'amour*

L'amour, l'amour, toujours l'amour. Spring has come to the city of romance. Love is blooming on the riverbanks, in the alleys of Montmartre. Park benches exist for lovers exhausted by excessive kissing. The frustrated and the satisfied grow equally misty-eyed as the little sparrows and oily Romeos sing their hearts out in the clubs. Strolling arm in arm, enchanted couples catch their reflection in the Seine, a rippling pas de deux.

If I vomit two hundred words of that onto the page, I can get five dollars from the *Jersey City Herald*! Has my hometown run out of spectacular murders, or do the editors want to distract their readers with a French fantasy strategically placed between the accounts of infants burned in tenement fires and young husbands stabbed in broad-daylight downtown holdups?

If the subject *has* to be love, this is what I should write:

L'amour, l'amour, welcome to the city founded by lovers strictly for lovers. No one else need apply. No one can squeeze past the couples hogging the sidewalk, no one can rest his weary behind on the seats on which the amorous grope and writhe. The poster-hangers can't do their work because those caught short by passion are humping against every wall. Did Haussmann design the boulevards so men and women could embrace in the road, and the motorists must scatter, honking, around them? A citizen can't turn a corner without being treated to the appetizing sight of someone's tongue snaking down someone else's throat.

You're stuffed, you're force-fed love like a goose, until your liver's ready to burst. And if you don't happen to *be* in love? You'd be better off somewhere else. Don't order *boeuf* bourguignon if you're a vegetarian, don't venture into the tearooms if you don't like ladies with lapdogs. Don't come to Paris if you're planning a solitary hike through a sexual desert. It doesn't help to tell yourself that love is fleeting, that most of these lovers will fall out of love by tomorrow, or that these Parisian couples are unemployed actors paid by the mayor to keep up the city's reputation.

Meanwhile we lie about this paradise to earn enough to afford the privilege of being the only love-starved fool in Paris. Or so the city would like us to believe. In any case, that's the lie we're paid to spread each spring in order to lure the tourists and boost the failing French economy. So let me add this to the list of my crimes. In addition to my other misdeeds, I have whored myself out. I have lied. Two hundred words of bullshit about the romance of Par-ee.

When Suzanne said she was leaving me, I refused to believe her. This was a few days after our dinner with the baroness and Gabor, after she stripped at Ricardo's party. Or anyway so I heard. I was outside being sick. That night she didn't come home with me. I couldn't find her. Probably she'd been looking for me and gave up and left.

Days, then weeks went by. When a woman avoids her lover for a month, he (unless he is me) might think she was sending a message.

I ran into her doctor friend Ricardo on the boulevard Raspail. I asked if Suzanne was all right. He said yes, very much so. He'd seen her just last night. I might have been jealous if I hadn't known that Ricardo worshiped at the other church.

Desperate, I rang Suzanne's doorbell. I knew her mother was home. But the old lady didn't answer. Suzanne worked hard. She had two jobs. Maybe she was busy.

I waited for her to come to her senses. Let her take her time. And if she really was leaving me, well, there were other fish in the sea, plenty of pretty French girls.

One night, after several cognacs, I admitted that I was out of my

mind with grief. The idea of the future without her made me semisui-
cidal.

When Gabor told me that his baroness had suggested he get help
with his French and work on his accent, I reminded him that Suzanne
gave lessons. He could put in a good word for me, tell me how she was
doing. The perfect arrangement for everyone: an excellent teacher for
Gabor, the baroness's money in Suzanne's pocket. A good meal, some
wine, a comfortable bed to make love in. With less worry about how
she'd feed Mama, Suzanne could rediscover the creativity—the sexual
creativity—she'd had with me at the beginning. Once we wore Venetian masks, once she had me turn her upside down like the guy in the
da Vinci drawing. It was agonizing to think about that now.

Blinded by vanity and grief, I couldn't see the obvious: My good
"friend" Gabor knew that Suzanne taught French. He'd waited for me
to suggest it. To give them permission. A few days later Gabor told me
he'd started "studying" with Suzanne.

If he didn't know better, he would have thought Suzanne had
grown up speaking Hungarian. She knew exactly what a Hungarian
needed. The slippery bastard went on. "What a shame that you and
Suzanne are having trouble. You *are* having trouble, aren't you? Not
that I heard it from Suzanne. We never mention you. She's your lover.
I'm your friend."

Still, the romantic idiot—me—failed to put two and two together.
Until one evening I took my self-pity for a stroll along the Seine and,
finding a bench, nearly sat down on a pair of squirming exhibitionists.

It was Gabor and Suzanne! Was it a coincidence? Gentlemen, I
think not.

No one wants to hear a pathetic middle-aged expat whining about
lost love. Especially not a *poor* middle-aged expat, or worse, an unpublished writer. Here in France they want Hemingway. That's what
American means. The grizzly bear thumping his chest. Not that I
wouldn't thump, if I had a chest worth thumping. Hemingway should
have stayed in the Midwest. He ruined things for the rest of us, telling
all those lies. The lie about courage, the lie about every red-blooded
male needing to kill a bull or climb Mount Kilimanjaro.

What about the red-blooded male who just wants to eat, drink, and fuck—and who has lost the love of his life to a short, homely, Hungarian "artist" *still living off his parents*? If only I could have warned Suzanne: the guy is good-hearted, talented, but self-involved, infantile, weak. Didn't a woman of her intelligence know better than to fall in love with an emotional cripple terminally stunted by his unmanly dependence on Mama and Papa?

What did my friend have going for him? Those crazy eyes? That hair? Did Suzanne imagine he *listened to her*, which she always complained I didn't? I knew how much fun it was to roam the streets with him all night, watching what he photographed, meeting the colorful characters who trusted him to take their portraits. Whom am I jealous of, really? Do I envy Gabor for sleeping with Suzanne? Or do I envy Suzanne for going on Gabor's midnight rambles?

All I can do is hoard my pain to pour into my next book: *The Loser's Guide to Paris.*

Meanwhile, a few words of wisdom for my friends in the States. Here are five things to do in the city of *l'amour* when you have a few centimes in your pocket and the woman of your dreams has left you for your best friend.

One: See the two of them everywhere. Contemplate suicide. Would it seem too tourist-y to jump off the Eiffel Tower? Wouldn't a real Parisian throw himself in the Seine? Forget suicide. Paris is for the living! Save the impulse to end it all until you get back to New Jersey.

Two: Distract yourself. Paris has something for everyone. Let's imagine you are feeling slightly disenchanted with women. Dozens of places will persuade you that a beautiful woman is nothing more than a beautiful man in a dress. At Le Cirque, a six-foot Texan named Barbette hangs from a trapeze by his teeth—in a tutu and a tiara! At the Ton Ton Club, you can watch the enchanting Tiptina Sisters. Or go across the street where the equally enchanting Rocky Twins, two handsome Norwegian boys, dance and sing exactly like the Tiptina Sisters, in the original register and wearing the same gowns. Depressed about the human condition? Head for the Bobino and watch a Ferris wheel powered by cats wearing tiny straw boaters, a man dressed as a gorilla playing classical violin, and a woman who danced with Pavlova removing, feather by feather, fifty pounds of ostrich plumes. Spend twenty minutes in the Louvre, you'll see twenty women more beautiful than the one who left you.

Three: You're in Paris. Go to whores. Visit the brothel where you used to go with your Hungarian friend who pretended he was only there to take pictures. Choose a girl who reminds you of her. It's happened to her before. You can cry on her shoulder. Or pick the one with the softest heart and tell her your heart has been broken. It might get you a little something extra.

Four: Drink an entire bottle of wine, then stand outside the hotel where your beloved has shacked up with your former best friend. Look up at his window. Imagine them in bed until you get hard. Fall to your knees with your hand outstretched and wail, Help me help me, like that crazy Spanish beggar in the rue de Rivoli. Repeat until the hotel manager comes out and threatens to call the cops.

Five: Invite your friend for a beer. Promise you're not going to punch him. Even if it's not true, say everything is forgiven. Spend your last pennies on alcohol until your forgiveness is real.

I've agreed to limit myself to five, but let me add one more.

See her, quite by accident, after a long separation. She is lying on the sidewalk, modeling for a series of photographs he is taking. Talk to her. Say the wrong things. Tell her that you are angry at him when you mean you are missing her. You want to say, He doesn't care about you, he only cares about his photos.

Restrain yourself from saying that. She loves him. She's not going to listen to you. And still you want to tell her that she was wrong when she said you didn't understand her and only thought about your writing. That was unfair and untrue. You know who she is, and you love her.

That's when your friend appears and explains why she's been lying on the sidewalk. It has something to do with ectoplasm, with the residue of the dead. He's been trying to catch it on film. In other words, some Hungarian bullshit that's the most interesting thing you've heard in ages. You think, Fuck it. The guy's a genius. He deserves her.

What is a woman, after all? You are alive and in Paris.

From the (Unpublished) Memoirs
of Suzanne Dunois Tsenyi
To be destroyed on the occasion of its author's death

HE WAITED TILL we were in bed, after sex.

He said, "Suzanne, I need a favor."

I thought, There is nothing I wouldn't do.

I said, "Like what? It depends."

He wanted me to play dead on the sidewalk across from his hotel. Some friends of his would pretend to be strangers gathered around me. They'd play it so straight that real strangers would collect around my corpse. He'd arranged for a hearse to take me away, while he photographed the scene in stages, looking down from his window.

Any sane, self-respecting woman would have said "Are you out of your mind?" But love, it seemed, had obliterated my sanity and self-respect.

Morning and night I thought about him. All day I waited for evening so I could see him again. When I got home from the language school or the life-drawing class, Gabor was waiting for me at his hotel. We made love as soon as I walked in and only afterward thought about dinner. His kitchen was a hot plate on which my repertoire was limited to a decent onion soup. There were only a few restaurants that we could afford. One café let us split an order of roast lamb and flageolet beans, the perfect meal for indigent lovers.

There were problems, small ones, but problems nonetheless. When he asked me to pose as the dead girl, I asked, "Who's paying for the hearse?"

"A friend," he said. I knew which friend. Let her lie in the street in her ermine coat! He pulled my head against his chest and gently stroked my hair.

"When?" I said.

"Tomorrow noon."

I said, "I'm giving lessons all day."

He said, "Come on your lunch break. The light will be perfect. It's supposed to be cloudy."

I said, "It's all the way across town."

He said, "Take a taxi. I'll pay."

I almost said, "She'll pay."

First he kissed me, then he said, "Let's go for a walk. Then back to bed. All right?"

"Yes," I said. Yes to it all. I had become a puppy that stands on its hind legs and barks when its master fetches its leash.

I had grown up in Paris. But now I saw my city with the clarity of the newly arrived. I followed him, stopped when he stopped and started again when he did. I'd always been the kind of girl who walked ahead of her boyfriend. Lionel used to complain that he'd had to skip, to keep up. What had made that quick, independent girl lag so meekly behind?

But why was I so hard on myself for changing in his presence, when each night, a city transformed itself into whatever he desired? I watched the darkness ask questions to which he always found new answers. I watched him finding the marvelous in the everyday. He used to say he wanted to raise himself to the level of the object, to the glory of the trolley track, the smokestack, and the tunnel.

He photographed a gutter: a cobblestone cobra winding between two trees. The shadow of a buttress underneath a bridge became the silhouette of a fat man in a crooked top hat. He caught the fireworks showering the welders fixing a tram. The workers greeted him by name and offered us coffee with brandy.

As we walked alongside the prison wall, he let go of my hand. How could there have been such interesting shadows on that same wall last night—and such dull ones now? I told myself it wasn't my fault if the shadows were less exciting. His gloom lifted at the entrance to a narrow street of hotels whose neon signs hung like the banners in a Shanghai bazaar. The hotel of the universe, the hotel of the world, the hotel of the princess, the hotel of the king.

Pausing on the bridge, he meant to say, Look at the Seine. But what he said was, "Regard the breasts." I was no longer a useful teacher for him. I'd stopped correcting his French.

We'd only had two lessons. He'd insisted I must be part Hungarian. How else could I know exactly what a Hungarian needed? That lesson ended abruptly. We were too shy to go on. At the end of the second class, he was just about to leave when he turned around and we clung to each other. Until then our loyalty to Lionel had kept us from acting on what, we later agreed, was decided that night I stripped—for him—at Paul and Ricardo's party.

As we gazed at the river, I wanted him to embrace me. But he wasn't there for love. Or anyway, not love for me. I'd never wanted to be the flattering mirror in which a man admires his talent.

But how could I stop loving a man to whom a city is saying, Tell me what you want. For him, two gendarmes shared a smoke by a streetlamp and traveled back through time to take a break from pursuing the serial killer Landru. For him, the magicians with their long wands lit the last gas lamps in our electric city. For him, an elderly prostitute in moth-eaten furs extended her spotted hand, and the ghost of her lost beauty flirted with the camera. A taxi paused long enough for him to catch the wink of its passenger's diamond bracelets. For him, for him, for no one else. And for me, if I was with him.

Often the dawn was coming up when we got back to his room. He pulled the shades, lit the blood-colored bulb, and made negatives from the plates. Watching our night alchemized into art swimming in clear liquid, I knew I'd become a very strange puppy, trained not only to wait for the signs of its master going for a walk but also to associate passion with the smell of developing fluid.

We went to bed at six. An hour later we fell asleep. I slept for another hour, then got up and dressed for work. On my way out I kissed him. Though he slept more than he admitted, this time he was awake.

Insomnia had a starring role in the drama he played with his parents. It gave him something to write about instead of telling them about me.

"Will you do it?" he said.

"Do what?"

"Play dead," he said.

No, I thought.

"Yes," I said. "Tell me again. What time, and where do you want me?"

The morning was cold and bleak. Walking to the Métro, I dreaded lying on the damp sidewalk. If Gabor loved me, he wouldn't make me suffer. He couldn't bear to see what I'd look like, brought down by an accident or an illness. I could never tell Mama. She would advise me again to leave him.

But wasn't it also possible that this *proved* how much he loved me? He was using his worst fantasy—his lover dead, surrounded by strangers—to inspire his art. I was doing him a favor, but he was giving me something too. I would live forever as the pretty corpse on the sidewalk. I also knew what Mama would say about a man who promised you immortality instead of a wedding ring.

That morning, at the language school, I was no longer Suzanne the Liar, assuring the rich, unteachable Portuguese widow that her French was improving. Or Spineless Suzanne, absorbing the casual insults the Austrian businessman lobbed my way. Or Saintly Suzanne, refunding the money of the near-mute Chinese boy who shared an apartment—and my classroom—with nine other waiters. I was only pretending to be the underpaid, duplicitous, ineffective, struggling teacher of immigrant French. The real Suzanne was the lover and muse of a brilliant artist.

By lunchtime it was drizzling. Surely Gabor would cancel the shoot. But when I got to his hotel, I saw him standing outside with three photographer friends. They nodded to me, just barely. I'd met them before, in cafés, where they'd ignored me and talked to Gabor.

They've all brought umbrellas. Gabor had known what the weather would be. He wanted the puddled sidewalk, the drenched corpse, the scalloped black discs of the open umbrellas, the mourners' shiny black raincoats. He ran to me and embraced me. My doubts and resentments vanished.

He handed me a coat. He'd traded a dozen eggs to a corporal in the Hungarian army for this double-breasted greatcoat. It was the coat a homeless girl might wear with only a slip underneath, a fringe of lace Gabor could catch on film from his window, if he used the right lens.

I asked him where he wanted me to lie. He said, "Over there beneath the plane tree where the pavement is dry."

I lay down beneath the tree. The pavement was cold and wet. He told me to roll onto my side, bend my knees, and shut my eyes. Lift the hem of my coat. Like that. He whispered that he loved me. He asked if I was all right. I said I was fine. He thanked me and said he was sorry.

I'd lied. I wasn't fine. Playing dead made me think about the dead who weren't pretending. I thought about my father and how, after he was killed, I believed I would always be counting the days till I saw him in heaven. I stopped believing in heaven long before I stopped counting. I remembered the letter from the army, edged in black. My mother said we were lucky to get it. After the war, she showed me a photo of unmarked graves. She said those were the unlucky ones. I said we were all unlucky. Mama's health was fragile. No matter where I was, I felt a pang whenever she had an attack.

Lying on the sidewalk, I wept for Mama, for Papa, for the widows and orphans, the maimed and wounded veterans begging in the streets. Lionel used to say it moved him to see women cry, but he was lying. I even wept for Lionel and for the unhappiness I'd caused him.

As the dampness seeped through the heavy coat, I thought how someday I would be dead and buried in the cold ground. Sooner than we could imagine, Gabor and I would be skeletons in distant parts of the earth. I would lie beside Mama, and he would return to his parents in the cemetery above the town he thought he'd escaped. He'd told me he wanted to be buried in Paris. But I didn't believe him, no more than I believed that Lionel liked to see women cry.

I fought back tears. A weeping dead girl would have spoiled the shot, though only Gabor would have noticed. Anyone else would have thought: raindrops.

Again Gabor asked if I was all right. I nodded. He said he was going upstairs. I heard him shout down from his window—but not to me. I lay still. The wet earth stank of dog piss. Gabor's friends stood above me. One knelt and felt my wrist for a pulse. He remained like that for a while. I heard the voices of strangers. Gabor's friends told the gathering crowd that the police had been called.

A woman said, "How tragic! So young!"

A child was crying, "Let's go, Mama! I'm cold! I'm scared." Obviously I couldn't tell the kid not to worry. The crowd's reaction to *that* would have been something for Gabor to film. But not the image he wanted. He would punish me by spending more time with the baroness. I didn't think he was sleeping with her. But she gave him money, bought his prints, introduced him to glamorous people. I was ashamed to be thinking about her when I was supposed to be dead. Was this how I would spend the afterlife, competing with my rival, worrying because Gabor had mentioned that the baroness had offered to set up a studio where he could work, instead of in the hotel room where he and I spent almost every night?

At last I heard a van pull up. Hands loaded me on a stretcher. It was even colder inside the van, which reeked of blood and poultry. The engine started, we pulled away from the curb, then stopped. Gabor was still taking pictures. The van turned a corner and stopped again.

Only then did I open my eyes. An elderly man was driving. His helper rode beside him, reading a magazine with a naked girl on the cover. The driver asked if I could walk back on my own.

He said, "Forgive me, Mademoiselle. But you look unwell, and your coat is soaked."

I said, "It's my boyfriend's coat." He seemed to find the mention of a boyfriend reassuring, though I could tell they both wondered why this boyfriend didn't take better care of a girl like me. I couldn't bear their pity. I'd rather they thought I was a whore who'd gotten paid for posing. I didn't want them knowing I'd lain on the sidewalk just because a man asked. Did they know that another woman had paid them to cart me away, a rich woman who was in love with him and could buy him whatever he wanted?

I walked back to Gabor's hotel. It wasn't far, but my legs shook. I felt as if I'd died on the street and been resurrected. The strangers had dispersed. Gabor's friends were leaving. Gabor looked ecstatic, though normally he was too superstitious to be happy until he saw the final print.

He said to me, "I'm glad you're alive."

"So am I," I said.

He took my face in his hands and kissed me. It was difficult to stop, and when we did, the looks we exchanged contained (or so it seemed to me) a promise about the future.

First I had to go back to work. I returned his wet coat. He seemed shocked by how heavy it was.

He said, "I'm sorry, I'm sorry, Suzanne."

I said, "Don't apologize. I love you."

I waited to see him appear at his window and wave. Someone grabbed my arm. It took me longer than it should have to recognize Lionel. How strange that, only months ago, this stranger had been inside me.

Gabor had said they'd had a drink, and that it was all right with Lionel if Gabor and I were together. Who was Lionel to approve or not? How sweetly old-fashioned of Gabor to ask his friend's permission. The thought was infuriating, and yet I had to admit that it pleased me to know they'd been talking about me.

Lionel hadn't changed much. But our lives had changed. I might have recognized him sooner if I hadn't known him so well.

I said, "Lionel, I was just thinking about you."

"Thinking what?" He was hoping I'd say I missed him.

"Thinking about your writing," I lied.

"Suzanne, I'll always adore you," he said. "But he's a thieving son of a bitch."

Lionel put his arm through mine. I wished that *we* were friends. I wanted to know what he thought about my loving a man whose bills were being paid by another woman. He was the last one I could ask. It would have been too cruel.

I'd asked my friend Ricardo, who said that one had to put up with a lot when one loved an artist. I knew he was talking about Paul, who was said to have slept with every eligible man, and many ineligible men, in Paris.

The baroness would have said I was being dull and provincial. If she thought about me, which I doubted. Whenever I ran into her, it took her a while to remember who I was. Or anyway so she pretended. There are some people who remain your best friends even if you haven't seen them for ages, and others with whom you start from scratch every time. The baroness was one of those. She and I always began anew, and we never got very far. Occasionally she called Gabor on the phone she'd had installed for him—and he had to go to her house, regardless of how late it was. She'd decided to hang a print of his work and needed him to tell her where it should go.

How long could I persuade myself that their relationship was all about Gabor's art? Would he leave me for her? She was still attractive. I couldn't forbid him to see her. What choice did I have? I couldn't support him. I could barely feed myself and my mother. If he had to go back to journalism, he would be miserable—and blame me. Our happiness depended on the baroness's kindness.

Lionel said, "That son of a bitch. First he stole my girlfriend, and now he steals my idea."

I said, "No one stole me, Lionel."

He said, "I was the one who saw the dead man on the street. Actually, in the Luxembourg Gardens. Where they have the pony rides. I told Gabor."

How typical of Lionel to think he was the only person who'd ever seen a corpse on a Paris street. Every night, some poor clochard dropped dead under a bridge. Gabor had seen plenty of them. He didn't need to steal Lionel's idea. And he hadn't stolen me.

I said, "I'll tell him you were here."

He said, "You two deserve each other."

I said, "Why don't you write about it? Isn't that what you do?"

"For all you know, I already have. Look! Your poor little shoes are wet."

Gabor and I deserved each other! I could have kissed Lionel for that.

Moments later Gabor appeared. He'd seen us from his window. He hugged me, then Lionel, then stepped back, a little shyly. Lionel and I were about to be charmed into not minding something we should have minded.

Gabor said, "I don't want to be rude, but can I ask you two dear friends to continue your conversation out of camera range? I'm still trying to get the final shot. I apologize, darling. I love you."

"I love you too," I said.

"Great," Lionel said. "Everyone loves everyone else. Everyone but me. Can I borrow a few francs? Just until my check comes from home. Two days at the most."

Gabor pulled out a bill and gave it to him. The baroness's money.

Gabor said, "Let's have a drink soon, Lionel. There's so much I want to talk about with you. For example, these photos . . ."

"What about them?" said Lionel, more interested than he'd been in anything I'd said.

Already they were forgetting me, my boyfriend and his friend, starting out on a journey I wasn't invited to join. In a way, it was sadder than playing dead on the street.

Gabor said, "They were never about the girl or the crowd. I wanted the afterimage of her presence and her subsequent absence. Remember the pictures you showed me at that creepy gallery with the homosexual pornography and the Victorian spirit photos? I swear, the girl's ghost had just appeared in my lens when I saw you two, down here. Give me a few minutes. Maybe it will return."

"Ectoplasm," Lionel said.

"Exactly," Gabor replied.

And who was *I*, exactly? The girl who'd lain in the puddle of frozen dog piss. The girl whose death hadn't mattered. Whose body wasn't the point. The point was some residue that my death had smeared on the rainy air.

Lionel said to Gabor, "Take the girl. Steal all my ideas. What can I say? What can anyone do?" He turned to me. "You know what, Suzanne? Your boyfriend's a fucking genius."

From *The Devil Drives:*
The Life of Lou Villars

BY NATHALIE DUNOIS

Chapter Four: Early Days at the Chameleon

LET ME START with a suggestion for my sisters in academia. Those of you who may be thinking about writing a doctoral thesis that bridges the disciplines of psychology and literature might consider an underexplored topic: the dream life of the biographer.

During the writing of this book, I attended lectures and bookstore readings by respected and/or successful biographers. Several times I traveled to Paris to hear a writer I'd seen on TV. I remember the author of a biography of the Goncourt brothers saying she'd started from the position that every word the brothers wrote was a lie, and she'd left it up to them to prove they were telling the truth. A man who wrote a life of de Gaulle said he'd always felt that the general had suppressed certain facts about crucial events in Algiers. His suspicions had proved correct, but we would have to buy his book to find out what they were. I watched a Hitler scholar, a Freudian—this was a book I bought—claim that the explanation for everything Hitler did could be found in the architectural model he built, during his last days in the bunker, for remodeling his childhood home, the Austrian city of Linz.

But not once in all those speeches did I hear the biographers mention the dreams they'd had while working on their books.

Every night for weeks I dreamed about the photographer Gabor Tsenyi giving Lou Villars the business card of the Chameleon Club.

Why was I fixated on that? It was hardly the most important event in Lou's life. At that time I couldn't afford a therapist who might have helped me understand the source of my obsession, and I had to puzzle it out on my own.

What if it *was* the most meaningful thing that ever happened to Lou? Didn't everything follow from that? The friends she made, the people she met, the disparate circles she moved in.

I realize that it is not the biographer's job to speculate on the meaning of dreams. In my case, it's been hard enough to construct a narrative from bits and scraps. How fortunate that detailed financial records were kept, tracking the income and expenses at the Chameleon Club.

We know that Lou Villars worked there and later frequented the club from the late 1920s until she was asked to leave in 1935; a side note in her file cross-references a visit from Clovis Chanac, the infamous police prefect who rose to head the Municipal Council of Paris until a series of scandals obliged him to become the gangster he had always been, in his criminal heart.

We know that Yvonne began every evening with a song about a dead sailor. Then she welcomed the audience to the Chameleon. She told them to think of the club's front door as a portal to a magic kingdom. Crossing the threshold, they could shed the false skin, the disguises they wore for the world. The butterflies inside them could emerge from their cocoons. They should think of themselves as infants restored to the family to which God intended to send them, before he misdirected the stork to their biological parents. Then because the weather got heavy when Yvonne talked this way, she joked about feeling free to take off their trousers and relax. Or *put on* their trousers, if they preferred!

Lou laughed along with everyone else, even when she felt like crying. She knew that Yvonne was telling the truth. Yvonne had created this place for her and for others like her: born into the wrong life, the wrong body, an innocent victim of God's mistake.

No one asked where she'd come from or what she expected to find. Every so often someone looked at her—as Yvonne had, at first—as if they recognized her from somewhere. Had they seen her face on the posters? Or watched her perform at the Vélodrome d'Hiver? No one asked, and she told no one. As far as anyone knew, she'd been born with blood on her white clothes, on the day when Fat Bernard mistook her for the wine boy.

She missed her life as an athlete. She missed waking every morning in a state of hope. She missed the speed, the sting of the wind on her face, the blur of the world flying past her. She missed the sensation of her arm and the javelin becoming one, then separating like a rocket shedding its fiery tail. She missed knowing that she was getting stronger and faster every day. She missed the promise of the Olympics, the travel, the friends all over the country. She missed the hockey field at the convent. She even missed the tedious Vélodrome demonstrations.

She missed Sister Francis, but not Dr. Loomis. She tried not to dwell on what he'd done, on what he'd tried to do. She could never go back to them. But how did one become a professional without coaches or promoters?

Asleep in the tiny cubicle behind the Chameleon Club's kitchen, she again dreamed of being murdered by bandits on a foggy country road. She woke in tears that lasted until she heard the clatter of dishes as Véronique, the bearded lady, began setting tables for the evening.

Meanwhile Lou enjoyed the jobs Yvonne assigned her. For a while she helped take coats and hats. She loved seeing what was hidden underneath the customers' street clothes: the evening gown made from playing cards clacking under a man's fur coat, the spit curls peeking out from the brim of a fedora, the Adam's apple beneath the necklace, the painted-on mustache emerging from a shawl wound like a harem girl's veil.

Lou had a gift for the cloakroom. She liked touching and stroking the clothes. And the smiles she gave the clients showed how much she admired their glamorous disrobings. She knew which coat belonged to which guest without using anyone's name. She herself wore the uniform of a hotel porter. She loved its rough material, the ruts it left in the crooks of her knees and elbows, the circular red hollows the buttons dug into her chest. The jackets fit more comfortably if she continued to bind her breasts, as she used to, when she ran. She learned to cut her own hair, like a man's.

After work she exercised in her room, as energetically as she could without disturbing the others. She had a tendency to gain weight, and she refused to let her body get rubbery and weak.

When bearded Véronique left the club to join the circus, Lou was given new trousers, a shirt, an apron, and sent out onto the floor to put out tablecloths and collect empty glasses. It was less fun than taking coats, but it was a promotion. In the cloakroom she'd made a friend named Vilma, a Polish girl who earned a few extra cents selling religious cards of Joan of Arc, dirty photos, and cartoons of hook-nosed Jews counting money and molesting children. Now Vilma pretended not to see Lou when they passed in the hall.

Lou had expected to be invisible as she cleared the tables, but she was anything but. Customers whispered as she walked by. She had no idea what they were saying, but she liked it that people were talking. Every time someone noticed her made it seem as if she wasn't doomed to remain a former Olympic hopeful working as a busboy. She told herself she was still in training, lifting heavy basins of dishes and lugging them to the kitchen.

At night she prayed to Saint Joan for guidance on the path of obedience without resistance, a road she trod with a bowed head except when a flash of biceps beneath a sequined sleeve or the sight of a sailorette practicing splits recalled her vanished hopes. Then a customer might yell something like, Hey, little cream puff, why so gloomy?

After Lou's first week as a busboy, Fat Bernard gave her an envelope and told her to sign her name in a ledger. In the envelope was enough money to buy cigarettes. This period marked the start of Lou's lifelong dependence on tobacco and alcohol. Those of us who have faced and failed the challenge of conquering our self-destructive habits will find it easy to understand and forgive her, if only for this.

Like her coworkers, Lou kept her money tucked into her sock. She was saving to rent a place of her own, as Yvonne suggested.

Perhaps she'd become a waiter. Some of the waiters were legendary for their efficiency, tact, and discretion. Yvonne made very few hiring mistakes, so no one was ever fired, though a few employees had stalked out after lovers' quarrels. During Lou's first week, a clarinet player left her drummer girlfriend for a young, masculine German banker whom everyone but the clarinet player knew was a penniless, middle-aged American woman.

That autumn the gossip was that a dancer named Amazon Rose had gotten pregnant, thus ending the long debate about whether Rose was a female. Yvonne was using Rose's departure as an excuse to up-date the revue. Monsieur Pavel, the choreographer, was seen going into her office. Which lucky Cinderella would exchange the scrub brush for the spangled sailor suit?

After closing, when the staff gathered to finish the wine in the bottles the customers had left, occasionally someone asked Lou if she liked girls or boys. She said she didn't like anyone. Ha-ha, was she a virgin? It was none of their business. These moments of group hilarity were briefer than they might have been if Lou hadn't been stronger than anyone except a few male dancers and possibly Fat Bernard.

She worked hard. Everyone liked her. When a customer slipped her a tip, she divided it with the others. Twice Yvonne absentmind-edly patted Lou on the head.

One afternoon the staff was ordered to stay away from the club. The exterminators needed privacy to do whatever they did. There was nowhere Lou wanted to go. Some day she'd look for Robert, but not now. Not yet.

Heading out for an aimless walk, Lou got as far as the corner when she spotted Yvonne alone at a café table. Should Lou pretend not to see her? Yvonne beckoned her over. She asked Lou if she wanted a coffee. Lou nodded. A coffee with Yvonne! She didn't trust herself to speak.

Lou stirred in three cubes of sugar. The coffee was delicious.

"You have a sweet tooth?" Yvonne said.

"No, not always," Lou said.

They sat in silence for fifteen minutes. Lou swabbed the sweet grainy sludge at the bottom of the cup and licked it off her finger.

Yvonne said, "Can I ask you something?"

Lou wanted to say no, but nodded.

"Weren't you on a poster for a performance at the Vélodrome d'Hiver?"

"That was me," Lou admitted, bracing herself. For what?

"Let's go back to the club," said Yvonne. "The rats must be dead by now."

A peppery cloud of pesticide hovered over the dance floor. The air tasted to Lou like the birthday cake that Robert had laced with pigeon poison. She'd just been thinking of Robert. Maybe that meant something. Yvonne asked Fat Bernard to air the place out, lest a customer have an attack. Many of them had weak lungs, as Bernard well knew.

In her office Yvonne motioned for Lou to push aside some silky garments on the couch. Lou sat on a high-heeled sandal. It was awkward, retrieving it and finding a place to put it.

Yvonne began to open her mail. Without looking up, she said, "Could you lift a small woman?"

"I think so." Lou was lifting fifty kilos when she ran away from Dr. Loomis, but it was always wise to be modest.

Yvonne reached into her purse and took out her lizard, which she'd brought with her when the poison was being sprayed. Lou never understood how such a smart businesswoman and talented singer could cherish those nasty, scaly creatures. Once Lou overheard Yussef the dishwasher explain to an Algerian busboy whom he had a crush on: the Nazarenes had their rosaries, Madame Yvonne had her chameleon. "Love is strange" was what everyone said. It was practically the club motto.

Yvonne said, "Would you like my little friend to tell your fortune?" It was the last thing Lou wanted. "Very much," she said.

Yvonne shuffled a deck of playing cards and scattered them on the floor. She dipped the lizard's feet in a rouge pot and set the creature down. Cupping her hands so he couldn't escape, she let him roam over the cards, then gently dropped the chameleon back in his glass terrarium. She selected the cards marked with tiny red claw prints and studied them, frowning.

She said, "You will move extremely fast. You will be greatly honored. You will inflict a great deal of pain. You will die a violent, early death."

Lou said "My God" as each sentence Yvonne spoke erased the previous one, leaving a few indelible words: Speed. Honor. Pain. Violent. Early death.

Yvonne said, "I am sorry to give you this troubling news. But isn't it better to be warned? Now thank me and my little lizard."

"Thank you both," said Lou. What did a lizard know? A reptile with rouge on its feet! No French person would do such a thing. This charade was an import from a barbaric land of Gypsy sorcerers and cavemen.

A pattern emerges in retrospect: a chain of large and small events that would turn Lou Villars against foreigners, a prejudice that made her an easy mark for the false prophets who seduced her and the demons that possessed her. Though it's also possible that these biases already existed, remnants from childhood, inherited from her father and impressed upon her by her British nanny. Someone else might have been alarmed by a lizard's dire predictions without concluding, as did Lou, that it was a dirty Hungarian trick.

Later, Lou would tell this story to her women friends in the regional sports clubs, the innocent dupes from whom she extracted information to pass along to the enemies of France. She'd laugh when she described the fortune-telling reptile, but with a wince suggesting that a shiver of foreboding rattled her every time. She would offer the story as a confidence, and the women responded with secrets of their own.

After she'd given Lou the bad news, Yvonne said, "Can you lift *two* women? I mean, one woman at a time. For the new dance numbers. Both girls are tiny. You will be perfect. It requires more strength than grace. And there is something about you. . . . The crowd will love it. Don't ask me why. Report tomorrow morning at ten to Pavel's rehearsal studio."

"How do I get there?" asked Lou.

"Ask Arlette," said Yvonne.

Arlette Jumeau sang in the chorus during the grand finale in which a wooden boat filled with sailors dressed as the opposite sex sang a saucy but touching chorus about leaving for a warmer and more hospitable climate. The customers knew all the words and sang along with tears in their eyes.

Arlette was also going to Pavel's for the first time, but she was Parisian and knew the city. She belonged to a small clique of girls who did errands for Yvonne, trips to the seamstress and florist. These girls were all very beautiful. Their principal job was to make male and female customers fall in love with them and get flustered and buy more drinks to relax. None of them was for sale. Prostitution was a firing offense. None of these girls had been fired.

In an early photo, a cheap publicity shot, Arlette perches cross-legged on a rock. She is wearing a modest bathing costume. Her head is tilted to one side, her chin balanced on one finger, a pose that, like everything in the picture, suggests a deficient imagination. Though the photo is in black and white, Arlette—clearly blond and blue-eyed—looks like a spoiled child's expensive doll.

Arlette had many admirers, but her heart belonged to a boy named Eddie, who worked in a cheese shop and wanted to be a boxer. On Friday nights he drank too much and got loud and stupid. At first Yvonne had Fat Bernard throw him out of the club. But the customers saw the sweet spirit inside the handsome tough guy who reeked of Camembert. Or maybe they saw the handsome face and invented the sweetness. When Eddie was sober enough to be charming, he and Arlette glided from table to table, and the customers bought them champagne.

To Arlette, Lou was a busboy. Lou wanted to say she was more than that. But what would she have added? She was not about to tell a stranger about her past as a sports star-in-training. How pitiful it would make her seem, to admit how far she'd fallen. But who did Arlette think *she* was? Her voice wasn't especially good, nor could she do backbends and midair somersaults like the dancers. Granted, she was pretty, which counted for a lot.

Arlette said nothing as they set off for Pavel's studio. In the tram, which was so crowded that they had to stand, an expensively dressed pervert plastered himself against Arlette and was stealthily fondling her breasts. Lou jabbed him with her elbow so hard that he staggered off at the next stop. But Arlette seemed not to notice, let alone feel grateful for having been rescued. At the studio, she motioned for Lou to go upstairs first, ostensibly from politeness but in reality so they wouldn't be seen arriving together.

Pavel shook their hands and wagged his head so that his pointed beard tipped back and forth like the second hand on a clock. Lou thought of Miss Frost's book about a flock of winged infants who subsisted on pollen and nectar. The blossoms sustaining Pavel were dancers in pink tutus. He treated his students like artists: future ballerinas. It was beneath him to mention the venues where they would practice their art.

Despite Arlette's efforts to distance herself from Lou, the class knew they were the new ones, the only ones who listened when Pavel cracked his stick on the floor and announced, "I am not Diaghilev. I am something else." The others continued doing bends and stretches while their teacher summarized his career. As a young man, he'd danced with Diaghilev, who'd fired him for some minor infraction. A heavy blow, but also a badge of honor that admitted him to the distinguished confraternity of the master's former slaves.

For a while he had worked with the great Josephine Baker. But they had a falling-out when she'd gotten tired of shaking her behind in a skirt made from bananas and of appearing on stage nude but for a single flamingo feather. He'd told her the fans insisted on it, and he had been wrong.

His students went on with their leg lifts and knee bends. Lou liked watching her classmates perform strenuous exercises more targeted and effective than lugging tubs of dishes to the kitchen. She didn't have to be an Olympic champion. She might not be graceful, but she was strong. She could be a dancer!

Warmed up, the students began the high kicks and splits, the cascading pretzels and contortions they'd made famous at the club. Pavel moved from one to the next, suggesting improvements, until he reached Lou and Arlette.

"Of course. Of course. I remember now. My little mermaid and her sailor."

Apparently Yvonne and Pavel had discussed a number in which Arlette would dance the part of a mermaid. Lou would play the sailor who caught the sea creature in his net and fell in love with her while the others swam around them.

Lou's other duties would include lifting a little Filipina named Florine, formerly the partner of the pregnant Amazon Rose. Surrounded by girls in skimpy kimonos, Florine would reprise her popular song about first love and cherry blossoms. Lou could wear the same costume she wore for the mermaid routine. They would see how the Madame Butterfly number worked without Amazon Rose.

Florine had called in sick today, so they could rehearse that later. This morning, they would begin with Lou and Arlette's pas de deux.

Before he allowed Lou to lift Arlette, Pavel put her through the motions: Stand there. Plant your legs like that. No, like that. Step behind the mermaid. Put one hand under her armpit, the other under her thigh. Stop when you have her at shoulder level. Then raise her over your head. Whatever you do, don't drop her. Now put her down. Yvonne was right. You'll be fine.

Lou might have been more pleased had she been less aware that Arlette was refusing to look at her. Poor Arlette! Lou pitied her for having drawn her as a partner.

Pavel apologized to the class because, like Florine, his accompanist was out sick. Something must be going around. Lou could tell from the dancers' faces that this accompanist had been indisposed for quite some time. A pianist's wages would have strained the choreographer's budget. The grand piano appeared to have been serving as Pavel's wardrobe, writing desk, and dining table.

He switched on an old-fashioned gramophone and turned the volume up high. Static rasped, an accordion moaned, then a woman crooned, "Under the sea, under the sea, embraced by the loving arms of my octopus sweetie and me."

Pavel said, "My pretty starfish, my adorable jellyfish, swim around our mermaid so the other sea creatures will see you and want to make love with you and spawn more little fishies."

The dancers stared at him until one young man ventured an uncertain salute.

"All right! I see the confusion! You are no longer sailors. You have slipped a few rungs down the evolutionary ladder. Now you are mollusks and fish. Artists, why should you care what species you play? It is all about movement. But in case the customers like tipping sailors and sailorettes better than oysters and cuttlefish, you can change into your sailor suits before you go out into the crowd."

Pavel looked at Lou, *through* Lou, then told Arlette, "Believe me, my dear, you'll get lots of tips no matter what you are wearing."

The others regarded Arlette with hatred. What were they seeing, exactly? A china doll with a chipped front tooth. How odd that Pavel's complimenting Arlette should make Lou feel flattered. Arlette ignored and snubbed her, so why should her beauty be a source of pride? Because they worked at the same club? You couldn't even call them coworkers. Because they'd traveled here together? Arlette was embarrassed to have shown Lou the way.

"So then, ladies and gentlemen, you are creatures of the sea, navigating the currents around our mermaid and her sailor boy." Pavel turned up the phonograph. Under the sea, under the sea.

At the convent, Lou had watched girls skip around the maypole. Now she was that maypole, standing awkwardly beside Arlette as Pavel urged the others on.

A tall girl Lou had seen at the club, Spanish or maybe Moroccan, waved her hips and arms in a way that combined treading water, a belly dance, and a shimmy. Pavel told the others to watch what Fatima was doing, then to grab each other's waists and form a line behind her. A few dancers spun out from the swaying row and bent backward till their heads touched their heels, then pulled their arms through the hoops of their legs. They twisted into a tangle, until it was unclear to whom the arms and legs belonged.

Adding new steps and gestures, they ran through the routine again until they fell to their knees, waving their arms in time to the final notes from the gramophone.

Pavel told them to rest, then returned to Arlette and Lou.

"You have seen what your loyal subjects can do. You understand your submarine kingdom."

He instructed Arlette to lie crumpled at Lou's feet, then told Lou, "You have found the mermaid almost dead on the beach. Now lift her in your strong arms and save her from the pounding surf."

Lou willed herself to imagine this scene, but she couldn't see it. She would just have to go through the motions. The fantasy could come later.

Lou put one hand under Arlette's back, the other under her thighs. As if someone were tugging up on *her* belly, Lou felt a warm pressure between her legs. Lou raised Arlette off the ground. If only she could hold her like that, in the air, forever.

"That's it! Straight over your head. Now swim!" Arlette began to flail her limbs. Lou held on to her firmly, supporting but not impeding her as she waved and kicked.

"Now try the backstroke!" Pavel shouted.

Arlette rolled around in Lou's hands and flipped over on her back. How did their bodies know what to do? It was as if they were speaking. Or so it seemed to Lou. For all she knew Arlette was counting the seconds until she could escape Lou's clutches. Arlette was getting heavy, yet Lou prayed to make it last, for Pavel to let her stay like that, holding Arlette while the dancers gyrated around them. Pavel told her to turn Arlette so she was on her side, half swimming, half waving at the audience. This took some acrobatic shifting, adjusting, and bumping. At one point Arlette's bony hip struck Lou's forehead so hard she moaned.

Dimly she heard Pavel ask if she was tired. She shook her head no, and then he said, "All right. Now lower the mermaid."

Climbing down, Arlette twisted around so she was facing Lou. As she slid to the ground, her stomach and breasts pressed against Lou's. Was it an accident? Arlette ground her hips into Lou's. It was not accidental.

Lou was having trouble breathing even as she made sure that Arlette was steady on her feet. Competing in an athletic event was nothing compared to this.

Pavel said, "Would you like some water? Mademoiselle, you are pale."

Lou Villars was praying: save me. Save me or let me drown.

Paris
January 1, 1932

Dear parents,
Lying awake, I torment myself by thinking of what has happened in the years since I left home. Would we recognize one another on the street? I have sent you my self-portrait, and you have sent me your picture, taken by the pitiful fellow I would have become if I'd set up a studio in our town and married the mayor's daughter.

How many childhood nights did I spend dreading the day when Mama and Papa would die? Now you are only a train trip away. And I never see you. I cannot explain—not even to myself—why I cannot come home for a visit, why some unforeseen obstacle always derails my plans to return.

Because of this, I am perpetually melancholy, though I know you love me too much to want me to be sad. Is misery good for my art? Aren't you lucky to have a son whose art requires that *you* suffer?

I'm sorry for forgetting Papa's birthday, especially a milestone year. It horrifies me that I needed Mama to remind me!

By now, seeing my handwriting, you must think: What is our ungrateful brat apologizing for now? If I tell you how pleased I am, now that all your generosity and my hard work is starting to pay off, will you assume I'm happy because I have left home forever?

You were always the only ones whose selflessness I could rely on: my happiness was your happiness. I know some people say that my work wallows in filth, that I couldn't pay the rent without the baroness's help. But there are others who wish me well. Don't be jealous. Aren't you glad I have friends? Shouldn't we thank the baroness for having let Papa again consider retirement, the goal from which he was diverted by my selfish ambition?

Guess who I spotted the other day, in a café? Remember, years ago, I interviewed a Hungarian diplomat for the *Magyar Gazette*—the old aristocrat falsely accused of counterfeiting francs to destabilize the French economy?

When I mentioned him to Lionel, he asked if the old guy could still be persuaded to mint a few bills. What could I say? I sent Lionel to the café where I'd seen him.

As you know, the economic situation here is grim. The jobs one took for granted no longer exist. The newspapers we used to complain about have fired their foreign correspondents. I might be as desperate as Lionel if not for the baroness—against whom you continue to warn me.

I'm not surprised that you have trouble believing in the purity of a cultivated woman's fondness for a talented man. I understand that our relationship would cause a scandal in our town. The baroness is married. Our friendship is purely platonic. She is my muse, the Charlotte to my Goethe, the Héloïse to my Abelard!

Will it reassure you about the innocence of our involvement if I tell you something that I hadn't planned on confiding so soon? I have been "seeing" a French girl, a teacher named Suzanne, who also, in her sweet way, inspires me. If you knew her, you would love her like a daughter, though I know you still hope that I will marry a Hungarian girl—preferably someone rich and local.

Rather than discuss my love life, I want to tell you about the satisfactions I have been finding in my work. I would say I have turned a corner. Corner after corner as I walk the Paris streets. Every night is an education in such critical matters as the timing of an exposure: I smoke a fat little "blue" for a short exposure, a slow-burning Gauloises for a long one. Don't worry, Mama, I don't inhale!

A few days ago, I watched a film being shot: a sailor and his girl were kissing good-bye on a corner. It was a bright afternoon, and the lighting men were setting up scrims to block the direct sun. It occurred to me to experiment with something like that at night: I could use the trees and walls to diffuse the glare of the streetlamps. I tried it last night. I applauded when the images came up in the tray!

And yet there is more going on than I can attribute to skill, logic, or reason. Two nights ago a substitute bartender replaced the stodgy regular at the Hotel Madison. After the bar closed we got to talking, and he let me take pictures from the roof. For a moment the cars appeared to vanish, and the traffic circle became a luminous galaxy spitting out tendrils of light. Is it luck—or technique—that the horse chestnut blossoms lining the boulevards and the tracery of glittering bulbs on the Eiffel Tower seem to have been dabbed onto the prints with a tiny brush dipped in white paint? Is it pure chance that I arrive at the Medrano Circus when the bareback rider is taking a break, and the sadness she exudes suffuses the half-empty arena? Or that I descend into the Métro just as a pretty girl is leaning against a wall, removing her high-heeled shoes, between two posters advertising a salve for aching feet? This last is not one of my favorites. Too obvious, Papa would say.

I've developed a reputation as someone who can't walk out the door without seeing something magical. There's nothing occult about it. I've trained myself to notice the details, and I do my legwork, pounding the sidewalks to double my chances of being present when a miracle occurs.

Sometimes I feel that there is a camera eye growing inside me: an alien feeding on the radiant bubbles that will shatter after I catch them on film. Have I been possessed by the outer-space monster that frightened me as a child? Now when I walk into a bar, the girls lick their fingers and snail the spit curls down on their foreheads. They're preparing for the communion of having their pictures taken, a sacrament in which their souls peer out from behind their eyes and through my lens into *my* eyes and through my eyes into my soul and through the camera into the soul of the viewer.

Yesterday, two men came to sit for their double portrait in the studio the baroness has rented for me to work in. Ricardo and Paul are friends of Suzanne's. But because everyone is so busy, we had to schedule their visit for a time when Suzanne was teaching.

Both arrived in the overcoats over the costumes they wore when I met them: silver paint and a few peacock feathers. For their portraits they wore masks, because Ricardo comes from a distinguished South American family, is studying to be a doctor, and was sensibly concerned about being immortalized in such an unusual outfit.

I am sending a print of their portrait. It's only an offprint, so please don't frame it or show it to anyone. I will give you a better one when you come to Paris. But I wanted you to see what came out of this session. Look beyond the fact that both fellows are practically naked. Focus on how much character streams from every pore. How little the masks conceal. How much of Ricardo's decency shines through, though not so much from Paul. The sinewy curve of their arms around each other's shoulders conveys the easy affection between them.

A while ago the baroness asked if she could borrow my studio for a few days. Her husband and brother-in-law needed it for a business meeting. I could hardly refuse her the loan of a space she is renting. And it was fine with me to see how it might affect my work if I went back to walking all night (Suzanne sometimes comes with me) and printing in my hotel room.

Two weeks passed before the baroness left a message that I was free to return to my studio, where she would meet me. I let myself in and walked upstairs to the warehouse with its intoxicating aroma of chemicals used to process sugar and salt.

My key opened the lock, as always. It was the right place. But how could an entire nightclub have moved into my atelier?

Not *exactly* a nightclub. The *simulacrum* of a nightclub. Of the Chameleon, to be exact. Mirrored banquettes, a dance floor, tables. Was all this some sort of stage set left over from the baron's business meeting? What sort of meeting could that have been? The baroness had said: a small conference for manufacturers of luxury auto parts pitching their wares to her husband and his brother, who are designing a new Rossignol roadster.

The baroness stepped out of the shadows. Have I mentioned that she is tall? She wore a black suit with a calf-length skirt and a fitted jacket topped with a collar that many small white animals had given their lives to create. Her platinum hair was tucked under a sort of beaded swimmer's cap. She looked like an animated version of the hood ornament that adorns the Juno-Diane, which the baroness's husband and brother-in-law produce in their signature line.

Do you think I have fallen in love? I haven't. One can appreciate beauty without having to possess it. Though why I am telling this to Papa, who (I feel sure) has remained faithful through decades of marriage despite the temptations offered by his students' more attractive mothers!

My relations with the baroness are more serious than romance. If I were in love with her, I would be crushed by the impatience that sometimes creeps into her voice and reminds me of Yvonne. Is there something about *me* that makes women sound like that?

"What exactly are you not understanding?" asked the baroness.

I mumbled something about her husband's business meeting.

"Oh, please," she said. "That was a trick to get you out of the studio while I had it redecorated so you can photograph customers from the Chameleon without upsetting your friend Yvonne. Invite them over, ply them with drinks. No one who's afraid of blackmail is going to volunteer. Yvonne won't have to worry about her customers' precious privacy."

Mama and Papa, my head spun. Images whirled through my brain: the dancers from the club transplanted to a place where I can have peace and quiet, where I can control the lighting and camera angle. A place where I can take my time and get what I need in three takes! My happiness runs too deep for words. I can only do my work and let the images speak for me.

Meanwhile, I kiss you.
Gabor

January 30, 1932

Dear Mama and Papa,
I should have known better than to think you would understand.
What was I expecting when I poured my heart out, trying to describe
this new phase of my work?

Did you even read that part? And if you did, how could you have
fixated on the most trivial detail? You point out that I never actually
interviewed the Hungarian counterfeiter. You refer to an old letter in
which I confessed that I fabricated our conversation. Did it slip my
mind that his regret about missing the birth of his family's pet bear
was *my own invention*?

Pardon me if a few facts are jumbled in my brain, rearranged by
the cornucopia of images and experiences I've absorbed during my
years in Paris. Perhaps *your* more accurate memory has something to
do with how little happens in our town.

And, Mama, could you really not stop yourself from making Papa
ask, *Was I no longer Hungarian*? That photo of the men in peacock
feathers! Did I really not recall that bringing peacock feathers in-
doors is begging for bad luck? Was I raised by wolves? Whose bad
luck would it be? Bad luck for the two young men? For me? Or for
everyone else?

Could you not see the image as *a work of art*? Could you not re-
frain from telling your tender-hearted son something that, though he
knows better, keeps him awake at night?

Forgive me for being unkind! But I need you to know that I was
wounded and confused by your response. *Did* I invent that conversa-

tion? Am I certain that those peacock feathers *won't* bring some dire fate down on us all?

Despite how I struggle to tell you what makes my heart beat, you fixed on one tiny smudge along the line between truth and fiction. Have you also saved the letters in which I described staging scenes to look more convincing than "reality"? Do you fear that this Sodom and Gómorrah on the Seine has turned your honest boy into a liar?

Before you consign my letter to that perfumed silk-lined box in which Mama has saved every word, please read it one more time.

Meanwhile I remain your honest and loving son,
Gabor

From *Make Yourself New*

BY LIONEL MAINE

Marxism in one word or less

THE FIRST AMERICAN I met in Paris, a guy named Sim the Griff, claimed he'd won and lost a million bucks at blackjack. He said he'd worked on the Oakland docks and as a private eye. He claimed to be a Marxist, the only one of his claims I believed. He had that Marxist passion for oysters and good Sancerre, and that Marxist paralysis when the waiter brought the check.

Already it's obvious how much the Communists got wrong, overbetting on human high-mindedness, lowballing human desire. But Karl Marx wasn't an idiot. He hit some nails on the head. For example, history. The professor had history's number. Preceded by a dollar sign. All history is the fabulous, filthy fairy tale of greed and money.

No one knows what became of Sim. Supposedly the Corsican mob caught up with him, but no one believed that either. I heard he went home to Poughkeepsie and moved back in with his mom.

If one could stand the boredom, one could map this century and a chunk of the last by tracing the craggy highs and lows of currency valuation. Certainly that determined the great population migrations. Why does someone leave country A for country B? And not just your poor huddled masses yearning to be etcetera. As my sainted Pop used to say, The rich eat chicken, it's cheaper. That's how they got rich. A millionaire always turns off the lights when he leaves the room.

Will the future believe that a generation of artists migrated to Paris purely for the privilege of pissing against the same wall Baudelaire pissed on? Or will anyone think to cost-compare the price of a hovel in Montparnasse with the equivalent dump in Newark—and *then* ask why so many American geniuses came for the free rent, free food, free wine, and—ta da!—free love.

None of this is lost on the French, who are not exactly the world's least mercenary individuals. When the first tourists are sighted arriving for April in Paris, the hotel rates triple. And the bona fide artists who'd made it through the winter fight for the coziest spot under the Austerlitz Bridge.

Then came 1929. No sooner had the stock market crashed than letters began arriving: Dear Artistic Genius, we regret to inform you that Mummy and Daddy can no longer send you the regular monthly pittance. As a matter of fact, dear Daddy has just jumped out the window! And on his way down he hit a pedestrian whose wretched widow is suing us for our last million.

So the "artists" went home to put their affairs back in order, to fire the remaining child-laborers and evict the holdout tenement dwellers. The Right Bank jewelry shops felt the pain. Real estate took a hit. There was a fire sale on châteaux whose owners were back in Rhode Island.

Some friends left, and some pretty girls who liked buying everyone drinks. Otherwise I hardly noticed the change except to register the blessed absence of that sinusoidal Yankee twang murdering English and switching over to murder tourist French. I still get teensy, sporadic checks from my ex-wife Beedie, God bless her. Her bootlegger husband has adopted little Walt. The gangster business is thriving.

Unemployment was nothing new. My visa had long since expired. I'd lost my proofreading job. Every once in a century I got a writing assignment. Poverty is a bulwark against being swept in and out by the tide of money coming and going. It's a kind of stability that no sane person would choose.

What's that sound I'm hearing? The slamming shut of books? You readers turning these pages on the increasingly slim chance that the payoff will be food and wine, Paris, sex, café life, and art—just about now you're thinking: I didn't buy this book so some loser could lecture me about economics.

Though what is as sexy, as sweetly taboo as money? So secret, so unspeakable even among dear friends? How much did Daddy leave you? How much did you get for that painting? How did you buy that fancy car with no visible means of employment? I have friends who tell me about every kinky sex act, the lies they tell, the crimes they commit, their intestinal complaints. But they shut up like bad shellfish when you ask what they paid for their house.

I understand. I do. You don't want to hear me talk about cash or the lack thereof. You already know what the smelly old pauper will say. He's going to try to make you feel good about how little you have, or guilty about how much. So to set your mind at ease, I'll return to the subject of sex and slowly work my way back to the topic of dollars and cents.

I'd gotten over my broken heart. I'd forgotten about Suzanne with the help of a dancer named Fatima I'd met at the Chameleon Club.

My friend Gabor and his baroness had been spending a lot of time there. And for some mysterious reason, they liked taking me along. I absorbed or diffused something. I didn't want to know what. I was like packing material, keeping something unbroken.

What made it even stranger was that the baroness didn't like me. From the minute we met, it was clear—for reasons too complicated and tedious to explain—that she and I had no sexual chemistry whatsoever. Which in a way was a relief, though we despised each other for it.

Was she so shallow that her only desire was to stave off boredom? Or shallower still: a spoiled, stylish automaton attuned to the frequency of fashion that only rich women can hear? Or was it all about narcissistic vanity and pride, so that when she looked at Gabor and me, or even at the dancers, all she saw was someone ignoring *her*?

And what was she, exactly? A pretty French girl from nowhere who'd worked as an extra in Hollywood and found herself a wealthy, good-natured, homosexual husband willing to bankroll any life she wanted, as long as she left him alone. Her brother-in-law was a right-wing religious nut with an opium habit he blamed on a bogus war wound.

For a woman I would never sleep with in this lifetime, the baroness Lily de Rossignol has staked out a great deal of territory in my over-populated brain. But power is always fascinating, power and (to return to my subject) money. Why do some rich and powerful people only like to be around other rich and powerful people, while others, like the baroness, prefer the artistic and eccentric?

Sometimes I watched her at the Chameleon Club. What was she seeing when she stared at the dance floor, predatory and alert, like an animal hunting? Hunting what? Information. One problem is, she's a woman. Really, what *do* they want? Gabor simply wanted to take everyone's pictures. He gazed at the couples like a kid too shy to ask for a date.

For a long time the Chameleon Club had a select, loyal clientele, but suddenly it was the rage. Business picked up when the Americans left. It was always too much for them, frankly. Now it drew crowds of upper-class French kids, artists, film stars, socialites, diplomats, and bankers. From time to time one heard that the old-time butches were threatening to relocate, but they were having too much fun being reg-ulars at a popular club with a famous floor show.

The show was called the Chameleon Review. Girls dressed as boys and vice versa. You needed a forensics expert to tell them apart. You might think it would be a challenge to find two six-foot African body-builders of indeterminate gender performing strenuous duets to a score that alternated Tchaikovsky with jungle drums. But Yvonne had done it, with the help of her choreographer, Pavel, who is an artist. Under his direction, cheap cabaret was pure surrealist theater.

The shows used to change fairly frequently, but the current program—"By the Sea, By the Beautiful Sea"—had been running for a while. Water sloshes on the stage, and as the dancers and acrobats flop around, their fish costumes get wet and so transparent they might as well be naked. But the appeal was not about nakedness. Paris was full of nudie reviews.

The show gave you a giddy, bubbly sensation deep in your chest, like a swallow of pricey champagne. It wasn't great art, you knew that. But you couldn't stop watching. You could feel your brain expanding with each tiny shock to your unexamined ideas of what it means to be male or female, an octopus or a human.

One bright star was bound to emerge. And that stellar creature was Arlette—a slip of a thing with the body of a wood nymph and the voice of the hag who lives in the tree trunk. She played the little mermaid and sang a song she'd written, in which dirty double entendres were mixed with obnoxious references to the brave, handsome, superior French and the cowardly, ugly, inferior everyone else.

The "plot" had something to do with the mermaid nearly drowning. Sailors from various nations and ethnic groups try to save her, or fuck her, or both. They all fail miserably—she bats them away like water bugs and goes back to drowning—until the French sailor gets the job done. Sex and patriotism are an unbeatable combination, even for people who imagine they are rebels because they like to dress up. Could a mermaid almost drown? No one bothered explaining. It's hard to describe the experience of hearing a pretty girl with a voice like a cat yowling in the alley sing a terrible song—and being equally and simultaneously nauseated and aroused.

When Arlette's song ended, she hugged and soul-kissed chunky Lou, who played the French sailor who saves her. Lou half squatted, half sat on the air, and the mermaid rubbed her groin between the sailor's open legs. It was dirtier than any sex show, hotter than any French postcard, though the models on those cards wear a lot less than the two girls onstage. The hard-ons their embraces inspired were intensified by gossip about their offstage affair.

The first time Arlette sang her song, Fatima was so offended by its poisonous *Frenchness* that she went straight to Yvonne and quit. But since Fatima's solo was also a popular number, Yvonne brokered an accord. She reminded Fatima that, in Arlette's song, no Moroccan sailors got the chance to save the mermaid. If they had, Yvonne said, they would have succeeded.

Fatima wasn't stupid, but she stayed on at the club. Feeling isolated and aggrieved made her more receptive than she otherwise might have been to the attentions of a poor, aging American writer who (alone in that adoring crowd) came right out and said that Arlette was a filthy little pig and that Fatima's belly dance was the best thing in the show.

At first I was worried that Fatima might be a man. It wouldn't have been the sneakiest trick played at the Chameleon. But lucky Gabor had photographed her naked and assured me that under her spangled bra and filmy skirts was a bona fide female.

By our second night together, I couldn't remember what life had been like with Suzanne. How could I have imagined that I would love her forever?

And so it happened that Fatima and I entered that zone of tranced-out bliss until . . . Do I sound self-pitying when I say that bad luck kicked in? Not Fatima's bad luck. Mine. But why should I blame myself? It was all Arlette's fault, and to a lesser extent Yvonne's, turning the club into a pigpen where French *cochons* went to feel *French.*

One evening two cops in cheap blue suits asked to see Fatima's papers. The next day her deportation order was delivered by a messenger with a mashed-in boxer's face. On the following night, Clovis Chanac, the proto-fascist police chief who would later rise through politics to a career in professional crime, came to the Chameleon, just after the show ended.

He drank on the house, smoked a cigar, and joined Fatima and me without being invited. In a tone that mixed the harsh vinegar of the interrogator with the oil of a flirt, Chanac asked Fatima if she'd ever read *Les Misérables.*

"The novel," he said helpfully. "The French classic."

I squeezed her hand: say yes. I would never have pegged Chanac for being much of a reader. Which he wasn't. He was a bully who knew the name of one book, and decided to mention it, because I was a writer.

Chanac said that if you read *Les Misérables* the right way, it was a story about Fatima's chances of staying in France. But Victor Hugo had gotten one thing wrong, and that was the cash amount for which poor Jean Valjean could have bought off Inspector Javert and gone free.

"How much would that have been?" I asked.

Chanac gave us a number. I could have bought a car for that!

"How long would Jean Valjean have had?" I asked. "To come up with the money."

"Two weeks," said Chanac.

As soon as he left the club, I took Fatima over to the table where Gabor sat with the baroness. I told them the whole story. Fatima's tears would have melted a heart of stone, but not the baroness's. She was staring at the dance floor. The band was playing a song called "My Little Pink Horse," and several dancers were giving their partners piggyback rides.

After a silence so long I thought she hadn't heard, the baroness said she would love to enable Fatima to bribe Chanac. But then she would have no money left to help Gabor with his art. In other words, to put it bluntly, she was a useless bitch.

Gabor stared into his ashtray. I didn't know what *I* would have done, faced with the choice between my art and my friend's girlfriend. Art, we'd agreed, was eternal. Girlfriends came and went. None of us should have to choose. The baroness wasn't making Gabor choose. She had already decided.

That night, after Gabor and I had seen the baroness to her car and we'd set out walking, he said he had an idea. He knew an old Hungarian who had gone to jail for counterfeiting. He told me some bullshit story about the guy's family keeping pet bears for generations, and the guy missing a baby bear's birth because he was in jail.

He said there was a café where the old geezer hung out. We should find him and ask if he could mint enough cash to bribe Chanac.

I said, That is *so* Hungarian. It didn't sound terribly smart to me, passing counterfeit bills to a cop, a more serious offense than staying in France on an expired visa. But Gabor said the cop wouldn't tell anyone, because it might lead to an investigation into how he got the fake money.

It didn't add up. But it was a better plan than letting Fatima be deported. The next morning, I picked Gabor up at his hotel. Suzanne looked down from the window. I waved at her and blew a kiss. Everything is forgiven!

How often does it happen that in a city the size of Paris an ancient Hungarian relict is exactly where your friend thinks he'll be? My heart sank when I saw the guy. If he was minting money, couldn't he have sprung for a shampoo and shave? He looked as if he'd slept in his coat, under a bridge. Closer up I saw that he'd worked on that look, the style of a raffish aristocrat: a greasy shelf of swept back hair, cheekbones you could balance your coffee cup on, the hooded eyes and beak of a hawk, an eye patch for good luck.

"Maestro," said Gabor. "Good morning. Can we buy you a coffee?" The old man said, "Please. A café *corretto*."

Gabor ordered coffee with brandy, then introduced me as his American friend. The counterfeiter grasped my hand in his tattered cashmere glove. The rest was in Hungarian. Gabor had said that a Hungarian couldn't refuse anything if you asked in his native language. But how could that be true? Hungary was a place like any other, full of citizens denying and rejecting each other.

Gargling those garbled consonants, Gabor was a different person: charming as ever but shyer and more quietly respectful. Perhaps he was just deferring to age or social rank, but the tenderness and humility with which he treated the elderly grifter made me think of his parents and the grand opera of their letters back and forth.

When Gabor got to a certain point, the old guy leered at me and said, "Ah, *amour*." I did my best to leer back. *Amour* was the issue, all right. *Amour*, money, power, and nationalism, to be exact.

Switching to French, Gabor said, "Didn't you mint all that money to paper your mistress's room?"

"I don't recall that," the old man said.

Could he manufacture a few francs more? The counterfeiter shrugged. He was out of practice. They switched back to Hungarian. Then Gabor produced a roll of bills, which, to paraphrase Karl Marx again, spoke the international language of *yes*.

Apparently, the old guy had a friend who had a studio. . . . How much money would we need? The old man whistled between his last few teeth, a sound like a Japanese flute. He'd see what he could do. He named an absurd fee. Gabor agreed. It was less than Chanac was asking.

A day went by, then another. Gabor was optimistic. On the fourth day we met the old guy at the same café. This time he had a briefcase. He insisted on getting his cut before he handed it over. And he suggested that we might prefer to inspect his work in the men's room. No point alerting the customers of a cheap dive to their sudden proximity to a million francs, fake or not.

Gabor paid him. Don't do it! I thought. But I couldn't interfere. It was a Hungarian business transaction financed with money that the baroness thought was being spent on photographic supplies.

Gabor and I took the suitcase and hurried off to the toilet. God knows what the barman thought. By the flickering light of a urine yellow bulb, we examined the ragged bills. This was surely the only time in the history of France that the fifty-franc note carried the portrait of an elderly Hungarian with long white hair and an eye patch. Gabor and I ran back out, but the old man was gone.

Gabor tracked him down and got back most of the baroness's money. Having run out of options, I took Fatima to the police station. We were crying our eyes out, but she stopped crying before I did. At least she would see her dear mama.

That was when she told me that she wasn't going to see Mama. In fact, to be honest, she wasn't leaving France. She pointed toward the handsome young guard assigned to escort her to the border.

For all I know, they're popping out half-Moroccan babies in some prefecture in the provinces. So I would like to ask Mr. Karl Marx about this part of the story. Could it be that there are more important things than money?

Gabor saved a few counterfeit bills. One night, at the Chameleon, he gave two of them to Yvonne. Apparently the old shyster was a Hungarian national hero. She was delighted to find out that he was still alive, though sorry that his efforts had led to Fatima running off with a cop. She loved it that the old man had put his face on the bills. She took the phony Hungarian francs. A lucky charm, she said.

That night she sent to our table a bottle of champagne, which I drank to get over Fatima and to imagine a heaven in which Karl Marx was wrong, and money didn't matter.

From *The Devil Drives: The Life of Lou Villars*

BY NATHALIE DUNOIS

Chapter Five: First Love

DURING THE WRITING of this book I have repeatedly tried to build a bridge I could cross to reach Lou Villars. What could make someone sympathize with a torturer and a traitor? If empathy and pity are unavailable, then which of the higher emotions is left? Kindness? Compassion? If one is looking for explanations or exculpation, one could cite Lou's troubled brother (heredity?), her gothic childhood, her lonely adolescence, culminating in the near rape by her mentor and trainer.

Then why do I feel most strongly for Lou when I think about her doomed passion for the little blond viper Arlette? Everyone knows what it is like to fall madly in love with an ice cube. Many women (including myself) imagine that only men are naturally incapable of showing warmth or affection. But this book has been an education for me—and, I hope, for the reader. As we learn from the story of Lou and Arlette, a woman can be as calculating and cold as the most chilly, self-centered man.

Arlette was a hustler of a type that has always existed. She parlayed a pretty body, a mediocre talent, intense ambition, and opportunism into modest fame and brief success. Did Arlette use Lou Villars? Arlette used everyone. She traded up from her handsome cheesemonger boyfriend to notoriety with Lou, whom she traded in for the Paris police prefect, Clovis Chanac. Arlette hooked her star to a comet that would shine its sickly light on the dimmed-down Occupied City.

The notorious Clovis Chanac clawed his way to power. He took Arlette along with him and set her up in her own club. After the war, Arlette would be tried for treason, but she was never convicted. Her lawyers, who specialized in defending entertainers, proved that it wasn't, strictly speaking, a crime to have been popular with the Germans. Chanac vanished into the ether and wasn't considered worth tracking to Buenos Aires or Detroit.

Arlette saw Lou as a way to get noticed. Not only noticed but talked about, not only talked about but immortalized in Gabor Tsenyi's photograph "Lovers at the Chameleon Club, Paris 1932." Which is not to say that great art meant much to Arlette. Immortality was for the weak. Arlette lived for the present: pretty clothes, fresh oysters, champagne, a nice apartment in which to sleep late, an audience that loved her whether she sang on key or not. Walking into a stylish nightspot, she wanted people to know who she was. What good would it do to get the best table after she was dead?

Inexperienced innocent Lou had no way of knowing what Arlette wanted or who she really was. I feel I can say with certainty: Lou believed they were in love. Together they moved into a cramped flat in the unstylish nineteenth arrondissement. On the nights when Eddie stayed over, Lou slept on the couch.

To Lou it was her first real home, and a happy home it was, though there wasn't much in it but overflowing ashtrays and empty bottles. Arlette's suitcase spilled onto the floor on her side of the bed, which should have told Lou something, if she'd let herself see an unpacked valise as evidence of anything but Arlette's adorable free spirit. Later, Lou would tell another lover—who has asked that her name not appear in this book—that she'd been moved and surprised by how intimately and fully Arlette was *present* for her, and only her, when they made love. She'd never seen a mouth as huge and soft as Arlette's when Arlette leaned in to kiss her.

All of us have observed how often our erotic attractions reflect a mysterious but consistent taste, almost as if we were ordering a favorite dish from a menu. The chicken, please, not the fish. The difference is that the menu of Eros is secret, even from us. Sometimes only in retrospect do we realize that we have wasted our best years looking for a lost, inappropriate first love, that our life-changing passion for a particular person was no more than the desire to finally kiss the crooked lower lip of an elementary school principal or the boy on whom we had an unrequited childhood crush.

In her lovers, Lou invariably chose surface over soul. She was drawn to beauty of a certain vulgar sort: skinny blondes with heart-shaped faces. Or perhaps she would search forever for whatever she'd seen in Arlette—a quest that would eventually lead to the most disastrous of her affairs, her romance with the (also blond) German auto racer Inge Wallser.

But love is strange, as they used to say at the Chameleon Club. Even those of us who value intelligence over appearance have discovered, to our chagrin, that a high IQ doesn't necessarily translate into kindness or even conscience.

My readers may find me guilty of special pleading, of making a case for my subject, of laying the groundwork for Lou's (inconceivable!) pardon, of spreading it on too thickly when I mention a tragedy that occurred at this time and that left Lou even more vulnerable to Arlette's evil influence.

One afternoon a gentleman came looking for Lou at the club. He was her family lawyer; she dimly recalled him from childhood. Abruptly, and despite the fact that other people were present, he said he was sorry to tell her that both parents had been killed in a car wreck. Her father was driving. The accident had occurred near their home. That was all the lawyer was authorized to disclose.

Lou said, "Poor Papa always was a bad driver." By then she had learned to drive. Arlette's boyfriend Eddie had taught Lou on the tiny Citroën he co-owned with a pal. One of their favorite pastimes was to motor out to the country, where Lou drove as fast as she could while Arlette sat on Eddie's lap and kissed him. Then they'd go back to their apartment, where Lou and Arlette made love all night.

The lawyer was also sorry to tell Lou that her parents had left the bulk of their estate to support her brother, who was still in a residential home. The lawyer was not authorized to disclose where Robert was. Lou thought that if he said *authorized* or *disclose* one more time, she would have to punch him. But if she did, Yvonne would have her thrown out of the club, and they would find another sailor to save the little mermaid. So she thanked the lawyer and bowed her head, as if he had come to award her a gold medal of condolence.

Now that they are out of the picture, we can more fully assess what sort of parents Henri and Clothilde Villars were. Neither the best nor the worst. Neglectful, cold, and self-involved, like so many mothers and fathers. But to their credit they found Lou a school where they hoped she might thrive. They didn't stand in the way of her sports career, nor did they protest when that career ended and she wrote home to say that she was working as a dancer.

But what about their decision to keep her brother's whereabouts secret? Did they think they were sparing their daughter the burden of caring for him? Or were they simply hypercivilized, garden-variety sadists, denying Lou the one piece of information she craved, keeping her apart from the one person she longed to see? Perhaps there were other reasons which, lacking access to Robert Villars's medical history, we will never know.

Lou vowed that she would find her brother or hire someone to track him down. For now it seemed wiser not to bully the lawyer into *disclosing* where Robert was.

I can imagine my readers—those with psychotherapeutic turns of mind—making vaulting Freudian leaps from Lou's inability to find her brother to the brutality with which she would later extract information from her innocent victims. And perhaps these same readers will draw another "direct" line between the manner of Lou's parents' demise and her decision to become an auto racer. Or between her betrayal by Arlette and her subsequent betrayal of her country.

But however tempting it may be to make these neat connections, these "logical" explanations seem overly facile. Not everyone who is denied some vital personal information will wind up burning innocent people with cigarette lighters until they disclose the identities of their comrades in the Resistance. Not every girl orphaned in a vehicular accident will wind up racing cars. And not every spurned lover punishes the world by telling the Germans where the Maginot Line ended.

Hours after Lou received the bad news about her parents, she insisted on going onstage as she did every night, though Yvonne—who knew everything that happened in her club—told her she could take time off. But it would have felt like another loss, a loss on top of a loss, to forgo the moment Lou waited for all day, the moment when Arlette flipped around in her arms so they were face-to-face, and Arlette slid down her body like a serpent slithering down a tree.

As they kissed, Arlette thrust her slim hips forward and pressed her groin into Lou's. The audience could read Lou's mind. This beautiful woman is mine! She has chosen me, only me, and together we have traveled to an undiscovered planet of pleasure and happiness, a private universe where the two of us dwell alone, needing no one but each other. There is nothing we are ashamed of. This dance we perform, six nights a week, is a testament to our love.

How ashamed most of us would be, if we were reminded of some past behavior, some attitude that we maintained while under the delusion that we were in love—and were loved in return.

From *A Baroness by Night*

BY LILY DE ROSSIGNOL

THROUGH MUCH OF the 1930s, the Chameleon Club was my favorite nightspot. I adored the clientele, the dancing, the costumes, and for a while, the floor show. It provided a soothing antidote to the more stressful aspects of my life, among them my hopeless love for the photographer Gabor Tsenyi and a (possibly related) rough patch in my marriage to Denis ("Didi") de Rossignol. It also offered a brief distraction from politics, history, and from the terrifying uncertainties of the moment in which we lived. Whenever I managed to rise above my personal problems, it was hard not to notice that half of France was unemployed, that Hitler had seized power next door, that murderous gangs of extremist thugs were rampaging through our city.

Because I counted so many talented artists—and foreigners—among my friends, I was alarmed, even repelled, by the rhetoric of the right. On the other hand, I feared that if the Communists won and the upper class went under, so would my husband's auto business—and all our employees. Though later, the news out of Soviet Russia made me realize that Rossignol Motors would have done fine, selling cars to party officials.

In an atmosphere so unsettled, one might think that something more was required to lighten our mood than a lively drag show, a noisy crowd, a room full of dancing same-sex couples. But one can never predict what will enable a person to get through the night.

The Chameleon Club has had a long afterlife—most importantly, in Gabor's photos. It also appears in the cult classics written by our American friend, Lionel Maine. I've seen it mentioned in books about the history of the period and popular culture in Paris. But unless you were there, you cannot understand why it was so beloved, why one felt so happy to stand in front of its door and whisper its well-known "secret" password: *Police! Open up!*

In part what made the club such a haven was its power to make each person feel temporarily less alone. As someone who has always abhorred crowds, a horror I shared with Gabor, it wasn't the crush of dancers I enjoyed, or the smoky air. Nor the illusion of community, the shallow unreliable reassurance of being together with strangers whom we want to believe are like us. What moved and gladdened me was that the club's popularity, its longevity, and its very existence seemed to prove that each of us leads a double life.

When we say *a double life*, what do we think of first? The mousy government bureaucrat selling secrets to the enemy? The hired assassin masquerading as a country housewife? No, when we say *double life*, we generally mean sex. Bigamy, infidelity, an infinite continuum of so-called kinks and perversions. The self who touches and is touched in the dark, between the sheets, is not the same self who gets up in the morning and goes out to buy coffee and croissants.

Or anyway, so I was told.

By the time I joined the Resistance, I'd had considerable practice in secrecy and stealth. As with most people, my secret involved sex. But in my case, it was the lack of it that could never be mentioned. All through those years, in fact until the early days of the Occupation, I remained a virgin, even as I projected the world-weary, jaded sophistication of a woman who has tried everything and experimented so freely that, with no new frontiers to cross, she has retired from her strenuous erotic explorations.

I suppose the reason that I was assumed to be a degenerate libertine were the four years I'd spent in Hollywood. In Paris, at least in the circles in which my brother-in-law Armand moved, that was the equivalent of fifty years in a brothel. California was where I'd met Didi, but no one ever suggested that it had corrupted *him*.

Possibly you have seen me in the films of that era. I was the blonde in the scanty toga shyly draping a wreath around the neck of the sweaty muscular Christian climbing out of a gladiator pit. I was the prostitute cradling her baby in the doorway when the mad scientist dashes by en route to his demented experiments. I was the handmaid who catches the third of Salome's tossed-off veils.

Then little by little, role by role, I faded back into the crowd. I was one of the cannibals fleeing the volcano that saves the explorer from being cooked and eaten. I was one of the Israelites fanning my arms in front of the Golden Calf, though not one of the dancing girls exuding guilt, in close-up, after Moses's sermon. I was pretty enough, but not *something* enough to fight the riptide pulling me out to the sea in which the pretty extras drowned.

Hollywood years are like dog years. And age is a funny thing. When I first met Gabor he and I were the same age. But I was always older. Didi also was my age, but we *were* the same age. Perhaps because we both liked men, to whom age is so important.

People used to ask Didi and me how we met. A question meant to remind us that we were an unlikely couple. But how little that mattered, at first. We had so much in common. We were French and far from home. We were young and attractive.

"At a party," I'd reply. "Across a crowded room."

Actually, it was a party at the home of Douglas Fairbanks. He had a private auto racetrack and invited movie stars to watch their famous friends drive. Didi knew someone who knew someone, I knew someone who knew someone else. We were the only French guests except for a costume designer who ignored us, afraid we might know that she had been a seamstress at home. It was lovely to meet Didi and chat, in French, about the Americans' disgusting food and infantile social customs.

It was Hollywood. Crazy things went on. But knowing that the actor who plays the charioteer can only perform sexually in the presence of a chattering ring-tailed monkey is not the same thing as going to bed with the actor and his ape. Despite the skimpy toga, despite the doll-baby I clutched as the madman rushed by, despite what all Hollywood assumed about a pretty blond French extra, I had never been kissed offscreen.

I knew that men loved other men, that women fell in love with women. But no one ever had told me that there were men like Didi, who only made love with other men but who liked kissing women. As he drove me home from the party in his gorgeous Bugatti, he pulled off the road and embraced me so forcefully that when I got back to my apartment, the seams of the upholstered front seat were imprinted on my back. Nothing about Didi's kisses suggested his heart wasn't in it.

Didn't it mean anything that he asked me to marry him on our first date? It was obvious he loved me, though he never said so. Sometimes we necked for hours, then he stopped and pulled away. He was controlling his animal instincts. Saving me for marriage.

We were married by a judge in the Los Angeles County courthouse. Then the auto business called Didi back to Europe. Chaste as two cherubs, we traveled by train to New York, and by ocean liner to Rome, where we were married again in St. Peter's. Then we went to Venice for our honeymoon.

Venice was wet and cold. I blamed everything on the weather. Didi wouldn't get out from under the blankets and wouldn't touch me beneath them. Would our lives have been different if we'd gotten married in June? Then—a little late, don't you think?—he decided to tell me the truth. So it wasn't the weather or the Venetian climate. He'd assumed I'd known all along. Apparently, everyone did.

Venice is a beautiful city. But I have never liked it.

Sometimes I minded that everyone knew about me and Didi. No matter how modern you think you are, how many conventions you flout, it's a trial of the spirit to have the whole world know that your husband cannot forgive you for not being a Swedish boy. Had I turned him against women? Back then, people still believed that the right woman could convince a man to change his sexual preferences—even though it's been proven how hard it is to modify a man's taste in cuff links.

Unless I drank enough champagne, and sometimes even then, I often suspected that people were making veiled comments about my marriage. I still remember Lionel Maine talking about a nightclub act he liked: two Norwegian brothers who dressed and sang exactly like two popular American sisters performing across the street. I remember feeling a shiver of irrational fear that Didi might somehow meet one of the Rocky Twins.

It was ironic, wanting people to think I'd married Didi for money, rather than the embarrassing truth: I'd been in love. Didi loved me. Also he liked the social cachet of having a stylish wife with famous and gifted friends. He respected and followed my advice about Rossignol Motors. Someone else might think that we had the perfect marriage. I could pick up the tab for everyone, and dear Didi would pay. We enjoyed our time together. We were like brother and sister, but happier and closer.

Later in life, I met other women whose husbands shared Didi's predilections. Though we never discussed it, such wives understand one another. We knew what attracted us to men of that sort: they were nice to us, they were gentle, they liked the things we liked. And most important, they listened to us the way women listen to other women.

Before I married, I used to imagine the amusing, intelligent children I would have. But how would I have done that without another Virgin Birth? Eventually I convinced myself that I was better off childless, without the slack belly and sagging breasts. I could stay out till dawn with my friends without worrying about nannies or diapers or those childhood illnesses that age mothers prematurely before turning out to be nothing. I always thought I would have made one of those glamorous, indulgent aunts. But Armand's wife protected her children from their godless Aunt Lily.

One night, after one of the rare evenings when we'd gone out together, Didi informed me that, after several glasses of wine, I'd turned to each of the gentlemen in the room and announced, in a plaintive voice, that I didn't have any children. Did I think they didn't know? Was I asking them to give me a child? Didi said that the men were appalled.

Humiliated, I apologized. He told me not to worry. Men had short memories, especially for what women said. But though he trusted me at home, where I never failed to rise to my responsibilities as a hostess, we would never again attend, as a couple, a social event at which alcohol was served.

Didi married me for the third time in a church in France, to please or to spite his pious brother who, when we met at one of those hellish French Sunday family lunches, asked Didi, right in front of me, "Are you sure it's even legal?" At that same lunch, Armand asked if he might have seen any of the films in which I'd appeared. I said no, most likely they had never been shown in France. Later I learned that Armand never went to the movies.

Apparently, the Church had no problem with opium. Or if it did, Armand ignored it. He only smoked at night. During the day, he was a sharp businessman, working beside my husband. He was also an excellent driver, having practiced his skills in the ambulance corps during World War I. He'd insisted on driving himself, even though he'd been a colonel, a rank that came with the family name. He'd been wounded in battle, which, he claimed, was how his drug use started.

Armand was one of the founders of the Order of the Legion of Joan of Arc, the right-wing veterans organization with a small private army and close ties to the military and the pope. Why direct your prayers to a loving God when you can have the crown of thorns and the martyred French soldiers flying up to Jesus?

Because of Armand's nationalism and his prejudice against foreigners, I was literally trembling the first time I invited Gabor to dinner. I meant to seat my friend and my brother-in-law at opposite ends of the table, but circumstances intervened. Armand was high, but not high enough to miss the fact that Gabor spoke with an accent. There was an incident involving a grape that mortified Gabor. Somehow he'd gotten the idea that polite society sliced grapes in half with knives, and his flew across the table and practically hit Armand. Luckily I was able to help Gabor see the humor in it.

It took me years to appreciate my brother-in-law's good qualities, but I will say that by the time of his death I loved him like a brother. We learned not to talk about politics or religion, and to put the past behind us. It was Armand who, in a sober moment, taught me how to drive and gave me, as a belated wedding gift, the beautiful Rossignol sedan that I still treasure and occasionally take for a spin, though usually now with a driver. Even then, when I went out with friends, I preferred to have a chauffeur. I felt obliged to keep up with some world-class drinkers. And the cocktails at the Chameleon Club were notoriously strong.

By then I had learned to have things my way—an accomplishment, for a woman. *My way* meant never being bored. Boredom frightened me as much as, or possibly worse than, death. Only later, looking back on that time, did I understand that boredom was a luxury and a blessing.

Didi and I were married for almost twenty years. Like every marriage, ours had its ups and downs. My husband was kind and gentle when we were alone, but with his friends he sometimes turned mean. They gathered in his library, and when I heard them laughing, I often felt they were laughing at me.

I knew they were wounded creatures. Many, including Didi, had been tormented by cruel schoolmates and intolerant fathers. But my sympathy for them decreased with every minute I spent at the Chameleon, where men and women with odder quirks and more troubled pasts could relax and have fun and laugh at jokes that were not about the hostess. When I heard my husband and his friends laugh that way, I felt as if I were back in Hollywood, in the crowd of extras, watching the other girls get picked to prostrate themselves in front of the Golden Calf.

The first years I knew Gabor Tsenyi were not the happiest in my marriage, but later I turned back to Didi, for reasons I will explain. I can't recall who introduced me to Gabor. I think we met in a café. He seemed like a charming man with an adorable accent and unusually lively dark eyes. Then he showed me his photos. After that all I wanted was to see what he saw.

That was partly why we spent so many evenings at the Chameleon. Gabor was always on the prowl for photographic subjects. Eventually I saw the world as a series of scenes that belonged in his photos, whether he knew it or not. Sometimes he took my advice, sometimes he politely ignored me. I didn't care. It didn't matter. Or maybe it mattered a little.

For Gabor, the Chameleon Club was a treasure trove. The beauty and style of those dancers! Watching them, I'd ponder what it meant, *really* meant, to be a man or a woman. Is it our clothes, our sexual parts, our bodies and brains and souls? In one of Lionel's books he describes me as staring at the dance floor in search of information. He had come closer to the truth than he could have known.

At first, I liked the variety shows, especially the sailors and sailorettes. Contortionists are like magicians: you never get tired of trying to figure out how it's done. The crowd was very appreciative. There was a lot of whooping and whistling. It was relaxing to let down your hair and make noise.

The club took a turn for the worse when it inaugurated a new revue, "By the Sea, By the Beautiful Sea," that produced two unlikely stars, Arlette Jumeau and Lou Villars.

Everyone had been excited when the owner, Yvonne, announced a show with an undersea theme. What delightful fish would her choreographer, Pavel, produce?

A girl costumed as Neptune, in a fake beard and trident, sang a scorcher about how lonely it was at the bottom of the sea. Then the lights flickered, cymbals crashed, a gale swept over the ocean, a belly dancer fell off a cardboard ship. She shimmied while Neptune leered, then the two women—the sea "god" and "his" spangled queen—fell in love. Fatima was a genius, as belly dancers go, and everyone missed her when she left to marry a cop from the provinces. Three girls and a boy played starfishes, and as they crawled across the stage, they seemed to have five legs apiece. Meanwhile a school of angelfish rippled their sleeves like gills.

No one could have predicted how distasteful Arlette's routine would eventually become. But I had a premonition, the first time I saw "The Little Mermaid."

The audience knew about Arlette and Lou. Theirs was a stormy romance, spiked by public brawls over Arlette's boyfriend Eddie, of whom Lou was pathologically jealous. Would the crowd have loved it so much without having heard the rumors?

Surrounded by squirming aquatic creatures, the mermaid and sailor danced. Rather, the mermaid wriggled, and the sailor shifted from foot to foot. Still, the heat between them was clear to everyone in the room. Lou, who wasn't especially tall but was broad in the shoulders and chest, lifted Arlette and spun her like an airplane propeller.

I told Gabor, "We've seen her somewhere. Remind me. How do we know her?"

He asked if I remembered the javelin demonstration at the Vélodrome d'Hiver. Was it really the same girl who'd thrown the spear? I recalled a British bore droning on about female organs. How long ago had that been, and how marvelous it was that Gabor and I had been friends all that time! He said she'd been working at the club, but oddly, I hadn't noticed.

Gabor said he'd given Lou the Chameleon's business card. He assumed that must have been how she got to the club. But he'd never brought it up, and she seemed not to remember. It was typical of Gabor not to insist on being thanked for the enormous favor he'd done her.

Lou tossed the mermaid from arm to arm. *By the sea, by the beautiful sea.* She gently lowered Arlette. Mouth to mouth, groin to groin, they kissed and mimed sex onstage.

Lou's calf eyes were moist with desire as she stepped away from Arlette. Was her sorrowful look put on? Had she threatened to kill herself again? Or this time was it Eddie who'd almost thrown himself into the river?

The spotlight found Arlette's bobbed hair, shellacked a metallic gold. Stretching out her soft white arms, she began to sing in a quavering adenoidal voice, nasal even by the standards of the day, a song about a drowning mermaid and the sailors who try to save her.

It was troubling, how quickly the spectators threw themselves into the game. During the verse about the Chinese sailor, Lou pulled her eyelids and pantomimed struggling to lift the mermaid. The crowd jeered until an Asian gentleman dressed as Anna May Wong cried from a banquette, *"Mes amis! S'il vous plaît!"* Several audience members shouted that they were sorry.

When the English sailor (Lou donned a British navy cap) also failed, everyone laughed. From the wings, a bass voice growled the opening bars of "Rule, Britannia!" When the German sailor (Lou in a Wagnerian helmet with horns) gave up, the Germans (who knew there were so many in the room?) made it sound like a good idea to let the mermaid drown.

I was afraid to ask Gabor why Yvonne allowed this. I assumed he would defend her. Yvonne had bills to pay. Would he think the only reason I could ask was because I was rich? Did he not believe that a rich woman could be as sensitive as a poor one? Would he wonder why I couldn't just relax and have fun? He would never have said that. He was tactful and kind. He might not even have heard me as he made a rectangle with his fingers and framed the audience and the stage.

My discomfort increased when the tone of "The Little Mermaid" got uglier. Maybe the fans were getting bored, so Arlette upped the ante by adding two new verses, one about an American sailor and the other about a Jew.

The American, in a top hat and a uniform spangled with stars and stripes, succeeded in saving the mermaid, though when it came time to have sex, the Yank couldn't perform and ran away. A few seconds later, the Jewish sailor shambled into the spotlight.

In a prayer shawl and a yarmulke, Lou shrugged and turned up her palms in the gesture that had become shorthand for the weak, fake-innocent Jew. There were plenty of Jews in the audience. But there was none of the protest, however mild, that Arlette got from the other groups. No one spoke, no one breathed. It was one thing to joke about Germans, but quite another to mock the Jewish sailor for refusing to save the mermaid unless he was paid in full, up front.

Arlette stopped singing. The band fell silent. Tension jittered the air.

Finally Arlette waved to the band and flashed the musicians a grin. They picked up their drumsticks and raised their trumpets. She sang

the verse about the French sailor who bravely jumps into the waves
and catches the mermaid in his muscular arms just as she's going under for the last time. He rescues her, they marry, and proudly produce
a half dozen healthy French babies. Everything is forgotten or at least
forgiven. The German, the Chinaman, the Englishman, the American, the Jew, everyone's in on the joke.

Lou picked Arlette up again and spun her in triumph. The shortest
of the dancers pranced out in baby bonnets, fish tails, and sailor suits.

"Bravo!" shouted the crowd. Why didn't anyone say anything?
Why did no one object?

It was Lionel Maine who finally made the fuss that the rest of us
should have made. Maybe it was his being American, without European manners or the European fear that a relative might be watching. Or maybe it was the fact that by the time Arlette added the extra
verses, his belly dancer girlfriend, Fatima, had been forced to leave
Paris for not having her papers in order.

Perhaps it was just that Lionel could get aggressive when he drank.
I never understood why Gabor loved him or thought he was so brilliant. He was the sort of cowboy-caveman other men admire. I always
had mixed feelings about him. I admired his spirit. But he annoyed
and insulted me, both. When he looked at me, he saw an old witch,
though I was younger than he was.

One night, as the applause for Arlette was beginning to subside,
Lionel started swearing. His French deteriorated. He shouted something about a military parade and puppets and Arlette not having a
soul, until Fat Bernard and one of the African dancers hustled him out
of the club.

Gabor looked as helpless as I felt. We should have followed Lionel
out. But what could we have done, a woman in very high heels, and a
short Hungarian worried about his camera? Later, we learned that Lionel had been beaten up. I will forever feel guilty for not having helped
him, though later I would make up for my momentary inaction.

Arlette signaled the musicians and repeated the last verse. The audience cheered, as if she'd staggered up from a knockdown. Why was I
surprised? Everyone wants to be on the winning side.

I looked across the table at Gabor. I wanted to tell him . . . what? That he and I were outsiders. We didn't carry on like maniacs every time we heard the word *France*. We had friends from everywhere, painters from Russia and Japan, Romanian sculptors, Jewish composers, Argentinean medical students.

Gabor was looking at Yvonne, who was staring back. I knew what they were thinking. What would they do if a Hungarian sailor failed to save the mermaid? That would never happen. Arlette knew who had the power, at the club and elsewhere.

After the show, Lou, who had changed into a tuxedo, sat in a booth with Arlette, in a sequined evening gown. They greeted the adoring pilgrims who trooped over to pay their respects. I watched for a break, then introduced myself.

I told them that the famous photographer Gabor Tsenyi wanted to take their picture. I said the session would take place in his studio, and that they would get paid. Arlette gave me a filthy grin. What would they be wearing, and what exactly did he want them to do?

I said, "You'll be sitting as you are now, dressed as you are now." All they had to do was show up, spend a few hours, and collect their money.

I waved Gabor over. We set a date. Gabor put his arm around me. Lou had her arm around Arlette. For a moment we remained like that, two couples, each entwined. Then we moved away and let the next group of fans approach to say how much they'd enjoyed the performance.

From *Make Yourself New*

BY LIONEL MAINE

The Guillotine

I DON'T WANT to name-drop, but Picasso told me a story.

One night, I ran into him at a café. It was four in the morning. I assumed he couldn't sleep either. By then it was unusual for him to appear without his entourage. We remarked on this and chatted about the pleasures of solitude. He invited me to sit down.

Picasso said that there used to be a guy who sat alone every night in a corner of the café Le Select. Long crazy hair, ragged coat, nursing one glass of headache wine, muttering to himself as he shuffled what looked like animal teeth from one pocket to another. Tiger fangs, it turned out.

It seems he'd been a painter who so worshiped Gauguin that he'd tried to walk in his idol's footsteps. He traveled to some exotic island and went native, but something went wrong. He came home to live in Paris on a tiny pension from the state. If the French know one thing about you, it's how you make a living, though they mock us Americans for being obsessed with money.

Picasso felt sorry for the guy but also a little nervous. He tried not to make eye contact, though for Picasso it's always a challenge to dim those glorious brights, as large and wild as the saucer eyes of the dog in the fairy tale.

One night, the guy was shambling back from the toilet when he stopped at Picasso's table and said he'd heard Picasso was buying tribal masks.

Picasso digressed from his story to talk about masks and carvings. He said they were not merely sculptures but sacred magical objects. They functioned as ambassadors—diplomats—between the human and spirit worlds. The artists who made them were natural Cubists, producing weapons for the arsenal of our war against the demons.

To be honest, I'd heard him say this before, in a different café. Word for word, with the same conviction. Now that Picasso was famous he'd distilled his repertoire down to a couple of subjects. Unless he was talking to a girl, in which case his range expanded.

But I hadn't heard the story about the guy with the tiger teeth. Anyhow, he and the guy climb up to the guy's airless, packed-to-the-rafters sixth-floor hovel, where it smells like the spray of a thousand male cats. The guy has been painting. Lurid tropical landscapes. Picasso sort of likes them. No one's doing anything like it. No one since Rousseau. And this guy's better than Rousseau.

They're not there to look at his work. The man shows Picasso a closet full of masks. Not all masterpieces, not all good. But some are terrific.

Picasso's knees are shaking. But he keeps cool and makes a lowball offer for the entire collection. Generous, he tells the guy. A steal, is what he's thinking. The man accepts.

A few days after the sale, Picasso feels guilty for having cheated the guy. It's not as if the maestro hasn't participated in some sketchy transactions. That great Iberian piece he bought from Apollinaire and claimed not to know was stolen. Those flea market dealers he charmed into selling him Benin heads for nothing. But for some reason this one gets to him. He can't get it out of his mind.

So he finds the guy in the usual corner and sits down and orders a bottle of expensive wine. The man drinks and drinks—a different beverage completely from the swill he can afford.

The funny thing is that the wine makes him more, rather than less, lucid. He asks Picasso if he wants to know about his time in the jungle.

Sure, Picasso wants to know. Should he ever want to sell the masks, a good story about their provenance might increase their value.

Well, somehow (Picasso forgets this part) the guy wound up in

Malaysia, installed among an especially sweet and attractive tribe of little brown people. And who did they think *he* was? An artist, an emissary, an outer-space alien? Regardless, they're so hospitable, they give him a beautiful wife. A goddess. He gets lucky: a ready-made household. He's never been happier in his life.

For a while a missionary lived nearby, but he was called back to Missouri. Before he left he told the painter that their new friends used to be cannibals, not all that long ago. But they'd been converted and saved by the power of Jesus Christ.

Picasso laughed. He said, "Lionel. You're a smart guy. Do I have to tell you the rest?"

Eventually, the painter discovered that his neighbors had kept up their tribal traditions. Every Sunday they head-hunted picnickers from Singapore. Picasso couldn't remember how the poor guy found out. Maybe some weird-tasting liver in the cassoulet he'd taught his wife to make. He had the wife growing flageolet beans! Learning the art of French cuisine!

The people whom this man lived with, slept with, his wife, the men and women he thought he knew—he hadn't known them at all. They were still killing and cooking and eating human beings!

The truth was too much for him. He went crazy. Disintegrated completely. Hallucinations, raving, the naked sprint through downtown Singapore at high noon on a weekday. Two months in the local jail. The family savings squandered on shipping him home from Asia.

At least he blackmailed his former tribe into bringing their masks to the boat.

Even now, he has attacks. Some days are better than others. Some days he remembers less.

Picasso finished his story. He said, "Lionel, what's that cut over your eye?"

"Is it bleeding?" I asked. It bled like a statue of a miracle-saint whenever I got excited or drank. I'd been beaten up by some right-wing hoodlums outside the Chameleon Club. I'd gotten fed up with the jingoistic floor show that whipped the crowd into a joyous frenzy. Even in a cross-dressers' club, where you might not expect it.

One night I decided I'd had enough and staged a little personal protest. I shouted that a chorus line was no better than a military parade. Like soldiers, the dancers were puppets who had lost their souls. And that phony slut of a mermaid never had a soul to begin with! As I was escorted out onto the street, I told my friends I'd see them later.

A half block from club, three thugs were leaning against a wall. The only question was how bad it was going to be. All in all, it wasn't so bad. A few kicks, and we were done. Mild, as warnings go. Even so, the message was clear: don't screw up again.

I explained all this to Picasso. I got the sense that he already knew about it. Maybe that was why he'd told the cannibal story.

He said, "The French are cannibals. Those Malays or whoever they are have nothing on the French. You can live with them and admire their food and culture and fall in love with their women. But finally they are Frenchmen. And finally you are not."

Picasso said that he and I, an American and a Spaniard, were the same to the French. They would eat us when they get hungry, when there was no one younger or juicier around to braise with carrots and red wine.

Picasso was a celebrity with important, powerful friends. He'd just had a major retrospective. No matter what, he would be safe. The cannibals wouldn't eat him. No one was going to kick him to the curb outside the Chameleon Club. Whereas I was a defenseless turtle without a shell. The French could boil me into a broth and slurp me down for breakfast. Sure, I had the American embassy, but to them I was fish food.

Picasso said, "That's how the French are. Like everyone else, only worse."

He said he hoped they left the Jews in peace, for the obvious humanitarian reasons and also for selfish ones. All his dealers were Jewish.

I told him, "Let's hope for the best. After all, Pablo, don't forget. This is the land of Baudelaire, of Rimbaud and Rodin!"

Picasso took out his pen and drew a few lines on his napkin. Then a few more lines. I watched the image take shape.

It was a guillotine.

He showed me the guillotine, and we laughed.

"That too," I said. "I know."

"Cannibals," said Picasso. "It's almost dawn. I'm tired. I'm going home."

I wish I'd taken the napkin. He probably would have let me. Though maybe he wouldn't, by then. He'd already gotten careful. He folded up the napkin and put it in his pocket.

In any case, this isn't primarily a story about Picasso, though I would like to thank him for the detail of the guillotine. I'm grateful for the drawing that I could have taken and *have* taken, but only in words on the page. Words, which turn out to be worth so much less than a scribble on a napkin. I could have been a millionaire if I'd picked up that drawing and sold it and invested the money.

I've included this anecdote only to give my readers a sense of the conversations we had as we neared the end of those brilliant, insomniac nights in Paris.

Yvonne

THAT FIRST DAY at the choreographer's studio, when the little slut asked permission to sing a song about a mermaid, Yvonne thought, Why not? The girl was cute. The customers were excited by her and the sexy boyfriend who smelled like cheese and couldn't hold his liquor.

Sometimes the crowd still clamored for Yvonne to perform. But she had stopped singing completely. She spared her customers the rasping crow's caw roughened by cigarettes, spared herself the reminder of the widening gap between her current self and the woman whose lovers had sailed into her arms and back out to sea. She learned to live without the adoration of the crowd, and without the grief of the crowd, mourning her dead sailor. She never even sang to herself, when she was alone, to see if, by some miracle, the damage had been reversed. If she counted her losses, which she tried not to, she resolved to transmute her grief into determination.

Across the border in Germany, clubs like hers were being shut down. And if the wrong people came to power here, the Chameleon would be closed.

Meanwhile she had a business to run. Her clients may have thought of themselves as the most loyal creatures on earth, but eventually they would hear about a new club with a more stylish crowd and a dirtier floor show. It was no longer enough to have a place where customers could dress up and know they would see someone more dressed up, a place where they could feel sure that the cops had been paid off, a place where they could cry their eyes out every time Yvonne sang.

She'd known the girl's song would be a hit. She was ashamed of the venomous spirit that had infected her club, and her shame increased exponentially when Arlette added the hateful new verses. But the register receipts consoled her.

Everyone liked feeling superior, and if something compelled you to dress as the opposite sex, it was pleasant to be reminded that you were still several rungs above the impotent American and the greedy Jew. On good days Yvonne thought, It's only a song. But in the hours before dawn she awoke hearing Arlette's squeaky voice and thinking, I will hear this song over and over when I am burning in hell.

One night, just before the show began, Yvonne noticed that her entire staff, except for Bernard, had taken a bathroom break.

Clovis Chanac, the prefect of police, had walked into the club.

For years, *Police! Open up!* had been the password to get in, but the humor had worn off. Since Chanac started showing up, Yvonne told her doormen to politely inform the customers that the joke was no longer funny. Chanac didn't come often, but whenever he did there was trouble. Fatima would still be dancing there if not for him. He was an unpleasant drunk: touchy, easily aggrieved, certain that he was being insulted. These qualities reminded Yvonne, oddly enough, of Lou. She would never have imagined that Lou and Chanac had anything in common.

Except for a few out-of-towners, everyone recognized Chanac, principally because of his trademark mustache, which he waxed into points and teased perpetually, with one finger, like someone plucking a violin string. Accompanying him were two detectives in suits, a uniformed cop, and two pretty girls with short skirts and long legs. An empty table appeared out of nowhere. Fat Bernard was a genius.

Yvonne herself took their order. Welcome, Monsieur le Préfet. Chanac ordered the best champagne. If he paid, which was doubtful, a cop would stop by tomorrow to pick up the envelope in which Yvonne would put what Chanac had spent, including his stingy tip.

The crowd was unusually lively. What bigger thrill could there be than making merry, all dressed up, beside the guy who tried to run Marlene Dietrich out of town for wearing pants in her hotel lobby? Paris liked Chanac. Street crime and auto accidents were down. Even though so many citizens were starving and out of work, the city felt safer than it had in years.

Chanac had almost lost his support when he'd tried to get rid of the public urinals. The population went mad! The Communists claimed that this proved he was a fascist, while the right insisted that it was just like the Bolsheviks to make a case about pissoirs, and the liberals accused Chanac of being dominated by his prudish, older wife, who had all the money.

As a Corsican, Chanac was officially one of the foreigners he despised. But Napoleon had been Corsican, which, Chanac claimed, made Corsicans more French than Parisians.

The musicians and dancers knew that the prefect was in the house. Most of them hated cops. And yet they found his presence mysteriously inspiring. The clarinetist played more melodiously, the starfish gyrated harder. By the end of the evening, several contortionists required medical attention. And lazy little Arlette outdid their most strenuous efforts.

From the first notes, she beamed her song directly at Chanac. Twitching her mermaid bottom, she pulled her eyelids into a Chinaman face, then flapped her hands like flippers to play the pitiful Jew, even though these gestures were usually part of Lou's role.

Lou looked on, bewildered. Was Arlette imitating *her*? Arlette was getting big laughs and applause. Why did she need Lou? To save her from drowning.

Rescued by the French sailor, Arlette gazed past Lou at Chanac. By the sea, by the sea, my darling French boy and me. The police prefect was Arlette's French boy, and the mermaid was everything that Clovis Chanac had ever wanted in a woman: blond, skinny, sexy, not too bright, with politics and ambitions closely matching his own. Arlette would go home with him, if not tonight, then later. And though Yvonne forbid her employees to have relationships with customers, she would make an exception.

Soon enough, Chanac would get tired of watching his mistress hump her lover—her *former* lover—onstage. He would not only make her quit the club, but he would also erase the Chameleon from Arlette's résumé. Still the Chameleon would survive. Or so Yvonne hoped.

Lou's heart would be broken. But it would heal. Pavel would find another way to use Lou's talents, or they would retire her from the stage and promote her; Bernard needed an assistant. Yvonne would hire another singer, someone more like herself, someone who could move the crowd with something besides the pride of being French and the shame of being anything else.

From *The Devil Drives:*
The Life of Lou Villars
BY NATHALIE DUNOIS

Chapter Six:
"Lovers at the Chameleon Club,
Paris 1932"

ENTIRE BOOKS HAVE documented the creation of a single work of art: a jazz recording, the Sistine Chapel, a film by Hitchcock or Truffaut. But nothing, to my knowledge, has been written about the making of Gabor Tsenyi's photograph "Lovers at the Chameleon Club, Paris 1932."

This silence seems all the more puzzling, given the forests sacrificed to pontificate on certain overpraised photos by white male Americans with their frigid Puritan aesthetic: churches, gnarled trees, battered storefronts. How can one compare those soulless images with a double portrait that communicates so much about the sorrows and joys of love, the complexities of gender, the birth and death of passion, the pain of the human condition. The genesis of evil!

Perhaps the general reluctance to explore the sources of this masterpiece stems partly from the feelings that Lou's image generates— even in viewers with no idea who she was. Does the subject—a pair of lovers, two women, one dressed as a man—inspire responses so unlike those produced by Tsenyi's photos of entranced heterosexual couples?

In the photo Lou and Arlette are anything but entranced. They've been drinking, but not enough. Motionless, unblinking, they look like two nervous wrecks who have been ordered to relax. Maybe they are sorry they agreed to sit for their portrait. Maybe only one of them thought it was a good idea. They're as stiff as newlyweds in a wedding photo, instructed to look brave, to make the best of what they both already know is a disaster. Somewhere in my own archives is a photo from my first wedding, a picture in which you can plainly see that same glazed look in the eyes of the young bride (me) and the groom whose name I will not dignify by mentioning it in these pages.

For a while Gabor Tsenyi had an assistant, a German-Jewish girl waiting to emigrate to the United States. She kept a journal, and it is to her that we owe our knowledge, however sketchy, of what transpired that day.

Tsenyi's studio was in a former salt and sugar warehouse directly across from Le Mississippi dance hall. On damp summer days, the cool air rising from the cellar was so briny and sweet that pedestrians stopped to inhale its scent of sea air and vanilla. The windows were blacked out so that Tsenyi could control the light.

It unnerved Lou to enter a building with black windows. Possibly this was another of her premonitions. Later she would work in the interrogation cells whose windows were also black, though for different reasons.

Lou wished Arlette had come with her. But they'd argued late into the night, and this morning Arlette had begged for a few minutes more of sleep. She'd promised to meet her here at ten. If it hadn't been raining Lou might have waited outside. But she was wearing a tuxedo under a heavy black cloak, and she had cut and pomaded her hair especially for the photo.

When she rang, the concierge sent her upstairs. The double doors to the studio were slightly open. Lou eased them farther apart. The baroness was tearing something—a photograph—into pieces while the Hungarian tried to placate her and pleaded with her to calm down.

The baroness wore a leopard skin hat and a leather jacket, dozens of bangles, and black harem pants tucked into high riding boots studded with shiny hardware. She was shouting as she tore up the photo. Scraps fluttered to the floor.

"Let me get this straight. I spent all that money, (tear) hired the phony hearse, went to all that trouble (tear) so eternity could see (tear) *her* legs sprawled on the pavement?" More fragments fell to the floor.

"Whose legs?" the photographer said.

"I'm not an idiot," the baroness said. "You think all women are stupid. You imagine that we idiots are paying you to (tear) immortalize stupid girls who will only hold you back."

Lou would not have realized that the baroness was referring to Tsenyi's photo: "Rainy Paris Street. The Dead Girl and Her Aura," for which the model had been his lover, my great-aunt Suzanne.

What *did* strike Lou was the coincidence. She and Arlette had also fought about a photo—in their case, the portrait for which they were sitting today. Arlette had said that a picture was like a tattoo: the permanent record of something stupid you'd done in a weak moment. It could follow you for the rest of your life, and you couldn't erase it. Arlette told Lou that she was being naive to underestimate the power of the past to come back and bite you.

Arlette was being unreasonable. They'd be making decent money for essentially no work. And the Hungarian was famous. His photograph of them might bring more customers to the club. When they outgrew the Chameleon, a professional studio portrait might help them take their act to a more glamorous venue.

Lou would have liked to tell Arlette how the posters for her show at the Vélodrome d'Hiver had attracted crowds. But no one could accuse her of being naive about the past. She never mentioned her own past, certainly not to Arlette. The less likely it seemed that they would be together much longer, the more Lou bored Arlette with her fantasies about their magnificent future.

When Lou realized that nothing more dramatic than a lover's quarrel was going to happen in the photographer's studio, she went back downstairs. She propped the front door open so as not to involve the concierge.

Lou's lips moved in silent prayer: please let Arlette show up. But to whom was she praying? She doubted that the God of her childhood approved of her love for Arlette.

It seemed to Lou that she and Arlette were still connected by the telepathy they'd developed as dance partners and as lovers. Because just as Lou emerged onto the seedy boulevard, Arlette appeared, wobbling toward her on perilously high heels.

Arlette had never looked so beautiful as she did then to Lou, with the platinum light glinting off her snail curls, rinsing the last traces of color from her anxious little face. The fringes of her evening gown hung below a heavy, red-fox fur coat. Who had given her that coat? How had Lou not seen it? And why was Arlette wearing a fur coat on a warm, rainy morning in May?

Maybe Lou was a little rough as she dragged Arlette into the building, pushed her upstairs, and knocked on the half-open door. The baroness crossed the loft in time to her clinking bangles. She welcomed them to the studio, then summoned over a waiter who offered them glasses of champagne.

Ashamed of how desperately she wanted a drink, Lou said, "So early? It's only ten-thirty." Then, suddenly afraid that Arlette might think she was commenting on the fact that she was half an hour late, Lou lunged for a glass before it could be taken away.

"Why not?" the baroness said. "It's always midnight here in the studio."

"In that case," said Lou, putting back the glass, "can we make mine whiskey?"

"Champagne, please," Arlette said primly.

The baroness took their coats and showed them to a table exactly like their regular table at the Chameleon. The same crumpled pack of Balto cigarettes, the same ceramic ashtray showing two English gents in a carriage beneath the words *Horsey and Smalley ltd*, the same glass of cardboard straws, the same straw wrappers, Arlette's half full glass of absinthe, Lou's decanter of whiskey, the bottle of champagne on ice in case a friend dropped by, ashes dusting the cloth. Lou's cigarette lighter stood on end, a tiny monogrammed silver tombstone, close to the edge of the table.

In an early draft of this manuscript, I was quite taken by the idea that people who look at the photo might react subconsciously to the cigarette lighter that was later used as an implement of torture when Lou worked for the Gestapo. Only in revision did I (fortunately!) realize that the lighter in the photo wasn't the one Lou used in her interrogations. *That* lighter was a present she got later, from her lover, the German racer Inge Wallser. I was so reluctant to sideline this interesting train of thought—the connection seemed so *perfect*—that even now I must remind myself that the cigarette lighter in Gabor Tsenyi's photo is neither notorious nor historic.

It took Lou and Arlette a few seconds to figure out how their table at the Chameleon Club could have traveled all the way across town.

"Fuck me, it's a duplicate," Arlette said, and they burst out laughing. How hilarious and strange that this wealthy woman and her pet artist should have gone to so much trouble to replicate their messy table. It occurred to Lou that the point was to keep the photo shoot a secret from Yvonne. And any secret she shared with Arlette strengthened the bond between them.

The waiter brought a whiskey. Lou lit a cigarette.

The baroness inspected Arlette and sent for a makeup girl to cover the blueberry-colored rings under her eyes and the bruise on her neck. All this exists in the diary kept by Gabor's assistant.

Arlette said, "I was out late last night." Her challenging look at Lou was lost on no one.

The baroness rolled her eyes at Gabor, then smiled. Their disagreement had been trumped by the strain between Arlette and Lou. So it often happens that a fighting couple is pacified, even cheered, by the sight of another couple with problems worse than their own. If the baroness worried that some tension between the women might sabotage the shot, she read, in Gabor's expression, his opinion that a lovers' quarrel might complicate it nicely.

And what was Lou thinking? How much they were getting paid. And where they could spend it on a delicious lunch that might improve Arlette's mood.

Lou knew that Arlette was seeing Chanac and was going to leave her. It made her even more determined to have their picture taken. When she no longer had Arlette, she would have this evidence: she

and Arlette had been in love. They had come here and done this together.

Lou sat at the table and put her arm around Arlette. How pretty
Arlette looked in her shimmering gown. And how soon Lou was going to lose her. The silkiness of Arlette's bare arm made Lou want to
weep. Lou asked for another whiskey.

"Later," the baroness said.

The photographer peered through the lens. He asked the baroness
to look, and the assistant came over. All three shook their heads.

Gabor said, "I can't use this funereal shit. Pardon my language,
ladies. It's fucking blue-period Picasso."

"What language is he speaking?" Arlette asked Lou.

"Don't worry about it," Lou said.

"You are a beautiful couple," Gabor said.

"Thank you," Lou replied.

Arlette giggled the way she always did around anyone she thought
might be rich or important. It had always annoyed Lou. Was it too
late to start to love it?

The baroness approached their table. "Remind me. How much did
we agree on?"

"Are these bitches Jewish?" whispered Arlette.

"No," said Lou. "Shut up."

"Seventy-five," lied Lou. They'd said fifty.

"That's what I remember," the baroness said. "How about a hundred? In return for which, you ladies are going to have to work. Not
physical work, *psychological* work. Put something behind those eyes.
Think about your hopes and fears, your regrets and disappointments,
your secret loves, your not-so-secret loves, your sweetest childhood
memories, the thing you most want and will never have. Shuffle these
thoughts and feelings around, in any order you wish.

"Gabor will take three shots of you and choose the one he likes
best. His interest is in permanence, in capturing the essence of the
face beyond its changing moods. The face at rest, when its owner's
soul has turned in on itself—"

Gabor said, "My dear Lily! Let's not get carried away. That may be more about *me* than the ladies will find helpful."

Gabor instructed Arlette to lean against Lou so her bony shoulder jabbed Lou in the breast. Lou hated it when anyone touched her there. She put one arm behind Arlette's back and with the other hand cradled Arlette's elbow, resting on the table. She tried hard to ignore the flashes of light, the gunpowder smell, the pain in her breast, the camera. The trick was not to breathe.

"Let's take a break," the photographer said.

The baroness brought more champagne and whiskey. When Arlette went to the toilet, the baroness asked Lou why she was so unhappy.

Gabor Tsenyi's assistant overheard Lou Villars saying that she had a brother in an asylum somewhere in Paris. She didn't know how to find him. Both her parents were dead.

The baroness said she knew whom to ask. She would help Lou track him down. When Arlette returned, Lou signaled the baroness to drop the subject.

Once more Arlette and Lou slid into the banquette. Lou snuggled close to Arlette and tenderly cupped her elbow. She felt Arlette's pulse beating softly. For the moment they were happy.

This time, when Lou stared (not straight at the lens, please, Mademoiselle!) into the middle distance, she gazed into a future in which she lived with Arlette and Robert. Perhaps they'd find a house in the country with wisteria over the pergola and a swing in the garden.

The lights flashed, the shutter clicked. The photographer and the baroness made pigeon coos of approval.

Afterward, when the baroness paid Lou and Arlette, she asked if Lou knew how to drive.

"Yes," Lou said. "Very well."

"My boyfriend taught her," said Arlette.

Ignoring Arlette, the baroness said, "And do you *like* to drive?"

"More than anything," Lou replied. How did the baroness know?

The baroness said, "I have an idea. We will be in touch."

From the (Unpublished) Memoirs
of Suzanne Dunois Tsenyi
To be destroyed on the occasion of its author's death

WE MIGHT HAVE been more anxious about the economy, the world-wide Depression, the political murders and reprisals, Hitler ranting next door, if day-to-day survival hadn't kept us so busy. The art school modeling had long since dried up, but the language classes were mobbed with immigrants trying to pass as French.

The French had been growing steadily more hostile to foreigners. The musicians' union demonstrated outside the opera because its pit orchestra employed too many immigrants. The doctors tried to purge the wards and clinics of the foreign-born. The French were closing ranks like a fortress under siege, though it is unclear why Polish violinists and Argentinean surgeons should have seemed like dangerous assailants.

The director of the language school tripled the tuition. But still the students came. It was the only job I had. I wasn't doing them harm. Many of my students seemed terrified, and I was frightened for them. For once I could buy enough food for myself and Mama, but thanks to the shortages, there was nothing to buy. There were riots at the market after people had waited for hours on line for some commodity that had run out.

We couldn't afford a telephone, but there was one at the corner café, and they'd send a boy to knock on our door whenever Gabor called. I'd rush across the city to meet him. We'd have a drink and go back to his room, or stay out and walk all night. It calmed and energized me at once, squinting into the darkness, trying to see, before he did, what caught and held the light.

Ricardo and Paul still gave parties, but they weren't as much fun. Gabor and I continued to go, for sentimental reasons and out of loyalty to Ricardo, who was barely hanging on to his job at the clinic. Many friends had left Paris, others were ill and unemployed. I kept hearing that Ricardo had been sent back to Argentina, but the gossip turned out to be false. Paul was making sculptures of fists clenched around pistols and knives. The few collectors left in Paris were buying up the Renoirs.

I remember their last dress-up party: come as the person you fear most. Gabor and I assumed that all the guests would come as Hitler. The silly mustache, the pasted-down hair: a cheap and easy costume. So we weren't surprised, but still we laughed and exclaimed when dozens of male and female Hitlers showed up. Quite a few guests came as Clovis Chanac. That too was a simple masquerade: a pair of curled, pointed red brushes pasted on one's upper lip.

Gabor photographed a painting of a blowsy Bouguereau nude and wore the print around his neck. He hadn't come as Hitler but as Hitler's favorite artist. Out of pure perversity, I came as the baroness, in ropes of cardboard jewelry and moth-eaten furs from a charity shop. No one but Gabor caught the reference. He hardly spoke to me all night. People asked, Was I dressed as the Dutch queen? Why was I scared of *her*?

Of course, the baroness didn't alarm me as much as Hitler or Chanac. She frightened me in a different way. I thought if I pretended to *be* her I might better understand who she was and what sort of threat she posed. I slunk around like a cat all night, but no one got the joke. That is, no one but Gabor, who didn't think it was funny.

He was spending long hours in the studio that the baroness had set up. She often worked alongside him, though I wasn't supposed to know. Afterward he returned to me, in his room at the hotel. I was glad he still used it as a darkroom, a place that was only his. There were still trays of fluids and fixatives, laundry lines hung with prints. The reason he'd been working so hard was that a prestigious publisher, to whom he'd been introduced by the baroness, had agreed to bring out a volume of his art.

One night, for a change, *I* couldn't sleep. And though I respected Gabor's privacy and never looked at his work unless he showed it to me, I got up and switched on the blood-colored bulb. He was sleeping soundly, though in the morning he would insist that he hadn't shut his eyes all night. There was just enough light for me to see the single photo hanging on the line.

He'd made a new print of "Lovers at the Chameleon Club, Paris 1932." He was deciding whether to use it on the cover of his book. I'd seen the photo many times, but something made me look again.

I am, and have always been, a sensible, down-to-earth person. I'd modeled, I gave language lessons, I supported my mother. Later I was an undercover agent in the French Resistance. I married Gabor Tsenyi and since his death have efficiently and conscientiously managed his estate.

I was never superstitious. But looking at the photo, I felt a warning chill. Gabor and his photographer friends were always talking about *the moment*: the fleeting, precious instant of unrecoverable time. But that photo made me think that I was seeing more than one moment. I was being shown the future: a glimpse of what Lou and Arlette saw as they gazed past the camera. A bleak and sinister shadow of what was to come.

Was it a warning about the night, a decade later, when Lou Villars would walk into the interrogation chamber in which I was being held at the Gestapo prison?

Even after I switched off the light, an afterimage of the couple floated in the darkness. I crawled into bed beside Gabor and lay awake for the rest of the night.

February 8, 1934

Dear parents,

It's kind of you to keep saying how much you love my book, that you've shown it to all the neighbors, and even the butcher, dependable Fritz, who gave you a rope of bloodwurst to celebrate my success. And Uncle Ferenc called it the greatest masterpiece since the *Mona Lisa*! Poor Uncle, whom you tell me is nearly blind, cannot be bothered, as I am, by quality of the reproductions. How dark and streaked the prints are, and that portrait of Madame Suzy—I flip past it so as to not see the leprous white blotch on her forehead.

Wasn't it thoughtful of the publishers not to show me the final proof until it was already at the printers? But why am I complaining? I should, as you say, take pleasure in getting what every artist wants: a chance to have my work seen by the public.

I'm glad you like the cover. I can't remember if I wrote you that Lou Villars, the woman in the tuxedo, is the athlete I wrote about, years ago, for the *Magyar Gazette*. I think I told you that I gave her the Chameleon Club's card.

Now there is talk of her going to work for the baroness's husband. Strange, how certain individuals keep appearing in our lives, though not necessarily the people whom we would have chosen.

I need to tell you a secret. I have been having attacks. Heavy breathing, skipping heartbeats. Paranoid terror seizes me, and I become convinced that Paris is punishing me for revealing her mysteries in my book.

On the night you left Paris after your heartbreakingly brief visit,

I took to the streets, as always when I am sad. I walked until dawn and came home with nothing. I felt that Paris was saying, Isn't a book enough? Now look at your book instead of me. I owe you nothing more.

I set up my camera near the Place de l'Opéra, but the scribble of headlights could have been the writing on the back of a tourist postcard. Or (joke) the writing on the wall. As photographic subjects, the inky puddles of rain had all the originality of a depressed adolescent's poetry.

The next night, I tried again. I'd see how a year had affected the clochards under the bridge. My pictures of those unfortunate souls are not only popular favorites but among my best. They inspired the government to offer the men shelter for the night, though that program was soon quashed by the Paris police prefect, Clovis Chanac, who thinks the poor should suffer more than they do. Chanac is a type we saw often in the Empire, before the war: the bureaucrat who sits in his office and, when no one is looking, tosses your papers in the trash, where they will never be found again.

Now those blanket-wrapped larvae roiling under the bridge made me think of my work with horror. How many pretty pictures of these miserable souls are, thanks to me, decorating the fanciest walls in the city?

The icing on the cake, or should I still say on the strudel, was what happened in the rue Quincampoix. The ladies scattered when I approached, though they'd always been glad to see me. Was it because of my book? I should have shown them the prints and asked them if they wanted to be included. No wonder Paris is angry. I'd exploited her hardworking daughters to advance my career.

At the Café Boum, I ran into Petite Marguerite, the one with the corkscrew curl. She'd heard I'd made a fortune off her and her friends.

I said, "Not a fortune. Pennies!"

I promised to give them copies of the book. Tomorrow night. I'd buy the drinks.

I'd given away all my free copies to you, Lionel, Suzanne, and Yvonne. Lou Villars has several times asked for a print of her portrait, but I have none left to spare. And now I've spent my entire advance on copies of my own book, for the girls.

I carted the books to the Café Boum. The champagne began to flow. I didn't know how I'd pay for it. I'd ask the baroness, if I had to.

Anyhow, the girls loved the book. I was flattered by the pleasure they took in how I'd made them look, how I'd captured how brightly our city shines during their working hours.

They insisted I take their picture. They lined up, as if for a class portrait. I didn't like what I saw through the lens, but I felt obliged. I went home and developed the film. My instincts were right. I had taken a photo of the dead, the soon to be dead, women on their last legs and at the end of their tether.

For me to begin to explain would take a complicated disquisition on my aesthetic principles, an unblinking examination of certain aspects of my art that have been secrets even from me. The photo was dishonest, cold, poisoned by everything I never wanted to see in my work. How exhausted the women looked! Could Marguerite be ill? I never aimed to flatter them, but I never wanted to destroy them.

I watched the picture come up in the tray. Can you guess what I did next? Having just seen the visible evidence that the muse had abandoned him forever, your insomniac boy lay down and fell fast asleep. Explain that, Papa, if you can, oh expert on human nature!

Of all the things connected with the publication of my book, my greatest joy is the fact that you two could finally come to Paris. Reunited at the station, we flew into each other's arms and managed to hide our surprise at how much we had changed (in my case, for the worse) during the years apart. All of us were crying, though Papa and I tried not to.

I will never forget the pleasure on Mama's face at that delicious Saturday lunch at the Orangerie, where the baroness made you both feel so welcome. Or Papa's ecstasy when he climbed the steps of the Louvre. Or the way Mama put her soft white hand over Suzanne's when Suzanne said she wanted to see the town where I was born.

If only you could have swallowed your pride and let the baroness put you up at the (admittedly expensive) hotel for more than the few days we could afford. If you'd agreed to camp out at my (admittedly uncomfortable) studio, you could have stayed longer. Yet despite my grief at having to say good-bye so soon, I admire you for this, as I admire everything you do.

Paris will forgive me, or I will go someplace else and find another subject. I forgot to tell you that I have begun to get work, shooting celebrity portraits for an American magazine. This may also take me elsewhere, geographically and artistically, though I will always remain near you, in spirit.

I live for another visit from you. Meanwhile, I kiss you.

Gabor

From *The Devil Drives:*
The Life of Lou Villars

BY NATHALIE DUNOIS

Chapter Seven: A New Job

WHAT IS ONE to make of Gabor Tsenyi's repeated refusal to give, or even show, Lou Villars a print of her own portrait? He pleaded absentmindedness. He was busy. Or he forgot. Can we ascribe his behavior to the typical self-involvement of the successful male artist?

So it was by accident that Lou finally saw the photo. It was on the cover of Tsenyi's book, in a bookseller's window. She stopped and grabbed Arlette's arm. She heard herself moan, a sexual moan that briefly froze Arlette's face in a grimace of distaste.

At first Lou saw only her radiant Arlette seducing the camera with her twinkly charm. An impartial viewer might think Arlette looks distracted, drunk, her makeup clownish. But Lou worshiped every wave in her beloved's hair, the polished but bitten fingernails, the tilted half moon where her skinny neck emerged from her collarbone.

It took Lou a while to recognize the woman dressed as a man, lucky beyond all creatures to sit beside a goddess and cradle the heavenly creature's elbow. Looking into her own eyes, Lou saw what she'd seen when the photo was taken: gardens, a swing, wisteria, all her loved ones together.

She would have stayed longer in front of the bookshop if Arlette hadn't pulled her away. Arlette had seen something quite different: two women who shouldn't have been at the same table, let alone in the same photograph, touching. A pretty girl squandering the last of her youth on an overweight butch whose only function was to lift her and twirl her around. A gorilla could have done better, with a minimum of training. Perhaps Arlette had an inkling of how she would live on, as the anonymous female half of the lesbian couple, the nameless girlfriend in the photo of the cross-dresser Lou Villars.

"We look like circus freaks," said Arlette. "Now we'll look like freaks forever."

Lou wished she could afford to buy the book. But she couldn't because, as Arlette often pointed out, Yvonne underpaid them, considering how much they did for the club.

Just as Lou predicted, the book was good publicity for the Chameleon. Yvonne forgave Gabor for photographing her customers without her permission. Though he never shot at the club, Yvonne said he owed her a set of prints. Gabor agreed on principle but said it might take months. Yvonne cut the pages out of the book he'd given her and had them framed, so Gabor's portraits of the regulars hung throughout the club. Now Lou could admire the picture of her and Arlette every time she walked down the hall to the toilet.

One night, Arlette told Lou she had a date with Eddie. But Eddie showed up at their apartment an hour after Arlette left. Lou ran to the window whenever she heard a noise. It was dawn before she realized that she had been deceived.

She had never loved Arlette so much as she did then, and, as if to cause herself more pain, she thought back to those first nights when they'd played out their passion onstage, how the mermaid had clung to her sailor, mouth to mouth, belly to belly, so light-headed with desire that it took all Lou's strength and balance to keep them from falling.

When Arlette got home the next morning, Lou asked where she'd been. Arlette said, With Eddie. Lou said she was lying. Finally Arlette said, Go ahead. Make me tell you. But don't leave a mark. We're performing tonight *in case you're too stupid to remember.*

Lou slapped Arlette's cheek. Gently first, then harder.

Finally, Arlette said, "Stop. Enough. I was in bed with Chanac."

Arlette fell asleep. Lou dressed and went outside. She wore a man's coat and walked like a man, with her hands in her pockets, head down.

The longer she walked, the longer it would put off the day she woke up to find that Arlette was gone forever.

Lou got a telephone call at the club. Baroness Lily de Rossignol would pick Lou up at her apartment, at nine on Tuesday evening, when the Chameleon was closed. Through the static Lou heard two words: *driver* and *job*. She assumed: chauffeur. Not exactly the most glamorous work, after starring at the Chameleon. But her days at the club were numbered.

During one of their fights, Arlette had mentioned Chanac's offer to set her up in a nightclub of her own. And she'd made it obvious that Lou wasn't coming with her.

Lou began to invent improbable stories about the bright prospects before them. Was Arlette aware that a Hollywood producer—Lou didn't want to jinx the deal by mentioning his name—had phoned Lou to ask if she and Arlette might be willing to take a screen test, the next time he was in Paris? No, Arlette was not aware of that. Lou should tell her when he called again.

It is not uncommon that, at the end of a passionate love affair, the rejected lover—trying to rekindle the beloved's interest—fantasizes and may even lie about her own importance. So throughout her romantic career, Lou would begin to tell tall tales just when her soon-to-be ex-lover stopped listening. Ultimately this character flaw or neurotic symptom would have dire consequences. It would, one might even argue, cost Lou Villars her life.

Predictably, Lou's boasting only alienated Arlette.

At nine-thirty, after a miserable half hour during which she was sure the baroness had changed her mind or forgotten, Lou heard an auto horn beep three times. Arlette was sprawled with her head hanging off the edge of the bed, her eyes shut, her fingertips grazing the floor.

Lou knelt to kiss Arlette's forehead and said she'd be home soon. Arlette said not to rush. She had a date with Eddie. She claimed she'd gone out with Eddie last night, but Lou had watched from the window as she slipped into a black police sedan.

Waiting behind the wheel of a burgundy Rossignol convertible, the baroness wore a picture frame hat with a rhinestone-studded veil swathing a pair of goggles. Was it safe to drive like that? She'd gotten here unhurt.

She said, "I usually take my Delage, which is prettier and faster. If you tell my husband I said that, I will deny it. In any case, I thought it might be smart to arrive in one of our own cars. And for you to be at the wheel. Not that my husband or brother-in-law will be watching us drive up."

The baroness slid over into the passenger seat. The only car that Lou had ever driven was Eddie's Citroën. But this was not the moment to tell the baroness that.

What Lou had learned on the Citroën worked on the Rossignol. She eased down on the pedal. They pulled away from the curb. Luckily, few cars or pedestrians ever ventured down Lou's street. Bicycles were easy to miss, as was the street-sweeper's cart.

The baroness gave her directions. The first two turns were tricky, but Lou got the hang of it after that. When they reached the Place de l'Opéra, she took a deep breath and dove into the traffic.

"Well done," the baroness said.

After twenty minutes they drove through a gate, around a circular drive, and stopped in front of a brick mansion covered with vines.

"My brother-in-law's house," the baroness said. "Note the giant, vulgar cross above the door." Lou started to get out of the car, but the baroness restrained her.

"This always happens," the baroness said. "He pays the servants nothing. He doesn't believe his household help should be paid at all. He thinks they should pay *him* for the privilege of washing the socks of the younger brother of a minor great-grandnephew of Louis the Something or Other."

Finally two uniformed men appeared, opened the car doors, let them out, and drove off. Swaying on her high heels, the baroness took Lou's arm.

As the baroness had suggested, Lou was wearing a man's suit, a pale tweed with a high lapel, trousers with shallow cuffs and a sharp crease. A white shirt and a light blue silk tie. The rabbit ears of a white handkerchief peeped from her jacket pocket. A woman's handkerchief, women's underwear, it wouldn't have been her choice, but the law (or so people said) decreed that it was illegal for a woman to wear more than five items of male clothing. Everyone knew someone who had been stopped and stripped by Chanac's thugs and had every garment counted.

Lou looked stylish and very handsome. Too bad Arlette hadn't even opened her eyes when Lou left the apartment.

Now, as Lou stood outside Armand de Rossignol's mansion, it struck her that there were other people in the world besides Arlette, a universe beyond the apartment where Arlette was probably still in bed. Unless she went out with Chanac, she'd still be there when Lou returned, waiting irritably for Lou to bring her to orgasm, which was taking longer and longer. There were more important matters to consider than who, or what, made Arlette come faster, or about whom she was faking it with, which amounted to the same thing.

Before they'd reached the front steps, Arlette had shrunk, in Lou's imagination, to the size of the tiny mouse that stole cheese from their cupboard. She winced to think of their dear little mouse, whom Arlette had christened Maurice.

"Is something wrong?" the baroness asked.

"Everything's right," said Lou.

If she took a job as the family chauffeur, she'd be using the servants' entrance. Miss Frost had complained bitterly about the humiliation of "going into service." But telling a little girl horror stories in a lonely country house was not the same as cruising the most elegant boulevards in Paris in the most luxurious cars. If her bosses weren't angels, Lou could live with that. They were part of French history. Lou would be proud to work for them.

A butler opened the door before they knocked, and a half dozen servants bowed as they entered the ornate front hall. Lou tried to project goodwill. She would be one of them soon.

The baroness said, "Don't worry. It's just family. Didi and Armand. His wife and children are nowhere around. Probably whipping themselves or praying facedown on the chapel floor. Unless Armand has murdered them. Relax. I'm only joking.

"During the day he's a fabulous businessman. But in the evening, when he's high, his creative side comes out. His vision improves. That's why I wanted him to meet you with a few pipes of opium under his belt."

Lou shrugged. She'd gone to an opium den with Arlette. Lou smoked a pipe, then another, but all it did was constipate her for days. Whiskey was her drug. For Arlette, opium was an aphrodisiac. On those evenings Eddie was instructed not to visit. When Eddie slept over, Lou heard them in bed, Arlette practically sobbing. Arlette swore she faked it with Eddie. Lou believed her real sounds were the sounds she made with her.

"Are you *sure* you're all right?" the baroness said. "There is nothing to fear. Didi and Armand will see what I see in you. And they will do what I tell them."

In the parlor a man sat by the fireplace, half sunk in a leather chair.

"Darling!" said the baroness, from across the room. "Lou, this is my husband, Didi de Rossignol. What are you reading so intently you didn't hear us come in? Don't get up."

"Suetonius." Didi stood. He was tall, and his skin glowed, a freshly scrubbed pink. His straightforward handshake was neutral. He wasn't trying to find out how male or female Lou was.

The baroness said, "This is Mademoiselle Louisianne Villars. She should be driving for us. The Rossignol 280. She could take it to Montverre and all the way to Le Mans."

Those were the names of racetracks. This interview was for a different position than Lou had imagined. Her acceptable fantasies— waiting at the florist's while the baroness bought peonies, cleaning up the ants that crawled from the peonies into the car, calling for the baron at his gentleman's club—were replaced by diesel fumes and sheer vertiginous joy.

The baron looked Lou up and down.

"I don't get it," he said. "Why bother? All the great drivers are men."

The baroness said, "Trust me. This is why you have me and Armand."

"Look, my dear," the baron told his wife. "You're making the poor thing nervous."

"I'm not nervous," Lou lied.

"Of course you're not," the baroness said. "There's no reason to be nervous."

"Please sit." The baron pointed at a chair across from his.

"Later," the baroness said. "Maybe. First we'll look in on Armand."

The baron said, "I like hiring designers, engineers, technical experts. I can tell when someone loves speed. The person is always tapping. You aren't tapping, Mademoiselle."

Lou looked down at her shoes, two twin black dogs asleep on the Persian carpet.

The baroness said, "Mademoiselle Villars was an Olympic hopeful. She's on the cover of Gabor Tsenyi's book."

"I realize that," said Didi.

"Suetonius," the baroness murmured. "I've always meant to read him."

She led Lou down a corridor to a large room, darker than the hall. A candle with a beaded shade gave off just enough light to see the figured carpets on the floor and walls covered with brocade. In one corner was a lacquered, canopied bed surrounded by Chinese carvings. The room smelled like a candy store or a pâtisserie.

A man sat up in the Chinese bed. In the flickering light, his eyes shone dully, like onyx pebbles. He said, "Well, hello. Look at *you*."

"My brother-in-law," said the baroness. "Armand, this is Lou Villars."

"I see what you mean," he said.

In a life like that of Lou Villars, so thickly populated with strange individuals, it signifies something to say that Armand de Rossignol was one of the strangest.

When he appeared at the 1933 convention organized by the Order of the Legion of Joan of Arc, before a crowd that overflowed the stands at the Vélodrome d'Hiver, he chose to appear on crutches, though he didn't need them. He was a decorated war hero. Also an aristocrat and the sort of Catholic who would have felt at home in the court of a Spanish king at the height of the Inquisition. He was one of the earliest converts to Opus Dei, which had been founded by Josemaría Escrivá a few years before Armand joined.

It was a miracle that his opium addiction had left his nervous system and his reflexes so intact that he could serve as the trainer and coach who taught Lou Villars the skills she needed to race at the most challenging tracks in Europe. He was, it would be fair to say, another mentor from hell, though ironically, hell was what his sect taught its members how to avoid, with unceasing prayer, constant penitence, and the vigorous and merciless mortification of the flesh.

Lou approached the Chinese bed.

"Come closer," Armand said. "Stop. That's more than close enough."

After a moment he said, "Lily is always right when it comes to the newest style. The trend about to happen. Myself, I have older values, among them the love of Christ. But faith, pure faith, is a luxury a businessman can't afford. Lily is correct when she says that people will talk if you are our public face, a driver and a fast one. A winner. A record breaker. Is my sister-in-law decadent? Does she dwell in Sodom and Gomorrah? Can one live in two cities at once?"

Why me? Lou wondered to herself.

"Why you?" Armand said. "Because female athletes are rare birds. It will be a coup if we catch one and keep it in our cage. Everyone will notice. As Dr. Johnson said about the dancing dog, just the fact that it can be done. And there is the example of Joan of Arc, whom, I hear, is also important in—"

He stopped in midsentence and slumped against the cushions. A clocked ticked off the seconds, irregularly, it seemed to Lou.

After a while he said, "How could the competition have gotten it so wrong? Bolshevik Jews thinking with their dicks. Hiring gorgeous photogenic girls who know their way around a track. The beauty who will sleep with you if you buy their automobile. Women can't win, is the problem. Women come in seventh, thirteenth. Pretty women get photographed. But it's men who buy the cars, and the richest men want the fastest. Women drive, but not as well or as daringly as men. It's a biological fact. Women set records for endurance. Who cares about endurance? Who wants to watch a marathon? No one has the patience.

"Speed is what matters now, and what will matter in the future. We want a winner. Someone fast. The one who takes home the trophy and whose face is in all the papers. What we want is that rarest of birds: a woman who can win."

"Like me." How idiotic Lou sounded! At least it was too dark for him to see her blush.

"Obviously." Armand sighed. "Like you. Most women are fragile flowers. My wife, for example, is mentally and physically incapable of having sexual relations without a crucifix clutched in her hand. We have three children. The cross is worn smooth."

Lou didn't know what to say.

"You're hired," he said. "Starting tomorrow. *Au revoir.*"

He pulled the blanket over his head.

The baroness was nowhere around when Lou left Armand's room. A maid showed her out. A taxi was waiting to take her back.

She arrived at her apartment to find it ransacked and nearly empty. Not only was Arlette gone but so was the suitcase she'd never unpacked, together with the few household objects—a corkscrew, two wineglasses, a shot glass, an ashtray—that comprised the domestic inventory of their happy home.

Later, Lou would say that this proved the existence of some basic decency in Arlette. She'd waited to finally leave her for Clovis Chanac until the night when Lou started a new life, when the safety net had been put in place to break Lou's fall.

Rossignol Motors had been founded by Didi and Armand's grandfather, a passionate anti-Dreyfusard who'd punched the French president—supposedly by mistake. For several years Rossignol Motors was banned from professional competition, a handicap from which the brand had yet to recover when they hired Lou Villars.

The Rossignol 240 had been the favorite to win the Paris-Madrid race of 1903, the first of the historic automotive disasters. Drivers and pedestrians were killed, cars twisted around trees, charred wrecks smoldered in ditches from Madrid to Monte Carlo. Not only did the Rossignol driver die when he ran into a herd of sheep that some boys in the Pyrenees herded onto the road, not only did he spray a half-mile course with wool and sheep guts, but after he was ejected from the car, his vehicle, minus its driver, struck one of the boys who had set loose the sheep.

So began the succession of mishaps that had kept the Rossignol from joining the first rank of its rivals: Mercedes-Benz, Bugatti, Rolls-Royce. For a fervent French patriot like Armand, the Rossignol's record was a source of shame. By the time they hired Lou, Didi and Armand knew that their business couldn't survive much longer without a steady transfusion of funds from the investments of their despised dead father. Didi hid this from his wife, whom he encouraged to live as if their resources had no limits.

From the day Lou showed up for practice at the track outside Paris, Armand de Rossignol combined her professional education with an indoctrination in his extreme political and religious views. He reminded her that she was working not only for her own glory, or for that of Rossignol Motors, but for the love of God and France. For decades, Armand said, auto racing had been controlled by special interest groups who wanted France overrun by the same foreign profiteers who were sucking the country dry and destroying her from within. The village where the Rossignol ran into the sheep had a Communist mayor who instructed the boys to sabotage the French driver for the good of the international proletariat and the profit of Bolshevik Jews.

Armand reminded Lou of her father and also of Arlette. She wished she could think of a graceful way to mention that she'd starred in a nightclub act in which a brave French sailor humiliates a Brit, a Chinaman, an American, and needless to say, a Jew. But for all she knew, Armand disapproved of cabaret, and her instincts warned her against disclosing too much. She often spoke of her devotion to Joan of Arc, eliciting from Armand a flicker of the smile that a teacher might give a slow-witted but eager student who, after getting everything wrong, finally guesses right.

From *Paris in My Rearview Mirror*

BY LIONEL MAINE

An Essay on Ambition

FEBRUARY 1934

YESTERDAY, ON THE rue du Bac, a boy ran past me with blood trickling down his face. I grabbed him and asked if I could help. He said a filthy fascist bastard had just thrown a Communist hero into the Seine. Minutes later, I stopped another bloodied warrior who told me he'd just seen a Commie son of a bitch toss a veteran off the bridge.

No one is surprised any more when a riot breaks out. *Demonstration* is a euphemism for some poor slob getting his skull cracked. And no bridge is wide enough for the problems streaming across it. Unemployment, inflation, mass bankruptcy, immigration, a crushing national debt, an increasing tax roll, and a diminishing tax base, political scandal, poverty, a shrinking middle class—and the high jinks, over the border, of our neighbor, Mr. Hitler.

Yesterday's demonstration was unusually violent. By the time the dust cleared and the blood was hosed off the pavement, the leftist government had resigned and the right wing had taken over.

Am I boring my readers yet?

All that anyone talks about is the riot and the handover of power. Is it any wonder that no one took the slightest notice of a book published in Paris that same day: the first volume of Lionel Maine's *Make Yourself New*. Only an egomaniacal American writer would view cataclysmic historical change through the narrow keyhole of his literary career. But couldn't the revolution have waited another week?

Couldn't the coup have held off long enough to give a few citizens time to read my first chapter?

When I say "a few citizens" I mean "a few." The week before my book appeared, one newspaper ran a survey claiming that the average Parisian bookshop sells less than one book a day. My publishers, two Catalan brothers with an inherited income, took me out to lunch to inform me that the first print run would be only five hundred copies. Five hundred readers? I accept! And the lunch was delicious. The Pixho brothers drink the best wines—in the middle of the day!

My hopes were endearingly modest. But the day on which my book was launched was still a red-letter day. I dropped a word from the string of negative adjectives that had trailed behind me like tin cans behind the village idiot. *Unappreciated, unloved, unmarried.* But no longer *unpublished.* I kept my expectations low, and yet when I had heard the pop of rifles being fired at the demonstrators, I confess that my first thought was: A twenty-one-gun salute to *Make Yourself New!*

In any case, my work is out there. It will find its readers. And if not? It's nice to have a riot to blame my failure on. Minor success is better than none. The fact that my book has appeared helps me resign myself to the fact that my friend Gabor's overproduced, outrageously expensive volume—*Lovers at the Chameleon Club, Paris 1932*—was a sensation the minute it hit the stores.

Gabor and the baroness will talk your ear off about why people admire his work: his surrealistic vision, his sly wit, his love for the dark side of Paris, his genius for revealing the city's nocturnal beauty, the sacramental nature of his relationship with his subjects. And Suzanne is in love with him, so there's no point asking *her* for an objective opinion.

Were I asked, which I am not, I might humbly suggest that one reason for his book's popularity is that Gabor has arranged the perfect union of serious art with the ever-beloved dirty French postcard. What red-blooded male wouldn't contemplate a quartet of naked whores bellying up to a bar and have his wife admire his taste in the visual image?

I know that it's *un*dignified to compare myself with my friend; it can only harm our friendship and further diminish my self-esteem. It is a far, far better thing to focus on my hopes for my own work. All I want is to say: I am here. I existed! No one else has led my life or seen the world through my eyes!

Just yesterday someone told me that James Joyce admired my book. First I was elated, and then I thought, Great. How will James Joyce's admiration help me repossess the hotel room from which I have again been evicted?

Enough! I hate to repeat myself, and as all of my five hundred readers will know, I have already written the last word on the subject of self-pity.

Yvonne

ONE AFTERNOON, FAT Bernard knocked on Yvonne's office door and said that the prefect of police, Monsieur Chanac, was here to see her.

The *former* prefect of police. Did Bernard not know that Chanac had been fired after the recent riots, accused of ordering his men to fire on the Communists and protect their right-wing opponents? Hadn't she heard that he was involved in the financial scandal that nearly destroyed the economy? Had no one told her that he had been implicated in the death of the swindler responsible for the scandal, the billions of francs stolen from small investors, a criminal who died—a suicide, supposedly—while in police custody? For weeks no one in Paris talked about anything else, not even at the Chameleon, where pains were taken to leave politics at the door with the umbrellas and galoshes.

"Monsieur the prefect of police," repeated Bernard.

Were the tips of Chanac's mustaches always so aggressively waxed? Perhaps he meant the sharpened ice picks curling under his nose to compensate for his recent loss of power and status. He shook Yvonne's hand and gave her his most penetrating interrogator's stare. His eyes were opaque and reptilian. Yvonne thought of her lizards. What a bother they had been, and how much she missed them!

Bernard brought Chanac a large whiskey, and a dancer skipped in with a brandy for Yvonne.

"Monsieur Chanac," Yvonne said. "To what do I owe your visit?"

She assumed it had to do with Arlette, with whom Chanac was living, across town from his wife and children. Now that he'd lost his job, Arlette was probably planning to leave him for someone richer and more influential. Had he come to ask Yvonne's advice? The country was falling apart, and she and an ex-cop were meeting to discuss the tender feelings of a tone-deaf gold digger.

Pushing some clothes aside so he could sit, he held a camisole to his lips and gazed over it at Yvonne. Was he flirting? She'd lost her intuition, along with her voice and her interest in romance. She no longer cared if she seemed like a fascinating woman, a pool of secrets that a man might want to plunge into. The red dresses had begun to make her skin look yellow. Now she more often wore black. Red was for the very young and the very old.

Chanac dropped the camisole and swatted it off his lap. "It's come to my attention that you have, displayed in your club, a tasteless so-called *work of art*, a heavily doctored photograph that purports to show a female friend of mine in the company of a degenerate."

"I know the photo," said Yvonne. "But *degenerate* is not a word we use here at the Chameleon." Now *she* had to flirt a little. She had to pretend she was joking.

Gabor's pictures had been good for business. Tourists—the few who still visited Paris—came to see the place where the photos were supposedly shot. It would have been pointless to explain that they had been taken elsewhere. Yvonne had been silly to protect the privacy of the customers who'd flocked to the studio where Gabor and the baroness had re-created the club. She'd failed to understand how times had changed. Everyone wanted to be famous, no matter how they dressed.

"It is my impression," said Chanac, "that shooting this picture involved coercion, deception, and ultimately, trick photography. I would like this offense to public decency taken down at once."

Lou will miss it, Yvonne thought.

Yvonne had worried that Lou would be devastated by Arlette's desertion. But Lou had been too busy with her new job, racing cars for the Rossignols. Still, every few weeks, Lou came to the club and got drunk and stood there, weaving, staring at the double portrait. Yvonne liked to think that the club had helped Lou, that it wasn't just a place where people went to drink and dress up, but a ship of storm-tossed souls that Yvonne offered safe harbor. Now Lou had found work she was suited for, a career Yvonne had helped launch.

The prefect wished to obliterate Arlette's entire past. The *former* prefect. He no longer had the authority to tell Yvonne what to do.

Yvonne said, "To be truthful, Monsieur Chanac, it's not even a proper print. Just a page I tore from a book." She'd never admitted this to anyone. Not that anyone, including Chanac, cared about the provenance of her decor.

"Mademoiselle," Chanac said. "I am first and foremost a police officer. And as a policeman it's my professional duty to know what you are thinking. Correct me if I am wrong, but you are thinking that I no longer have the power to tell you what you can and cannot hang on your walls. But let me be the first to inform you that *you* are the one who is wrong."

Chanac smiled each time he said the word *wrong*, as if it were a joke, but Yvonne understood that he would rather kill than be wrong. He would rather murder someone in cold blood than have someone think he was wrong when he wasn't wrong, or even when he was.

"Surely you realize that the crimes committed against me will be exposed, that these perversions of justice will be reversed, and I will be restored to power. I've had some bookkeeping problems, I'll admit. But my replacement—my *temporary* replacement—is a murderer and a fool. When the demonstrations resume, he will shoot into the crowd. The rioting will escalate. Our pathetic excuse for a government will collapse. The people of Paris will beg me to return and restore order.

"Perhaps I should also warn you that the laws are about to change. Degeneracy won't be as freely tolerated as it is now. It would be in your interests to protect yourself against the crackdown that, I promise, will occur."

Was Clovis Chanac bluffing? Yvonne didn't think so. It was humiliating to take orders from a bullying petty crook. But she had to safeguard her business. She owed it to her clientele.

"Could I trouble you for another taste of that delicious whiskey?" Chanac asked. Yvonne was reluctant to leave him alone in her office. She went to the door and yelled for Bernard, and Bernard, her fat angel, appeared.

Turning, Chanac scooped more room for himself out of the mess on the couch, and settled back against the cushions, with his drink. He was silent for a while. Then he said, "People say I am Corsican, but that was only my father. He died when I was seven. We returned to France when my mother inherited a tiny plot of land. She asked an uncle for enough money to buy one male and three female rabbits. By the time I was fifteen, I was killing seven hundred rabbits a week."

Yvonne gave flirtation one last try. "Poor man! We both grew up too young."

"It's not that I don't trust you," Chanac said. "But I would like to take the photograph with me. As a memento—a souvenir—of our pleasant conversation."

Yvonne called Bernard, who returned with the photo. Chanac examined the picture, then gingerly turned it over, as if something even more disgusting might be stuck to the other side.

Yvonne pictured Lou at the wheel of a race car. Drive faster, Yvonne thought.

Part

Two

From *A Baroness by Night*

BY LILY DE ROSSIGNOL

The Race at Montverre

BEFORE THE WAR, our family firm employed Lou Villars, first the famous auto racer and later the infamous spy. Years earlier, I'd seen her throw a javelin at the Vélodrome d'Hiver. After walking away from a promising athletic career, she resurfaced as a "dancer" at the Chameleon Club. There her duties involved clumping around in a sailor suit and lifting Arlette, her tramp of a girlfriend, in their crude but popular Little Mermaid routine. Later Arlette would become the toast of Nazi-occupied Paris.

At the beginning, nothing, or almost nothing, hinted at the fiend that must have been lurking inside Lou. There was that time she punched a referee after a race in Louvain. But I'd missed the confrontation, having been kept in Paris on business with Gabor Tsenyi. Apparently Lou apologized, and the matter was forgotten.

Lou was never a normal person. A woman athlete who dressed like a man was in a class by herself. Sometimes she reminded me of a twelve-year-old boy balancing on the razor's edge between baby fat and manhood, hiding his insecurity beneath a veneer of surly aggression.

Anyone could see how unhappy Lou was. Her love for Arlette was like a dog's love, but so is all love, in a way. Arlette broke Lou's heart when she ran off with Clovis Chanac. He and Arlette were made for each other. Macbeth and Lady Macbeth. In any case, I believe that Lou's unhappiness went deeper than romantic heartbreak, that it ran like a vein of coal through the dangerous mine of her soul.

Once or twice I considered broaching the subject of psychoanalysis, which was becoming fashionable in our circle. I assumed that Lou must have suffered some childhood trauma. I vaguely recall her mentioning an invalid brother. It also occurred to me that rage and sadness were part of what made Lou such a maniac behind the wheel: fierce, focused, apparently fearless. As a patron of the arts, I'd learned that it could be counterproductive to *fix* whatever was "wrong" with an artist.

By then I'd helped many artists. But Lou was the only athlete whose career I advanced, whose success might not have happened without my help. For better and worse, I take partial credit. By which I mean *blame*. Partial blame.

Writing in full knowledge of the result, I add this entry to the catalogue of Good Intentions Gone Wrong. Could psychoanalysis have helped Lou? Would history have been changed if I hadn't asked Lou and Arlette to sit for Gabor? If I hadn't seen, in Lou, a person who would get noticed, photographed, talked about, and—to be honest—who could sell cars? Could a war have been averted had I not introduced her to my husband and brother-in-law?

The same things would have happened, regardless. Anyone could see that.

Our small but influential family business was always ahead of its time. Didi and Armand hired Lou to race our cars and to be the modern, semiscandalous face of Rossignol Motors. And so we became the first luxury brand to consider, as they all do now, the commercial value of a company's public image.

We were not like the Renaults, who made tires for German tanks. If you insist on blaming someone for Lou's crimes, blame the government. Blame Clovis Chanac and his thuggish Municipal Council for turning her against her own country, when all she ever wanted was to be its twentieth-century Joan of Arc.

Could I have seen what was coming? I suppose I could have paid closer attention on that day when Lou came to the studio so Gabor could photograph her and Arlette. He and I were arguing. I can't remember why. Suddenly, I looked up and saw her in the doorway. I wondered how long she'd been there, watching. But neither a psychiatrist nor a psychic could have made the connection between a bit of rude social eavesdropping and telling the German army where to breach the French defenses!

When Rossignol hired Lou, it was assumed—and Lou agreed—that she would end her professional association with the Chameleon Club. After a while, Didi, Armand, and I decided that we would work toward the 1935 Women's International, in June, at the Montverre track, near Paris. That race would open the door to the rest, to winning major backers and earning a chance to compete in the important, formerly all-male races. There were other women drivers, but Lou would be the best. It would take months of training. Lou would compete in local rallies and qualifying events throughout France and elsewhere.

I began bringing Gabor to the track, and he started taking pictures. He'd been having a bit of a dry spell since his book appeared, and especially after a visit from his adoring, adorable parents. He was paralyzed by grief at how much they'd aged since he'd seen them last. For a few worrisome weeks he stopped working altogether. He'd begun to say that his muse had left Paris and that he might have to leave the city to find her again.

How fortunate that the racetrack was one of the milieus in which Gabor would reinvent himself as an artist. He was able to sell his racing photos to *Auto* magazine, where circulation was booming. This lessened Gabor's dependence on me, which in turn was good for our friendship.

My brother-in-law found Lou a cottage near the track, to which, he told me in confidence, she brought a succession of women. That my pious brother-in-law permitted this was proof of his high hopes for Lou. In her sitting room Lou set up an altar to Joan of Arc, which may have consoled Armand for her unholy romances.

Armand hired an assistant, Fraulein Schiller, a Prussian who'd coached the German swim team in the '28 Olympics. Starched up, sporting a monocle, she was straight out of *Madchen in Uniform*, a German film about lesbians that was a big hit in Paris.

It was the fraulein's idea—rejected—that Lou exercise outdoors, naked. In fact she did jumping jacks in a man's shorts and undershirt. A farm ox would have mutinied from exhaustion and boredom. It was painful to watch Fraulein Schiller counting to a hundred while Lou did knee bends in the cold. Lou boxed, ran, jumped, swam in the icy lake, and worked out on parallel bars. She lifted weights to strengthen her arms, for better control of the wheel. We all understood what had to be done so she could drive on instinct without her body or brain interfering.

Like all of us, Lou loved speed. And she wanted to win. I wouldn't have wished—I wouldn't have dared!—to compete against her.

When I was asked if I'd glimpsed warnings of what was to come, I could have mentioned the look of transport on Lou's face when Fraulein Schiller shouted orders at her, in German. Later I observed that gleam on the faces of the Hitler youth in the film of the Nuremberg Rally, faces that Lou must have seen when she attended the Berlin Olympics.

Months passed before Didi and Armand let her drive the Rossignol 280, which they'd kept under wraps. They allowed her to take it around the track and push it up to the highest speed she could. Armand let her get a taste for it, then told her she had to work harder. I noticed the envy with which Lou watched the men sliding in and out of the driver's seat, behind the wheel—always a problem for buxom Lou.

My husband and brother-in-law hired a physics professor to teach Lou about gravity and motion, an engineer to analyze the geometry of the track. At Fraulein Schiller's suggestion, they brought in a Japanese monk from a temple in the Dordogne. The monk blindfolded Lou and walked her around the course, telling her to follow his voice and feel the earth under her feet. Sometimes he would make her crawl. When the blindfold was removed, Lou lost her balance and stumbled, and the Japanese monk, the Prussian coach, the physics professor, the engineer, and my brother-in-law would laugh.

The intervening years have long since put my own trivial problems into perspective—miniaturized them, you might say. Considering what I lived through and the person I proved myself to be, I feel I can speak more freely than I could have when Didi was alive. Also it is easier to write about such matters at a time when it is widely, if not everywhere, understood that true love can exist outside the bounds of conventional marriage.

I loved my husband, but I also knew what kind of boys he liked. I enjoyed our evenings home alone, but when we went out together, I never had any fun. I was always on guard for that special boy. Often I spotted him first. It was more relaxing to be with artists, especially Gabor, whom I can say, also from this safe distance, was not only my great art discovery but the love of my life.

Didi should never have married me, but he wasn't foolish or cruel. He too had been lonely in Hollywood. He'd been thrilled to find me.

In many ways Didi was loveable. And we loved each other. I've mentioned that we met at Douglas Fairbanks's private track. Later, back in France, we joked about those soap-box derbies where movie stars played at driving. It brings a couple closer to find out that their pasts have become the same past. Who could have predicted that our marriage would turn out so much better than so many unions that burn with the flames of (heterosexual) passion and see those fires burn out?

It was always a challenge to be with Didi and his brother Armand, knowing that Didi was cruising for boys and not knowing when Armand would spiral into some rant about Bolsheviks and Jews, about whipping one's self bloody and surrendering to Christ. People pretended not to hear, but conversation stopped. I used to worry that someone might physically attack him, but no one ever said a word or even asked him to be quiet.

The races were a fantastic distraction. The caustic fumes of auto fuel and burnt rubber took one's mind off one's problems. The noise was excruciating. We yelled along with the crowd for Lou to beat her opponents, the clock, her previous best.

Only at the track was I able to forget my marriage, my brother-in-law, my unrequited love for Gabor, the riots, the crashing economy, the threats from Hitler across the border. There was plenty of entertainment available in Paris: the symphony, the opera, the all-boy *Mi*-

kado at the Chameleon Club. But in the midst of those performances, one's mind could begin to wander. At the track I never thought about anything but the race.

Drivers had died at Montverre. Part of the track was a wooden bowl called the Tea Cup, another section an obstacle course, known as the Gates of Hell. And a rutted, bumpy stretch was nicknamed the Snake Pit. The course was banked so that the fastest drivers could hit 220 on the curves. I told Armand and Didi that I didn't want Lou getting hurt, but they only made fun of me for being female and weak.

One reason our marriage lasted so long was that Didi and I never talked about money. I didn't ask how much it cost to rent the track so Lou could practice. Didi never asked how much I spent on Gabor and his friends.

Once Didi did say, For all the funds I was laying out, where were Gabor's pictures of *me*?

I laughed and laughed. How hilarious. I was upset for days.

I don't remember how our understanding evolved: Gabor was never to take my picture. I don't think we discussed it. He never asked me to sit for him. I didn't want to know why. The few times I wandered into the frame, my image stayed in the darkroom. Did he fear that an unflattering likeness might affect my support? I preferred to think so, rather than to suspect that he worried a photo might reveal something too personal—too unflattering—about how he saw me. How old, un-attractive, how dried up compared to his toothy tomato, Suzanne.

When Lou began to race professionally, Gabor traveled with us. He took pictures for the auto journals and kept me company while Didi was pursuing his Swedes, and when Armand sequestered himself with Lou to indoctrinate her with his madness.

Gabor and I stayed in the same hotels but never in the same rooms. Many nights, I couldn't sleep, knowing how near he was. I felt we were growing closer, though I couldn't have said how. In my mind I talked to him in such vivid detail that I occasionally got impatient with him for forgetting something I only imagined I'd said.

Lou lost the first few races, then began to come in third, then sec-ond, then first. She was glad to reconnect with women she'd met touring the sports-association circuit. Invited to speak at regional clubs, she made many new friends, women with whom she spent the night and later kept in touch.

Once I watched her address a cycling society in Toulouse. I was amazed to hear Lou, so taciturn in our company, talk so eloquently about the suffering and sacrifice required of female athletes. I was taken aback by the audiences who mobbed her and asked how soon she could return.

Lou had thrived on the applause at the Vélodrome d'Hiver. She'd enjoyed meeting her fans at the Chameleon Club. She liked talking to reporters and seemed flattered by the attention. When they asked, as they always did, why she dressed like a man, she repeated that everything she did was for God and France. When they asked her to elaborate, she said it was self-evident.

I knew my brother-in-law had told her to mention France whenever she could. I tactfully suggested that we would also like her to say more about the Rossignol. Not that it would have mattered. The reporters were less excited by our car, or a victory for France, or even by how Lou drove "like a man" than they were by how she dressed. But our name would stick in people's minds. Especially if Lou won, the next car they bought would be ours.

We needed the papers to print those stories. But I worried. Cross-dressing was technically illegal, thanks to some archaic remnant of the absurd Napoleonic code. And Lou had a serious enemy in Clovis Chanac.

Around that time, Lou requested a three-week leave from practice. She claimed she was in urgent need of a medical procedure. I assumed it was some female disorder related to the male hormones, extracted from bulls, that she was said to be taking. So naturally I was irritated when I had to read in the papers that she had voluntarily undergone a double mastectomy in order to fit more comfortably behind a steering wheel.

I never saw Lou naked. Before and after the surgery she wore the same loose jackets and jumpsuits. Obviously, I was curious. Had her operation really been entirely about the driver's seat? Or did she want

to look more like a man? Not asking felt like the right thing to do: virtuous and decent. I didn't assume the right to pry into Lou's personal
life just because I was her employer.

What mattered to her was racing. The seat belts were constricting;
the straps had crushed her breasts. Had Armand paid for the operation? Had he and Didi known and not told me? Did they assume I
would have objected? I would never have dissuaded Lou from something she wanted so badly that she was willing to face the combined
assault of physical pain and vicious gossip.

The lead-up race to Montverre was the rally at Brooklands. We
accompanied Lou to England, where she spent several weeks training.
Gabor experimented with angles, light, and exposures to capture the
strain and exaltation on the drivers' faces. Critics have remarked that
his grimy, sweating racers resemble the martyred saints in the work of
the Spanish Old Masters.

The Montverre Women's International was being promoted as the
contest of France against Germany, Britain, and Italy. Just as I tried to
stay out of the political aspects of Lou's relationship with my brother-
in-law, so I tried to ignore their idea of racing as a nationalistic blood
sport.

A British girl, Alice Ascot, would be driving the Rolls-Royce, an
Italian named Elisabetta Todino was piloting the Bugatti. But Lou's
most formidable competitor would be the German, Inge Wallser, pit-
ting her Mercedes against Lou, in our Rossignol. My concerns about
Lou's prospects increased when I saw Gabor's photo of Inge sitting
on the hood of her car and smoking a cigarette. Only Gabor's genius could have made it clear that behind those dark glasses were the
eyes of a woman who would stop at nothing to win. Perhaps his photo
alerted me to a resemblance that I would register consciously only
later. Something about Inge Wallser reminded me of Arlette.

The photo I admired most was one that I can hardly bear to look
at now. It's an image of Lou Villars, suited up, wearing goggles, peering under the hood of her car before the start of a race. To me, and
to many others, that photo represented the essence of Modernism. I

thought it was great art. Now I know that it was a photograph of the nightmare that would be our future.

On the morning of the Brooklands race, I saw Gabor taking my picture as I got out of my car. I was driving the sensational bi-color black and burgundy Juno-Diane, the luxury top of the Rossignol line, the sleek but substantial coupe whose generous curves and forward slouch always made me think of a lion crouched on its paws, ready to spring forward.

Was Gabor photographing the car? His camera seemed to be focused on me.

This so unnerved me that the race was well under way before I could give it my full attention. How pitiful I was to be thinking about a photo as Lou Villars and Inge Wallser outdistanced the Bugatti and the Rolls.

Lou ran second for the next few laps, never quite catching up. But during the tenth lap, Lou tromped on the gas and cut toward the inner lane, swerving and nearly sideswiping the Mercedes. For one horrific moment it seemed as if Lou and Inge might crash. At the last instant Lou swung away and pulled out in front. Inge seemed to regain control. Then her car skidded across the track and smacked into the wall.

Lou sped on as if nothing had happened. The spectators gasped, then fell silent and stared at the twisted, smoking Mercedes.

Inge stepped out of the wreck, straightened up, and waved at the fans. The crowd was on its feet, cheering Inge—and Lou, the new champion of Brooklands.

The race was over, but Lou never let up as she sped through the final circuits. She crossed the finish line, then did a slow, ceremonial victory lap. Finally she coasted to a stop, climbed out of the car, swept off her helmet, and bowed. We shouted. Armand whistled. I heard myself—was that really me?—yelping like a greyhound.

Lou Villars was a hero. Didi, Armand, Lou, Gabor, and I were champions together.

Would we have been so delirious if disaster hadn't been nearly averted? What if Lou and Inge were killed? It would have been a tragedy. Senseless carnage. *Our fault*. The death of two gifted young women drivers. The loss of a colleague and friend. And the end of our hopes for Rossignol Motors.

All of France would have mourned Lou Villars. Germany would have worn black for Inge Wallser. It would have been another nail in the coffin of our family auto business, a warning against speed and recklessness, against the determination to win at any price.

On the other hand, if Lou and Inge had collided and died in the wreck, many more people would be alive than are alive today.

Paris
June 1934

Dear parents,

Mama, I've been thinking of a story you used to tell about your courtship. Evenings you would wait for Papa at your parents' door, and you'd smell his pipe smoke and know he was approaching, and that he'd started smoking because he loved you and hadn't yet found the nerve to say so. You said you felt as if you'd drunk a glass of plum brandy distilled just for you by God. Don't get married, you used to say, until you meet someone who makes you feel that tipsy.

By that definition, I have fallen in love with a car. Race cars, to be exact. The minute we reach the track I feel a giddy intoxication. The crowd around me senses it too. We are all punch drunk with excitement. Some chemical surges inside us when the cars roar off. My heart learns a jazzy new rhythm that makes me happy to be alive! I know what you are thinking. Why does our son never sound like this when he's talking about a girl?

But lest you think I've been going to the races to squander the pennies I've squirreled away in this bleak economy, let me reassure you. My relationship with the races is like my connection to the brothels. I don't go to participate but to document a way of life.

It's some of the best work I've done, and for once my interest coincides with that of the larger culture—which is *very* interested in fast cars and their drivers. I've been selling my work to a journal with tens of thousands of readers.

Auto has money to pay an artist—me!—who would be taking the same pictures whether they paid him or not. Speed is the greatest challenge I have faced so far: how to render it in black and white and in two dimensions. I have gotten more abstract, turning wheels and windshields into arcs of light. Meanwhile my curiosity and love for everything human has inspired portraits of trainers, mechanics, gamblers, and their molls, characters as fascinating as my old friends the thieves and pimps.

The baroness's husband and brother-in-law are sponsoring a driver, Lou Villars, the woman in the tuxedo on the cover of my book. If I have time, I'll send you a print I rather like: a photo of Lou checking her engine, as she does before every race.

Last week *Auto* ran, on its cover, my picture of Lou winning the women's competition at Brooklands, in Great Britain. The event occurred on the name day of Joan of Arc, which had special meaning for her. How alive Lou looks, how victorious and proud, a savage goddess painted with road grit and motor oil. France needs a heroine, as do we all. And wouldn't you agree: better a race-car driver than a general or a dictator.

If only Lou's success could bring her the happiness it has brought me. But according to the baroness, Lou is a tormented soul.

Yesterday evening, the baroness and I went to the Chameleon Club to see *The Mikado* sung by bearded men in kimonos. It was supposed to be hilarious, but I wasn't laughing. I'd noticed that my photo of Lou and Arlette was missing from the wall. It gave me a queasy feeling, like glancing in the mirror and seeing I'd lost a front tooth. I searched the club. My other pictures were there. But not the double portrait.

Clovis Chanac had insisted that Yvonne take down the photo. Arlette is his girlfriend now, and he doesn't want her and her Amazonian sweetie, or ex-sweetie, on a wall outside a toilet in a cross-dressers' club.

What if my book, with Lou on its cover, is declared obscene and confiscated from the shops, where it's still selling nicely, if not quite so briskly as before? Speaking of censorship, have I told you that my friend Lionel has been put on the literary map by his government's efforts to prevent his memoir, *Make Yourself New*, from being imported and sold in the States? A judge ruled his masterpiece obscene!

I couldn't stop myself from asking Yvonne if she thought something might happen with *my* book. And what if it didn't end there? Men like Chanac are always looking for foreigners to deport.

Yvonne said, "Chanac isn't thinking about you. He doesn't care about books enough to burn them, like the stupid Germans. Lou's the one who had better watch out. Chanac *is* thinking about her."

That same night, Lou appeared at our table drunk, though she was supposed to be in training. The Rossignols had asked her to stay away from the club. Everything depends on her winning at Montverre.

Always the diplomat, the baroness pretended not to notice her presence. Lou asked if she and I could speak privately. We went outside for a smoke.

Lou said, "Do you remember when Yvonne used to keep those disgusting lizards? Do you know she told fortunes with them?"

I told her no, I didn't. I knew about the lizards but not the fortune-telling.

She said, "Is that a Hungarian thing?"

Such is the mood in Paris now that I bristled at the word *Hungarian*. I said, "No, it is not a *Hungarian thing*."

Lou said, "I should have stomped the damn reptile."

I said, "You shouldn't drink, Lou."

A few weeks later, when the baroness and I went to watch Lou practice, I spotted Chanac at the track. Having been fired from the police and subsequently elected to the Municipal Council, he had every reason to be there, to keep an eye out for foreign spies disguised as drivers and coaches.

Chanac wasn't looking for spies. He was watching Lou. He'd come to the track a few times and several times sent his men. They stare at Lou, and not in a friendly way. They should be rooting for her to win and uphold the honor of France.

For the moment, we are probably safe. One can't go around arresting people for training to race the world's most innovative car, about which I hesitate to write in detail, in an international letter.

By the way, in addition to my work for *Auto*, more American magazines are hiring me to take celebrity portraits. Last week I went to the Ritz to photograph Gary Cooper, who was in Paris to promote his new film.

The baroness mentioned she'd known him in Hollywood. I asked her to accompany me, and at first she agreed, but at the last minute she called to say that something had come up. Should I give Mr. Cooper her regards? No, she said. Don't bother.

Mr. Cooper's photo practically took itself. He was a perfect gentleman, professional and polite. He knew precisely how to pose to give the editors what they wanted. He even knew where to put the lights to accentuate his cheekbones.

However far apart we are, we should thank God that things have worked out. Though I know you miss me, you must admit that Gary Cooper is in every way a more rewarding subject than the graduating class of our town's Academy for Young Men.

Mama and Papa, don't bother refusing, but soon I will be sending a check for a fraction of what you sacrificed to help a son who never dared imagine he would be able to a make a living, doing what he loves. I thank you, I kiss you. Keep me in your prayers.

Your devoted son,
Gabor

From *Paris in My Rearview Mirror*

BY LIONEL MAINE

A Season in Hell

PARIS 1935

WHEN I WAKE at 3:00 A.M., alone, as I often am now, I must try very hard not to think that one day, in the near future, I will have to leave Paris. If I let the thought cross my mind, I won't sleep for the rest of the night.

The gloom and doom economy, the coming war, unemployment, riots, street crime, financial scandals, serial killers, Nazis at home and next door—what red-blooded Parisian male would admit to noticing or caring? The women worry constantly, as women always do.

Life goes on, as always. If you can scare up a franc or two, you can still go to the Café de la Rotonde, and it's fun, like trawling, casting your net on the waves. You never know what you'll find: lovely mermaids, tasty perch, or a shark like Lou Villars.

I never understood Lou. She always wanted to talk about cars. She assumed an American guy would be conversant with the fine points of camshafts and piston thrust. Once she asked if I had the inside dope on what Detroit was up to. As if I gave a shit about Detroit! Did I ask Lou Villars about Rimbaud's *Season in Hell*? Not that anyone talks poetry anymore. The conversation is all about speed and miles per hour. Lou's language.

When Lou realized I had no idea, she considerately changed the subject to some esoteric carburetor problem. I pretended to know what she meant. After all, she was in charge. Too bad I couldn't bring myself to charm her into bed. It would have been the closest I came to having sex with a man. Lou had balls on the Hemingway scale. Bigger than Hemingway's, maybe.

Every few months there was a nasty crash at the track. But Lou never seemed afraid. She drove like a lunatic on Nazi speed. No one could predict how high and far she would rise. Whatever it took to win, she had. It was thrilling to watch her.

I could never figure out how much Lou knew about the Rossignols. The right-wing lunatic junkie brother-in-law was her mentor and idol. People said Lou took elixirs distilled from bulls' balls. I wish I'd had the nerve to ask her for a dose. That would have steered the conversation away from the secrets of Detroit. But Lou decided what we talked about. It was a new experience, for a guy like me to admit that a woman was, so to speak, in the driver's seat.

From *The Devil Drives:*
The Life of Lou Villars

by NATHALIE DUNOIS

Chapter Eight: Teacher

ARMAND OFTEN REPEATED himself, yet Lou was never bored. In fact she found it soothing. Repetition made it easier to memorize what he said, which she could then repeat to herself, like a catechism.

He said, "No human wants another human to be smarter and stronger. It's instinctive to want others to be stupider and weaker. Teachers have lost that instinct. They hope their students surpass them. Teachers are unnatural, if not actually insane. It's proof of my insanity that I have taken on your education."

Whenever Armand spoke like that, Lou felt as if he'd taken her hand and led her out of the shadows into the sun. She was starting to feel lucky. She'd found the guidance she needed when she needed it most. So what if her helpers weren't all saints? Human beings were imperfect.

That was another of Armand's subjects: certain races were more imperfect than others. The Communists wanted equality, everything fair and the same. But how did they plan to level the unequal playing field that was God's plan for Creation?

Armand rambled on about trust and the fellowship of the like-minded, about the chaos that will ensue if white men wait for the tortoiselike progress of natural selection to save the race from being overrun. He told Lou to trust no one. No one, not even him. Not even the mechanics.

Before every race, Lou should inspect the car herself. Armand showed her what to look for. He made her take apart every bolt and screw and put the vehicle back together. High or sober, he knew everything there was to know about engines. He designed and manufactured automobiles. He'd driven an ambulance during the war.

He said, "If things don't work out at the track, you can always be a mechanic."

He and Lou laughed long and hard at that. She wasn't going to be a mechanic.

Armand never mentioned the possibility that Lou could get hurt. Those were the chances you took. Your chances improved if you were smart and skillful and driving the best car. The worst that could happen didn't scare Lou. If she had to die the violent death that Yvonne's lizard had predicted, let it be on the track.

After months of training, Armand let Lou drive the 280 again. She pushed it hard, then harder, slipping into a dream from which she was jarred awake by Armand waving his arms and shouting to stop unless she wanted to blow the engine.

The Rossignol went back under wraps, and they brought out a two-seater. Armand sat beside Lou and guided her around the course, pushing her to drive faster until the wind flattened their faces against their skulls. Each morning, Fraulein Schiller counted off jumping jacks and ordered Lou, in German, to murder the punching bag. But it was Armand who was teaching Lou how to win.

Armand had driven an ambulance through the slaughter fields of World War I. Slaughter fields were easier to picture than the rivers of mustard Miss Frost had described. Armand explained what mustard gas did to men's faces and lungs, the agonies into which it twisted the soldiers' tangled corpses. A weapon, not a condiment. Lou understood that now. No matter how much opium he smoked, Armand was lucid about numbers. The numbers of wounded, the numbers of dead at the Ardennes and Verdun. Lou could never remember: Was it thousands, or tens of thousands, killed in one day at Charleroi?

When Armand talked about the war, Lou could tell how much he missed the excitement, the camaraderie, the brotherly love. The Order of the Legion of Joan of Arc was made up of former soldiers whose spirits would never again burn as hot as they'd blazed under fire. They would never feel such passion. They would never be that young or that lucky, twice.

They held meetings and staged rallies at which they tried to recapture what they had lost, but marching in a veterans' parade was an enraging substitute for the real thing. They didn't know what to do with their rage. Armand put a little of it into shouting at Lou to drive faster.

Lou never minded his yelling. She envied Armand and the other veterans for having had experiences and felt emotions she would never know. Racing might come close. But she was alone in the driver's seat, and they'd had each other. She imagined the men in the trenches squirming like litters of newborn kittens.

Of all the things Armand repeated, this was what he said most often: "Drive like you're driving the wounded over a muddy battleground pitted by bullets and shells. Each wasted instant, each idle second means that a soldier will die."

As soon as Armand said that, Lou knew how to drive the track. If only someone had said it before and skipped the crawling blindfolded with the Japanese priest. But it was thanks to the priest that Lou knew every pit in the road, every crevice and bump.

Drive like you're driving the wounded over a muddy battleground pitted by bullets and shells. Each wasted instant, each idle second means that a soldier will die.

Lou would remember that all her life, until the hour of her death.

Armand said, "Listen to the engine." And Lou heard it speak. Too fast, too slow, too loud, too soft. She felt like a conductor, attuned to the voice of each instrument in a symphony of machine parts. Lou's harmony with the Rossignol was what the musicians in the Chameleon's jazz band had with each other. Did it matter that her duet was with an automobile?

Armand let her drive five, six laps. Then he'd make her stop. He'd take off his helmet and goggles and talk about autos and auto racing. The lives of the female drivers and the records they'd set. He paraded them past Lou like beauty pageant contestants.

There was Elsie Dobbs, whose newspaper-sponsored effort to be the first woman to cross the United States by car ended on the first day, with the engine stripped bare by souvenir hunters outside an Albany church; Grace Welling, eaten by grizzlies when her car broke down in the Rockies; the millionairess, Ida Greene, whose older husband ignored her affairs with men and women she met at the track, where her specialty (Armand snorted) was endurance.

What could one expect from American women? British girls were as bad. The English Jewess who came in third at the Isle of Man but was better known for the poses she struck when she pretended to change her own tire for the cameras. The Londoner, Agnes Richards, who drove to the Arctic Circle in a cocktail dress.

At least the Brits had Fay Taylour, disqualified from a race for not stopping until she ran over a flagman. To her credit, Fay was a friend and follower of Sir Oswald Mosley, who, despite his nationality, had political views that Armand found congenial. *Sympathique.* Then there was the Italian girl, whose name Armand forgot, who drove the Mille Miglia backward, the same race after which poor Florence Kelly required so much reconstructive surgery.

French women had been pioneers. Armand called them road workers. They'd paved the way for Lou. They could drive, but they weren't serious. They were sabotaged by their hearts. They fell in love with mechanics. Lou would not have that problem. Their promoters fell in love with them, also not a worry for Lou. She shared Armand's contempt for the publicity-hungry girls who freshened their makeup as they crossed the finish line, the ones who wouldn't drive without a Pomeranian drooling in their laps.

Even before Lou won a race, the papers were running her photo. They bid for the pictures Gabor Tsenyi took of her checking the engine. Armand liked Lou to talk to the press. He told her what to say. She should say, I plan to win. I have talent. I work hard. I believe in God and France. I'm driving the Rossignol for God and France. The baroness told her to say *Rossignol* as often as she could.

When the smoke and fumes became too much, Lou and Armand repaired to the cottage the Rossignols had rented. There Armand would smoke a pipe or two while Lou drank American whiskey, and he'd talk, first calmly, then more heatedly, about the enemies of France.

He said France was a beautiful apple, the fruit in paradise. The serpent would not appear again until the apocalypse that Revelations predicted. In these dark intervening years, the country was infested by worms gnawing it from the inside, until the fruit was rotten beneath the skin. But the damage could be reversed. Unlike a real apple, France could regenerate and become crisp again—but only if the worms were eradicated. Lou felt surges of righteous anger on her country's behalf. What if the solution were near? What if she could hasten it with every race she won?

Sometimes, when Armand spoke about their wounded country, Lou felt he was talking about himself—about the pain of his war injury or a childhood hurt that would never heal. Lou wanted to comfort him, pat his arm. But she was afraid to touch him.

After that first evening, Armand never again mentioned his wife polishing her crucifix during sex. There were many topics that Lou and Armand avoided, among them the fact that Lou dressed as a man and liked girls. When Lou decided to have her breasts removed, Armand gave her time off. He paid for the operation without asking what it was for and hired a nurse to care for her until she recovered.

Lou had always hated the mirror, but now she liked looking into it when she applied the salves and ointments the doctors gave her to flatten her scars. But she hadn't had the surgery to change what she saw in the mirror. Driving was safer and easier without two hazardous encumbrances bulging out of her chest. Now she had a better chance of escaping a crash without waiting for the mechanics to pry her out of the wreckage.

As a feminist historian, I should devote more attention to the role that breasts played in Lou's psyche, to her gender dysphoria, her sexual confusion, her lifelong discomfort with the restrictive female role. But the subject becomes much simpler when I try to think as Lou did: her breasts would make her suffer and, in her worst fantasies, kill her.

Sometimes, in the evening, Lou drove Armand around Paris.

Excepting those summer afternoons when she'd played in her parents' garden, and her first nights in bed with Arlette, these were her happiest moments so far. The lavender light parted like veils of gauze as they wound their way up from the river to the highest points in the city. How strange and sinister Paris had looked when she first arrived. Now the crooked alleys seemed like the beckoning fingers of old friends. Come closer, they hissed. Don't be afraid. We want to tell you a story.

Everywhere she and Armand went, people stared, first at the car, then inside to see who was lucky enough to ride in that splendid machine. Sometimes strangers recognized Lou from her picture in the papers. She smiled and waved, and once, caught in traffic, she autographed a boy's notebook, all of which pleased Armand.

One evening they drove up to the cemetery of Père Lachaise and parked and looked down at Paris winking at them through the twilight.

Armand said, "Dear God, what a view. Wasted on the dead!" He said the artists should be exhumed and moved to lower ground, and the cemetery rededicated to the warriors who died fighting for their country, Frenchmen who had earned the right to spend eternity in this beautiful place.

Nights when Armand preferred to be alone, Lou went to the clubs—the Safari, the Zebra, the Rio Grande—and met girls she brought back to her cottage near the track, but never for more than one night. Arlette had taught Lou about the danger of letting down her guard. Like many who have been wounded in love, Lou made rules for her own protection: No girls from the racing world. No dancers or singers. No girls who knew anyone she knew.

After Lou won the medal at Brooklands, Inge Wallser sidled up to her and whispered that she was free for the evening. But even though Inge was blond and pretty and very much Lou's type, Lou refused to break her rule about mixing business with pleasure, and she told Inge that she had a previous engagement.

She was having dinner with Armand in the bar of their hotel. He brought along a crucifix he'd bought in a curiosity shop, in the cathedral town where the child martyr, Little Saint Hugh of Lincoln, was murdered by the Jews for the blood they used in the ritual recipe for the Jewish Passover bread.

Armand said, "Look closer. Do you notice anything strange?"

Finally Lou saw it: the two nails in Jesus' legs. One at the ankle, the usual place. And above it, midcalf, a larger nail, protruding at a sharper angle.

Armand said, "The organization to which I belong has uncovered secret information proving that not one, but two, nails were driven into the ankles and legs of our Lord Jesus Christ."

Lou said, "Why two nails?"

Armand tapped his forehead. "One wasn't enough for the Jews."

From the (Unpublished) Memoirs
of Suzanne Dunois Tsenyi
To be destroyed on the occasion of its author's death

I NEVER LIKED the photos Gabor took at the track. I would never have told him so, and I never did. I couldn't have explained why the images moved me so much less than his earlier work. Besides, I worried that any criticism might be taken as an attack on the baroness, who'd introduced him to the world of auto racing, as she did to so many worlds through which the two of them moved more freely without me around to impede them. Had I been less selfish, less possessive and small, I would have been purely glad that he'd started taking pictures again after the dry spell that began when his book was published and his parents visited him in Paris. Had I been less self-centered, I might not have been so hurt by how little Gabor's parents seemed to have heard about me.

After the Austrian chancellor was murdered, one disaster followed another. Hitler, always Hitler. The Abyssinian crisis. Every morning we woke up and thought, How much worse will it get today? At home we had labor demonstrations, strikes, riots, right against left, each side afraid that the other would seize power and take revenge. Cracked skulls, sirens, ambulances, murders, a police force instructed to make sure that we were as frightened as possible.

In the midst of this, what frightened *me*? The thought of my boyfriend at the racetrack with another woman, watching a woman dressed as a man drive a car that had been designed by the family of my rival. I imagined (wrongly, as it turned out) that I understood why I'd been so disturbed by Gabor's portrait of Lou and Arlette. In her new incarnation as the Rossignols' driver, Lou had joined the conspiracy to steal Gabor away.

If Gabor was going to fall in love with the baroness, wouldn't it have happened? But they had never spent the night in luxury hotels so far from home. All night I stayed awake, imagining them together.

How many times had Gabor and I walked the streets when *he* couldn't sleep. But I had no one to walk with. I was perfectly capable of going out by myself. But now the dark streets were only dark, as if Paris were blaming me for his absence and making sure I knew: it had confided its secrets in me only because I'd been with him.

Having eaten well, stayed in downy beds, and spent his days at the races, he returned to the cranky girlfriend who had been teaching French and standing in line for bread so her mother could enjoy a stale crust with her vegetable broth. What fun that must have been! How romantic! Was it any wonder that we began to get on each other's nerves? Suddenly awkward, we broke glasses, dropped and spilled whatever we touched. At the end of a tearful conversation we should never have had, he swore he loved me, only me. I wanted to believe him.

He insisted that he and the baroness had separate rooms and behaved like sister and brother. Did he mean the incestuous siblings in *Les Enfants Terribles*? He said the baroness was too old for him. Somehow I found this a comfort. I never asked myself if someday I would be too old for him too. In fact, I was lucky in this regard, as I was with everything about the man who would become my brilliant and loving husband.

A wealthy American woman would have been less of a threat. But the baroness was French. We'd learned the same tricks from the soil in which our food grew, from the air and wine and water. If a woman complains about another woman and waits for her lover to agree, she has already lost. The only way to win was to pretend not to notice or care.

The only person I could tell was my friend Ricardo. Stay calm, he said. Be brave.

I examined Gabor's photos of the track for covert messages from a man who didn't yet know he was planning to leave me. After the war, these images were published in a volume entitled *At the Speed of Light*. But more time would have to pass before I could look at them without recalling how I'd come home from a day of teaching to share a meager supper with Mama, knowing that my lover and his beautiful patron were at the Savoy in London, dining on tiny succulent lamb chops and discussing Lou's prospects.

Only now can I say with conviction: they are not my husband's best work.

For several years I fought to suppress his portrait of Inge Wallser, the repulsive Nazi goddess. But the legal case—argued for some reason in a Danish court—dragged expensively on. Perhaps it was better that I lost. Today, anyone can see wicked Inge perched on the hood of her Mercedes: a pinup that, I've heard, adorns the bedroom walls of the most violent right-wing adolescents.

On principle, I still avert my eyes from that photo. I was angry at Gabor for taking her picture—though at the time for the wrong reasons. You can't be a photographer's girlfriend and object to pictures of beautiful women.

Was Inge Wallser beautiful? *Cute* is the word I would use. Cute as a baby snake. Why should pictures of Inge bother me more than photos of Lou Villars? Was it that Lou was French? Or that Gabor never found Lou attractive?

In retrospect, the book's title (not my choice) says it all. Speed and light were the stars of the drama Gabor caught on film. The drivers, mechanics, and spectators were only supporting actors. How airless and one-dimensional the world of racing seems compared to that of the brothels, the gangsters, the cops, all those shimmering incandescent ghosts haunting the Paris nights.

It wasn't only Gabor. Everyone was obsessed with Montverre. Times were tough, the races were a welcome change from the Depression. Newspapers everywhere ran interviews with the drivers.

At the Speed of Light contains Gabor's only known portrait of the baroness Lily de Rossignol. Taken at Brooklands, it shows her getting out of her convertible. Over her shoulder, one can see the magnificent

Juno-Diane with its hood ornament fashioned in her image, a tribute to her glamour and her sense of style. On the prow of the car, as in life, her profile slices the air. Her hips are slung forward, her handsome head arched like a cobra preparing to strike. Though she often went to the track dressed in a fashionable version of the protective gear worn by the drivers, she is wearing a filmy, feminine polka dot dress and a velvet hat in the shape of a mushroom.

Clearly she has no idea that her picture is being taken. Alone in the world, purely self-possessed, she acts the part of a beautiful woman, a star performing for her fans, even though no one is watching. No one but the photographer, whom she loves. If she'd been aware that he was nearby, she couldn't have thought about anything else. But for that one fleeting moment, she didn't know he was there.

Even after everything that happened later, events that would so drastically alter my view of the baroness, the image still fills me with the dread of a woman who fears that her lover will leave her for the woman in the photo.

From *The Devil Drives:*
The Life of Lou Villars

BY NATHALIE DUNOIS

Chapter Nine: A False Memory?

LIKE ANY ARTIST, the biographer has moments when the creative process taps directly into the unconscious, forging new associations or repairing old ones, dredging up buried memories silted over by time. One such memory surfaced when I was writing this part of my book.

I have written that I first heard the name of Lou Villars spoken in hushed tones, at the home of my great-aunt, Suzanne Dunois Tsenyi. But one morning, while writing, or *trying* to write, I rose from my desk and sleepwalked down to the corner café. With shaking hands, I lit a cigarette. I ordered a café filtre and, as I drank it, recalled a story my great-aunt told my mother about having been hired by a certain baroness to accompany Lou Villars to an exclusive mental asylum outside Paris.

The story had appealed to me for all the reasons it would fascinate the romantic girl I was then. An asylum for wealthy lunatics with glamorous nervous conditions! Just the word *baroness* was enough to inflame my imagination. Somehow I intuited that my aunt and this baroness were rivals for the same man. It is at once heartening and depressing to discover that our ancestors have been in fixes much like those in which we find ourselves, decades later.

Lily de Rossignol paid my aunt a large sum to help Lou search for her brother, whom the baroness's agents had tracked to the hospital in the suburbs. Why had Lou needed the baroness? Why did a woman who could race cars at terrifying speeds lack the wherewithal to locate her own brother? The only logical answer is that, all her life, Lou exhibited a strong, even self-destructive respect for authority, tradition, and established institutions.

The baroness must have known what Lou would discover. She didn't want Lou going alone but had no desire to go with her. And so the baroness offered my aunt an unpleasant job in return for a fee that she knew my aunt would accept.

When my aunt and Lou arrived, they were told that the brother was dead: a victim of powerful seizures. In the café, that phrase came back to me: *a victim of powerful seizures.*

Apart from this early memory of my own, I have been unable to find any evidence proving that these events occurred. Shockingly, there is no record of the fate of Robert Villars after he was admitted to the Institute Notre Dame de Miséricorde, which in the 1980s was dynamited to make way for a hideous mall. What happened to those children during the Occupation? How can we live in a country in which such things are "not known"?

Nor do we know for a fact that this traumatic discovery was made in the company of my aunt, whom Lou may have held responsible—as people do, blaming not only the messenger, but also the witness. Even in the absence of conclusive documentation, it seems likely that learning this sad truth, in such a shocking way, would surely have contributed to the person Lou became and influenced how she treated my aunt when their paths crossed again.

For a long time I pictured Lou being told the bad news by a clerk. I imagined Lou refusing to believe it and searching frantically through the wards, yanking the blankets off slumbering catatonics, staring into the faces of slobbering psychotics while my aunt trailed helplessly behind, until a team of guards subdued Lou and ushered her out. Perhaps I found it easier to sympathize with Lou than I might have, were I not an only child, unacquainted with the mixed feelings siblings can inspire.

In any case, my impression of this scene—not of the emotions involved, but of the circumstances—changed when I happened to find, in a flea market, a vintage postcard, thick as cardboard, softened by time. A sepia image, lightly stainèd. A group portrait of the nursing staff at Notre Dame de Miséricorde.

Not only does creative work mine the rich veins of the unconscious, but it also has an uncanny ability to obtain what the artist needs, from the world. My shock on discovering the postcard was so obvious to the vendor that he charged me ten times what it was worth. I paid without protest, then retreated to the nearest café, where I ordered a coffee to calm my nerves but continued to tremble as I stared at the hospital: a looming dark brick castle, in the English Victorian style. In front of the hospital stood two rows of women in white robes and enormous starched winged headdresses, like satellite antennae.

Which was the one who informed Lou about her brother's death? Lou could not have looked at these women without remembering her time with the nuns, Sister Francis saving her life and then handing it on to her brother. The sight of the nun would have triggered Lou's reflexive, schoolgirl obedience. Instead of punching the messenger, Lou thanked the sister for her trouble. She and my aunt rode in silence all the way back to the city.

Paris
November 1934

Dear parents,
Last week I had a visit from Clovis Chanac, our former prefect of police, who came under a cloud of scandal but was soon back in power and now heads the Municipal Council. Chanac asked to see the prints of every shot I took at the track. He flipped through them, pausing over my pictures of Lou. He said he had agents and operatives whose secret identities would be compromised if anyone saw them in a photo taken at the race course. I didn't see how this could be true, but I nodded as if it made sense.

I wish I could tell you that I was mature enough to keep silent as he shuffled through my work like a deck of playing cards. But finally I couldn't bear it.

I said, "What are you looking for? Why?"

He said, "Do you think this is Communist Hungary, where every comrade is entitled to a detailed explanation of secret government affairs?"

Papa, you could have set him straight. I myself was speechless, which was probably just as well. Just before he left, he saw a photo of Lou hanging from the clothesline, a picture I took just after her victory at Brooklands. Chanac tore down the print, threw it on the floor, ground his heel in it, and spat on it for good luck.

Mama and Papa, pray for Lou. Chanac wants to destroy her. We are all uneasy. We live in frightening times. It calms me to think of you, and of all the changes and upheavals that you have survived.

Your loving son,
Gabor

From *A Baroness by Night*

BY LILY DE ROSSIGNOL

MY BROTHER-IN-LAW INSISTED that every outing, however informal, be choreographed with all the pomp and rigmarole of a military parade. Perhaps he'd watched too many newsreels from Italy and Germany, gotten too many overheated letters from his British friend Oswald, heard too many reports from like-minded acquaintances who'd been to Berlin and developed crushes on Hitler. He'd loved his time in the army. I sometimes forgot that about him.

Whenever Lou competed, Armand demanded that we all arrive at the race course together. Though it would have been more convenient for us to take separate cars, our short trip to Montverre became a precision maneuver. Armand and his driver picked up Didi and me, then we stopped for Lou, whose cottage was down a dirt path half a mile from the track. Maybe Lou would have liked to walk. But Armand said she should ride.

It was a beautiful morning in June. The grass glittered in Lou's front yard.

Lou always looked her best before a race: bright eyed, confident, calm. But that morning, she looked tired. That morning, of all mornings! Armand noticed too. Even Didi remarked on it, though my husband was hardly the most observant creature.

"Did you sleep?" Armand said as Lou climbed in the car.

"Like a baby," Lou said.

"Meaning you woke up screaming every hour," said Armand. Everyone laughed politely, though I always felt that Armand's references to children were veiled criticisms of Didi and me for not doing our part to increase the pureblooded French population. It was a source of great sorrow for me that Didi and I never had children, a pain that ebbed and waned unpredictably, over time.

Lou's path joined the main road not far from the track, near the parking area, surrounded by forest. We were turning the corner when we saw the scatter of black police cars angled like toys thrown down by a careless child and left wherever they landed.

As we drove up, the police fanned across the road with their weapons pointed at us. Through the window I saw Clovis Chanac, flanked by a gang of cronies.

Didi said, "Disaster."

"Not necessarily," said Armand.

But I knew that Didi was right, and I sensed that Lou did too.

We got out of the car. Armand's driver remained at the wheel. As Chanac twirled his mustaches like a melodrama villain, his men grinned at the spectacle of how distraught we were.

I put my hand on Armand's arm.

The cops gripped their guns as they watched Lou march up to Chanac. It was satisfying, but disquieting, to see him take a step backward. We were too far away to hear. I don't know why we didn't go closer. We were stunned, I suppose. Chanac produced an envelope and handed it to Lou, who stared at it. She was never a confident reader. Lou asked Chanac something. Then he said something else, and Lou shouted, "You bastard!" releasing us from the spell.

My brother-in-law asked what the problem was. Chanac gestured at the envelope, which Lou handed to Armand.

"Read it aloud," Didi said. But Armand read it silently and summarized its contents. It was an official document revoking Lou's license to compete in public athletic events, starting with, and including, today's race.

I said, "Did she *have* a license?"

Didi and Armand nodded.

"Right," I said. "This is France."

Armand said, "Don't be unpatriotic, Lily."

I noticed Chanac regarding me with malignant interest.

"Whether or not she had a license," Chanac said, "she doesn't have one now."

"And why not, may I ask?" said Didi.

"Look at Mademoiselle Villars," said Chanac. "Look at how she's dressed." We all did, as if we didn't know that Lou was wearing trousers and a blazer. Before the race she would change into her jumpsuit, helmet, and goggles.

Chanac said, "It goes against the laws that Napoleon passed down to us and are part of the heritage of France." I expected that to wake up Armand. The heritage of France. But he was poring over the document.

Armand said, "It's not just Chanac. It's the French Legion of Decency, the Movement for the Family, the Cross of Fire, the Order of the Legion of Joan of Arc, the French Women's National Athletic Association, etcetera and so on." All these groups had joined together to protest the threat that Lou Villars posed to the morality of the nation in general, and to young French women, in particular.

Armand belonged to at least two of these organizations. Why hadn't someone warned him? Chanac's power was on the rise. No one wanted to cross him over a female pervert in trousers.

"We're calling our lawyer," Armand said. "If you'll let us by, we'll phone him from the track."

"Call anyone you want," Chanac said. "Your girlfriend—or should I say *your boyfriend?*— isn't driving today."

Armand said, "This is treason! Who will drive for France?"

Chanac motioned toward his black sedan. Arlette got out of the car, wearing a black leather trench coat unbuttoned to the base of her cleavage. What did the Legion of Decency have to say about *that?* Arlette's lips and cheeks were slashes of red, her lashes a shelf of mascara. Life with Chanac had been unkind. Her face had grown harder and sadder.

Lou and Arlette looked at each other, then looked away before I could decipher what, if anything, passed between them.

Armand said, "Who is *that?*" No one bothered answering. Even Didi knew.

Armand said, "You're joking. Is *she* driving?"

Chanac said, "I *am* joking. Maybe she'll drive in the future. France doesn't need to win this race. France will win all the rest. We will win when it's important." He'd brought Arlette along to mock us. She was never going to drive. He didn't want to go to bed with the muscles she'd need to compete.

Didi said, "Our lawyer will contact you."

"By all means," said Chanac. "We have the government behind us."

Lou stood there, trembling, murderous. I thought about the referee she'd punched in Belgium. But Lou was not an idiot. Her career was at stake. She was the first to get back into Armand's car.

Armand's instincts had been correct. It was good we were all there, so we could retreat together. His chauffeur made a smooth full turn. He was an excellent driver.

Later, people sometimes asked how things happened the way they did: Hitler breathing down our necks, threatening France, and the French doing nothing but fighting among themselves. When they asked, I'd sometimes tell the story of Lou's expulsion from the athletic federation. How her license was revoked because she dressed like a man.

I'd say, That was what we were focused on as Hitler made plans to surprise us.

From *Paris in My Rearview Mirror*

BY LIONEL MAINE

WHEN THE DESK clerk said I'd gotten a 4:00 A.M. call from Jersey City, my first thought was that something had happened to Beedie or little Walt. The caller left a number. Hooray, it wasn't theirs.

When I phoned back, a secretary informed me that I had reached the desk of the international editor of the *Jersey City Herald*. I assumed he wanted to interview me about my book. How had my life changed since *Make Yourself New* was banned by the court? Had my purity been tarnished by fame? Did it bother me that my American audience was limited because my publishers, the Pixho brothers, refused to pay the second round of legal fees? Why waste good money they could spend on white wine at lunch? What did they care if a famous American poet—now mostly forgotten but at the time touted as the new Walt Whitman—had written that *Make Yourself New* should replace the Gideon Bible in every hotel room?

If the editor in New Jersey asked, I'd say I was writing a sequel filled with filthy stories I'd hesitated to put in my first book. Now I had nothing to lose. I was more determined than ever, thanks to the ban imposed by the New York judge whose brain had been softened by backed-up sperm. Thanks also to the lovers of literature who smuggled *Make Yourself New* home in their luggage. I'm going to tell *everything* in the second volume. If the truth is too obscene for my fellow Americans, so be it.

I'll admit I was disappointed when the editor from the *Herald*, Chuck van Something or Other, asked if I'd be interested in covering the trial of Lou Villars. A short piece, six hundred words, about a lady auto racer he'd heard about, suing to get back a government license that had been revoked because she dresses like a guy. Was this even true? Were people in Paris talking about it?

"Round the clock," I said. How much was the paper willing to pay? Twice as much as I expected.

I said, "So, Chuck, does this mean happy days are here again?"

Chuck said, "We're dying. The circulation guys are all over me for a sexy story like this."

Sexy? Chuck didn't know Lou. I tried to see the sexy part. Lesbians. Fast cars. Was I supposed to mention Lou cutting off her breasts? The *Herald* was a family paper. How could I phrase *that* so no one in Jersey got their panties in a twist? Who would think a voluntary double mastectomy was sexy? Maybe a few deviants. Not enough to boost circulation.

I say, "Well, you know, Chuck, it's funny. I know Lou pretty well. I'd been planning to attend the trial." That part was a lie. I was planning to harass the clerks at American Express in case Beedie had wired a few bucks. Then I planned on hunkering down in my favorite café to work on the book that has become *Paris in My Rearview Mirror.*

If I was writing about the trial, I could get in to watch. And the baroness would be grateful. Any press was good for the Rossignol brand, even in New Jersey. Given the state of the world, it might be a smart idea to have the well-connected baroness—finally!—in my corner.

I didn't blame the Rossignols for turning Lou's misfortune into publicity for their car. They'd invested time and money. In fact I admired the baroness for spreading the word that the Joan of Arc of the racing world had been destroyed by a moronic bureaucrat on trumped-up charges designed to safeguard the moral health of the French—an oxymoron, if there ever was one.

Had she been allowed to compete, Lou would have won, instead of Inge Wallser, who brought home the gold medal for Germany in the Mercedes. A story about Lou's trial was better than no story at all. If life was handing the Rossignols lemons, they'd make *citron pressé*.

The Rossignols should have seen what was coming. They should have cared about Lou's career. They knew Chanac wanted her dead. They knew that cross-dressing was technically illegal. They should have hired a chic designer to tailor some unisex culottes. Didi and Armand could have fixed this. Now they'd found her a lawyer, and everyone hoped for the best, which, as everyone but Lou seemed to know, would not be all that good.

When I discussed the case with Gabor, he defended the baroness. That worried me, needless to say. You don't want to watch your friend selling his soul to the devil. You don't want to see a decent, talented guy fall in love with a rich, controlling, neurotic snob who's been trying to buy him for years.

I hadn't planned to write about Lou for *Paris in My Rearview Mirror.* But I could work on the newspaper piece and my book at the same time. I'd earn a few bucks and get something for my memoir. Maybe a three-way sex scene involving Lou, the baroness, and me.

Neither woman attracted me, but the orgy they had in my fantasies was exciting. I hadn't gotten laid in so long I was fantasizing about Beedie, in Jersey City. Her gambler husband had been shot dead and left her comfortable, if not rich. Maybe that was why I'd thought of her first when the editor called.

So I told Chuck, Yes. Absolutely. I'll cover Lou's trial so the good citizens of New Jersey can be distracted from their catastrophic unemployment rate by the story of how the supposedly permissive and sexed-up but actually snooty and prudish French are keeping Lou Villars out of professional racing because she wears pants.

There was a lot I couldn't fit into six hundred words. Would the writer inside me erupt and blow apart the obedient reporter?

How could I convey the bizarre, Old World formality of the French court? You would have thought the guillotine was at stake instead of a racing license. A rising politician was using a women's sports federation and a fortune in French taxpayer money to ruin his mistress's ex-girlfriend. Wouldn't it have been simpler just to have her killed? People were being murdered every day, for political reasons. Chanac had already massacred dozens of blameless Parisians.

In France, cases took decades to come to trial. Money must have changed hands, favors been promised or called in. Chanac rushed the case through the system. He knew he was going to win. It was just entertainment for him—and a lesson for Arlette.

There were plenty of reporters, which pleased the baroness. Lou also enjoyed the attention, though she seemed not to know what it meant.

Another thing I couldn't include in the article was my personal opinion. I think people should be allowed to dress however they want. I like low-cut dresses on women, but I wouldn't make it a law. Nudity would be the best, though perhaps not for gents of my age. Women should drive as fast as they like and be free to mutilate their own bodies.

Obviously, I omitted the sex scene I'd imagined: me and Lou, then Lou and the baroness, then the three of us together. Six hundred words for a family newspaper gave me no room to observe that the judges from Dreyer's *The Passion of Joan of Arc* were sitting on Lou's tribunal. I didn't know if the film had been released at home, and I would have had to explain.

But why am I tantalizing my readers with the fun bits I couldn't fit into the piece? Here is what I wired the *Jersey City Herald*:

All of Paris is talking about the case of Lou Villars, the talented auto racer currently suing the French government and the French Women's National Athletic Association to force them to reinstate her professional license to compete.

Ever since last spring, in a dramatic public encounter, Villars has been barred from the track. She had been slated to represent France, driving the Rossignol 280 in the Women's International at Montverre. Since then Villars and her mostly female supporters have been holding weekly demonstrations on the steps of the Third Tribunal, where the trial began today.

This morning the judges heard from the defense, arguing that Villars sets an unhealthy example for young woman athletes—and all French women. She smokes three packs of cigarettes a day, swears like a sailor, drinks whiskey to excess, punches referees, and corrupts innocent girls. (Could I say this in the paper? Let the editors decide.) In addition she dresses in trousers, an offense to public decency, and has gone to the extraordinary length of surgically altering her body to look more like a man.

As evidence, the prosecutors introduced a photo of Lou Villars in male attire.

When the buzz subsided, Lou's lawyers presented their case. She should have her license back. Had the judges heard of Joan of Arc? Would they have ruled like *her* judges?

Their client admits that she underwent an elective operation, but not because of vanity and certainly not perversion. Like everything she does, it was for sport, which, along with God and France, is her reason for existing. And what was wearing trousers compared to the treason committed by the government and the French Women's National Athletic Association by not letting the French auto industry prove itself against Germany, Italy, and Great Britain?

All eyes were on Lou, who was seated between her attorney and Armand de Rossignol, the scion of the auto manufacturing family. Dressed in a man's white cotton suit, a silk tie, and a white fedora, Lou was a model of gangster high style. When her lawyer pronounced the word *treason*, Lou's arm shot up in the salute of the French far right. The judge instructed Lou's lawyer that his client would be removed from the courtroom unless she behaved.

Highly sensational testimony is expected to follow, though the word on the boulevards is that the bookies are offering ten to one *against* Lou Villars. Meanwhile the racing-world star has announced that, if she loses, she will move to Italy or Germany or even the United States, any country that accepts her—and knows how to treat its athletes.

In fact Lou Villars never mentioned the United States. And she never gave the fascist salute. But no one in Jersey City ever found out or complained.

September 16, 1935

Dearest Mama and Papa,

Imagine Papa learning that his favorite student had grown up to become a killer of children. Or Mama paying a Sunday social call and bringing her most delicious strudel, and when no one is watching, the hostess's beloved toddler chokes to death on a slice of Mama's cake.

That is how I felt at the Third Tribunal when my photo "Lovers at the Chameleon Club, Paris 1932," was introduced as evidence of Lou Villars's decadent manner of life.

I know you two have doubts about Lou. You warned me that such pictures could get me in trouble. I should never have told you what powerful enemies she has. Nor did your opinion change when I wrote you that Lou is a fan of my work. No other photographer got the access she gave me at the track. No one else was allowed to shoot her inspecting the engine before the races.

Lou thought she was letting me show the world what she was doing for France. The baroness thought that Lou and I were working for Rossignol Motors. I thought that Lou was helping me make a living from my art.

Lou used some of her prize money to purchase my portrait of her and her former girlfriend, Arlette. She'd asked for a print many times, always when I was most busy. Now she has paid full price, without trying to get a bargain. However she dresses, Lou has proved herself to be, in this regard, a lady.

The baroness says that beneath the swagger, Lou is a tragic soul. That will not stop people from seeing a woman who has crossed the line men draw, a woman who not only competes like a man, but who dresses and loves like one too. Do I sound like a feminist? You taught me to listen to women. And women appreciate the attention, not only the baroness but also Suzanne. If I see less of her than I used to, or anyway so she claims, it is only because I have become so involved in the crisis that, thanks to Lou's involuntary retirement, is currently facing the baroness and her husband's firm.

When it comes to viewing Lou Villars without prejudice or preconception, the eyes of Paris are not so unlike those of our provincial town. People share the same narrow view: men should be men and women should be women—meaning that women should do what men tell them.

Please try to understand how I felt when my portrait of Lou was used against her in court! I wish you were here, so you could rout the demons buzzing around my head like monsters out of Goya. The demon who says that Yvonne was right to forbid me to photograph at the Chameleon. The demon who says, Everything you told yourself about the *sacramental transaction* between you and your subjects—every word was a lie. You have exploited these people for your so-called art. The homeless sleeping under the bridge should have tossed you into the river.

If only I could have photographed in the courtroom. I would love to have an image of the judges' faces as they inspected my portrait of Lou and Arlette. Were they all really seeing it for the first time? Hadn't one of them seen my book? They were disgusted by my photo, more than they would have been by my shot of the half-naked prostitute awaiting her customer in bed. I'd like to put a picture of the judges up in my studio and look at it every day as a reminder to never take another picture without warning my subjects that their portraits could be used against them.

Lou came up to me after the hearing and told me she didn't blame me. It was nice of her to say so. We shared a peaceful moment of something like understanding.

Lionel is a real friend. He tried to cheer me up. He said they would have ruled against Lou with or without my photo. He said it's a badge of honor when the courts hate your work. What clearer sign does an artist need that he's on the right track?

As usual, Lionel was talking about himself. His own life changed for the better when the judge in New York decreed that his book was filth. Many more people have heard of his book than if it hadn't been banned. I thanked Lionel and told him our situations were very different. Lou let me take her picture, and I returned the favor by destroying her life.

Lionel said, "You paid her. It was a job."

Lou took the stand in her own defense. Whatever skills I'd developed writing for the *Magyar Gazette* fail me as I try to describe what made the start of her speech so touching. Her eyes shone with tears as she told the court that she lived only for sport, God, and France. When she asked the surgeon to remove her breasts, it was to avoid danger and pain. She never wished to marry and have children she might have to nurse. I could tell that Lou's lawyers wished she hadn't said that.

Her breasts had been a handicap and a hazard. Having them removed had nothing to do with wanting to look like a man. She was proud of being female and of the God-given chance to show women what they could do. They needn't live the way she lived. But they must be willing to suffer as she had—to nearly drown swimming against the current, to drive on winding mountain roads at high speeds without a rail between her and the abyss. To lose a part, two parts, of her body. There was no way to win that didn't require gritting your teeth and telling yourself, Faster! Harder! Stronger!

When she talked about suffering, I felt that I was hearing an artist speak about art. But apparently the role of my "art" had been to undermine Lou's case.

Mesmerized, as we all were, the judges let her continue. Lou spoke briefly about how the Maid of Orléans was her patron saint, how she tried to emulate her, on and off the field of battle. She went on too long. She gave the judges too much time to slip back into seeing what they'd seen at the start: a young woman with a man's haircut, dressed like a man, in a suit. They'd seen my photo of her with her arm around the bare shoulders of a pretty girl in a party dress. A lovely girl who might have been *theirs* if this Amazonian predator hadn't seduced her with her secret female sex tricks!

In a more honorable world, Arlette might have come to her old friend's defense. But Chanac's team had told Arlette to stay away from the courtroom.

When the probable outcome of the hearing finally dawned on Lou, her demeanor took a sudden, shocking turn for the worse. She began to rant about the hypocrisy of her accusers, how the women of the athletic association were trying to take away the thing she loved most as punishment for the "cardinal sin" of wearing trousers. They themselves were only pretending to be innocent and pure.

Lou had spied the French Women's National Athletic Association President, Madame LeNotre, with her tongue down the throat of a swimming coach twenty years her junior. And the vice president, Mademoiselle Blanc? Lou had caught her in a men's locker room with her behind in the air, doing a "favor" for a soccer star. Before they ruled against Lou for wearing the comfortable clothes of the opposite sex, let the court consider how many men become priests only because taking holy orders allows them to wear skirts!

The judges banged their gavels. Order in the court! It took them fewer than fifteen minutes to decide against Lou.

Her license will not be restored. She cannot compete. She has no way of earning a living.

As Lionel said, her enemies would have won, no matter what. But my photos helped destroy her. The baroness begged me not to take it to heart. This was not the first time that great art had been used for evil purposes. I thanked her for her kindness, but I remained inconsolable.

The baroness, her husband, and her brother-in-law went off with Lou and the lawyers to figure out the next step. Out of politeness, they asked me to join them. I appreciated the gesture, but I was in no mood to attend a meeting to which I could contribute nothing but shame over my (innocent) mistake. A meeting at which everyone ignored the fact that my "art" had not only harmed Lou but also Rossignol Motors, which has always supported my work. As have you!

Lou's defeat is bad news. I've sold a picture of her meeting with a lawyer and another of her practicing to keep up her skills. But the papers only want so much of that. And those pictures only remind me of my role in Lou's downfall.

I can still do celebrity portraits for French and American magazines. But they have started to bore me. The stars all have assistants who know how to set up a shot. I'm just there to click the shutter and sign my name on the credit line. My muse found me again at the races and has left me once more.

Auto magazine asked if I wanted to go to Germany and photograph Inge Wallser training in the Mercedes. But I refuse to take pictures that could be used by Hitler. It's bad enough that my work has ruined an innocent woman's life.

The Rossignols dropped me off at my studio on their way to the baroness's house. I walked into my haven, my home, the site of so many discoveries, the place where so much of my life has tiptoed past so as not to disturb me.

It was changed beyond recognition. All around me were pictures of people with guns to their heads. And I was holding the gun.

I wrote to you. I closed my eyes. I lay like a corpse for two hours.

I was awoken by the phone. The baroness was calling to see if I was alone. She knows it can be awkward when she and Suzanne are together. In fact I'd chosen to be alone, even though Suzanne, who knew how I was suffering, had offered to come over.

I heard the baroness's car shriek to a stop beneath my window. The desk clerk sent her up. She had come to assure me that Lou would land on her feet, and that my portrait of her and Arlette was a work of art. We talked for several hours. We shared a bottle of wine. I made the baroness coffee so that she could drive home.

As she was leaving, I asked her to wait. I found a reasonably decent print of my photo of her at Brooklands. I examined it to make sure that it was an appropriate gift. I was astonished all over again that this woman was my friend, this streamlined radiant sunbeam of sleek modern beauty.

I'd had an argument with Suzanne when she first saw the picture.

She'd insisted that I and the baroness . . . She accused me of having feelings for the baroness that I do not have. Unlike Suzanne, whom I care about deeply, the baroness would know better than to misread an image that way.

I gave the baroness her photo.

"In gratitude," I said. "In gratitude and love."

She stared at it for a long time. Then she burst into tears.

For several minutes, we were both too overcome to speak. Then she thanked me. I thanked her. We kissed.

I watched from the window as she got in her car and drove away.

And finally now, to sleep. I promise to write you soon, dear ones.

                    Till then and forever, I am your loving son,
                    Gabor

From *A Baroness by Night*

BY LILY DE ROSSIGNOL

IF THERE IS an afterlife, I hope they will throw a party for the angels who on earth were the subjects of famous photos. There will be a carousel for those tragic little girls who sat for Lewis Carroll, nourishing meals for the Dust Bowl families. The lovers Gabor shot in cafés can devour each other forever. We'll visit with Baudelaire and Bernhardt, courtesy of Nadar, and with that funny Lartigue lady wearing more fur than her dogs. No need to invite Lou Villars and Arlette, who will be in hell.

We will recognize one another, angels with faces fixed forever in black and white and in two dimensions. There will be many things that we won't need to say, though I wish that we would. I would like to know how the other angels felt when they saw their pictures, or when (just for a laugh) they read some critic's ruling on what their image *meant*. Is immortality a sufficient reward for being tethered eternally to one moment in a whole life?

Gabor's photo of me at Brooklands became a symbol of the Machine Age. Many critics had the stunning originality to compare my profile with the hood ornament on my beautiful Juno-Diane coupe, a decorative tribute to me that my husband and brother-in-law designed. Do they really imagine that the resemblance was accidental, or that it took Gabor's eye to discover the likeness?

There must be other angels who, even in heaven, can't look at their portraits without having to fight back tears. I wept the first time I saw mine. How shy and proud Gabor was, almost apologetic.

"In gratitude," he said. "In gratitude and love." He wanted me to know how much it meant to him that I'd stopped by on the evening of the verdict against Lou. I'd known he would be upset about how his work was used in the trial. In fact he was very blue—and *very* happy to see me. It was almost as if my presence was a sign that he would be absolved for whatever sin he thought he'd committed.

I had convinced myself that I hadn't been imagining the new erotic tension that had lately arisen between us. I hadn't known what to make of it. I'd decided to wait and see.

Knowing how grateful he would be if I visited that night, I'd dared to imagine a seamless arc, a rainbow of desire and pleasure we had only to follow from the first tentative, awkward touch to a kiss to the heights of passion. I had no idea how we would scale those heights or how rarefied the air would be, if and when we arrived.

But when Gabor showed me my photo, I focused on the Juno-Diane. Only after that did I think: who *is* that old woman? The car looked ageless and very beautiful. I looked tired and tightly wound. I understood that my fantasies would never come true in this life.

He said he wanted me to have it. He said, in gratitude. He said, in gratitude and love. He was the one who used the word *love*. I heard it the way I wanted.

Though he and I were the same age, it's different for women and men, as it is for dogs and humans. His Suzanne wasn't yet thirty and had the breasts to prove it. What could I have been thinking when I went to his house that night? I suppose I'd hoped to cheer him up. I'd succeeded, if only slightly. It was time for me to leave.

Gabor and I would never be together. We would never fall in love. Perhaps it could have happened when we were twenty. We were twice that now.

Then why, you might ask, had he said *love*? In gratitude and *love*.

I was about to thank him and say good night when he took me in his arms. All I will say is that it would have been better for our friendship—and much better for my pride—if I hadn't gone there that night.

How can a woman surrender to love, transcend her reserve and hesitations, immolate herself in the heat of her lover's body, when all she can think of is how to hide the fact that she has never done this before? The only thing that mattered to me was that Gabor not find out that his sophisticated patroness was a middle-aged virgin.

We were gentle and patient with each other, kind and forgiving as we tried something that didn't work. Tried something else and failed. I wanted time to go backward and start again, so I could fix what had gone wrong.

We were still friends. We would always be friends. But we would never be lovers.

As soon as I saw Gabor's photo of me, I'd known what was going to happen, and what it would be like. But I tried to put it out of my mind as we went through the motions of love. Or *some* of the motions. Maybe it was the photo's fault. Maybe I was distracted by what I'd seen in the image, and Gabor sensed that distraction, and that was the end of that.

After we stopped trying, we laughed, as if to reassure ourselves that this was just the newest of the little private jokes that formed the bedrock of our friendship.

The next morning I showed Didi my portrait. I said, "You've been asking where is the photo of me? Well, all right, here it is."

I turned and gazed out the window. An organ grinder had stationed himself directly across the street. His shriveled monkey in its tiny bellhop's uniform hopped into the arms of a girl who screamed, and the monkey screeched back.

"A beautiful photo," Didi said, "of a beautiful woman. It's striking, really, how our fabricators were able to make that hood ornament on our Juno-Diane look so much like you."

I cried when my husband said that. I pretended that they were tears of laughter at the mayhem the monkey was causing.

For days, I'd look at the photo and sob. At last I filed it away. I think it got lost in the war. It resurfaced in a collection of Gabor's racetrack photos, *At the Speed of Light*, and later in a gallery show near the Spanish Steps in Rome. By then he'd been dead for a decade, having succumbed to a heart attack in the arms of his beloved Suzanne.

When I saw it on the gallery wall, even all those years later, I broke down and wept. Elegant Romans edged away from me. But I didn't care. I cried for what happened that night and for what didn't happen and for everything that happened later. For Gabor, and for what we'd lost, for the years since I'd seen him.

In the gallery near the Via Condotti, I stared at Gabor's photo through the blur of tears. How young and pretty that woman was! By *that woman* I meant *me*. It had taken all that time for me to understand that the subject of the photograph was not the car but the woman.

Do the other photographed angels grieve for the irretrievable past? When I look at that photo, I think: too bad that woman doesn't know that she is still young and beautiful enough to make the photographer love her. What a pity she doesn't know that he already does.

From *The Devil Drives:*
The Life of Lou Villars
BY NATHALIE DUNOIS

Chapter Ten: After the Trial

BEFORE HER PROFESSIONAL license to race was revoked as punishment for challenging traditional gender roles, Lou Villars was the favorite to win the 1935 Women's International race at Montverre. She'd trained to drive the Rossignol 280 for France, against an Alfa Romeo, a Rolls-Royce, and a Mercedes-Benz, each driven by a woman representing her home country. After Lou was disqualified, the competition was won by Inge Wallser, in the Mercedes.

The Rossignols promised to help Lou get her license restored. They hired lawyers to argue her case in the Third Tribunal. And they continued paying the rent on her cottage near the track.

Not long after the trial, the Rossignols arrived, unannounced, at her door. Lou had been expecting them. She'd heard they were talking to other drivers: men. They wouldn't make the same mistake twice. It had been reckless of them to bet that the racing world was ready for a woman in trousers, though they'd been right about Lou's ability to get attention for the brand. Unfortunately for Lou, the Rossignols were selling cars, not newspapers. A win at the track was worth more than a driver people gossiped about, a minor celebrity whom the public had already forgotten.

Lou opened her door to find the baroness wearing the racing-inspired outfit—goggles, leather, hardware—she'd often worn to the track. She brushed wispy kisses onto Lou's cheeks and gave her an affectionate hug, which seemed odd, considering she'd come to fire her. Maybe they weren't firing her. Or maybe it wasn't odd. Sometimes Lou trusted the Rossignols. Mostly she trusted no one. Armand had said to trust no one, not even the mechanics.

The baroness's husband looked Lou up and down and said, "Mademoiselle Lou, allow me to say that you are looking terrific."

Lou had always liked Didi. She admired how he'd found a way to love boys without anyone much objecting. No one objected to anything if you were rich enough. Only now did Lou realize that. It made her like Didi less.

Didi and the baroness strolled into Lou's cottage without waiting to be invited. They were paying the rent. They assumed Armand was right behind them, but he stalled in the doorway, swaying slightly, like a building in an earthquake. At the same moment Didi and Lou lunged, caught him, and propped him up. He walked between them, on his toes, with his back stiffly arched. He paused at Lou's altar to Joan of Arc, where he shuddered, crossed himself, and lurched on.

Lou and Didi deposited him on the sofa. He slumped and closed his eyes. A soft, rhythmic, nasal whistle was the only sign of his presence. Lou was grateful to Armand. She'd loved him, in a way. She regretted to see the condition in which he'd been brought to witness the end of her association with his family and their cars.

Lou invited Didi and the baroness to sit, but they chose to stand, as if their vigilant postures might counterbalance Armand's collapse. The baroness prowled the background while Didi spoke to Lou in the language of business: reassessment, trial, direction, avenue, approach. They *had* come to fire her. But Didi used every word except that one.

It was what Lou had anticipated. What good was a racer who couldn't race? Still, she was caught off guard by the plans they had made for her future.

"Confidentially," said the baroness, "our friends are always complaining that it's impossible to find a good garage mechanic in Paris. There isn't one you can rely on in the entire city. Lou, you know more about cars than anyone. You're a celebrity driver and a famous . . ." The baroness's impish grin expressed the impossibility of attempting to define what Lou was famous for.

The Rossignols would lease Lou a garage with a reasonable rent. It would be an investment. Their friends would bring her their autos. She could fix cars and sell motoring accessories at a substantial markup. Her clientele would grow. The Rossignols could quit supporting her, and Lou would be set for life.

They'd trained her to drive fast, to win races, pose for photos, talk to reporters. And now it turned out that her destiny was crawling under some fat lazy banker's sedan and selling him doeskin driving gloves for his plump *boudin blanc* fingers.

If things don't work out at the track, you can always be a mechanic. How she and Armand had laughed at their little joke. Was it something his family discussed? Had this been their fallback plan from the start? It only made Lou angrier to realize that she should be grateful.

Armand's eyes were rolled back in his head. Of course she would agree to their plan. The country was in the midst of history's most prolonged Depression. There was no money, no work. Lou would be lucky to have a job. Not just a job, but a business. She knew one former driver who was sleeping under a bridge.

Lou said, "Thank you. What a brilliant idea. When can I start working?"

The Rossignols found Lou a windowless shack near the Gare du Nord. At first it reeked of dead mice. The stench of gasoline was an improvement. She could live above the garage. Her sheets and pillowcases stank of motor oil.

The first six months were paid for. After that she was on her own. The owner was a Russian Jew who kept raising the rent. Each incremental increase confirmed Lou's negative view of his race.

One evening Lou went to have a drink at the Chameleon Club. Yvonne asked Fat Bernard to let Lou know, gently and diplomatically, that she was no longer welcome. Yvonne was sorry, but the trial had attracted too much attention. The club had lasted as long as it had because everyone was discreet.

Lou's exile from the Chameleon was only mildly surprising. She shouldn't have expected a Hungarian to be loyal.

Lou saw Armand at political rallies, supported by an entourage of handsome, strapping veterans hired to keep him upright. Sometimes she wasn't sure if Armand recognized her or not. When he did, he was friendly and polite. How was business? Fine, thank you.

In fact Lou had plenty of business. She worked fourteen hours a day. The baroness and Didi stopped by to remark on how well she was doing. After their visits, bile rose in her throat.

Occasionally she closed the garage for a few hours and went to meet married clients. Sometimes these women rented hotel rooms. Sometimes she visited their homes. In accordance with her rule against mixing work with romance, Lou always ended these affairs after one afternoon.

Most mornings, the only way that Lou could get out of bed was by telling herself that she was fortunate to have a bed to get out of. The only rays of light that brightened her dark night of the soul were the trips she still made, once or twice a month, to speak to provincial sports clubs. The Rossignols had sold her a sedan destined for the junk heap that she restored and got on the road. She loved the long solitary drives, the cheap traveling salesmen's hotels, the attentive crowds of women unconsciously stroking their biceps as she spoke.

One evening, in Nantes, the audience was so large that the venue had to be moved from a church hall to a barn. The ladies of the Nantes Gymnastics League showed off their fitness by rushing across the cowshed with stacks of folding chairs.

A few minutes into her lecture, Lou felt a new spirit move through her. In a brave and confident voice, she told the crowd that she knew they'd heard her sad story. But she hadn't come all this way just to rehash a legal scandal. Nor did she plan to compromise their dignity and her own by explaining, yet again, why she chose to dress like a man and why she had every right to do so.

That was *exactly* why they had come. But before they had time to be disappointed, Lou promised them a chance to rise above all that. She would tell them how their government, corrupted by foreign influence, had stolen her God-given right to make an honest living. The very same government that, by raising taxes, permitting uncontrolled immigration, weakening the military, failing to control the national debt, and fostering skyrocketing unemployment, was making it impossible for them to feed their families and provide better lives for their children.

She'd come to tell them that their problems could be solved if they were willing to sacrifice, to transcend their personal interests and become part of something larger. Their needs would be met, their nation restored to its former glory—a process that could start with sports and physical fitness. Who didn't want their destinies to be more heroic, to surrender to something higher than the question of who cheated which sibling out of an inheritance and who was sleeping with whose husband?

In a spiffy suit, with a cigarette idling between her lips, Lou Villars was promising that something different could happen. But what? She ended before she had to explain what this new world would look like. Armand had never elaborated, so why should she?

After her speech, she was mobbed by more fans than she'd had when she raced or when she and Arlette had played the Chameleon. It made perfect sense that the women of France would respond so openheartedly to a woman in a suit. After all, she wasn't the first. Joan of Arc had paved the way. The vision to look beyond what a person wore was deeply rooted in the French, paradoxically the most fashion-conscious nation on the planet.

Lou made friends wherever she went. Soon there were so many she had to organize them in her mind, alphabetically and by region. There was Abelia from the Ardennes, who told her husband that the money she made teaching tennis came from selling aubergines in the market. Berthe from Bordeaux, whose lecherous choirmaster had shown her drawings of a Greek discus thrower. Clara from Caen, who told no one but Lou how often she swam too far out in the ocean, Danielle from Drancy, who ran to escape her dread that a catastrophe was about to befall her town. They took up collections to bring her back and boldly ignored the censure of the French Women's National Athletic Association.

When Lou spoke to these sisters in sport, when she shared their nutritious regional delicacies, smoked their cigarettes, drank their wine, and spent the night in their beds, she was content, or almost content. But on Monday morning a grumpy Cinderella was back in coveralls at the garage.

Lou tried not to imagine a future in which she'd be fixing cars after the local clubs tired of her and wanted to hear a new voice. For example, the voice of an athlete who'd competed in next summer's Olympics. She tried not to think about the games from which she'd been excluded. Regret was for cowards and weaklings.

On good days, she convinced herself: there was honor in hard work. Then a client would mention a sporting event, or she'd see a flyer for the Garden of Eden, the club Chanac had opened for Arlette, and which, she'd heard, was popular with right-wing journalists and city officials.

One morning a Delage pulled into the garage: a midnight blue ocean liner piloted by a uniformed cop with another cop beside him. In the backseat was Clovis Chanac.

Lou knew he must have approved her license to operate the garage, a mystifyingly generous act. Now the spiteful pleasure visible on his face told Lou he'd been waiting, calmly planning the fun he was going to have today.

Chanac eased himself out of the car. "Mademoiselle Villars! How long has it been?" Both knew precisely how long: Chanac had last seen Lou at her trial. Lou extended her hand to Chanac, but he smiled and demurred. Her palm was black with grease.

"Sorry," Lou said, hating him, and herself for apologizing.

Chanac's mustache was half pink with the dye he'd used to bring the gray hairs in line with their faded red neighbors. He told Lou he had a problem. A personal problem. Several acquaintances, satisfied customers all, had told him that Lou was his man, ha-ha. The perfect *person* to fix it. Some liquid had accidentally spilled on the backseat. He'd heard that Lou had a magic touch with upholstery stains.

Lou leaned into the Delage. On the rear seat were dried smears of thick white fluid. Even if the two cops hadn't been snickering, Lou would have known that Chanac meant her to think that the crusted substance was semen.

She forced herself to look again. Too much, too thick. It was library paste. Though Lou had never, strictly speaking, gone to bed with a man, she was sure Chanac could never have shot that much, not in his dreams, not with a dozen Arlettes. It must have been a slow day at the city council. Chanac and his pals were having fun with a woman whose mechanic's license could be revoked in a heartbeat.

Lou got a cloth and solvent. The glue spread and stuck to the leather, but she cleaned it all off. The two cops applauded. Lou wanted to grab their guns and shoot them.

Chanac thanked Lou and said he'd be back. He reached inside his jacket.

Lou said, Please, it was on the house. It had been her pleasure.

Everyone who has ever written a biography, everyone *who has ever lived*, will have noticed how often a dark thread runs through the weave and weft of a life. Clovis Chanac was Lou's dark thread, almost from the beginning, or at least from the moment Arlette directed her mermaid song at him. And everyone has, at some point, met a man like Chanac: those lucky individuals who continually fail upward, who are fired for incompetence or for some abuse of power and instantly find a better job. We ordinary mortals would have wound up in jail or on the street! But these chosen ones rise higher—in politics, business, or even at a sleepy provincial high school. And so this pattern repeats itself: promotion, crime, exposure, failure, bigger crime, bigger failure, bigger promotion. In Chanac's case, the skills required for the three phases of his career—police prefect, politician, gangster boss—were so alike that he could excel at all three.

How unfair that, of all the men in Paris, Chanac kept crossing Lou's path. When she heard that he had lost his job as the head of the city council, she was at first delighted until she learned that he had gone into partnership with the leader of one of the gangs with whom she was obliged to do business in order to run the garage.

In an era of shortages and limited import-export trade, auto parts were only available on the black market. Dealing with the racketeers was like buying fan belts and exhaust pipes in a store, except that the store was a bar called Le Hippo, and the salesmen were killers and thieves.

The gangsters didn't intimidate Lou. She knew their secrets. She'd slept with the wives they neglected. They knew who she was and what she'd done. They admired her for having balls. A convenient arrangement all around. Lou liked holding her own among the toughest of the tough. And these hardened criminals treated Lou Villars with more civility and respect than certain high school administrators show their teaching staff.

Lou had private names for them. Carburetor Sammy. Patsy the Piston. Marcel the Manifold. Alex "Tires" the Greek. It was fine with her if they wanted to funnel rich people's money into their own pockets. The real criminals were in the government, the banks, and the foreign fifth column composed of Communists and Jews.

For a while she dealt exclusively with the Gasparu gang, led by the petty crook and car thief Pierre "Crazy Pierrot" Gasparu. Then when the government fired Chanac for laundering a fortune in bribes through Arlette's club, he made a deal with Gasparu, offering his contacts in industry and the police in return for a half share of Gasparu's business. A group of former police officers whom Chanac took down with him accompanied him to the negotiations, to help persuade Gasparu.

At first Lou thought it might be awkward to work with a man who had stolen her first love, destroyed her career, and humiliated her in her own garage. But these were challenging times. Slates were being wiped clean. Compromises were required. One climbed into bed with people whom one wouldn't have spit on before. If Lou had to work with Clovis Chanac, she could let bygones be bygones. The equally pragmatic Chanac was perfectly glad to do business with the cross-dressing Amazonian grease monkey who'd tried to ruin his beloved's reputation by spreading the ridiculous rumor that they'd once been lovers.

The Gasparu-Chanac gang had turned Le Hippo into a social club of which they were the only members, an emporium where, despite the absence of visible merchandise, everything was for sale. Chanac had an office in the back, from which he rarely emerged. Even when alcohol and tobacco were not to be found anywhere in Paris, the criminals always had liquor and cigarettes and were willing to share.

They enjoyed having Lou as an audience when they drank and boasted about how big and bad, how tough and mean they were, and about the less tough, less mean guys they'd bullied into submission. They'd ask Lou what she needed. She'd name an auto part, and the next day a kid would deliver it to the garage. They trusted her to pay them when the client paid her, and she knew not to test their trust. It ground her down to depend on Chanac and his men. And for Lou, every ounce of energy that didn't go into fixing cars was spent fending off what today would be diagnosed as clinical depression.

Once Lou had dreamed of being a star. But she was a reasonable person. Meaning, she was French. She could lower her expectations and get through the day. Like Saint Joan, she could accept, even glory in, shame and degradation.

Looking into the sources of evil, as I have in writing this book, I have developed a profound respect (if *respect* is the word) for the power of resentment, the corrosive acid produced by the conviction that a person has been overlooked, cheated, or betrayed.

Lou Villars had plenty to resent, or anyway so she thought. A psychologist colleague has written a monograph proving that each member of the Gasparu-Chanac gang (including Pierrot Gasparu and Clovis Chanac) held some smoldering grudge against the state or a particular cop, a landlord, a woman, someone who'd done him wrong. And with such people, as we know, nothing is ever their fault.

Lou's misery lasted through the winter and well into the spring. The election of the Popular Front only made her feel worse. On the night of the election there was dancing in the streets. Lou stayed inside and heard, outside her window, the sounds of a party to which she had not been invited.

The progressive new laws didn't apply to her. What good was the promise of a forty-hour week when she worked fourteen hours a day and barely survived on her earnings? So what if French citizens were guaranteed the right to strike and bargain for better conditions? Whom would she have struck against? People whose cars needed fixing? The cars? And when was she supposed to take her two-week paid vacation? Who would run the garage when she was away, and where did Léon Blum and the other powerful government Jews think she would go *on vacation*?

The invitations to lecture at the sports clubs had stopped, but Lou didn't care. She would only have turned them down. The friends she'd made weren't real friends, the lovers not real lovers but bored provincial housewives, the most daring in each crowd, nervy enough to spend the night with a failed auto racer. Even though whiskey was scarce and expensive, Lou drank more than she had since she and Arlette drank for free at the Chameleon.

She slept with married women who paid her to hammer out the dings in their fenders. After these amorous afternoons, the women expected Lou's rates to go down, but not one of them protested when Lou charged them double.

Sometimes, when Lou drank, she imagined jumping in front of the Métro or joining the desperate citizens who, if one believed the papers, were waiting in line to end it all in the river. She stopped eating and on Sundays rarely left her apartment above the garage. Her existence was shrinking. Maybe her life would grow small enough to disappear on its own.

One afternoon in late June a cream-colored envelope arrived in the mail. On the top right-hand corner were two German stamps. A runner with the Olympic torch sprinted across one, while, on the other, a diver, a half-naked Greek god, jackknifed in midair.

Written in brown ink, with only a few mistakes in French, the letter said:

Dear Mademoiselle Villars!

I hope you will remember "Little" Inge Wallser. You won the race against me at Brooklands. You deserved to win! I'll admit!

I won at Montverre after your government prevented you from doing what you worked so hard to accomplish. Otherwise you would have won. I know an athlete should never say that, but when you get to know me, you will find out that I value truth above all things! Even above my career! I live for truth . . . and love.

We spoke at Brooklands, remember? I would have liked to talk more. But you were "busy" that evening! Too bad!

Never a fast reader, Lou decoded the words she'd already smudged with oily black smears. Of course she remembered Inge flirting with her at Brooklands. How pathetic Lou had been, how many chances she had wasted with her ridiculous *principles* about mixing romance and racing.

For a German, Lou thought, Inge used a lot of exclamation points. Well, sure. To be an auto racer you had to be a passionate person.

Inge wrote,

I have thought about you since then, and I followed your case with interest, in the German papers. I am not a poet! So I will put it simply: your story obsessed me. It moved me to tears. Remember that interview in which you said you'd always loved France, but you wished you lived in a country that respected its athletes. Since then I have wanted to write you a million times, to send you my warmest wishes, assure you of my faith and support, and say,

"Dear Mademoiselle Villars, Germany under the Führer is the country of your dreams!"

I have told your story to government officials I've been lucky enough to meet through my (modest!) fame as a driver. I say, Look who this woman is! And look how the French treat her! Such stories travel upward, and (are you sitting down?) your story has reached the Führer!

At a recent reception the Führer remarked that (meaning no insult) it was just like the French to worship nightclub singers no better than prostitutes and let their taste in art be dictated by Jewish dealers. Yet they mistreat their athletes, whom they're too blind to appreciate as symbols of national pride. If only Lou Villars could see the glory the Reich heaps on its sports stars!

To say nothing of our government program, Strength through Joy, which encourages every worker, every student and village housewife to develop powerful bodies along with healthy minds. In the past there has been some prejudice, here as elsewhere, against female athletes whose destiny as wives and mothers might be harmed by strenuous exercise. But our Führer so opposes this ignorant thinking that he has formed a commission to reeducate our population.

I'm digressing. Let me get to the point: would you consider joining us at the upcoming Olympics as the Führer's special guest? This is a real invitation! We hope you will say yes.

As with every little thing that concerns the Führer, many people are now taking credit for the idea to invite you. Let the censors object, but I assure you, I thought of it first! And yet I could only imagine such a thing, only dare to come up with such a plan, because the Führer believes that this is how we will change the world: one heart and mind at a time.

We hope you will come and see for yourself how our athletes live under the Reich! Please write back if you are interested. I hope to hear from you soon! Until then I remain your loyal fan,

Inge Wallser

Already conscious of the role she would play in history, Inge Wallser kept copies of her letters. This one can be found in the State Archive in Berlin, though the original is believed to have been lost with Lou's possessions, after her death.

Between the day she got Inge's letter and her trip to Berlin in August, Lou lost the fifteen pounds she'd gained from drinking. She closed the garage for an hour each day and ran in the Bois de Bou-logne. She lifted weights every morning. She lived on salad and rice. She corresponded with Inge, who sent her sports news and political gossip, train tickets, schedules, and practical information.

Lou would stay at the Hotel Kaiserhof, where the Führer used to go at teatime for milk and linzer torte, though he had given up this simple pleasure, because Hess was paranoid about pastry. Besides, the Führer wanted to look trim in his uniform for the Olympics.

Inge would be Lou's host at the games and guide her through the busy social calendar that she described in detail so Lou would bring the right clothes. Several times Inge mentioned how much the Führer liked pretty girls. And though Inge didn't—and, Lou felt, would *never*—suggest that Lou dress more like a woman, Lou was inspired to have a tailor alter her suits to look less masculine, more like the sex-ually ambiguous but still fetching clothes of Marlene Dietrich.

Lou could pretend to be pretty. She could crimp a wave in her hair. Painting her lips red was harder than it looked. It had to be mastered, like a sport.

Lou's rules could be bent without breaking. She was not about to waste her chance to meet the Führer by insisting on wearing fireproof racing boots to a formal dinner. She bought new shoes laced like a man's, broad in the toe, but with thick high heels. And she learned to walk in them: more athletic training. How impressive that women balanced on stilts—for beauty! She found it practically effortless to make the concessions for Hitler that she had so ferociously refused to make for her mother.

A muscular gamine edged her way into the mirror, and the tough garage mechanic stepped aside to make room. Lou worried about Inge, who'd flirted with the more masculine Lou. What if she pre-ferred that type? Lou would take her chances.

She would have liked to tell the baroness about her upcoming jour-ney, but something warned her against it. Armand would have been happy for her, but maybe also jealous that she was the one meeting Hitler. If Armand was still capable of understanding who anyone was. She considered writing and asking her friends in the sports clubs along the route—Lola the soccer player from Liege, who pretended to be Portuguese, Astrid from Alsace, who liked Lou to squeeze her around the waist till she fainted—to come to the station and wave to her as her train to Berlin sped by.

But because she feared that the ticket Inge sent her wouldn't work, and that she would be laughed at when she presented it at the station, she told no one. She was genuinely surprised when the conductor smiled and showed her to a sleeping compartment that made her thankful she'd lost weight. Even so, she was glad that she'd kept her plans secret, so she could sit undisturbed by the window of the dining car, sipping whiskey and smoking. However bleak Lou's future had seemed, something must have been guiding her. Everything in her life so far must have followed some grand design if fate had engineered this moment precisely halfway between perfect calm and wild excitement.

When Inge met her at the station in Berlin, Lou could tell that Inge liked her new, girlish look—or anyway, girlish for Lou. Inge wore a summer dress, stitched from the palest pink petals of beaded silk. Inge kissed Lou's cheek and lightly encircled Lou's wrist with her fingers.

Lou had made a new rule for this trip. She would take whatever was offered.

Secretly she suspected that she hadn't been asked to Berlin just so the Führer could win one more heart and mind. A more logical explanation was: she was being interviewed for a job. Maybe the Germans wanted her to race. Would a patriotic Frenchwoman, mistreated by her country, consider driving for Germany, if only to show her deluded homeland that it had made a mistake? She couldn't race a Mercedes, which would always be Inge's. But maybe she could test-drive some newer, muscular model, better suited for someone like Lou. She would push it to victory until France fell to its knees and begged its prodigal daughter to come home.

In person, Inge was, like her letters, a fountain of exclamation points. But her punctuation was oddly timed, and her voice rose in the wrong places. How wonderful to see . . . *you*!

Inge chattered nonstop. In the chauffeured Mercedes that took them from the station, she told Lou how lonely life was at the top, without another auto racer—another *woman* racer—to talk to, a friend who could sympathize with her losses and celebrate her successes. Lou wanted to say: I'm that person! as she had to Armand. But she felt inhibited by the presence of the chauffeur, a pretty young woman in an army uniform, watching them in the mirror.

They sped along a boulevard hung with giant red and black flags. Streamers hung from the plane trees that canopied the road. How much pride and hope and energy the banners exuded, beating in the hot wind so their swastikas spun, an optical illusion one can see in films from that time.

Lou was not given to flights of imagination, probably because, as she and Inge had agreed in one exchange of letters, their work, their *lives*, depended on staying focused. In the moment. Even so, Lou told Inge, she almost felt as if she were traveling back in time. Their Mercedes was a chariot whisking her into the thumping heart of an empire as great as Greece or Rome.

A page in a history book—from the convent?—turned over in Lou's mind. Pillars and temples, horses, drivers with garlands encircling their foreheads. The male charioteers wore dresses. Lou remembered that.

Encouraged by Lou's enthusiasm, Inge leaned across her so that her breasts, beneath her silky dress, brushed against Lou's arm. She pointed out the landmarks, and the improvements the Führer had made. How wide the boulevards were!

Lou said, "Everyone's smiling."

Inge laughed. "An order came down from the Führer. This is the week of smiles. But is that this week or next week? No one can remember. So we're smiling both weeks, just to play it safe!"

She smiled at Lou, who smiled back. Why shouldn't everyone smile? Everyone they passed on the street looked prosperous and well fed. Lou couldn't help comparing them with the depressed, malnourished Parisians. The French had brought it on themselves. They shouldn't have taken away her license.

Lou took Inge's hand to communicate her sympathy for how the Germans had suffered. Inge's hand was surprisingly calloused, her grip unusually strong. So was Lou's. They were drivers.

Inge said, Look around! Despite the lies Lou had probably read in the anti-German press, there were no signs prohibiting Jews from entering public buildings and private establishments. Did Lou see any? No! Nor were there any laws against Jewish-owned businesses or stores.

Lou said, "So what if there were?" With that, she and Inge reached a deeper level of understanding.

When Lou had traveled the racing circuit with the Rossignols, they'd stayed in first-class hotels. But nothing had prepared her for the Kaiserhof. The spasm of bows and *Heil Hitler*s their arrival set off among men in top hats and tails made Lou wheel around to see whom the men were greeting. There was no one behind them. Touched by her new friend's skittishness, Inge squeezed Lou's arm.

In the vast domed lobby, more banners and swastikas swayed above the frosted glass, the iron braziers, the Persian carpets. Lou thought it was a good sign: the same grandeur inside and out. Inge showed Lou to the door of her room, kissed her on the cheek, and let her fingers trail against Lou's forearm when she said she'd pick her up at seven.

Inge had written that, on Lou's first night in Berlin, they would be dining at the Chancellery. With the Führer! Though if the Führer changed his mind and canceled at the last moment, Lou shouldn't be surprised, or take it personally, or think it was about her.

Lou bathed and rubbed her skin with the perfumed oils the hotel provided for free. She fixed her hair and changed into an attractive, if uncomfortably feminine, tuxedo. She was tying her bow tie when the front desk called. Fraulein Wallser was waiting downstairs.

If Inge had looked like a flower today, tonight she was a snowflake that melted on contact as she hooked her arm through Lou's. The black Mercedes was driven by the same severe driver, but this time she nodded coolly at Lou and said, "*Guten Abend, Fraulein Villars.*"

Inge talked all the way there, repeating things she'd said that afternoon and pointing out yet more positive changes the Führer had made. Again she complained about the foreign press and its lies, among them the preposterous falsehood that, under the Reich, one could no longer have a fabulous time at the city's nightspots. Inge would be happy to show Lou around, if she liked. Speech failed Lou when she tried to say how much she would like it.

Admittedly, the nightlife wasn't quite what it had been in the old days, when there was something for everyone. By which Inge meant *everyone*. People said it was paradise, but what is paradise without a serpent? And they'd had more than their share of serpents!

Lou nodded so hard her neck ached. That had been her experience too. Maybe someday she could tell Inge about those vipers, Arlette and Clovis Chanac. How Inge would laugh when she heard that evil snakes were running an establishment called the Garden of Eden.

The clubs in Berlin had been sanitized, Inge said, which was a pity, though it was probably good that they had closed the places that degraded honest Germans. The degenerate Jewish lesbian bars should never have existed! All the grand old establishments with a respectable clientele—the Monte Carlo, the Heaven and Hell, The Cockadoodle, the Stork's Nest, the White Mouse—were alive and well and in business, thank you very much. At Rio Rita, you could still telephone a girl or boy at another table. If Lou wanted, she and Inge could take a night off from official functions. Have a few drinks and relax!

Inge's voice rose in a birdlike trill that wobbled on the high notes, then pitched her over into unrelated subjects. When Inge stopped racing, she might go to work in the party's public relations office, because the truth wasn't getting out. Especially in America, where Jews controlled the press. Hadn't it been awful, that pathetic attempt to boycott the Olympics because of how Germany was supposedly treating its Jews. In fact a Jewish fencer, Eileena Mayer, was probably going to bring home the gold, or at least the silver, medal for the Reich. It was a pity that Herr Goebbels didn't like Eileena. No matter what happened at the games, her career would go nowhere, because stupid Eileena, arrogant like the rest of her tribe, refused to fuck him.

Lou laughed, as she was supposed to. She was trying to remember what she'd heard about Goebbels.

During her trial, the youngest and most hotheaded lawyer had wanted to read an item that had appeared in the French papers. Goebbels had said that a government should not concern itself with whether a woman wore trousers or skirts. Eventually the more moderate lawyers persuaded him that their case would not be helped by quoting the Nazi minister of propaganda.

Though the statement went unread in court, Lou had, ever since, felt a fondness for Herr Goebbels. But now Inge was telling her that Goebbels was not their best friend in the higher echelons of the party. Conceited about his education, he looked down on sports and games. Inge would like to see what good all that education did him if she challenged him to a couple of laps, one on one, at the track.

Was Inge on some sort of drug? Lou thought fondly of how Armand had rambled when he was high. It was odd, how life kept throwing a person together with a certain other kind of person. Lou had never heard someone make fun of education. Inge was her soul mate.

Inge said, "Everything here is the opposite of what outsiders think. Everything except the rare good reports, which happen to be true. Do you know that Frederick the Great is the Führer's idol? Why doesn't the foreign press ever mention the genius of modeling yourself after Germany's greatest king?

"And speaking of the Führer . . ." Inge grasped Lou's arm with both hands and gazed into her eyes. Her own eyes were a matte gray, like the backs of two pewter spoons. "People see those awful newsreels and imagine he is scary. Jumping and yelling and jerking around like some crazy marionette. I can tell you, the Führer is a sweetheart *and* a great leader, a hero to whom we owe everything. We will die for him, if we have to."

Inge giggled, released Lou, and sank back against the seat. "But oh, dear God, how he loves the sound of his own voice! He can go on for a whole dinner, boring everyone silly. Once he brings up vegetarianism, you're in for forty minutes of recipes for his mother's Bavarian nut cutlets.

"Obviously, no one says this. Tell a joke about him, even a nice one, and you'll wind up in jail. A Berlin woman was *executed* for telling a story about Heydrich saying to the Führer that if he wanted to make the German people smile, he should jump off the roof! I know I can trust you, can't I, Lou?"

Lou grinned like a maniac. Trust me.

"Sometimes after the Führer goes to bed, always early, the young officers get together with the prettier girls (there are always pretty girls around the Führer) and a junior officer will drink too much and say, 'There are two possibilities.' And everyone will almost die laughing, because it's one of the Führer's favorite phrases. Just the words *nut cutlets* give everyone the giggles."

Inge told Lou that she shouldn't worry if she felt nervous around the Führer. Everybody did. After all this time, even though Inge saw him almost as a friend, she still got the shakes in his presence. Usually, her trembling fits subsided within a few minutes.

"Until then I quake like a leaf. Something just comes over me There's nothing I can do."

Lou was starting to be alarmed that her translator and guide to an evening among the highest German officials was an auto racer on drugs who had fits in the Führer's presence. But Armand had proved how well the impaired can function. It was too late to worry now. How would Lou choose, if she had to, between having sex with Inge Wallser and meeting Adolf Hitler? Maybe she wouldn't have to choose. Maybe she would get it all. Inge, the Führer, a driving job, and an adopted homeland that respected its athletes and would understand the need for a racetrack Joan of Arc.

Inge said, "I think one reason the Führer is so eager to meet you is that cars mean the world to him. *The world.* He's infatuated with his Mercedes! Even though—can you believe it?—he never really learned to drive. Whenever he can, he rides in front beside his driver.

"Unless he has to stand in back of the open car to greet his millions of fans. Millions! For a while he had a mechanic . . . the Führer's tire had a blowout. Bang! Bang! Everyone panicked! We thought: an assassination attempt! Only our Führer kept a cool head. That mechanic left Munich and has never been heard from since." Inge giggled.

An awful thought occurred to Lou. Was *that* why she'd been brought here? To work as a mechanic?

She said, "I assume the Führer has a good mechanic now."

"Naturally," said Inge. "Herr Boehm and his men were required to pass top security clearance. I knew them from the racetrack until the Führer stole them. But it was an honor to sacrifice the country's best pit crew for the safety of our leader."

As they pulled up in front of a sort of fortress, uniformed men swarmed the car, peering into the windows. When they saw Inge they opened the doors, and two soldiers escorted Inge and Lou through the magisterial gate that swung open as they approached.

They made a handsome couple, two champion women drivers, one in a filmy white dress, one in a black tuxedo. Picturing them, on that fateful night, one can't help conflating the image with that of Lou and Arlette in Gabor Tsenyi's portrait.

Arm in arm, Inge and Lou made their way (Inge bouncing and skipping, Lou gently holding her back) along a corridor, past rows of gilded columns. Lou decided not to drink tonight. She could no more let down her guard here than behind the wheel during a race.

A queue of guests had formed outside the door of a ballroom. "Don't be afraid," said Inge as Lou looked through the door at a receiving line of smiling men in suits or uniforms, and a few women, also smiling, also beautifully dressed. Inge fluttered into action, chatting with the minders whose job it was to tell the dignitaries whose hand they were shaking. The Germans and most of the athletes knew Inge. For the diplomats, lady racers were a welcome change from ministers of war.

Everyone was polite to Lou and intrigued to see a woman in a tuxedo. It was well known that the Führer liked men to be men and women to be women, and people wondered why he had made an exception in Lou's case.

Lou was happy to follow Inge's lead. The line moved so slowly that Inge had time to tell Lou who everyone was. Lou was impressed, *enchanted*, by how much Inge knew.

Inge said to stand up straight and pay attention as they approached Hans von Tschammer und Osten, the Reichssportsführer. The minister kissed both women's hands and asked Lou if she knew how lucky she was to have, as her friend, Berlin's "It Girl" of the moment.

Inge blushed. "Oh, *please*, Herr Minister."

"*The moment*," said the minister's wife, urging them down the line.

"We'll talk again," Von Tschammer und Osten promised, leering clownishly at Inge.

Hess, Göring, Himmler, Heydrich, von Ribbentrop. It was hard to remember who was who. Lou recognized names she'd heard before, and a scatter of new ones. She found it easier to tell the women apart, because they were women, and also because there were so few. Among them was Wagner's widow and the Berlin socialites, who, Inge whispered, had raised fortunes for the Führer and whom he still visited faithfully, if less frequently, for tea and the linzer torte he nibbled when Hess wasn't watching.

Inge introduced Lou to a pair of statuesque British sisters with blond hair, red lips, fixed smiles, and no interest in Lou. One spoke a German so basic that even Lou understood when she asked Inge what she was doing after dinner. Inge said she was taking Lou back to her hotel.

But the sisters were already raising their arms in the National Socialist salute (from which Lou, as a foreigner, was officially exempted) as a man with a chest full of medals edged Lou and Inge along.

During the wait to shake Fraulein Riefenstahl's hand, Inge said, "Don't take it to heart if the skinny bitch looks right through you. She thinks she's the queen of the universe because she's filming the games!" Inge would have liked to be included in the film. But she hadn't been asked, from jealousy or some political reason, though it was also possible that someone just forgot.

As promised, the film director was ice, pure ice, and they moved along to Herr Goebbels, standing beside her. When Goebbels heard *auto racing*, his face stiffened, and he absentmindedly, though it wasn't absentminded at all, rested his hand on Fraulein Riefenstahl's bony behind. Before Lou could think of a subtle way to call this to Inge's attention, she spotted the Führer at the end of the line.

She leaned against Inge for support, but Inge was already trembling. Her tremors were so contagious that Lou almost lost her footing and silently thanked Fraulein Schiller and the Japanese monk for her balance training.

Could some German scientist have found a way to install a high-wattage lightbulb inside the Führer's head? He emitted ten times the radiance of a normal human being, and his eyes were a hundred times brighter than the cloudy lenses through which ordinary humans peered. Lou had never seen a man exude such simple modesty combined with such charisma. He was like a temple idol! How strange that his guests were shaking his hand or saluting him instead of doing the logical thing: flinging themselves at his feet. The air around Lou seemed to thicken. A grainy nausea rose into her throat.

The Führer took Inge's hand and kissed it, then did the same to Lou. Everyone was watching. Even those still waiting outside the door craned for a better look. Lou had driven a race car at a hundred miles an hour. But standing before the Führer as he kissed her hand was like driving faster, around a curve, in a typhoon.

She looked down. She and Inge were holding hands like schoolgirls, like siblings in a fairy tale.

"Fraulein Wallser," the Führer said. "And Fraulein Villars." Then something else in German. Lou glanced at Inge, whose face was red, her breathing shallow.

"What did he say?" Lou asked, more sharply than she meant to.

"He says he is looking forward to chatting with you at dinner."

The Führer studied each of them, staring into their eyes. Then he turned to a man in a top hat and tails who came up behind them.

Chatting with her at dinner? Had Inge translated right?

Inge looked as shocked as Lou. Because it made no sense. The guest list included champion athletes, ambassadors, Olympics committee members, artists, party officials, European royalty. The Führer was looking forward to talking to *two girl racers*?

"Don't ask me," said Inge. "Sometimes the Führer does something apparently for no reason. Later it turns out to be the most brilliant, inspired thing that anyone could have done. That's why he's a great leader. Everybody knows that."

Weak with excitement and nerves, Inge and Lou helped each other through a doorway into another, larger room. Near the door stood men with crystal goblets of wine. Lou took one, but Inge shook her head, and Lou gave it back.

Inge said, "Whatever you do, don't get the Führer started on drinking. Not unless you want to spend the evening hearing that beer is the hereditary enemy of the German people, right up there with the Jews. If we didn't need the export income, he would close all the breweries tomorrow. No one drinks when he's around. Later we all get smashed." Lou loved it when Inge assumed she could speak freely about the Führer because she knew that Lou adored and revered him as much as she did.

By now they had worked their way among the knots of partygoers who made room for the "It Girl" and her French friend, knots that unraveled because the guests had seen the Führer kissing the women's hands. Lou nodded when she was supposed to, smiled when she was supposed to. The Führer was looking forward to chatting with them at dinner.

Not until they went into the dining room, and Inge found their place cards flanking the Führer's, did Lou and Inge believe it.

"It still might not happen," warned Inge. "He often changes his mind at the last minute, for security reasons, just as he changes the route he takes from his home to the airport. . . ."

The guests sat down, but when the Führer came in, everyone rose, most with outstretched arms, Lou among them. It felt good to do what the Germans did, saluting the Führer as he deserved. How else could she show him that she believed in him too? A bodyguard pulled out Inge's chair, another pulled out Lou's. It was awkward, but after lifting their behinds several times, they were settled on either side of the Führer. It was also clumsy when the Führer spoke to Lou, and Inge had to lean around him to translate. But ultimately it had the effect of bringing them closer together.

The Führer went on for so long that Inge seemed anxious that she would forget what he'd said.

Inge explained she'd told a friend that Lou had remarked that entering Berlin was like driving into the heart of a great empire. Her gossipy friend had told someone, who told the Führer, who liked what

Lou said very much. He says that it is exactly how he wants our guests to feel.

"*Merci*," said Lou. "*Danke schön*."

The Führer asked if she liked the hotel. Lou nodded. The Führer seemed pleased and said something about Herr Hess.

Inge said, "The Führer used to love the linzer torte at the Kaiserhof, but Hess has forbidden it because the cook is a Communist. Hess thinks he might poison the Führer." The Führer added something that included "Fraulein Villars," then laughed.

Inge said, "He says you can eat all the cake you want, Fraulein Villars. You seem like a good soul who might be very fond of cake." Inge laughed. Lou laughed. She should have lost twenty more pounds. The Führer laughed again. Laughing together set them apart. It was the sort of laughter that would have made the other guests envious, even if Lou and Inge weren't laughing with the Führer.

The Führer said he was glad Lou liked Berlin. In his opinion (he smiled) Berlin was the only city since Imperial Rome that could call itself a city. He had been to Paris. A pitiful Alpine village.

This was tricky for Inge to translate. Paris was Lou's home. And everyone knew that the Führer had a lifelong love for Paris.

Lou was being tested. Inge and the Führer wanted to see if she could take a joke.

Lou laughed. No hard feelings! The heavy mood lightened again.

A waiter approached with bottles of wine. Inge shot Lou a warning look, but the Führer, master of surprises, motioned for Lou's goblet to be filled with red wine. How thoughtful! How could Lou ever thank him for letting her have a glassful of help with the social demands of the evening.

Lou said, "Berlin is beautiful."

Inge said, "*Berlin ist schön*."

More waiters interrupted them, proffering mountains of food. The waiters looked like Olympic athletes, blond, with broad shoulders and narrow waists. A tray of sliced meat bypassed the Führer, and this time, when Inge signaled Lou to say no, the Führer didn't countermand her. Lou would have loved some meat, which had been scarce in

Paris, even if one could afford it. The juicy slabs of beef looked better than anything she'd seen all summer, but Lou shook her head. No, thank you. Following Inge's cue, she lifted her chin in a welcoming nod at a platter of breaded schnitzel.

"Nut cutlets," explained the Führer.

Inge didn't, *couldn't*, translate for fear of dissolving in giggles. It thrilled Lou that she and Inge were already sharing private jokes about the Führer's diet. Inge was right to trust her. The Führer wolfed down half his cutlet and pushed his dish away. The plate was removed, along with Inge's. This allowed the Führer to talk and Inge to translate more freely, though Lou held on to her plate and, as she listened, masticated tiny mouthfuls of oily fried-sawdust croquettes.

Now the Führer spoke at length, and after some pouting and a theatrical sigh, Inge said, "The Führer says his views on nutrition are well known to me and probably even you, but still he wants to say: try a simple experiment. Put two things in front of a child—a dead animal and a pear. The child will reach for the pear. Because the child is in touch with its instincts. Now put a sausage in front of the child, who will scream and cry. What brilliant anthropologist can explain why chewed-up regurgitated flesh, stuffed into a pig's gut half-cleaned of excrement, is the most beloved delicacy of the German people?"

"I don't know," Lou said. Inge didn't bother to translate.

The Führer seized Inge's forearm, gesturing as he spoke, as if he were a ventriloquist and Inge his pretty dummy.

The Führer said, "That is why the German people desperately need a leader. This is one of many things for which we can thank the Jews, turning herbivores into practitioners of ritual sacrifice addicted to animal flesh, all because the Jews could make a bigger profit from sausage than from salad."

"I love salad," Lou said.

"She loves salad," said Inge.

Now the Führer focused on Lou, talking to her as if he could *will* her to understand German. But not even he could do that.

Afraid of disappointing him, Lou turned to Inge, who said, "In the early days of the party, when the Führer was in jail, do you know what got him through?"

"You wrote *Mein Kampf,* my Führer," Inge went on, covering for Lou.

"Obviously," said the Führer. Again he spoke intently. "During the day I wrote. At night I dreamed of cars. I could hear them driving past my cell window. The prison was on a curve. Cars were all I thought about. I swore that, when I got out of jail, I would get the biggest, fastest Mercedes money could buy. Which is what I have now. Though who would have predicted that by the time I got my dream car, Germany would need me so badly I couldn't risk driving it myself."

Inge continued translating, but now Lou had the eerie sense that she was understanding German without Inge's help. The Führer motioned for Lou's glass to be refilled, a gesture that shocked Inge and two hundred other guests up and down the table.

"What did he say?" Lou asked Inge.

"Do you want to hear about his favorite thing in the world?"

Lou nodded. Certainly! The Führer's favorite thing!

Inge said, "His favorite thing is racing American cars in the middle of Berlin. Sometimes when he and his driver are alone in the Mercedes, and an American vehicle pulls up beside them, the Führer orders the driver to step on the gas—and they leave the big fat hairy American buffalo in the dust. The Führer laughs till his sides hurt. They are idiots in Detroit!"

"That's what *I* always say," said Lou.

The Führer said, "Inge also loves cars. Like we do." Lou felt as if she and Inge were receiving a benediction. No wonder the Führer had sat with them. Everything made sense.

Lou had something she needed Inge to tell the Führer, but her glass had refilled itself, and she forgot what she wanted to say. The Führer asked about the Olympics. Was she looking forward to the games? Wait till she saw the stadium! "Ladies, listen! When we began to plan the games in Berlin, my architects informed me there were two possibilities only. On one hand . . ."

Inge winked so only Lou saw. How joyous Lou felt, spotting the Führer's favorite phrase: another private joke.

"One possibility was a stadium costing eleven hundred thousand marks. The other was a stadium costing fourteen hundred thousand marks." The Führer smacked the table. Lou and Inge should have seen the ministers' faces when he told them that he was allotting fourteen million marks!

"The stadium has already brought in twice that much in foreign currency, which Germany needs to rebuild. And still they complain that our stadium wasn't constructed *exactly* to Olympic specifications! Let the weaklings whine. The next Olympics will be held in Japan, but after that the games will take place every year in Berlin, and Germany will decide what Olympic proportions are."

The Führer asked Lou something about France. Inge said, "He wants to know if France has a network of local sports associations. Like we do here."

The Führer leaned toward Lou. Lou covered her wineglass when the waiter came round again.

Speaking slowly, Lou said there were thousands of sports clubs, all over France. There was hardly a village that didn't have its own men's and women's tennis or gymnastics, bicycle-racing, swimming, or golfing society. And Lou had friends in every one! This was an exaggeration, but only a slight one. Lou wasn't so much describing the present as making a promise about the future.

The Führer told Inge to ask what Lou knew about the early history of the party.

"Nothing, I'll bet," said Inge.

"Not much," admitted Lou.

The Führer said that when the party was outlawed by the parasites, cowards, and thieves who nearly destroyed the homeland, the old soldiers went underground. And the patriots who helped them were often members of sports associations, exercise clubs, gun clubs, and village teams.

The party would have succeeded without them. Destiny was on its side. But it would have been harder. And besides, it was only right. Athletics was the pure expression of the National Socialist ideal. Perfect bodies, perfect souls. Youth and strength and hope. The sacred beauty of nature uncorrupted by civilization!

Though some of his less progressive advisers argued against strenuous sports for women, the Führer believed that physical fitness would empower Aryan mothers to bear a healthy, revitalized nation. The Aryan girls' associations required its members to schedule, during each meeting—the Führer counted on his fingers—a five-minute run, twenty-five minutes of gymnastics, forty-five minutes of track and field, and at least that much of games. Did Lou know that the older girls' groups operated under the direction of the Faith and Beauty League? Did Lou know that their nationwide Strength through Joy program had tripled the average productivity of the German worker?

Lou was thrilled that she could say yes without lying. These were among the first things that Inge had told her about the Fatherland.

The Führer was glad the Olympics were being held in Berlin because it let Germany show off the youth that National Socialism was producing. The world would come to appreciate their drive toward excellence, their optimism, and their belief that Germany will outshine every star in the constellation of nations. Inge had heard this so often that she could translate before the Führer finished speaking.

Then he said something else about France, which Lou had to prod Inge into translating, and possibly (Lou got the sense) toning down what he said. France was a once great nation. But now it was like a child who had wandered off the path. And its kindly older brother, the Reich, could help the child find its way home. With Germany's loving guidance, France could again become the thriving society it was before it was attacked by enemies from outside and by parasites from within. This answered a lot of questions for Lou. Since she'd arrived, she'd noticed that the Germans seemed better off than the French. It bothered her. She *was* French. She loved France. But the Führer also loved France and was offering to repair her country and restore it to the French people.

Just then a young man in uniform tapped the Führer's shoulder. Rising, the Führer thanked Lou and Inge for their time and attention. He made a sweet, almost childlike face, blinking both eyes as he apologized for leaving. He assured them that his men would try to make Lou's stay in Berlin enjoyable and productive.

He was gone by the time Inge finished translating that, and before Lou could thank him. But what would she have said?

She would have said, I will do anything. Anything you ask.

Would that have seemed excessive? Would it have embarrassed Inge? Would the Führer think she had drunk too much, as in fact she had?

Anyway, the evening was ending. The party was breaking up. Inge reminded Lou that the Führer liked to go to bed early.

In the car going back to the hotel, Inge took Lou's hand and brought it to her lips. She said she wanted to kiss the hand that the Führer had kissed.

In the middle of the night Lou and Inge shared a cigarette. The curtains to the balcony fluttered in the warm wind. They sat up, naked, cross-legged, on their canopied bed. They joked about how nervous they'd been at dinner, how hard it had been for Inge to translate the Führer's words when her teeth were chattering because they were with the Führer, and she'd been so attracted to Lou.

Lou said she was surprised by the lack of formal speeches or toasts. Inge said she too had expected speeches. But the Führer was famous for doing the unexpected. Who could have foreseen that the Reich's sovereign leader would spend all evening talking to *them*?

Then Inge sighed and said that she and Lou could have been together like this, they could have been lovers since Brooklands. If only Lou hadn't acted like the stuffy German and forced Inge to behave like the slutty French girl.

Lou didn't like apologizing. But for the first time she liked the *feeling* of saying she was sorry. It was like being pushed, too high and too hard, in the swing.

Inge hoped that Lou hadn't been offended by the Führer's remarks about France, and Lou said no, not at all. It was always a relief when someone told the truth.

Inge said, "When the Führer wants to win you over, he calls you 'a good soul.' After the Führer calls you that, your heart belongs to him forever." Inge touched Lou's cheek and said that in her opinion Lou really *was* a good soul. No one had ever called Lou that. Nor had any-one touched her like that.

That night Lou and Inge exchanged the stories of their lives. They spoke in quiet voices, sometimes in a whisper, pausing when tears welled in their eyes and they didn't trust themselves to go on. At moments Lou recounted her history as if it were a tragedy, or a joke, or a true story she couldn't believe herself. She described her chilly mother, her disappointed papa, her sweet grandmother, the cruel British governess, but not the mad brother. She included the jav-elin demonstration at the Vélodrome d'Hiver but left out the boxing match and Dr. Loomis's attack.

Inge stroked her shoulder, a soothing repetitive touch that smoothed the rough edges of Lou's life so far and hypnotized her into feeling a tender forgiveness for everyone who had hurt her. There were plenty of things she regretted and wished she could do over. But tonight she felt reluctant to disturb the fragile ecology of the past that had brought her to this moment, in this pretty hotel room, with Inge.

Inge had grown up in a family in the foreign service. She had lived all over the world, never feeling at home anywhere except behind the wheel of a car. Just the names of the places Inge had traveled—Siam, Abyssinia, India, the Belgian Congo—gave Lou the shivers. How could such a brave, adventurous path have led Inge to *her*?

Inge asked Lou when she first knew that she wanted to dress like a boy. Lou said ever since she knew what clothes were. Inge told her that in India there were men who dressed as women. They sang and danced professionally and blessed weddings and new babies. When a boy was born that way, he found these troupes, and the men embraced him and took him in. Sometimes a boy's parents brought him to them because he was that way, and they embraced him and took him in.

"What about little girls?" asked Lou.

Inge said, "They're taken care of. They're allowed to be their true selves, strong and brave citizens of their ancient country."

It made sense that India, with its vast expanse, its deep spiritual wisdom, and its historical role as the cradle of the Aryan master race, should have a vision broad enough to acknowledge and accept every aspect of human nature. Lou had never talked about these things with anyone, not even with Arlette. She was grateful, even blissful, to discover that people like her had existed since the dawn of civilization. Inge *saw* her as no one ever had. Inge loved her, body and soul.

It was almost dawn before Lou Villars finally took off her shirt. She held her breath as Inge gently traced one manicured fingertip along the scars where Lou's breasts had been.

In the morning, a blond youth in a uniform with gold epaulets rolled their breakfast in on a cart. Lou jumped up and pulled on her pants, but he didn't seem fazed to see two women in bed. This wasn't what Lou had heard about Germany under the Führer! She'd heard there were harsh penalties for loving one's own sex. But she'd also heard that coffee and sugar were even scarcer than in Paris, and here was Inge, pouring Lou a large cup of coffee and stirring in three sugars, just the way Lou liked it.

Inge said, "It would kill the Führer to see us eating sausage!" And she burst out laughing as she swallowed a juicy morsel of *weisswurst.*

Before Lou could begin to express her happiness, Inge tore off the soft inside of a hard roll and ate it. A feather of bread hung out of Inge's mouth. Lou tried to remove it, a gesture that started out clumsily and ended in a kiss.

Later that morning they were woken again by noise from the street. With their arms around each other's waists they stood on the balcony watching soldiers, workers, and schoolchildren in uniform, marching in perfect columns. From above they saw the caps and hats all turned in the same direction, the angular geometries of raised arms and uplifted knees.

It was drizzling, but no one minded. The wet banners must have been heavy, but the flag bearers held them high. Lou saw a boy stumble under a flagpole, and instead of tormenting him, as older children do, two big boys rushed over and helped him.

In the afternoon a car came to take Lou and Inge to the stadium, past masses yearning to glimpse the Führer, lining the roads so

thickly that soldiers had to push them back, out of danger. Inge said
that whole families had been camped out all night.

"In the rain?" Lou asked.

What was a little rain? This was something the German people
would remember all their lives and tell their grandchildren about. After a while Inge said, "Look, the Olympic towers!" The towers came
into view, two stone monoliths with a chain of Olympic circles float-
ing in midair between them.

Look! Inge kept saying. Look! She'd begun to sound hysterical, in-
fecting Lou with her panic as Lou tried to figure out what Inge was
telling her to look at now.

An enormous zeppelin, like a giant inflated shark with swastikas
on its tail, hovered over the stadium.

"The *Hindenburg*!" said Inge.

"Beautiful," Lou said.

They would not be watching from the Führer's box. But they had
an unobstructed view of where he would be sitting. In the seat beside
Lou was a familiar-looking man. Max Schmeling! The heavyweight
champion had just returned, in that very same zeppelin, from beating
the Negro Joe Louis. He and Inge greeted each other like old friends,
though they seemed confused about what to do first, kiss or say *Heil
Hitler*. Inge introduced Lou in French as a famous auto racer. Schmeling (also in French) said he was honored to meet her.

"The honor is mine," said Lou.

Inge asked if the voyage had been comfortable, and Schmeling said
yes, thank you, and Inge said he was the hero of the German people
and the Aryan race, and Schmeling said thank you again.

Lou's attention lapsed. Why really was she there? What could
a garage mechanic have done to deserve this? Was it all about Inge
and how popular *she* was? Had she been invited to be Inge's imported
French plaything?

The spectators had found their places when the Führer arrived,
surrounded by guards. The entire stadium rumbled. Lou grasped
Inge's hand. *Heil Hitler Heil Hitler Heil Hitler* she chanted along with
the crowd until she could no longer tell if the chanting was inside

or outside her, until the pounding hearts around her were pumping blood through her veins. Exalted and hypnotic, the incessantly tolling bells summoned her from the pasture and sent her into battle. The crowd roared and fell silent and roared again, the roaring crested and subsided, only to rise and fall. Many people must have been hoarse, but they kept on yelling. Tears streamed down Lou's face, and she was embarrassed until she saw that Max Schmeling was weeping too.

Lou's arm lifted on the cyclonic wind of arms rising around her. The steadiness with which she held it straight defied gravity and exhaustion. This was what she had trained for, lifting weights for the track. A magnetic current pulled her body and soul toward the body and soul of the Führer. A trumpet fanfare roused the crowd until it seemed that the shouting would go on forever.

The Führer motioned for silence. The crowd cheered him for having the power to dam this flood of feeling. It was thrilling to obey: so many, so strong, every individual unified in a single obedient being.

The band struck up the German national anthem, and after that the Horst Wessel song, which Inge translated, in a whisper, breathing wetly into Lou's ear. Listening to the sad story of the German hero murdered by Communist thugs, but only after writing this stirring hymn about the flag and the battle, a future of bread and freedom, Lou felt pride and sadness, along with a wayward impulse to silence Inge with a kiss.

As the teams marched toward the reviewing stand, the sun broke through the clouds. Had the Führer arranged that too? The colorful flags of the nations flapped in the summer wind. New shouts and cheers erupted. All eyes were on the Führer. Once more he held up his hand, quieting the multitudes with a flick of his wrist.

Lou's heart filled and overflowed. How beautiful the games were, how glorious the tradition that inspired each country to send its swiftest and most graceful to compete in contests that went back to ancient Greece. The bond Lou shared with these women and men went deeper than culture or costume: the turbans on the Indians, the funny caps on the Japanese, the Americans' straw boaters, the white pleated skirt the Greek captain wore—and Lou's dark suit and fedora.

How proudly they paraded, knowing that the crowd understood how hard they had worked to get here. Surely it was a miracle, a foretaste of salvation, that Lou could watch from the stands and not feel sick with resentment because she wasn't marching with the French athletes. She would rather be where she was. Greater things were in store for her than winning a gold medal!

Last night in bed Inge had told Lou that it was a controversial question: how would the national teams salute as they passed the Führer's box and what did this imply about the relations between Germany and their home countries?

Out of politeness, Inge said, every athlete should honor Hitler with the Nazi salute. After all, they were Germany's guests, on German soil, breathing German air. When in Rome, etcetera. Why didn't their coaches inform them that the party had adopted the salute *because* it was how the earliest Greek athletes hailed their gods? Ignorant of history, some of the athletes were expected to choose the so-called Olympic salute, their right arms raised to one side at a forty-five degree angle.

Lou had ended this slightly tedious conversation by trailing one finger from Inge's neck down the length of her back. But now that the teams were marching past, she was acutely aware of how the athletes held their arms—and the Führer's response. The British, the Indians, and the Japanese turned their heads toward the Führer. The American men removed their straw hats and placed them over their chests. Lou could tell that the Führer was torn because it seemed overly jaunty and disrespectful, though the straw hats may have reminded him of the Hollywood musicals that, Inge said, he loved. When the Austrians saluted him openly as their leader, Lou watched paternal pleasure soften the Führer's stern face.

The Italians gave the fascist salute. But having caught a glimpse of the French flag fluttering in the distance, Lou lost interest in the codes being transmitted by the athletes' tipped hats and tilted biceps. She braced herself for the pain of seeing the French athletes and not being among them.

The music became less military, more like a dance hall tune. In their tailored white flannels, dark blazers, and berets, the French held their arms to the side at an unmistakably Olympic angle.

Lou was prepared to feel angry, envious, and betrayed. Instead she felt pity and sympathy for her French brothers and sisters. How long would it take them to see the light, to know they were headed for ruin, to admit that their German neighbors wanted to save them from falling into the open grave their enemies were digging? If only Lou could make them see what she saw and understand what she understood. Newly in love, respected, welcome, watching the games in comfort, about to be offered a chance to start over, she had no desire to trade her life for theirs.

Her heart went out to her dear countrymen in their farmer's berets, the symbol of their peasant roots, of their love for the land and its traditions. Their visit to Germany would show them that a nation could be healed. They would learn from the Germans how human beings could treat each other with care and loving kindness.

Hitler's face was unreadable, but Lou thought she glimpsed the trace of a frown as the stadium erupted in cheers for the French neighbors with whom the German people hoped to live in peace and friendship. Lou added her voice to the others and wept again as she shouted, *"Vive la France! Heil Hitler!"* Listening to the noise of the crowd, she seemed to hear each person saying: there will not be another war. She and Inge could be together.

The Swiss marched past in clockwork time, followed by the Germans, the women in angel white, a squad of captains and coaches in military dress, the athletes in snowy linen suits, like the army of God. Inge told Lou to look at the Führer making an effort to be fair and to not appear excessively proud of the beautiful young Germans. But at last he smiled, despite himself. He lowered his hand and, deeply moved, put his fist to his heart. He stepped forward and solemnly announced that the Berlin Olympics, celebrating the Eleventh Olympiad of the modern era, were officially open.

The loudest trumpets yet played a fanfare, and a flock of twenty thousand white birds took off and soared, fluttering, into the sky. Then the honor guard fired off a volley, scaring the pigeons so badly that they all simultaneously lost control and defecated on the athletes standing at attention.

Everyone in Berlin heard about this regrettable event, which would not appear in *Olympia*, Fraulein Riefenstahl's film.

That evening, the pigeons were the talk of the private dinner on Peacock Island given by Herr Goebbels. From across the room, Lou spotted the Führer, who tonight was too busy to pay attention to Inge and Lou. Lou didn't feel slighted. She'd gotten so much last night. Inge hung on Lou's arm, translating the gossip and jokes, which were mostly about pigeon droppings.

Apparently, the bird shit had landed on the American athletes, the British, the French, but . . . are you ready? Not the Germans! The Führer had a good laugh when his press secretary said that by tomorrow the foreign press would report the Germans had trained its pigeons to bomb with the same deadly accuracy as its air force, which, as everyone knew, did not exist.

Of course the German air force existed. That was part of the joke. Bombers had flown over the stadium. Lou's ears still rang, hours later.

After the Peacock Island dinner, Inge told Lou they'd been asked to a small, exclusive cocktail party, to be held tomorrow evening at the villa of Sturmbannführer Heydrich, the head of the state police. Herr Himmler and Reichssportsführer Von Tschammer und Osten had been invited, and a few more guests, though sadly, not the Führer.

This was it, thought Lou. This wasn't just a social event. They were going to make her an offer. They would ask her to use her skills and training to help the Reich restore the glory of France.

The next day, Lou watched the javelin competition won by German girls without feeling any, or almost any, resentment. Nor was she envious when Hitler gave his autograph to Helen Stephens, the American winner of the 100-meter dash, one of several female athletes suspected of being men.

Even as hosts, the Germans were fastidious record keepers. A ledger preserved in the State Archive in Berlin notes that on the evening of August 20, 1936, Lou Villars and Inge Wallser were on the guest list at a gathering at the home of Reinhard Heydrich, who, in addition to his police work, had been a major organizer of the Berlin games.

Heydrich, who would go on to become an architect of Kristall-nacht and the Wansee Conference, at which he and Eichmann ham-mered out the Final Solution to the Jewish Question, lived in a simple, even sterile villa, done entirely in black and white. The floor of the re-ception room was covered in checkerboard tiles. Lou felt like a chess piece, a bishop, in a tuxedo.

Whatever happened after this, the fact remained that she had been chosen. She had been here and seen this. Nothing could take that away. A genie had lifted her out of a garage in a Paris slum. A magic carpet had transported her to Berlin.

Heydrich offered Lou a glass of wine (Don't tell our beloved Führer!) and began by saying (in German, which Inge translated, as she would throughout the evening) that they had discussed Lou's character, her intelligence, her gifts. How could she be most useful to her country and theirs?

Lou couldn't help saying, "You talked about *me*?" Inge shot her a kindly but stern look and didn't translate her friend's girlish lapse.

Heydrich said, "You are a driver."

"That I am," said Lou.

Heydrich said, "Our hope is that you will agree to drive for the Reich."

"I would love to," said Lou. "But it might take me a few months to get back up to speed. No, I mean a few weeks. Or even a few days. Just give me a fast car—"

"We all love fast cars," Von Tschammer und Osten said. "Who doesn't love fast cars?" His laugh was like the high, sharp bark of a small, ill-tempered dog. "But for the job we have in mind, speed is not the principal qualification."

A race without speed? Were they suggesting she compete in en-durance courses, the traditional slot into which women drivers had been shunted? Armand had contempt for marathons. But maybe Ar-mand was wrong.

Unless they didn't mean racing. Maybe they wanted her to test-drive new models. In France, retired racers often became consultants. Why hadn't the Rossignols hired her to do something like that? If they had, she might not be here. Now she was glad they hadn't.

Heydrich explained that what interested them were Lou's connections with sports clubs throughout France, athletic associations, which, as everyone knew, formed an important and vibrant network. Such groups had played a critical role in helping the early heroes of the National Socialist Party.

Lou remembered the Führer telling her that. It made her feel that the Führer was here tonight, if not in body then in spirit.

Heydrich said, "We believe that you could be a valuable source of information." Translating, Inge had to pause for breath before she could continue.

"Information about . . . ?" asked Lou, though she knew what was being asked. As a child she'd played at being a spy. Be careful what you pretend.

"About your magnificent country," Heydrich said airily. "Information that will help foster peaceful international relations and cement the ties between Germany and France."

Inge's eyes were shining. Had she been in on this from the start?

Inge wanted the best for Lou, for Lou and herself—and the world! Why not? Inge loved the Führer and Germany. She loved Lou, and she wanted Lou to love the Führer and Germany too.

Heydrich said, "Let's say you're giving a talk to the soccer club of Reims. And on the way you notice that the road is full of army trucks. Well then, let us know. *Someone* ought to know. Your government is wasting good money that its hungry citizens need. Squandering precious resources on defending itself from an invasion that will never happen."

Von Tschammer und Osten said, "*Soldaten.*"

"Soldiers," translated Inge.

"Exactly," said Heydrich. "Soldiers. Suppose you're at dinner with the ladies auxiliary of the Lyons hunting club, and they say their husbands—the best shots in town—have been drafted into the army.

Or you're advising the women's basketball team of Clermont-Ferrand, and someone mentions that her husband's factory has gotten a massive order for truck tires."

"Fortifications," prompted Von Tschammer und Osten.

"Right," said Heydrich. "Fortifications. Imagine you're driving through the countryside, and you see a new building project in an unexpected or unlikely place. A fortification meant to strengthen the border that, we promise, will never be breached by us. In other words, we would like you to shine some light on areas that should be transparent."

Now they were all looking at Lou, to see if she understood. Did they think that she had never seen a spy film? Or didn't they show such films in the Führer's Germany?

"Will I have a contact?" Lou said. "To whom will I report?"

Inge said, "I can personally guarantee all the contact you want." Her tone was lewd, but genteelly lewd. Everyone laughed. The men loved it. That the Germans so liked to laugh was another surprising thing about them.

Inge said, "Pillow talk is the oldest and safest way to exchange information."

"Of course we will pay you," Heydrich said. "Obviously, in francs."

"And a budget for travel," Inge suggested.

"Of course, a budget for travel," said Von Tschammer und Osten. "All this will be under the auspices of the sports ministry."

Heydrich said, "We have worked out a scale of payment for our advisers and consultants. A certain amount for identifying a troublemaker, more for a conspirator, still more for the location of a weapons cache. Other sums will be determined based on the quality of the information."

"I'd be honored," said Lou. "Money is the least of it." Was that even true? She no longer knew. She had no idea what she was saying. She was talking to Heydrich and Von Tschammer und Osten, in a language that passed through Inge and emerged as speech. But her audience was much larger than Inge and the men in the room. She was saying yes to everyone, to the French and German people, from the humblest peasant all the way up to the Führer—the one to whom she was saying yes.

From that date on, pay stubs in the files of the German secret police document checks deposited directly into the Paris bank account of Lou Villars, who was listed as the president and treasurer (the only other recorded member was the secretary, Inge Wallser) of the Franco-German Athletics and Brotherhood Federation.

Paris
April 1937

Dear parents,
You are the only ones who can see into my heart, who will not judge
and condemn me as a selfish monster for indulging in a little harmless
boasting at a moment when it seems as if the world is about to topple,
like Mama's china shepherdess, off the mantel and shatter.

In the past months my photographs have been included in five
international exhibitions, including one (can you believe it?) in New
York's Museum of Modern Art. The waiting list of would-be collectors has grown so long that it no longer makes sense for me to waste
my time working for magazines: the gardener's newsletter, the hairstyle monthly, the journal of home improvement, the erotic publications that ran my nudes for the wrong reasons. If I never mentioned
these publications to you, it was only because I didn't want you to
know how I was prostituting my talent.

By the same token, I'm tempted not to mention the insomnia that
has returned, worse than ever. I am too old, and you are *way* too old,
to trouble yourselves about it. I can only tell you what keeps me up at
night. I wonder: am I benefitting from the misfortunes of others?

Could it be that everyone suddenly wants photographs of Paris because they fear that this eternally beautiful city may not be so eternal?
What if Hitler isn't just bluffing? And what is the connection between
these terrors and the fact that Paris and I have fallen in love all over
again?

Last night I attended a costume party for people in banking and
finance. The invitation instructed guests to come as ordinary kitchen
objects. Despite the shortages, my hosts and their friends hired de-

signers to fashion medieval collars from pastry tubes, encrusted tiaras of forks and spoons twanging like antennae. Another lavish party started off with a waltz performed by a couple dressed in real paper money and gold coins. They were delighted to have me transform their merriment into art.

Every night, I could, if I wish, attend a different party with Suzanne or the baroness. I reserve time to spend with each one. And it's fine with the women, with whom I have very different relationships. But that is a bit too personal to put into a letter to my parents!

The list of painters and sculptors I know would make Papa green with envy! Dufy, Derain, Maillol, Giacometti, and Papa's special hero, Matisse, all have invited me into their studios because word has gotten out that I am good at photographing artists and their work. Matisse has invited me to shoot him sketching girls in the nude! There is talk that Picasso and I might collaborate on a book.

The world is approaching a precipice. In the pit are snakes, twisted corpses, bloodshed and death, and meanwhile I am thinking, *It's fabulous for my art.* Is it my fault that desperation looks so stunning through the camera lens? I have been taking photos not only of upscale Parisian soirées but also of refugees traveling north from Spain. When we first saw *Guernica*, all the artists were inspired by the brilliance with which Picasso had managed to pack so much tragedy onto a single canvas.

I am photographing how my beloved, threatened city looks now. And it looks very beautiful indeed, as if it knows how many tearful good-byes its citizens will soon have to say. Isn't it a lesson, reminding me always to return and try to rekindle the love that I think I may have lost or exhausted? Doubtless that is a lesson you have learned in your long marriage, and that I am only beginning to absorb in my relationship with the endlessly patient Suzanne.

And now, a little matter that you must be wondering about: when will our son mention money?

Enclosed you will find a substantial check, in francs, which I hope you can still convert into whatever currency will be most useful. I know that accepting money from me goes against everything you believe. But I insist.

I used to promise that I would repay you, but I never imagined I could. Every time I swore to return some of what you sacrificed, I was preparing to ask for more. But now that my earnings are probably triple Papa's salary, I want to give back a fraction of what you've given me.

If there is a heaven, this should be the first item in my application for admission. This sinner repaid his parents! Let's hope that this fact is established before the devil describes how my work was used in court against Lou Villars. I know I should get over that, but I will never recover, though, as you say, worse things now happen daily.

I plan to send you more checks along with my next letters. I fear there will come a time when it will no longer be so easy for us to send and receive mail. And we need to prepare ourselves for that sad eventuality.

> Through everything, I remain your loving son,
> Gabor

From *Paris in my Rearview Mirror*

BY LIONEL MAINE

An Essay on Fear

IN THOSE DAYS I had a girlfriend, Jasmine, a widow with two kids. She worked as a receptionist at the Hotel Ritz. She was kindhearted, everyone liked her. She got us free rooms when business was slow, which that winter it was.

No sane human being doesn't love sex in a fancy hotel room. Also there were extras: the barely tasted bottles of wine and the American newspapers guests left behind, papers you could no longer count on finding on the stands. For Christmas I got a *New York Times*, only lightly puckered from having been on some movie star's bathroom floor. Foreign guests were rarer now. Jasmine was lucky to have a job. She might not have one for long. I had no money. We had no plans. The Nazis were in power. Why not enjoy the moment?

Christmas morning, we lay naked in bed. So what if there were fuel shortages and the room was cold? The kids were with Jasmine's mother. We'd had crazy sex and would again. The holiday was ours.

The Sunday *Times* ran a survey that I read aloud to Jasmine: what subjects were the American people most interested in this year? In 1937, the ladies were most interested in the marriage of the Duke of Windsor and Mrs. Simpson. This year men and women alike were interested in the German annexation of Czechoslovakia, and in whether there would be another world war.

Sixty percent of Americans thought appeasing Hitler meant that war was more likely. Forty percent disagreed. Sixty/forty were the chances of war in the estimation of the citizens of Buffalo and Sheboygan. In Paris the numbers were different. One hundred percent in the heart and mind, zero on the face.

I want to get paid to do surveys. I want to take my notebook out to the boulevards and explain that I'm an American reporter writing a story on how many hours a day Parisians spend in terror. Not the old everyday fears—failure, poverty, loneliness, old age, disease—but major historical dread. Will we go to war? Will our cities and homes be bombed? Are we all going to die?

I'd ask, How many of you Frenchies think about war, first thing in the morning?

No reporters have asked the French that. They can have fun debating these questions in Cleveland, but here it's much too close. Life must be business as usual.

A friend of mine sold a painting. We went out to celebrate. We all got fined for having Chateaubriand on a day when meat was rationed. Busted after one bite. Guess who ate the rest of the beef? Not the dogs, I'll tell you that. The cops are having a field day, crown roast every night. If you have any money, you can still live like a king—like Marie Antoinette on the eve of the revolution.

Last week I went to the Chameleon Club for the first time in a while. They have a new revue called "Tout va très bien, Madame la Marquise," after a popular song from a few years back that they are reviving. In the song, a marquise calls home, and her servants tell her that everything is fine, except for one teensy problem, the death of her prize stallion, but everything is fine, except that her château has burned down. Everything is fine except for the suicide of her husband. But everything is fine.

Yvonne's revue consists of the same song performed, in a different way, by actors dressed as horses and stable hands, girls in firemen costumes, pretty boy policemen, all manner of suggestive and comical combinations. It's hard to believe how much entertainment and sexy surprise could come from hearing the same bad news sung fifteen different ways. Beneath it all was the obvious joke. Everything is *not* fine. Our horse is dead, our château in ruins. Our husband has hung himself in the attic.

Things are being sorted out in the most despicable fashion. Where you are born means everything. Either you're French, or you're not. God had better help the Jews, because their French friends won't. Many of my Jewish friends have already left the country, lest they wind up in the same pickle as their German relatives.

So what if I've been here fifteen years? I'm the American writer. The Spanish are all tragic, the Russians all Bolshevik Commies. All the Italians I know call Mussolini the Little Martian. They say he landed from outer space in that wedding cake he built in the Piazza Venezia. The palazzo was a spaceship that touched down and got stuck in Rome, and the Martians thought, What the hell, since we're here, let's invade Abyssinia.

Gabor called Jasmine at the Ritz and told her to ask me if we could get together for a drink. We agreed to meet at the Café Voltaire.

We greeted each other warmly. I hadn't seen him in weeks. He looked sleek and well fed. Had the baroness found a genius to cut his hair?

Lately, in my opinion, he'd fallen in with the wrong crowd. He'd been taken up by the race-car set. He'd always been a bit of a social climber, but he'd hidden it before. His photos were shown around the world. I'll admit, that was hard for me, though I'd had some success of my own. Someone told me about a Yakuza who'd had a sex scene from *Make Yourself New* translated into Japanese characters and tattooed, in microscript, on his back.

We drank our first glass of wine in silent, companionable comfort. It was too early to ask about Suzanne. It still hurt to recall how he'd stolen her. Not that Suzanne could be stolen. She'd left me for him. Which was worse. I wanted to hear about his work, but not about his money and fame.

After the second glass I said, "How's the baroness?"

He said that he saw the baroness regularly, though slightly less often than before.

I said, "Can I ask you something? Did you ever fuck her?"

He fell silent. Then he said, *Almost*. Once. If I told Suzanne, he'd deny it. In any case, sex was not the bond between him and the baroness. I don't know why I suddenly hated him. He hadn't said anything wrong. Maybe I felt that his reputation and social connections meant he was *safer* than me. When the war began, the baroness and her family would do more to protect him than anything the American embassy (which was already urging us to go home) would do for me. It was as if we both suffered from the same disease, but he had better doctors.

How *was* Suzanne? Terrified. Depressed. She was sure there would be a war. He blamed her pessimism on the widowed mother. I said the mother was probably right. He said he thought she was right too. And then for some reason we laughed.

I said, "Will you stay in Paris?"

He said, "Maybe it won't happen."

We ordered another round and drained our glasses in one swallow. Then he told me that he and the baroness had gone to Biarritz. The baroness had promised that it would be relaxing. And maybe it would have if the town hadn't been full of Spanish refugees. Filthy, starving. Sick kids. Hadn't the baroness known that it would spoil their vacation?

I said, "She knew. Didn't you get some good pictures? Refugees are so photogenic."

"Fuck you, Lionel," he said. "Actually, I did."

According to the baroness, it might not be smart to show them until it was clear which way the wind was blowing.

I said, "The baroness always was a slut."

Gabor said, "First of all, she is not a slut. And secondly, everyone who isn't a whore wants to be one. Even you, Lionel."

"Actually, not me." The truth was, I would have been a whore if I could have found a client.

He said, "Everyone has problems."

Gabor's personal torment was the mail service between Hungary and Paris. What would happen to his parents if war broke out? I said they would be fine. Unless he wanted to move them to Paris, there was nothing he could do. And there was no guarantee that they would be safer in Paris.

He said he might have to stop writing them, sooner rather than later. He was already under suspicion for being foreign born, and now the constant communications with a country about to be under German rule might get him sent to a prison camp. For writing to his parents! It would kill them if they found out. How exactly would they find out? Logic was never Gabor's strong suit when it came to his mother and father.

By now I was drunk enough to say, "I've always believed that relations between a man and his mother are sacred. Off limits even for close friends. Which makes me a better person than Freud, but that is another story. Still I would be lying if I didn't say that, often over the years, when you would tell me something your parents wrote or something you wrote to them, I'd ask myself: How old is this guy?"

"Forty," Gabor said.

"I rest my case," I said.

He said that he could tell his parents things he couldn't tell anyone else.

I said, "Really? What, besides boasting about yourself?"

He leaned across the table and hugged me and ordered another round.

We drank until almost dawn, alternately calming each other down and riling each other up. I wish I could remember half the things we said. Only as we were saying good-bye did he realize he hadn't explained why he'd wanted to see me.

He said, "Remember Lou Villars?"

I said, "Of course. She's in my book. Have you read one word I wrote?"

"I'm sorry," he said. "Of course I remember. Last week Lou showed up at my studio. I was nervous because of my photo . . . her trial."

"That was a while ago," I said.

Gabor seemed not to hear me. "In fact she couldn't have been friendlier. She wanted to buy a photo. Maybe more than one. I felt it would insult her if I told her how much my prices had risen. Was she sure she could afford them? I asked which photos she wanted. Did I have any pictures of bridges, tunnels, fortifications, armories, that sort of thing? I said I would look. She said don't worry, she had money. What does this sound like to you?"

"Nothing good," I said.

"That's what I thought," Gabor said. "And not just because I am a paranoid Hungarian. There's more. She wanted to learn to take pictures. She would pay me to teach her."

I said, "She was always a creepy broad."

Gabor said, "I told her no."

"Bravo. Smart boy," I said.

After that we said good night. Gabor went back to his studio, where, though neither of us said so, Suzanne was waiting. And I went to the hotel. Maybe Jasmine would still be awake. If not, if I could still see, I would write a letter to my editor in New Jersey.

Did the paper want eight hundred words on "Paris on the Brink"? I could go out on the boulevards and conduct my own survey. I would ask the French if they were as frightened and as willfully blind as my Hungarian friend.

From *A Baroness by Night*

BY LILY DE ROSSIGNOL

AFTER MY BROTHER-IN-LAW was killed, it put a strain on my marriage.

Armand was shot in September 1938. For weeks his murder went unsolved. All that anyone knew was that he'd gone with Didi and some friends to the Garden of Eden, the club that Clovis Chanac had set up for Arlette.

It was a bachelor party for one of Armand's pals in the Order of the Legion of Joan of Arc. Edith Piaf had been hired to sing "Mon Légionnaire" and a medley of other rousing paramilitary hits.

Chanac must have bribed Arlette to let Piaf have the spotlight for fifteen minutes. I imagine the crowd was relieved when Madame Macbeth returned to the stage. Piaf asked a lot of you, but Arlette asked nothing. All that she and Chanac wanted was to rule the world, starting with Paris.

My brother-in-law went home early, to get a head start on the days of fasting and penance with which he and his wife and children scourged themselves after every time Papa went out. Perhaps he had some errands to run on his way home. At that time my brother-in-law was, like St. Anthony, fending off an army of demons, though in Armand's case the desert was in his veins and his mind.

Armand left without the entourage that accompanied him everywhere. Later, this was looked into, and the men were exonerated; Armand had dismissed them. None of Armand's health problems were in evidence that night, and his minders assumed he was capable of making it home alone. According to his driver, he asked to be let out on a rather unsavory corner in the tenth arrondissement.

Didi was home by two. At five in the morning my sister-in-law called, hysterical because Armand hadn't returned.

It took them several days to find him. Someone had picked his pockets where he lay under the Pont d'Austerlitz.

The crime was immediately classified as a political murder because of Armand's position in the Legion of Joan of Arc. The Legion owned newspapers and lawyers; they had the government's ear. The police said that a Communist was almost certainly behind Armand's death. I was angry at how humbly Didi acted toward the cops, how graciously he thanked them for their brilliant detective work.

I understood: my husband's only brother was dead. But why did he want to be lied to? The Communists weren't after Armand. His circle of acquaintances ranged across many quarters of Paris and included criminals and addicts, any one of whom might have killed him, over money or drugs.

Eventually the police got lucky. Armand's killer was not just a Communist but a Bolshevik Jew! Herschel Grynszpan, 17, the same boy who shot Ernst vom Rath, a junior official in the German embassy in Paris.

That murder, of course, was the crime that set off Kristallnacht, the German people's "spontaneous" response to hearing that one of the Reich's finest young lives had been cut short by a Jew. Goebbels himself came to Munich to say he wouldn't be surprised if the Germans took it upon themselves to revenge this outrage by smashing up Jewish businesses, synagogues, and homes.

One last unpleasant detail: my brother-in-law was killed by the same caliber bullet—a 6.35 caliber revolver—that struck vom Rath. So it was decided that Grynszpan had plotted the crime in advance, trailing and killing my right-wing brother-in-law as a trial run for the main event. It was rumored by people "in the know" that Grynszpan had asked my brother-in-law to fund a Jewish sports club like the one he'd belonged to back in Hanover. He'd shot Armand in a fury when Armand refused. But no one who'd ever met Armand would imagine that even a lunatic would approach him to ask such a thing. And Grynszpan wasn't a lunatic, just an unhappy, angry young man.

I never believed that Grynszpan killed Armand, whom he had nothing against, as opposed to the German diplomat, whom the poor boy held responsible for deporting his parents and leaving them, cold and starving, just across the Polish border. And for making him an orphan, a stateless person, and a wanted man.

Everyone was lying, fantasizing, inventing, spouting improbable theories. Later, Grynszpan's lawyers would base their defense on the claim that the killer and his victim were homosexual lovers. Thus it would no longer have been a political assassination, a capital offense, but a crime of passion, which under French law, was perfectly legal or pardonable, I can't remember which.

Armand's memorial service was our homegrown mini-Nuremberg rally. Columns of veterans and policemen marched to solemn dirges played by military bands. The flag-draped casket was hauled forward, one agonizingly slow hoofbeat after another, by a team of white horses with bridles and plumes that matched the flag.

I kept my arm around Didi's shoulders. My poor husband wept without restraint. He cried as the casket rolled by. He sobbed during the "Marseillaise."

My memories of that day are blurred, but one image I clearly recall is the tear-streaked, swollen face of Lou Villars, bobbing toward me through the sea of mourners. I pretended not to see her. I felt sorry for her, but I was afraid that her soggy sympathy would drown me. I was having enough trouble keeping Didi afloat.

Didi wanted to believe that Grynszpan had murdered Armand. That the killer had been apprehended. And it drove a wedge between us, though it was less like a chasm than like a large oily puddle, too revolting to cross. Everything Didi did and said began to get on my nerves. It was the same for Didi, I'm sure. I could tell how much I annoyed him.

I didn't want to leave Didi, and he didn't want that, either. It seemed simpler if I left Paris.

Anyway, Paris was no longer fun. Did no one see what was coming? No one discussed an invasion. But everyone smelled it on the air, like the first depressing whiff of autumn. Gabor complained that his friend Suzanne did nothing but worry about the war. Maybe it would have made me feel less lonely to talk to her. But she wasn't the sort of girl I spoke to, at that time. Later we would be in constant conversation, ironically at a moment when any words—the wrong words—might have been fatal to us both. History would prove me wrong about her, as it would about so much else.

I decided to leave for the south of France and establish a refuge to which my friends could escape. I suspected that I wouldn't have long to wait. And once again I was right. Even before I had settled in, Parisians were fleeing the city.

It would be a lie of omission not to admit that I purchased a great deal of art and arranged to have it shipped south. I hesitate to mention this because of the nasty gossip one still hears about collectors, especially female patrons of the arts. It's been implied that we took advantage of the crisis and acquired treasures at bargain rates. As if it were a crime to redistribute family wealth, to allow artists to stay or escape: as if we were exploiting our friends instead of saving their lives.

From *The Devil Drives:*
The Life of Lou Villars

BY NATHALIE DUNOIS

Chapter Eleven: A Deadly Duo

COUNTLESS ACCOUNTS HAVE tracked the careers of murderers and thieves who might have gone to their graves with clean hands, had fate not thrown them together with the one person who could awaken the fiend inside them. Often serial killers prowl their corpse-strewn landscapes in pairs, the strong and the weak, the merciful and the merciless, each playing the agreed-upon role, sometimes trading off. The result is like a laboratory experiment gone hideously awry, an explosion set off by an accidental mixing of chemicals, volatile and deadly, but only in combination.

That was what happened when Lou Villars fell in love with Inge Wallser. No one can say for certain whether Lou would have done what she did without Inge. But the reports of people who knew them at the time, and of those Lou met later, suggest that the lovers were energized by a sense of themselves as an outlaw couple, desperados on a crime spree that would leave Europe in ruins.

This was not what they said aloud. Out loud they were helping their countries.

The spring of 1938 was the sunniest season in Lou's life. The warm weather arrived early. Pollen blew in on the breezes that rattled the plane trees and covered the pavement with pearlescent chartreuse dust. Overnight, the daffodils and forget-me-nots bloomed, followed, hours later, by purple drifts of Siberian iris. When no one was looking, Lou knelt to admire the red tracery on the yellow tulips in the park. Who had given the flowers these capillaries filled with blood? What inspired artist had selected the pink of the apple blossoms, the scarlet of the poppies? Armand would have said that God painted the tulips, but Armand was dead. Did he wonder, at the last minute, why a merciful Christian God had sent a Bolshevik Jew to shoot him? Armand believed in martyrs. Was he surprised to become one?

Everywhere lovers kissed and embraced. But their shameless self-display no longer irritated Lou. She too was in love. It was all the sweeter that her love involved a hidden intrigue. She and Inge shared important secrets. The thought of what they alone knew made life seem doubly delicious.

Inge stayed for long weekends and sometimes into the week. The Germans paid Lou enough to hire an assistant, Marcel, whom she'd known at the track. Competent and incurious, he was ideally qualified to take over the garage when Lou was away.

Lou and Inge traveled in the restored Rossignol sedan that Lou had bought from Didi at a discount, though it annoyed her that, after the sacrifices she'd made, her former employer had the nerve to charge her for a wreck. She and Didi had embraced at Armand's memorial service, even as the baroness pretended not to see her.

Sometimes Lou and Inge drove to distant parts of France. In July, they watched the Grand Prix from their hotel room near Lyons. How could Lou have minded not competing in the race when she was struggling to catch her breath between Inge's kisses?

In the past, Lou had never let anyone drive her car. But she let Inge take the wheel, a gesture of trusting surrender, intoxicating and naughty. Inge drove too fast, and the formerly safety-conscious Lou began to do the same. Once Lou ran over a duck; once Inge struck a goose. Both times they took out some cash and weighed the bills down with a stone beside the mangled poultry. Once a low-flying guinea hen nearly hit them. It was hilarious, really! A bird had tried to kill them, but they survived because they'd been chosen for the destiny they were fulfilling.

Every new experience brought them closer. The game they played for the Germans heightened their pleasure in being together. Their happiness was infectious. Around them, women who might have been jealous of their love convinced themselves that their own hard lives were easier, their chilly marriages warmer. They were often shocked to go home to discover the same old grumpy husband instead of the doting prince they'd imagined. It was thrilling to ferret out vital information that friends, acquaintances, and strangers vied to confide in two good-time girls: a couple of glamorous lady auto racers who appeared one day and vanished the next, in a fancy car.

Everywhere they went, Lou knew women she'd met when she'd lectured the sports clubs. Everyone was delighted to see her, even former lovers, who gracefully withdrew when they sensed the strength of the bond between Lou and Inge. Their arrival was like the circus coming to town. These bored provincial Emma Bovarys could enjoy themselves and have fun, even though, in their regular lives, fun was scarce or nonexistent.

In the bars and cafés, Inge bought round after round. No one seemed bothered by the fact that a German had all the money. Actually, they liked the idea, and with every beer Inge bought, Lou's old and new friends felt more secure that a war with Germany was unlikely.

Lou and Inge's passion *proved* that the two nations could coexist. These visits became a currency that the local women could spend after Lou and Inge left, and the talk turned, as it often did, to the threat of war. There was not going to be a war, except in the minds of their paranoid leaders. And the women had proof: the relaxed and enjoyable evening they'd spent with a celebrity racer from Paris and her famous German friend.

While they spoke to these women, Lou and Inge conducted a parallel conversation in glances. Who would ask the first casual question? Who would follow up with another? They felt like a pair of historic swindlers from the glorious annals of crime. The confidences they won and betrayed had a noble purpose, a selfless goal. Their playful little con games would forge a lasting peace and begin the hard work of making France as healthy as her next-door neighbor.

The electricity between Lou and Inge lasted long after the parties ended and they were back in their hotel room. They went over what they'd learned, the information they'd gathered. It was like counting stolen loot. Theirs was a bandit romance.

It was amazing, how much people would say, and how rapidly Lou learned to interpret and evaluate tidbits of gossip. The women had husbands, and the husbands talked, and the wives wanted something interesting to add to the conversation. The wife of the man who man-ufactured truck tires remarked that she hadn't seen her husband for months, he had so many orders to fill. A woman confided that she was making pocket money bringing sandwiches to the workers building additional landing strips at an airfield nearby.

The universe seemed to *want* them to know certain things. When Lou took a detour near the Normandy coast, they were stopped on the highway by a soldier, beyond whom they glimpsed a traffic jam of tanks and military vehicles. Once they were sunning themselves on the beach near Caen and Inge said, "Look, out there!"

"Where?" said Lou.

"There," Inge said. "It's a submarine. Poking out of the water."

Lou wasn't sure she saw it, but she agreed that she did, and the submarine went into the suede-bound notebook that Inge carried everywhere. A girl in Alsace told them that her boyfriend's hunting club was called out on a secret mission, to shoot all the carrier pigeons trained by the communications squad of the local army regiment. The pigeons had finally been replaced with radio and telegraph, and it was feared that the homeless, unemployed birds would betray the squadron's location.

Taking turns, like a loving couple, Lou and Inge described how the pigeons shit on the athletes at the Berlin Games. The Alsatian girl laughed. Imagine that! They'd been to the Olympics!

For the Alsatian girl's boyfriend, it was a hunter's dream. The girl wrinkled her nose. Feathers and blood and death. But here was the punch line: the radio and telegraph didn't work, and it was too late to fix it. All the carrier pigeons were dead. And the funniest part was: the communications system along the segment of the French line of defense ran on electricity from the German side of the border! By that point the French were glad that the pigeons were dead, so they couldn't carry information about this unfortunate situation.

To mark their six-month anniversary, Inge brought Lou an expensive Leica camera that, Inge said, might prove useful in their work. Lou said she wanted to practice taking pictures on her own. She was ashamed to let Inge know that she had no idea how to use it.

Inge also gave Lou a silver cigarette lighter: elegant, slim, old fashioned, engraved with Lou's initials.

After Inge left, Lou went to see her old friend Gabor Tsenyi, who had gotten rich and famous, partly thanks to his portrait of Lou and Arlette. But this old debt meant nothing to him. When Lou asked to see certain photographs and suggested he might give her some pointers on photography—lessons for which she was willing to pay—he practically kicked her out of his studio. What was Gabor's problem? His problem was not being French. A problem that would soon be solved, for him and many others, whether they liked it or not.

When Inge was in Germany, Lou worked diligently in the garage. But now she was cheerful and patient, with endless sympathy for her customers' concerns. Her business did better than it had when the garage was all she lived for. Now her secret life held her aloft, like Papa, just before he'd tried to teach her to swim by throwing her into a pond, from which she'd been rescued by her grandma just before she drowned. Or like Robert, before he let her drop to the ground.

Lou tried not to think about her brother. For a long time she let Inge believe that she was an only child, but one night, feeling especially close, Lou told her the whole story—and Inge wept real tears. Several times since then, Lou had mentioned Robert, but Inge changed the subject, looking bored and fretful in a way that made Lou reluctant to spoil an otherwise amicable conversation.

Once in a while she wished that she could tell someone what she and Inge were doing. How she could have brightened the worried faces around her, how she could have comforted her anxious French neighbors! She and Inge were making sure that their worst fantasies didn't come true. But for now it was essential to keep their mission secret.

Inge seemed pleased by the quality of the information they were gathering. And Lou was also satisfied, even when she judged herself by the standards she imagined had been set for her by the Führer. How much faith he had shown in her! What a sacred duty he had entrusted her with! Even when she was tired, the memory of that dinner made her feel rested and ready for whatever was required.

One brilliant autumn Saturday, Lou and Inge were driving through the Ardennes near the Belgian border.

Inge said, "Shakespeare's magic forest."

Luckily, Lou was behind the wheel and could smile and nod without betraying the fact that she had no idea what Inge meant.

In a café halfway between Sedan and Longuyon, Inge and Lou had arranged to meet a middle-aged woman named Elise Becker, who had briefly been Lou's lover when Lou was the darling of the Northeastern Women's Sports Club.

Lou and Inge had worked out a system. They always arrived late, and they always called ahead and told the café owners to let their friends drink on their tab until they arrived. At first, some owners hesitated, but Inge made it worth their while. By the time Lou and Inge showed up, the women were so tipsy that no one had to waste time getting them into a state in which they would say things they ordinarily might keep quiet.

When Lou spotted Elise Becker sitting alone at the table in back, Lou tried to recall how long it had been since their brief affair. Surely less than two years. But how could Elise have so totally lost her looks since then? Nothing like an unhappy marriage to ruin a girl's complexion. Elise's face was pale and covered with blotches and welts. Lou searched for a memory of something, anything: a smell, a touch, a caress. But the nights she'd spent with Elise merged with so many others, and the effort to retrieve it made Lou feel irritable and guilty.

Lou and Inge had met with Elise twice in the last six months. Each time, Lou was saddened by how Elise had aged.

Elise looked up when they came in, overjoyed and puzzled by Lou's desire to see her again and to bring along her lovely German companion. Elise's husband, on whom she'd cheated with Lou, was in the cement, earth, and stonework business, with a special interest in sewers and excavations. She'd already dropped several intriguing hints about his new job, building some sort of fortification.

A nearly empty bottle of red wine sat on the table in front of Elise, and it seemed to Lou that the whites of her eyes were lightly stained pink. Elise half rose to kiss them, and then asked, as she had the last time, if she smelled like a latrine. She laughed a little hysterically when they assured her she didn't. The stench was in her house, her bed, her husband's clothes. Elise smelled it and tasted it no matter how often she did the laundry. All of her husband's business these days involved digging sewers and trenches. As always, before going out, she'd bathed three times, then doused herself in lavender water to kill the odor of Pascal's hands and breath.

As they sipped their drinks, white wine for Inge, whiskey neat for Lou, Elise reported on her husband's latest business misadventure. He'd been hired to dig the latrines and sewer lines for the Maginot Line, the French border fortifications. He'd calculated the mileage, then ordered supplies and hired workers based on his calculations. He'd been surprised and, frankly, put out to find himself with tons of extra cement, dozens of shovels and unemployed laborers, lazy bastards who expected to get paid for doing nothing.

The government had decided to end the defense line at Sedan and to rely for protection on the dense Ardennes forest. Not only was this foolish, and, speaking personally, bad for business, not only had Pascal been left with idle workers and unusable cement, but the idiots in Paris were leaving the country undefended. And how had Elise's husband reacted? As he did to all business setbacks. He got drunk and beat Elise.

Elise was crying so pitifully that Lou wanted to console her. But she didn't know how, and besides, it would have angered Inge if Lou had somehow caused Elise to stop talking. None of this was her fault. Why should she feel responsible and ashamed? Then she saw Inge's look of exultation. This was news that the fellows back home would be pleased to hear!

Lou said, "There won't be another war. You and your husband won't have to worry."

"I love you." Inge mouthed the words so that only Lou could see.

From *Paris in My Rearview Mirror*

BY LIONEL MAINE

On Falling in Love with a City

SAYING GOOD-BYE TO a city is harder than breaking up with a lover. The grief and regret are more piercing because they are more complex and unmixed, changing from corner to corner, with each passing vista, each shift of the light. Breaking up with a city is unclouded by the suspicion that after the affair ends, you'll learn something about the beloved you wished you never knew. The city is as it will remain: gorgeous, unattainable, going on without you as if you'd never existed. What pain and longing the lover feels as he bids farewell to a tendril of ivy, a flower stall, the local butcher. The charming café where he meant to have coffee but never did.

Magnify those feelings a thousandfold when the city is Paris. Every bridge is a pirate's plank the lover walks at his own peril, watching the twinkling Seine and giving serious thought to jumping and losing himself in that seductive, sparkly blackness. Every spire pierces the heart. Every alley, every smoky tabac, every fountain was killing me. I was going to Jersey City.

I decided on a departure date. September 1, 1939. Things were getting too crazy with the nonwar about to start and Germany breathing its beery sausage breath down the Frenchies' necks. Each day brought urgent communiqués from the American embassy telling me to go home or they couldn't guarantee my safety. If you've ever gotten such a note, you know: it is not a comforting feeling.

In the meantime I tried to live as I always had. Eating, drinking, picking up girls, making love, seeing friends, talking, writing, having fun. Supporting the final days of my habit by doing little money jobs for the papers back home.

The assignment I was most grateful for was one I almost turned down. The editors in Jersey asked me to cover the last public guillotine execution. No one knew it would be the last. But afterward, everyone did.

The condemned man was a mass murderer. To the folks in the States, his most hideous crime was strangling an American girl he buried in his basement. The paper offered to pay me double my usual fee.

Back home, I'd be off the Paris beat. I'd have to find a new subject. Also, to put it bluntly, a nice messy execution would take my mind off my own problems. I'd be joining the long line of literary lights who had followed the masses to watch the guilty brought to violent justice. Byron, Dickens, now Lionel Maine. As the not-so-immortal Byron once said, I would have saved them if I could.

The news of the crimes had sold millions of papers worldwide. With the economy crashing, this was what people wanted. Forget the political assassinations, the invasions, wars all over Europe! The story that made readers salivate for every juicy detail was about Eugene Weidmann, the depraved German maniac who strangled an American dancer he lured to his house to talk about . . . are you ready? . . . *Wagner*! Afterward the guy went on a murder spree that left six people dead, among them a chauffeur, an unemployed chef, and a real estate agent. This criminal genius left his business card in the real estate agent's office, though in the end that hardly mattered. His accomplices, their parents and girlfriends, all knew about the murders. I sympathized with one thing: the guy could not shut up.

The execution was scheduled for June 17 in Versailles. Everyone wanted a close-up look at the blood spewing out of the guy's neck. When the government got wind of how many people planned to attend, they did some calculations and decided that only a select group of reporters and special guests were invited. The lumpen proletariat would just have to buy the paper. And if the movie-going public wanted to watch it in the newsreels? Too bad! Filming this news-worthy event was *absolument interdit*! The French had been chopping heads off for centuries, but now, on the eve of another world war, they'd gotten squeamish.

Somehow my editor got me a ticket. Two hundred of us chosen ones were permitted to wait in line for an hour. We shuffled past the checkpoint, stopping to make way for VIPs, among them Clovis Chanac, who, in his seamless transition from cop to politician to gangster, had kept his front row seats at sold-out entertainments.

How theatrical—how French—of them to give the dead man a drumroll. The prisoner was marched out. Wearing dark trousers and a white shirt, he was trussed like a duckling with his arms behind his back.

It was lucky they had him tied up in the neatest possible package. Because everything that could go wrong did. To be more blunt than I was in my article for the folks back home: it was a regular goat fuck. Naturally, I thought of myself to take my mind off the horror. I recalled my former fascination with the French Revolution and its ingenious method of decapitating unwanted aristocrats. What a fool I had been to imagine such things were romantic! Then I remembered Picasso's drawing of the guillotine, which I had so desperately coveted and which he'd snatched from my grasp.

When a plank jammed, the executioners panicked. There were hurried consultations. Someone gave an order, someone struggled with the rigging. Finally (it seemed long to us, so imagine how it seemed to him!) it was decided to stuff the prisoner through the opening. They draped his legs up over the board and crammed his head through the space, but it didn't work from that angle either, so they had to shift him around.

Ladies and gentlemen of the jury, I ask you: was there booing from the crowd? Was there any sign of moral revulsion or even disapproval? The answer is no. There was not. We'd worked hard to get our tickets, we didn't want to get kicked out and spoil everyone's good time. Besides which, what could we have done? I would have saved him if I could.

Finally they got it right, or almost right. What would *almost* mean if it was *your* head on the block? Regardless of our personal views on capital punishment, everyone was praying that the repulsive contraption would function.

Finally God—or something—got the blade to drop. The body fell into a bin. The head rolled onto the cobblestones. A guard picked it up. The crowd was silent. No one prayed or said "God Forgive Us" or "*Vive la France!*" or any such bullshit. We pulled our hats down over our eyes and shuffled off toward the railway station, only to face the part of the story that no one warned us about.

A mob had gathered in Versailles. Thousands of people were only now hearing that the murderer was dead. They'd missed the main event.

Beet red was the median facial hue of the assembled citizens, who proceeded to get drunk and destroy "downtown" Versailles. Needless to say, they left the palace untouched. They were French. As I made my way toward the station, sirens started to wail. Shards of glass were flying. A café table just missed me. The faces I saw were frightening. I had never seen, never want to see, expressions like that again.

I looked at the people around me and thought, Enough. *Adieu. Au revoir.* It's been fun. But now it's time for this Jersey boy to go home. Maybe I'd try the West Coast. Hollywood, here I come!

From *A Baroness by Night*

BY LILY DE ROSSIGNOL

EVEN THEN, WITH the sky falling in, there were still warm spring mornings when the greatest pleasure was to sneak out early and do errands, like a normal person in normal times. The lilacs were never as fragrant as they were that year. I'd buy an armful of snapdragons, put the flowers in my bag, along with cheese and a loaf of bread. There was rationing throughout the city, but less so in my neighborhood. All the merchants knew me, and if the authorities checked, I had a letter from Didi's doctors saying that we were ailing and needed a bit more butter than our neighbors.

It was outside the baker's, on one such morning, that I saw Lionel Maine for the last time. By which I mean the last time until years later, after the war, when I gathered my old friends for a reunion at my château in Ménerbes, before the American tourists ruined it.

Lionel had plastered himself flat—arms out, like Jesus—against the baker's wall. Spread-eagled over the hot air duct, through which the ovens piped delicious smells onto the street. Lionel was breathing rapidly and deeply.

I tapped him on the shoulder. He wheeled around, red-eyed and still bleary from the night before.

He said, "My dear Lily, do you know how, when you've run out of cigarettes, sometimes, when you wake up, you can cough hard and get some of that good smoke taste in your mouth?"

"Lionel, you smoke too much. That's disgusting," I said, even though I smoked that much too, and I knew what he meant.

He said, "I'm inhaling Paris. I'm leaving tonight for Cherbourg. Somewhere over the ocean I can go on deck and cough, and the breath of a Paris bakery will still be in my lungs. I'll give it an ocean burial."

"How romantic," I said.

I've said that I never liked Lionel, but it wasn't that simple. It was partly the sexual element, or the lack of a sexual element. The insult of knowing he'd tried to seduce every woman in Paris but me. He was Gabor's friend. I'd spent time with him. And everything that had happened—my sad misunderstanding with Gabor, the death of my brother-in-law—had so toughened me that I no longer cared whether an aging American poseur happened to find me attractive. Except that a woman is never immune to insecurities of that sort.

Lionel said, "I'm leaving Paris."

"You mentioned that," I said.

Then he told me he'd attended the public guillotine execution in Versailles. I remember his exact words. He said it was a goat fuck.

I said, "You went to see a man's head chopped off. What did you expect?"

He'd written about the execution to earn a little money. But he was glad that he did. What he'd seen in Versailles had finally enabled him to leave Paris.

I said that sounded like something he would put in a book. Surely he had other reasons for leaving.

I had always expressed a certain contempt for Lionel's writing, though to be honest I'd never read it. I assumed it would be the literary gushing of your typically self-involved, hard-living, tough-talking "man's man," madly in love with his penis and with no understanding of women. They are all repressed homosexuals, as one still sometimes hears, mostly from feminist academics on literary TV talk shows.

When I finally read his work, not so very long ago, I discovered that I'd been right. Though by then the formerly shocking stuff seemed as mild as milk. And by then I was doing my own "literary gushing," writing, or trying to write, the memoir you hold in your hands. Curious to see what Lionel said about me, I skimmed his books for my name. I was especially interested in how he described our nights at the

Chameleon Club. That I'd studied the dancers for information about sex was one of the few things about me that Lionel got right.

That last morning, outside the bakery, I felt I owed Lionel something. I suppose I still felt guilty for not defending him when he spoke up, as Gabor and I should have, against Arlette's disgusting song. Also he'd written a useful piece for an American newspaper about Lou's trial; the story was widely reprinted. He'd always complained that he'd gotten cheated on the fees. Thanks to his essay, several rich Americans custom-ordered Rossignols, but the war interceded before they could be delivered.

Standing with Lionel in the delightful cloud of yeasty vapors, I felt warmer toward him than I ever had, and not just because we were surrounded by balmy gusts of fragrant air. It certainly wasn't because he kept repeating that he was leaving Paris, in that aggressively tragic tone, as if his departure was my fault. The thought of him leaving made me sad; that is all I can say.

I told him, "We'll see each other again. I know."

He said, "Maybe if you're paying, baroness, we can all get back together." He really could be a bastard.

I said, "By then, Lionel, you'll be able to pay for us all."

Lionel gave me a vigorous hug, the way he might hug a man. He kissed me on both cheeks.

"Good-bye," he said.

"*Au revoir*," I told him.

"So they say," he called over his shoulder.

Lionel's shirtsleeves were rolled above his elbows. I noticed that, as he left. At what age do men start walking with their shoulders turned out, so their elbows are facing backward? A man walking like that has crossed the line from a young man to an old one.

It depressed me to watch him, bent over, walking away from the bakery, from me, from Gabor. From Paris. I too left, very soon after. For the rest of my life I would remember the sight of Lionel walking away, his elbows receding into the distance. And happily, he was still walking that way, healthy and vigorous, at our reunion, after the war.

PART

THREE

From the (Unpublished) Memoirs
of Suzanne Dunois Tsenyi

To be destroyed on the occasion of its author's death

A FEW DAYS before the German invasion, I saw a group of people gathered on the corner near the Sèvres-Babylone Métro station. Everyone was looking at the sky, silent except for one boy whining that his mother was squeezing his hand so hard that it hurt.

"Fighter planes," his mother informed me. I looked up and saw a flock of swallows catching the silvery light.

"Birds." I said it louder. "Birds." It was like one of those dreams in which you shout but no sound comes out.

I'd been on my way to the language school for a two o'clock class with a trio of obese German businessmen who had bullied the director into charging all three the customary rate for one student. They were importers, they said. When I asked what they imported, one of them—the fattest—imitated a cuckoo clock, and the others laughed. Ho ho! Their joke was on me.

Since the start of the phony war, many German citizens had been interned in French prison camps. But my students were well connected. They came and went as they pleased. The words they wanted to learn belonged to the lexicon of governance, prison, industry, civic control. The only way I could live with myself was to teach them mistakes. They left my classroom convinced that the French word for *curfew* was *parsnip*. I made them repeat it until they got it right.

On the day I saw the crowd watching the swallows, I understood that disaster was really about to occur. Now it seems like hindsight. But I remember the ominous certainty. Though I knew that the director of the language school would be angry, I canceled my lesson with the Germans. What if they were the ones who would call in the fighter planes behind the swallows? The ones who would order the soldiers to impose an early, strict *parsnip* on the citizens of Paris?

I walked to Gabor's studio. He was working in the darkroom. I paged through a book of Rodin drawings as I waited for him to finish. We went back to his room and spent the rest of the day in bed. I can still see the striped sunlight sliding over his shoulder. I watched him sleep in the zebra light.

Until then we had been acting. The drama of the baroness, the comedy of my playing dead on the sidewalk. The war put an end to the theatrics and made things very simple. What did we want to keep? What couldn't we stand to lose? For me, it was Mama and Gabor. My mother was old and not well. And Gabor was foreign. Many foreigners had been deported, though not yet famous artists, like Gabor. The baroness had protected him. But she had left Paris for a mountaintop in the south and was constantly writing Gabor that we—Lady Bountiful included me—should join her.

Germans are like bears, she wrote. You can escape them by climbing.

Gabor and I decided to leave for the baroness's. We would go back as soon as we could. That is how I tell the story: a mutual decision. The truth is, I wanted to stay. Paris was home. My mother was there. Gabor refused to remain in the city and wait and see what the Germans would do about his being Hungarian. And I wanted to be with him. Time makes it hard to remember how the racket of passion drowns out the measured voices of loyalty and common sense.

Ten, twenty times a day, I promised Gabor that his prints and plates would be safe. We worked for weeks, packing and storing everything in waterproof, fireproof containers in his basement. Every friend, acquaintance, and former assistant was enlisted to help.

The baroness had sent ahead several crates of plates and photos. But we tried not to talk about that, not only to avoid the subject of the baroness but also because we knew what a small fraction of the whole she had managed to save.

That might have been the moment to finally insist that Gabor tell me the truth about his relations with the baroness. Had they been lovers? Did she resent me? How could I be her houseguest unless I knew? But it was the wrong time to ask. Our country was being invaded, our city was in danger. I was ashamed to be taking orders from my jealous heart.

What *were* we afraid of losing? For Gabor, it was his life's work, his negatives and prints. I didn't want to leave Mama, but she refused to leave Paris. She was stubborn, either from bravery or fear, I never knew. She insisted we go without her. She made me promise to stay with Gabor until after the invasion she'd been expecting since my father was killed. The only thing that surprised her was that it had taken so long, and that anyone was surprised.

The sirens made it scarier, though we knew they were wailing to warn us, not panic us, which they did. Stalled cars and frightened pedestrians stoppered the streets. Overloaded baby carriages and horse carts fell off their wheels and slammed to the ground. The horses balked and reared up, and we navigated around them. Bicycle riders straddled their bikes, walking bowlegged and cursing. It was a miracle that more people—more children—weren't trampled. Every so often I had to bend over and take a breath because my heart was jittering like a drop of water on a griddle. Before I could collect myself, someone shouted at me to move on.

Was it wrong that, amid all that suffering, I was proud of how well my lover knew Paris? Far from their own neighborhoods, most people kept to the boulevards so as not to get lost, but Gabor took back alleys. I wanted to compliment him. But I didn't want to remind him of how he'd acquired that knowledge, taking pictures, many of which he was leaving behind. All those rainy nights when I'd struggled to keep our cigarettes lit as I handed him the plates guided us out of the city and onto the open highway. Only the bicycles outdistanced us as we headed south, well ahead of my terrified countrymen and the German planes strafing us from the sky.

Farm families gave us milk still warm from the cows. We slept in the meadows beside the road. The fireflies watched us make love. We'd fallen in love all over again, more intensely than before.

The prospect of death is a strong aphrodisiac. Years later, I read a novel about refugees from an earthquake who take shelter in a theater; all day and night the orchestra pit roils with couples making love. And many years after that, on an airplane, I sat beside a hospice nurse who told me the most delicate part of her job was fending off the amorous, grief-stricken relatives of the dying.

During those anxious nights before the invasion, Gabor and I had stayed awake staring into each other's eyes, as we used to when we first realized we were made for each other. On the road south from Paris, all Gabor had to do was take my hand. Was it a sin to be thinking of sex, surrounded by so much death? I was embarrassed by how my body responded, despite or because of the suffering that we knew was about to get worse.

The baroness's garden teemed with reptiles, and I wandered among them in the haze of the displaced, a stupor induced by troubled sleep and nightmares about my mother. Once I made the mistake of announcing I'd seen a snake. The baroness became so hysterical she had to be sedated.

After that I kept quiet about my game with the lizards. The geckos sensed I was watching them and went totally still, so that my observations were more meditation than research. Finally I'd throw a pebble, not to hit or tease them but just to get them moving. Then I'd watch them run. They'd come back to the same spot, and we'd play again. Stasis, pebble, escape. Any routine was soothing compared to the mood in the château.

The lizards made me think of Yvonne. Was her club still open? Her chameleons belonged to another life, when people had the energy and time to work at becoming legends. With her songs about a dead sailor, her lizards and red dresses, Yvonne had been as brilliant as any artist (except Gabor) who'd frequented her club. Her customers trusted her to protect them by knowing when to stand up or back down. Moral courage, talent, and business sense are a rare combination.

What would the Germans do about a club for chic transvestites? They might think it was like Old Berlin, but they would say it was French. Loathsome French degeneracy. The Chameleon would stay open. But no more jokes about Germans.

Unwilling to leave his auto business, the baroness's husband had stayed in Paris. Every few minutes the baroness said, "I am worried about Didi." She didn't know or didn't care that she'd said it minutes before.

It is always shocking, what the rich can do. Despite the downed communication lines, Didi managed to phone every evening at six. When the phone rang in the main salon, the rest of us left until we heard the baroness sobbing, and we returned to console her. That is, Gabor comforted her, while I and an audience of artistic refugees watched.

Each of us adapted or not, in different ways, or not. None of us were "ourselves." No one knew what to do with our time, though Gabor took some pictures. Days of gloom were brightened by lavish dinners. The baroness found local farmers to sell her scarce, delicious food.

The champagne was exquisite. Legendary. People talked for hours about the magical champagne. And it did work magic. If we drank enough we believed that the Germans would be defeated soon, and we would be back in Paris.

It bothered me, how we were living compared to the rest of the country. I'd get angry at the baroness, as if it were her fault. But I didn't leave, and I said nothing, not even to Gabor. We weren't hurting anyone by drinking good champagne.

Even as she indulged us and tried to foresee our needs, the baroness exhausted us. All those white Shetland puppies she bought from a breeder nearby, purebreds that ate only special food and had diarrhea on the silk sofas. The scenes about their behavior! It was her house, her sofas, her silk. Who else could have procured all those lobsters, so far inland and in wartime? When we cracked the shells, an oily black liquid oozed onto our plates. The dining room fell silent but for the grating of the chairs being pushed away from the table.

In light of what happened later, I wonder if I would have liked the baroness more if we'd met under different circumstances. Without the competition over Gabor. Without her power and money. Meanwhile I became obsessed with the way she stubbed out her cigarette in her picked-over food. I waited for it, all through the meal. She put it out and left it there for someone else to clear away.

Whenever the subject of children came up, she would tilt her head and turn to one of the men and say, in a little-girl voice, "I don't have any children." As if he didn't know! Was he supposed to feel sorry for her and to find her pathos sexy? Or was she informing him that motherhood hadn't wrecked her boyish body? I didn't have children either, but I didn't feel the need to say so.

Periodically, she would emerge from her fog of worry and distraction and organize excursions in the two Rossignols she kept in the garage. She also had the magic power to make gasoline appear. I often felt that her fear about Didi and her anxiety about France were competing with her terror that she, or one of her guests, would get bored.

Life at the château was . . . bearable, I would say. Years later, I read about how Samuel Beckett worked with the underground in Paris and had to hide out in the south. Near us, though we didn't know it. He went insane from boredom until he found the local Resistance and carried out secret missions. Boy Scout stuff, he called it.

There was no anti-Nazi cell near the baroness's château, or none that trusted us. We were always outsiders. City people, waiting.

I longed for the smells of Paris, for the damp cold, the mildew, the rats. It is not a vacation when you can't go home. The only slightly happy guests were the landscape painters. I missed my mother terribly. When the phones worked, I could call the café next door. Her friends and neighbors took care of her, and she was as well as could be expected, given the shortages of food and fuel and everything she needed. The baroness offered to ask one of Didi's employees to check on her, but she never remembered to tell him, and I couldn't bring myself to remind her. I was afraid of how much I would hate her if she forgot again.

I missed watching strangers on the street. I missed seeing, in a pâtisserie, expensive cakes baked with imitation ingredients. I missed the displays of shoes made from cardboard and chewing gum, baby clothes stitched from old napkins: whatever could be scrounged. I missed never knowing who I might run into. I missed passing a window and hearing a child practice piano scales. I missed organ grinders, carousels. I missed human beings! My homesickness deepened each time someone said that the Paris I missed was gone: it was only a memory now. The cafés were empty, the newspaper kiosks boarded up. Everyone interesting had left. The only people one met now were spies, soldiers, or German civilians.

And Gabor? He missed Lionel, who had gone back to the States. Everything reminded Gabor of the loss of his friend. When I showed him the lizards in the garden, he told me that Lionel used to speculate about whether Yvonne had sex with her pets. I too was surprised by the size of the empty space that Lionel's absence created.

Gabor stopped writing his parents, who must have been frantic. He was afraid that his letters would be read. He said that the postal system was an easy way for the Germans to keep track of our whereabouts. Why attract attention until we knew what they had in mind?

For once he was not being paranoid. New arrivals showed up at the château, en route from Paris to Lisbon, artists, musicians, longtime Rossignol customers, a steady stream of Jewish friends. That was how we learned what was happening to the French Jews. In the middle of nowhere, we heard what was going on, so those who say they didn't know must have never gone outside or had one conversation with another person.

I know this is not a popular view. No French citizen wants to hear it. That is one of the reasons I have repeatedly changed my mind about whether I want my memoirs destroyed after I am dead.

One day a Jewish violinist arrived at the château. He'd been loaded onto a boxcar in Vienna and traveled, without food or water, alongside the dead and dying. When the doors were opened, he found himself in Toulouse.

Our problems seemed trivial compared to those of the Jews. No matter how our hearts ached for them, we were relieved when they left, not only because we hoped they would be safe but because of our guilt. Being unable to help them increased the strain on our nerves.

That Gabor was Hungarian was a constant worry, but as the baroness reminded him: he was a famous artist. When new arrivals told stories about violence and close calls, I knew that Gabor was thinking, My negatives! My prints! Should I have been angry at him for caring so much about pictures when so many people were suffering? It wasn't as if we'd just met. I knew who he was, and I loved him.

Instead of gifts, the guests brought horror stories. The black jazz musicians had been rounded up and sent to camps. An official decree declared that jazz was a Jewish plot. Swastikas flapped from every monument, as the Nazis shoved our faces in the shit of defeat.

But eventually we began to hear that life was returning to normal. Or almost normal. Though obviously not for the Jews. I was sure, or almost sure, that the Germans weren't crazy enough to destroy our beautiful city. Hitler had always wanted to visit Paris in triumph. If there was no Paris, there would be no triumphal visit.

The Germans didn't want trouble. They wanted to smoke on the Métro, cut the lines at the theaters and opera, and look at naked girls. They adored the cafés and clubs, the Bal Tabarin, the Cigale, the Select. The overpriced tourist traps in Montmartre rose like phoenixes from the ashes.

The curfew was lifted, then clamped down again after a German official was stabbed. Did my German students say *parsnip* to mean the hours after which people could be shot for being on the street? A strict nine o'clock parsnip was imposed throughout the city.

Ultimately, the baroness was the one who suggested returning. At the time she had other guests, but she took Gabor and me aside.

She said, "Didi is there. Gabor's photos are there. Everything we love is in Paris."

Four of us traveled together in the Rossignol. Gabor and I rode behind the baroness and her Italian driver, Frank. I suspected that they were having an affair, but they were very discreet. One night, at an inn near Avignon, I thought I heard them in the room above ours. Gabor got annoyed when I asked him if he thought they were lovers. He was furious when I woke him to listen to them upstairs. I asked him if he was jealous. He said I knew him better than that. It made me happy to hear him say that I knew him better than to ask him what I'd asked.

There were roadblocks everywhere. The Germans examined our papers and calculated how much fun they could have. The luxuriousness of the baroness's car and the presence of a chauffeur said fun maybe, fun certainly, but possibly repercussions. It was easier and safer to have fun with the poor.

Later, those of us who survived were often quoted by journalists and interviewed by documentarians. We wrote best-selling memoirs and consulted on feature films. And if we were away from home when the Germans invaded, we made sure to say so. We wanted it known that we weren't trapped but *chose* to return and fight from within. One of the boldest heroines of the Resistance was in California on an academic fellowship with her husband and child. They came back to Paris from Berkeley. And the husband was Jewish! You can't blame people for wanting credit, for wanting the world to know how bravely they faced the threat of torture, prison, and death.

Didn't we do enough without also having to be humble? What does ego matter, even an ego like the baroness's, which burbles up through every word of her memoir, *A Baroness by Night*, and which must be part of the reason why her book has done so well.

Was everyone's motive pure? One didn't ask why people did what they did. I wish I could take credit for courage, pure and simple. But the truth was less exalted. I wanted to stay with my boyfriend. Gabor's life's work was in Paris. And I needed to be with my mother. It still shames me that I left her. Even after she'd outlasted the war by a decade and died peacefully in her own bed, even now I am certain that if there is a day of judgment, all my good deeds will be weighed against my having abandoned Mama during those critical months.

It was November 1940, when we got back to Paris. The city was foggy and cold. Even the cobblestones seemed tender, melancholy and fragile.

Rattling over the streets shook Gabor from sleep. He mumbled, "Mama, Papa. We're home."

I'd seen him do that before. The baroness turned around. It was an awkward moment. I was the one who knew what he said, half conscious. I was the one who squeezed his hand, hard enough to wake him fully.

Gabor said, "Look at that!" But we were already looking. Paris was dressed, like a stolen child, in the kidnapper's clothes. That our city had been humiliated only made us love her more.

I asked Frank to let me off a few blocks from my apartment. I ran the rest of the way with my cardboard suitcase banging against my shins. Mama rose to greet me and kissed my forehead as calmly as if I'd just returned from an afternoon at the language school.

How neatly the Germans sliced through our lives, separating past from present, so that the most tedious daily chores shimmered with nostalgia for a time when we hadn't appreciated how sweet tedium could be. What foolish things we'd worried about: breakups, sugar, tobacco. We'd taken for granted the freedom to go through the day without someone reminding you that he can spit on you, or shoot you, or send you to the Gestapo headquarters, where, one heard, interrogations had begun.

At first I thought I could keep my head down and wait out the Occupation. By now all my students were German. I told myself I could stay sane by playing those little jokes, sending them out with the wrong words for what they stole, for what they could force us to do. The Allies would win. Gabor and I would go back to our lives, our love deepened by what we'd been through.

Then I took the Métro and sat next to the German soldier, smoking.

Before the Occupation, a Métro ride was simply a trip from point A to point B. All that mattered was how far you were going and how well you knew the route. I was constantly back and forth from Gabor's studio to the language school to Mama's apartment. I was always going far, I always knew the route.

Even during those anxious months, there was plenty to look at: a child with a pig nose made from a pincushion tied on with ribbons. A woman in a red hat with a comet of pheasant feathers. A man in a cashmere overcoat with a doctor's bag and a black eye. A fur stole with a weasel's head missing one eye. A girl applying lipstick while the train pitched and rocked.

I'd always loved watching the students acting out their little dramas. When the kids exploded into the car, it was a welcome distraction from the grown-ups' faces on which, as the war approached, all one saw was worry. It felt wrong to be *interested* in how frightened people were.

But after the invasion, even the teenagers were afraid. They lost their natural boisterousness and became quiet and watchful. Worse things were happening. French boys were being deported. The Germans were murdering Jews, and French people were helping them do it. But when I saw the school kids, I thought, Their youth is being stolen, the only youth they will ever have. Instead of being focused on themselves, like normal adolescents, all they saw, all the rest of us saw, were the German soldiers smoking.

Surely it cannot be possible that during the entire Occupation I never once rode the Métro without seeing a German light up. But that is what I remember. I remember you couldn't avoid it.

Smoking in the Métro became illegal during the Occupation. But even before, no French person did it, except for the rare lunatic or drunk, whom their fellow passengers gently but firmly reprimanded. It was an unusual clause in the social contract, because in those days we smoked as we sang our children to sleep, smoked on the street, at the beach, in the bath. It was unheard of to have sex without afterward smoking in bed. And this was when tobacco was so scarce you smoked each stub till it burned your fingers, and then you went through the ashtrays and rerolled the butts. When the tobacconist could no longer be charmed out of a few strands, we smoked dried nettles or artichoke leaves, though it was hard on the throat.

Everyone on the train watched the smoking Germans, and when new passengers boarded, that was all they saw. After that the entire ride was about how each person reacted, whether we ignored it or rolled our eyes, too subtly to cause trouble. The smoking soldiers made a point of sitting next to elderly people, children, and pregnant women.

There was no point switching compartments. Not unless you wanted to ride with another German smoking in another car. How could we not feel defeated? Perhaps it was a low-cost form of psychological warfare.

It helped us build the Resistance. We learned how to communicate down the length of a Métro car with hardly an observable glance and not a word spoken.

One afternoon, a German officer sat beside me and lit up a cigar. He puffed a thick cloud in my face. He took off his glasses and wiped them to observe my reaction more clearly. He wasn't smiling, just looking. To see how I enjoyed it.

I liked the smell of cigars. Mama said that Papa used to smoke them in the toilet, which may explain why the smell of certain cigars can still make me burst into tears. But sitting beside the German, I thought, I am going to vomit. The door opened, and I rushed out, though it wasn't my station. I headed for the stairs and fought my way toward light and air.

There was my friend Ricardo, waiting to cross the street! My stomach felt instantly better. We were thrilled to see each other for the first time since the invasion. I asked Ricardo if he was working. Thanks to some miracle or bureaucratic oversight, they were still letting him practice surgery at the American hospital. Most foreign doctors and South Americans had been interned or deported.

I said, "They're letting you work because you're so good at it." He shrugged, then asked if I'd been in Paris the whole time. I said I'd been in the south with Gabor.

"Oh," he said. "You're still with him?"

I said, "Yes, we are very happy."

The moment I asked about Paul, I knew. It was terrible to see Ricardo's eyes glisten with tears. He said, "He's been deported. We assume he's somewhere in Germany."

"I'm so sorry," I said. *"We?"*

He took a closer look at me. A diagnostic look. I felt the anxiety one feels in the doctor's office. He asked why I'd seemed so upset when I surfaced from the Métro. I said it was nothing. A trivial annoyance.

In Gabor's portrait, Ricardo and Paul are costumed in silver paint and peacock feathers. The photo had always spooked Gabor. His mother had given him the crazy idea that peacock feathers were bad luck. His mother had been right.

I told Ricardo about the German soldier, smoking on the Métro. I said I'd had it up to here. I raised my hand above my head. He looked to see how high.

He said, "We think Paul is in a labor camp, but we can't find out where. The Red Cross is useless."

I couldn't stand to think of Paul being afraid or in pain. I hugged Ricardo for a long time. People walked around us. Ricardo looked at me again, and we had one of those moments of silent, 100 percent understanding.

He invited me to a party. A gathering of some friends. I knew what he meant: a party. I knew what he meant: some friends. I'd always had a gift for languages. Now I was learning a new one.

I should thank the cigar-smoking German, whoever he was. Perhaps he died in the war, or in prison, or years later in a hospital bed, from smoking-related causes. I'd like to tell him: you did me a favor. You and your filthy stinking cigar pushed me over the edge.

If it hadn't happened that day, it would have happened later. I would have reached the breaking point. Even so, I am grateful for the smoke that blew me out of the tunnel and into the arms of my old friend Ricardo de la Cadiz Blanca, a great hero of the Resistance.

From *A Baroness by Night*

BY LILY DE ROSSIGNOL

TO SAY THAT it was a confusing time is to put it mildly. No one knew what to do about the war and the Nazis and so forth. Later hardly anyone knew *why* they did what they did. Or *what* they did, for that matter. Most French people, including myself, settled on a story, stuck to it, and more or less believed it. I wish I could say that I returned to Paris from the south because my country was being trampled by swine. I wish I could pretend that I burrowed into the belly of the pig to fight the pig from within.

But the truth is that I went back to Paris for personal reasons, out of loyalty and love for my husband, Didi de Rossignol.

We'd heard that people were trickling back. Paris was safe, if you were French and rich and white and of course not Jewish. One needed a permit to return to the capital. As a Hungarian, Gabor needed a special permit. I reminded him that one could work miracles by offering the lawyers triple their normal fees. It was easier for his girlfriend. Her mother was in Paris, and Suzanne planned to resume her "career," teaching French to Nazis.

For some time I had been feeling the breath of that old dragon, boredom, toasting the back of my neck. There was nothing to do in the south, unless you liked to garden. After the war I saw Sartre's play *No Exit*, about those hysterics brutalizing one another in their one-room hell. I remember thinking we'd been fortunate at the château. At least Sartre wasn't there to lecture us about the meaning of existence. Hell, in that case, really would have been other people.

One night Didi phoned and said, *Good news!* We'd sold a car to some big shot Nazi. Then he said it again. *Good news*. He was trying to tell me something.

I remembered a dirty joke he used to think was terribly funny. I'd forgotten the details, but it was about sex and hell. The punch line was the devil saying, *Good news*, and describing an eternity of some grotesque sadomasochistic torture. Didi was telling me in code: he'd sold a sedan to the devil.

My husband wasn't a fanatic like his late brother Armand. But he was a loyal Frenchman, and it shamed him to do business with the Germans.

Were we traitors? I don't think so, and neither did the French government. After the war no charges were ever filed against us. We weren't making tanks but luxury cars of a breed so rarefied and expensive that Didi insisted on presiding over every sale. We never produced military transport vehicles, as did our competitor Louis Renault, who was prosecuted as a collaborator and died—*under mysterious circumstances*, as they always say.

What harm did selling a few cars do? Enabling a few porky Germans to take their mistresses out for a "picnic" in the country. It was an act of sabotage against high-ranking German wives and by extension their husbands. I always hoped that some wurst-stuffed fattie would screw his girlfriend in one of our cars and have a heart attack. We knew that it was only a matter of time before the Germans seized our factory and our business.

Everyone has an explanation for why they did what they did. Why they *had* to do what they did. My husband's factory employed over four hundred workers. Should their children have starved because Didi and I had *principles*? Should we have planted bombs or weakened the brake lines of the cars we sold to Germans? Four hundred families would have been on the street. Or in jail. How innocent we were compared to, let's say, our former employee, Lou Villars!

I decided to go back to Paris and help Didi face the stress. Later I found ways of reinvesting some of our profits so as to make up for who our customers—*some* of our customers—had been.

It was oddly pleasant, the drive back to Paris, considering that we were constantly being stopped and harassed by uniformed hooligans. Gabor and Suzanne sat in back. I rode up front with Frank, our driver, whom I would like to thank for, among other things, teaching me how to take sedative pills without water.

We made the trip in four days. I spent every night with Frank. If the Rossignol money ever runs out, and the value of my art collection plummets, I plan to fund my retirement with one of those books French women write for their American sisters. My book will describe in detail how a middle-aged baroness with a history of sexual and romantic disappointments could, at the eleventh hour, find erotic fulfillment with her Italian chauffeur, twenty years her junior. With Frank, I understood why people make such a fuss about sex, why they would do anything to lose themselves in that fog of bliss, to feel as if they are sharing a dream with another person.

I know there will be readers who can only see through the reductive lens of social class, wealth, and power. Such small-minded prudes will naturally conclude that a woman like myself could only let down her defenses and experience pleasure with a social inferior. All I can tell these bigoted snobs is that, if kindness, patience, imagination, and sexual know-how are the exclusive territory of the working classes, then I had been born—or rather, married—into the wrong province.

Not for one instant did Frank or I imagine that our fling would last beyond the moment we saw the roofs of Paris. But our on-the-road affair was a lovely surprise.

In memory, the warmth of desire fills the luxury sedan as we sped along those misty country roads, past oily black trees, rubble, the muddy earth scarred by war. I remember the touch of Frank's hand against the small of my back while our passengers slept like babies. It was the closest I have ever come to a conventional domestic scene: Frank and I playing Mama and Papa, while our children, Gabor and Suzanne, snoozed in the backseat, and we headed into the wicked heart of Nazi-occupied France.

Bounced awake by cobblestones on a suburban street, Gabor and Suzanne leaned forward. Frank returned both hands to the wheel.

Half asleep, Gabor mumbled, "Mama, Papa, we're home."

Back in Paris!
December 1, 1940

Dear parents,

As you know, you and I have now become official allies, or unofficial enemies, depending on whether one thinks that Hungary's being forced to join the Axis puts us on the same side, or in opposing camps. What if this letter were read by the censors in France or in our homeland? Would they come after me, or—my hand trembles—would they hunt you down? My fear of that is so profound that this letter will never be mailed but will join the growing pile of aerograms I put aside to send when we can again communicate safely. Before my courage failed, I sent you a few letters. But they were returned, and I have stopped trying.

You must know many Hungarian boys who have been drafted to fight for the Nazis or to work in German factories. For the moment I am, believe it or not, above the age of conscription. But every day the parameters are widened to fill the need for cannon fodder and free labor. I know you would not want that for me, though I suspect there are times when you think, At least a soldier's parents get letters home from the front!

I am keeping these unsent letters in the box in which I have saved our correspondence. That box was among the things that drew me back to Paris from the south. I couldn't bear to imagine your letters falling into the hands of the vandals who might invade my studio and help themselves to my prints.

Everyone knew that I worried about my work. But I could tell no one, not even Suzanne, how I feared for a box of letters. Leaving them behind was one of the foolish choices that I, like so many Parisians, made in panic and haste.

A blazing poker pierces my chest when I open the box and Mama's potpourri rises from the blue paper strudel. I would give *anything* to wake up tomorrow and find a letter fretting about my insomnia, which is worse than ever since the curfew was reimposed. Now, as we move from shadow to shadow, we can be shot at by drunken soldiers.

I cannot describe the longing I feel to see you. Only with you can I recall certain incidents from my childhood. Only you will understand that I am telling you the *real* truth about what life is like now. The incident of the caterpillar. The incident of the landlady's goose. The incident of the algebra teacher. The incident of the butcher boy and the broken bottle. The incident of the hotel maid. The incident of the beehive. Especially the beehive.

I have forgotten how to pray, but I entrust us all to Mama's prayers, if prayers are permitted under the new dispensation. Papa, you would know the name of the poet who said, "Shorter are the prayers in bed, but more heartfelt." A poem about a medieval knight on the eve of a battle. I think you'd translated it from German, but I am not even sure of that.

I should throw this letter in the fire. But though I am a coward, I will keep it with the others and give it to you when the war is over and I can deliver it in person.

Till then, from your son who thinks of you always,
Gabor

From *The Devil Drives:*
The Life of Lou Villars
BY NATHALIE DUNOIS

Chapter Twelve: A City at War

LOU VILLARS HAD mixed feelings when Germany invaded France. As a patriotic Frenchwoman, she was naturally less than delighted to see a giant swastika hanging from the Arc de Triomphe, German soldiers goose-stepping down the Champs-Élysées, and signposts in German measuring the distance to Berlin from the Bastille. But she understood that this was a temporary situation. A temporary *inconvenience*, like leaving one's car in the shop for repairs.

The Germans weren't annexing France but *fixing* it. Their ministers and soldiers were visionary mechanics. In a reasonably short time they would leave her country—tuned up, restored, cleansed of grime and grease, strong and efficient enough to function as an essential component of the engine propelling a Nazified Europe into the future. As she told the customers who brought their vehicles into her garage, These things can't be rushed.

Lou and Inge and doubtless quite a few Germans were the only people who knew what Lou had done to help bring this about. Lou's opinion was that she deserved neither blame nor credit. Well, maybe a little credit.

Sooner or later, the Germans would have found a way to breach the French defenses. More soldiers might have been killed. She had done France a favor, even if others might not see it that way. Eventually, they would find out—and thank her. She would be a heroine, the Joan of Arc of the Franco-German peace détente.

Meanwhile, she and Inge would resume their glamorous prewar life in France and Berlin. There would be invitations to parties, delicious food, champagne, a generous travel budget in return for the occasional item of local gossip.

When she heard that the Führer had paid a surprise visit to Paris, Lou felt as if a close relative had come to town without letting her know. It consoled her that he'd arrived at dawn and stayed only a few hours, just long enough for a whirlwind tour of the high spots. Most likely the thoughtful Führer didn't want to wake her.

When the clocks in Paris were set ahead an hour to run on the same time as Berlin, Lou thought it would be easier to call Inge, who was getting harder to reach. Often Inge's maid said that she was out and would call back. She was busy.

Lou checked the mail several times daily, but the invitations to the diplomatic parties never arrived, a mystery that she had more (too much!) spare time in which to contemplate. Because of the gasoline shortage, many of her former customers kept their cars garaged.

Now her clients were mostly Vichy officials and high-ranking Germans. Lou knew that some of her neighbors disapproved. Let them turn up their noses! A carburetor had no politics. Who cared whose engines needed work, as long as their owners paid? If Lou were making more money, she could afford to be choosy.

Inge still came for long weekends of road trips, espionage, and increasingly rushed, tepid sex. Lou and Inge had documents that allowed them free passage, but being stopped at the checkpoints and roadblocks made travel slower and more stressful.

Everyone was wary, even Lou and Inge's friends. The most trusting souls in the sports clubs were suddenly curious: why did Lou and Inge want to know? Fortunately, alcohol—even the homemade wine and beer, which was frequently all they could get—still worked magic. Two glasses of wine, a few mugs of beer, and everyone remembered the good times, the confidences they'd shared.

Now the gossip typically involved someone harboring a British soldier or a Jew, or distributing an anti-German pamphlet.

"Boring," said Inge. "Why should I care?"

Why? Because the outcome of the war might turn on the information they provided. Because they were saving innocent French and German lives. More than ever, the future of France depended on the alertness, the courage, the steadfastness of its citizens.

Just as she had with Arlette, Lou responded to her lover's growing coolness by inventing unlikely scenarios on the theme of her own importance, tall tales meant to remind Inge of how lucky she was to be with her. Did Inge know that Heydrich had sent Lou a message expressing his personal gratitude and the Führer's best wishes? No, Inge did not know.

Partly thanks to the shortages of laundry soap and fuel for heating water, the country inns that had once seemed so charming now seemed merely unclean. Lou tried not to think about those first balmy nights in Berlin, when she and Inge had longed to stay awake forever. Now Inge seemed sleepy and impatient for the sex to end. Afterward she rolled to the far edge of the bed while Lou stared into the darkness, resolving to drink less and earn more—enough money to buy the gifts that might show Inge how much she was loved.

In Paris Inge did nothing but complain. It was dull compared to Berlin. Didn't Lou know one amusing person in the entire city? Lou heard from a customer, a German general's wife, that Inge's racing career was not what it had been when the party came to power. What did Inge expect? There was a war going on. Though the Führer had promised that German drivers would beat the rest of world, even loyal racing fans had turned their attention elsewhere. Whenever Lou felt overwhelmed by worries about the garage, or depressed by the widening distance between herself and Inge, she recalled her dinner with the Führer and vowed to remain the person he'd entrusted with a sacred mission.

One rainy weekend Lou and Inge went to Rouen, where Lou was scheduled to speak to women who had stayed focused on physical fitness even as rationing made it a challenge to eat well. The hall was chilly, the lecture underattended. Just as Lou was talking about the honor of being invited to the city where Joan of Arc died for France, someone's stomach grumbled. More intestinal noises chorused around the drafty room, as if the women's digestive systems were having a parallel conversation.

Lou ended her speech to a scatter of relieved applause. She and Inge dined on greasy sausage and overcooked peas in a café where the lighting made its customers look like victims of liver disease. Having drunk more than they should, they returned to their hotel room. Dressed in a bulky sweater and a stained lime green slip, Inge sat on the edge of the bed, paring her toenails and cursing when her manicure scissors nicked her toe and blood dripped onto the sheets.

It depressed Lou to remember the time when so many of Inge's sentences had ended with exclamation points. Now they were bursts of anger or ellipses of vague complaint.

Later Lou would try to recall how the argument had started. What had possessed her to suggest that Inge had never loved her, that she'd only been with Lou because of . . . because of their work. She couldn't bring herself to say what exactly their work was. If Inge left her, she would never again find someone with whom to share the guilt and the pride.

Their next trip was to Angers to check out a tip about a Resistance group infiltrating a factory that manufactured parts for tanks. They waited for hours in a smoky café, but the women—their friends and informants—never showed up. Inge took it personally. Not even ignorant peasant gymnasts wanted to waste an evening with them, though Inge would have bought the drinks.

The weather was bad, the road slippery, the drive back to Paris slow. Inge missed the last train to Berlin and had to stay until Monday.

On Monday morning Inge slept late. Lou went down to the garage. That afternoon, when Inge came downstairs to say good-bye and tell Lou that she would be busy for the next few weeks and not to bother calling, Lou was occupied with a regular customer, a man by the name of Jean-Claude Bonnet.

Several books have been written about the career of Jean-Claude Bonnet, focusing on his activities during the Occupation. Though each author argues for a slightly different view of his role in the most despicable crimes committed against the French, they all agree that he excelled at maintaining a false identity, staying behind the scenes, and serving (at least nominally) as the deputy minister of information in the Paris office of the Reich. He was an excellent recruiter and an exacting boss. His photos show a tall, thin, dapper aristocrat dressed in tailored suits and paisley silk cravats, always wearing sunglasses, which along with his pallor and his white-blond hair, fed the (in my opinion, false) rumor that he was an albino.

During intense conversations, Bonnet would remove his glasses, revealing two ordinary (if rather small) blue eyes, perpetually pink rimmed, like the eyes of those ghostly marsupials that lumber onto the highway at night. Soft-spoken and impeccably polite, he had many eccentricities, among them an obsession with cleanliness and germs, so that he was unable to shake someone's hand without interposing a handkerchief between his palm and theirs. He was sensitive to cigarette smoke; no one could smoke in his presence. Though in public places, Bonnet made an exception.

Despite these oddities, Bonnet was known for his personal charm. During the interrogations at the French Gestapo headquarters in the rue Lauriston, he would knock politely, enter the cell, and try to persuade the prisoners to tell him what they knew. Bonnet knew that he wouldn't succeed. It was a form of theater.

He would mime disappointment before he left the cell and sent in the torturers to try another approach. So one might say that his theater of charm was the first act of torture. That was what the courts ruled, though it had little effect, since by then Bonnet was gone, some said to Paraguay, others said to Argentina, where he was later hired, by Stroessner, or Perón, once again demonstrating that the truly evil never stay unemployed for long.

During his time in France, Bonnet modestly acknowledged that he was the grandnephew of the late Eduard Bonnet, a decorated veteran of World War I and the founder of several influential right-wing organizations. Eventually it would come out that he was neither a nephew of *the* Bonnet, nor was his real name Jean-Claude Bonnet.

In fact he was a German, Fritz Schreiber, a name under which, after the war, he was found guilty of crimes against the citizenry of France and sentenced to ten years in prison, a judgment never carried out, his escape to South America having been facilitated by the Church.

What had brought Bonnet to Lou's garage was his 1939 black 540K Mercedes-Benz Cabriolet B: a gorgeous vehicle, very rare. Hermann Göring drove one. Considering how expensive Bonnet's car was, Lou was appalled to discover that it suffered from more problems than she would have expected to find under the hood of a cheap Citroën. In peacetime Bonnet could have sent it back to the manufacturer, but thanks to the war, the company had other things to do besides finetune a custom-made roadster.

Bonnet soon became Lou's best client, if such a thing could be said about the owner of a car on which, as soon as something was fixed, something else broke down. He never once complained about the cost or the inconvenience.

Whenever he had to leave his car in Lou's garage, he was driven away in a sedan with windows so dark that Lou couldn't tell if the driver was military or police. Lou never asked what Bonnet did, and he never said.

On the afternoon Inge stopped by the garage to tell Lou that she'd be unreachable for the next few weeks, Lou and Bonnet were watching the Mercedes emit ominous curls of black smoke. Bonnet held a handkerchief soaked in cologne over his nose and mouth.

When Inge appeared, she and Bonnet regarded each other with such avid interest that it would have seemed rude not to introduce them. When Bonnet shook Inge's hand, he pretended he'd absentmindedly forgotten to put his handkerchief away.

Bonnet said, "*The* Inge Wallser? The famous auto racer?"

Inge flashed him her public smile, perfected in the glare of flashbulbs. "*The* Bonnet?"

Bonnet said, "His unworthy nephew." Then he asked Inge a question in surprisingly good German. Inge glared at Lou, as if she should know the answer. Bonnet chuckled and said something else. This time Inge smiled. What was Lou supposed to do? Break up the intimate German tête-à-tête between her customer and her girlfriend?

She said, "Friday evening at six, you can collect your car."

Bonnet thanked her and told Inge, in French, that it had been a pleasure to meet her.

Bonnet's sedan had barely left the curb when Inge exploded.

Lou didn't understand why *she* was behaving like the injured victim. Inge had been the one flirting with Bonnet.

It was unbearable, Inge shouted, she simply couldn't endure it! Apparently Bonnet had said he couldn't understand why he hadn't run into Inge at any of the fabulous parties that Ambassador Abetz was giving on the rue de Lille, or the Luftwaffe General Hanesse's marvelous soirees in the former Rothschild mansion. Inge was too ashamed to say she hadn't been invited. She'd let him think she was too busy. But she wasn't busy! She never went anywhere or did anything. And all because of Lou!

No wonder they had no social life! Who would want to spend time with a not very bright, not very pretty, alcoholic mechanic in filthy coveralls? A bore with only one story, which she told over and over, about how she was almost a champion until her racing career crashed and burned because of her gender and how she dressed. Who wanted to hear *that*? Whenever Lou got really drunk, she'd maunder on about the dead crazy brother. Had no one informed her about the Führer's views on the insane and feebleminded? These vampire parasites could not be allowed to continue sucking vital energy from the healthy population. Hadn't Lou heard Hitler's plan? After the Olympics were permanently relocated to Berlin, only German athletes would be allowed to compete, and only after they'd passed a blood test establishing the Aryan purity of every drop of blood in their veins.

Inge lit a cigarette and flipped the match onto the floor.

Lou said, "Darling, be careful, please, don't smoke in the garage."

Inge started ranting again, this time on the subject of France. Didn't Lou know that the Führer had called the French a Negroid,

Yiddified race? Or that he'd sworn the two countries would never in a million years merge under the flag of the thousand-year Reich?

Lou felt something she'd never felt before, not when she'd fought the boxer in the shed in Amiens, not when she'd punched the referee in Louvain. She wanted to smash Inge's face in, just until she stopped talking. An animal impulse to silence a sound: a sound attached to a person.

When, in my research, I realized this, I allowed myself to hope that I had found a major clue to the mystery of Lou Villars. Isn't wanting to smash someone's face another step along the path that would take Lou from one circle of hell to another, until she ended up smashing faces in the infernal headquarters of the Gestapo? Yet as I continued writing, certain events too personal to be mentioned here made me begin to think that no normal woman does what Lou Villars did just because of a failed romance. Besides, she'd already committed what were arguably her most serious (indeed historic) crimes when she and Inge were still in love—or anyway, so Lou thought.

Inge left Paris, presumably for Berlin. That evening when Lou returned to her flat, she found that Inge had taken all her possessions and quite a few of Lou's.

The next days were among the saddest yet. Lou was lonely, underemployed, worried (along with everyone else) about getting enough to eat. It didn't help to remind herself that she'd weathered hard times before, to recall the day when Chanac had forced her to clean library paste off his upholstery, or how blue she'd been just before she was invited to the Olympics. Once more God had abandoned the lowliest of his creatures, an auto mechanic in a city whose residents rode bikes. How could she convince herself that life would improve when she could still recall every cruel, true word that Inge had said?

On the night after Inge left, Lou headed for the Chameleon Club without having decided what to do when she got there. The sounds of laughter and conversation drifted across the street. Lou pulled up her collar and hurried off, afraid that someone might see her.

The only people she talked to that week were Carburetor Sammy and Marcel the Manifold, whom she found playing a melancholy game of double solitaire at the Le Hippo, where she'd gone to find the parts for Bonnet's Mercedes. Even the gangsters had run out of alcohol and tobacco, so that the business transaction was brief, subdued, and to the point.

That Friday, dreading the weekend ahead, she was preparing to close the garage when Jean-Claude Bonnet returned to pick up his car. Lou showed him how the engine purred when she turned on the ignition, but Bonnet seemed distracted and asked if they could speak in private.

Lou took Bonnet to her office behind the garage. On the wall was a calendar on which a young woman wearing only an ermine hat and collar was ice-skating, balancing on one leg, the other knee cocked behind her, looking back over her shoulder with a devilish smile

Lou would have liked to offer Bonnet a drink, but on account of the shortages . . . Bonnet said that the shortages were something they could discuss. He hoped he wasn't presuming if he said he thought it was a pity that a woman with Lou's talents should be working (or *not* working) as an ordinary mechanic. Not to undervalue the importance of mechanics! When something went wrong with your car, you needed a mechanic more than a movie star or a champion athlete or even (dare he say) a military or political leader. But an individual with Lou's experience and skills . . . Again Bonnet didn't mean to pry. But could he ask how Lou's business was doing?

Lou said she had no complaints.

Bonnet said he was glad to hear that; he disliked complainers. "So perhaps we should get to the point. I have been appointed deputy minister of information and public relations. I report directly to the German ambassador, Herr Otto Abetz, a civilized fellow whom I know from the world of journalism, long before the war.

"We want you to work for us. You were among our most resourceful and valuable agents. We know you worked with a German citizen. But you were the heart and soul of the operation."

Lou *had* been the heart and soul of her partnership with Inge. No one had ever said that before. No one had ever noticed.

Once more, Lou's private disaster had turned out to have a bright side. Doubtless, meeting Inge in the garage had made Bonnet suspect that there might be more to Lou than was visible on the surface. He must have done some research and unearthed certain facts that, Lou hoped, would be harder for an ordinary person to discover.

Bonnet said, "The Führer has not forgotten you. He is grateful for your support."

An hour before, Lou had been feeling as if she had disappeared from the surface of the earth. And all that time she'd been present in the mind and heart of the Führer!

Bonnet explained that he was putting together a team of community liaison workers. And because of Lou's connections in the auto business, the athletic community, the racing world, and (to be frank) the underworld, she was perfect for this program, which had a budget large enough to let Lou live modestly, but well. And she might find the job interesting. Most of Bonnet's team did.

Her information-gathering duties would resemble the work she had done with Inge. The Occupation forces—the *temporary* Occupation forces—would find it helpful to know who had cars. Who went for a drive in the country. Who was trying to sell an automobile. Who was looking to buy one. Who had money. Who was offering what goods, for how much, on the black market. Who possessed more gasoline ration cards than they should.

Bonnet assured her that no one would get in trouble as a result of Lou's reports. On the contrary, she would be helping to maintain the peace. The idea that she was saving lives enabled her to overcome her disdain for snitches, along with the suspicion that she was being asked to be one.

In the absence of diaries, firsthand sources, or reliable informants, no one will ever know what Lou Villars told herself or what she thought she was doing. She was not, as she'd always feared, a stupid woman. She was, however, limited. Subtleties enraged her, and anything ambiguous seemed to conceal a possible insult. Also she was resentful. Life had not gone her way.

Bonnet asked if she knew Louis Renault, the auto manufacturer.

Lou said she'd met him briefly when she worked for the Rossignols. Bonnet said that was perfect.

Her first assignment would be fun. At least he hoped she would think so. He wanted Lou to approach Louis Renault and say she needed his help. His advice. A group of German archaeologists were planning an expedition to the basin of the Tigris. They needed the latest technologies for making rubber tires for the vehicles that would transport them to the ruins of ancient civilizations.

Everyone knew that this was not about archaeology but about the invasion of whatever desert country the Germans were planning to invade next. Lou didn't say this to Renault, and she didn't have to. Everyone knew that his factories would be requisitioned if he refused.

Arguably, Louis Renault wasn't nearly so guilty as the manufacturers of Zyklon B or the V-2 rocket. Or for that matter, Lou. But even if the crimes he was being asked to commit were relatively minor, no one wanted to tell Louis Renault that the Germans needed tracks for their tanks.

They sent Lou. She said *archaeology*. She said *ancient civilizations*. Everyone went home happy. Except Monsieur Renault.

Lou had a good laugh at that. *Archaeology* meant *invasion*. The Germans were translating French into something better than French. You had to admire their nerve.

Bonnet gave Lou his solemn word: no one would know about their work. He would continue to bring his Mercedes in for repairs, a cover for their debriefings. Secrecy was a matter of life and death, considering that Lou would be reporting on the activities of the Gasparu-Chanac gang. Lou was tickled to have found a way of revenging herself on Chanac—and getting paid for it. Though for now she thought it best not to probe too deeply into what the gang was doing, aside from fencing auto parts. She wasn't getting paid enough to cross them.

Bonnet brought his Mercedes into the shop whenever something went wrong. Something was always going wrong. As promised, he helped Lou deal with the shortage of basic goods. He made sure she had extra ration cards for food and coupons for whiskey, which he viewed as a work-related expense. A drink now and then would help her deal with the stress of taking on an additional job.

Sheltered from prying eyes by the raised hood of the Mercedes, Lou told Bonnet that a grocer had brought in a Citroën with bullet holes in the passenger door. Why did Bonnet think a museum curator would ask a gangster if he could procure explosives? A nervous stranger had come in with a decommissioned military ambulance. Could Lou build some storage space underneath the chassis?

Even as Lou's downward slide was gathering momentum, she prided herself on maintaining certain standards and on not losing touch, as so many of her neighbors were, with basic human decency and compassion. She was slow to come on board with the measures against the Jews, however much she personally disliked them. She knew that harsh tactics were sometimes required. She'd waited on line at the Palais Berlitz to see an informative exhibition entitled "The Jew and France," where a display confirmed what she'd long suspected: behind every historic scandal lurked a Jew. Still, she didn't enjoy seeing children herded through the streets at gunpoint. Once she was almost hurt by some idiot cops hurling crockery down from an apartment at a terrified Jewish family being loaded into a van.

At the same time, she believed that an elastic adaptability was one hallmark of adulthood—of being a *French* adult. And so she acclimated herself to disturbing sights. She was relieved and frankly glad when the Jew who owned her garage was forced to sign it over to her and subsequently deported.

Lou became a good citizen of Nazi-occupied Paris, working for the Ministry of Information, glad that she was no longer an obscure garage mechanic but a person of importance with a respectable, if secret, position. No longer did she look in the mirror and see a former champion reduced to rotating tires. The philosophers can say what they want about the banality of evil. But for Lou Villars, obtaining information, eventually with violence, was in every way less banal than replacing a radiator hose.

Picasso and Me
With a preface and photos by Gabor Tsenyi
(Revised for the 1970 edition)

THROUGH THE WORST of the Occupation, publishers survived. There was never enough toilet paper to wipe the asses of Paris, but books were still printed and sold to a fortunate few. Early in 1942, the director of Editions du Nord commissioned me to take the photographs for a volume of Picasso's work.

Like everyone but a few artistic rivals and disgruntled former mistresses, I idolized Picasso, the genius of our age. I'd met him in cafés, and several times at the home of my friend the baroness Lily de Rossignol. But not until we began working together did Picasso and I ever have a serious talk about art.

We'd had one brief, unsatisfactory exchange, which was already our little joke. That was in the late 1920s. Picasso was already famous. But it would be years before my first book, *Lovers at the Chameleon Club, Paris 1932* established my reputation.

It took an entire bottle of wine for me to get up the nerve to invite the great man to visit my studio. I was shocked when he showed up, though, on the chance that he might appear, I had bought a bottle of Spanish brandy, ten times what I could afford.

He would have loved some brandy but was in a hurry and couldn't stay. He shuffled through my photos, then glanced at some pencil sketches and told me that, in his opinion, I would be better off sticking to drawing. After he left I sat on the floor and drank all the brandy. Later we would laugh about this. He'd blamed it on a bad mood. But this hasty judgment passed by the master on the younger artist's work was, for several years, a source of uneasiness, even tension, between us.

But all that had ended long before 1942. The war and the Occupation had put our trivial ego and aesthetic quarrels into perspective. I was flattered because Picasso asked the publishers to hire me. I was, and still am, proud to have helped create the volume that is being reprinted in a handsome new edition.

My friends were less thrilled by the project. The baroness de Rossignol, and my future wife, Suzanne, both heroines of the Resistance, warned me that I was being used to produce a catalogue from which the Germans could choose what they wanted when they raided Picasso's studio and took the best pieces, just as they'd cherry-picked the gems from Jewish collections. I told them that if the Germans wanted an inventory of Picasso's sculptures, they could take their own photos; the pictures would just be worse. If the work was stolen, at least we would have an accurate record of our looted patrimony.

Opinion was divided about how safe Picasso was. Some people said he was too famous for the Germans to touch, too rich, too well connected. On the other hand, he was a foreigner, a Spaniard who never bothered hiding how much he hated Franco. If Franco demanded his extradition, France might turn him over.

It was rumored that he gave money to the Resistance and hid refugees in his apartment. And what was this *world opinion* the Germans didn't want turning against them? The Allies wouldn't drop one bomb more or less if a painter was arrested. The Germans preferred to keep him in Paris, to pacify the public and enjoy the sadistic pleasure of making the rebel genius be polite to the Nazis, though he never went that "extra mile," as many artists did.

Always in civilian clothes, Germans showed up at Picasso's studio—once, sometimes twice a week. Picasso was famously picky about who he would admit: only friends, friends of friends, sometimes not even lovers. But he let in the Germans. He'd hired a pretty,

German-speaking girl whose only job was to follow them around and monitor what they were looking at and saying.

The whole time we worked together, I was afraid that a Nazi would arrive and force me to watch a human gorilla pawing through pure gold. But it never happened, whether through luck or because we were being watched. They chose their own times to visit.

Lots of gossip was circulating about Picasso and the Germans, all of which made him look good. There is always one person the dictators allow to thrive, if only to make everyone else feel worse. Some people said these tales of courage were true, some said that Picasso made them up. He gets credit for making them up. We needed them, true or not.

We liked the story of how the German "guests" asked about Picasso's Afghan hound, Kazbek, and he claimed that the Afghan was a eugenically purebred dachshund. We laughed about how, when the Luftwaffe officer looked at *Guernica* and asked Picasso, "Did you do this?" Picasso said, "No, *you* did." People said he used to talk about Hitler riding on Mussolini's shoulders through a swamp of shit.

We'd say, The Spaniard has balls! We needed him to have balls. No one who wasn't alive then can understand what those stories meant to us. Humor was in short supply. Picasso's presence in Paris—like mine, I must say—was a political act. It made it an even greater honor that I was chosen to document his work.

Although my parents raised me to be as superstitious as only a Hungarian can be, I was by then semirecovered from my Oriental childhood. So I wasn't entirely paralyzed by a portentous event that happened en route to my first professional visit to Picasso.

I was passing the Hotel Lutetia, which had been requisitioned as luxury housing for Nazi counterespionage and military intelligence agents. Normally, I went out of my way to avoid the hotel that, in happier times, had let better-dressed artists drink in the bar, on credit. Picasso had stayed there, which may have been the force that drew me, unconsciously, into its evil orbit. So intent was I, so focused on the meeting ahead, that I suddenly looked up and found myself beneath the hotel's facade, which resembles a palace constructed of melting ice cream.

I crossed the street. A mistake. Opposite the Lutetia was the Santé prison. I'd photographed it late one night when the shadows were especially dark. Now its fortress walls looked threatening even in broad daylight.

On the corner a grizzled old fellow was selling black market ladies' silk stockings stretched out on a filthy white towel. I *had* to take a picture of that chorus line of ghost legs against the frayed terry cloth curtain. But first I had to pay off the guy and promise that his face wouldn't appear in the photo. As I set up the shot, I asked why he didn't just cross the street and sell inside the hotel, to the Germans.

Two Maltese toughs controlled the territory. They would beat him senseless.

Both of us were nervous. We sensed a hundred pairs of eyes—the eyes of spies and secret operatives—watching us from the windows.

I should have thought a million times before picking up my camera. Was that what people mean when they talked about being willing to die for your art? Taking pictures of *anything* carried a serious risk. Any German could knock your camera out of your hands if he'd had too much to drink or just didn't like your face. I'd gotten good at ducking into doorways. Several friends had had their cameras smashed.

I didn't care. I wanted that shot. I wanted to buy a pair of stockings for Suzanne and another for the baroness. Small tokens of my gratitude. How patient and kind those women were!

Someone grabbed me from behind. Two helmeted German soldiers tossed me between them like a rag doll. Eventually they got bored with the game and demanded to see my papers. Was I by any chance a Hungarian spy?

I said, No, I was an artist. On my way to visit Picasso.

One of them pulled a gun on me and said if I moved he would shoot me.

He said, "Admit you're a Hungarian spy."

I said, "All right. You've got me. I'm not really *an artist*. I'm an *amateur* on my way to a private studio where I plan to take . . . *certain pictures*."

The older soldier asked what did I mean by *certain pictures*?

I said, "Artistic pictures of naked French women." The older guy looked at the younger one, who, after a brief hesitation, asked if this studio was nearby. The older one explained that this was precisely the sort of filth that needed to be mopped up. I said I had the address, which I would be happy to give them. I had in mind a real place, which made the conversation easier. But the address I gave them was that of the government office that monitored resident aliens in Paris.

The older German returned my camera. He said, "Go on, get out. We don't want to see your ugly mug again. And you'd better keep away from that whorehouse you mentioned." I promised yes on both counts, and they let me go.

It took another twenty minutes to walk to Picasso's. I had time to calm down. But my shoulders hurt where the soldiers had grabbed me, and I was still breathing hard when I climbed Picasso's famously steep, dark staircase. I promised myself to quit smoking. Such was my state of mind as I pulled myself up to my full height and knocked on Picasso's door.

Picasso appeared, grinning up at me with that white, startled-clown face. I felt my knees bend on their own, to equalize our heights. The last thing the world needs is another description of what a shrimp Picasso was. So let me say that I was short. But Picasso was shorter.

As I looked into those blazing anthracite eyes, I thought of my old friend Lionel Maine, who had gone back to the States. Lionel, my lost brother. I tried to remember what he'd said about Picasso's eyes, something about a magic dog in a fairy tale.

Picasso wore a gray jacket, gray pants, gray cotton shirt. Another thing one heard was that he dressed to match the dust that collected in his studio, the dust he called his alarm system because it alerted him when anything was touched. His suit was costlier than it looked. I'd been around enough to know that, though my own fashion taste ran to baggy overcoats with pockets I measured by how many glass plates they held.

Picasso slapped me on the back. I winced. I considered telling him about the incident with the stockings and the German soldiers, because it was a good story, and because it might impress Picasso, who had shown such bravery in painting *Guernica* and letting it be shown. Picasso and I were resisters. We worked on a small scale, on our own. Soldiers armed with art. I decided against it. I was afraid that Picasso would figure out how scared I'd been.

During the months after the invasion, when I'd stayed with the baroness in the south, Picasso was at the beach in Royan. But he'd run out of canvas. He decided he would rather die than not paint. He'd keep working and hope for the best.

Ever since the day I'm describing, I've had a recurring dream of wandering through a portal into a glittering, cobwebbed chamber filled with treasure, a magical curio shop. I wake from these dreams in bliss, knowing that the god of sleep has carried me back to that studio, dismantled decades ago, which now lives only in memory—and in the photographs that I and others took.

How could such a place vanish? Why can't I go back, even once? I dream of walking through a door, and there they are, waiting for me, like guests at a surprise party: the brothel girls, the gangsters, the thieves. Where have they disappeared to? I might think I had imagined it all if I didn't have my photos to remind me that Picasso's Paris studio existed—and that I, Gabor Tsenyi, was there.

I thought I'd photographed the range and variety of the nests that artists build in which to hatch their ideas. Giacometti with his Etruscan tomb; Kokoschka's grand white parlor empty but for one painting, a huge mirror, and his life-size Alma Mahler doll; Brancusi cooking succulent lunches on his roaring forge; Monsieur Matisse with his giant birdcage and the naked models who were always in attendance, and who made his studio my personal favorite.

But I had never been confronted with *so much* to look at, such a profusion of *things* crammed into the labyrinths connecting grand salons, pyramids of empty cigarette packs piled against gilded mirrors; corners arranged like shamanic altars to an animal god who demanded moth-eaten taxidermy, skeletons, and seashells. Canvases were stacked everywhere, on easels, against the wall. Painted faces peeked at me from behind the crude votive idols dressed in artists' smocks, holding brushes and palettes.

I could write this whole preface about how the light shone down from the mullioned windows, onto the tables piled with papers and books, the heaps of metal scraps, the plaster cast of the artist's hand. It didn't require a palm reader to trace the lines of his greatness. The African figurines, the pitch-covered goddess bristling with nails, the Cycladic nude emitting the sharp, salt-and-vinegar smell of something brined on the ocean floor.

I had often participated in that ritual of the studio visit, with its special chemistry of the professional and the friendly, the casual and the official, its ballet of how the visitor moves through space, where he stops, what he passes, says and doesn't say. It was a test of one's tact, judgment, aesthetic, not to mention one's ability to come up with a perceptive or witty remark. It was even trickier when so many of the paintings were portraits of Picasso's mistress Dora Maar, her face sliced apart and reassembled, weeping, wracked with psychic pain. What could I say? Are these Dora? You've made her look so . . . what?

At last I came upon an earlier, happier portrait of a woman holding an artichoke. I suppose I must have chuckled.

"What's so funny?" asked Picasso.

"That artichoke," I said. "The most Cubist of vegetables."

"My point, exactly!" Picasso said. "From now on, everyone who eats an artichoke will be dining on a Picasso!"

From the corner of my eye I saw something that I was never able to capture on film. My photo of it exists. But now that every grade-school art-class student knows that a bicycle seat can be made to look like a bull's head, I can no longer describe what it was like to discover, for the first time, that an artist could see a mythical *toro* where the bicyclist puts his ass.

Picasso said, "It's a miracle that it doesn't take off and trot back to the pasture."

I laughed to convey my admiration for his imagination, his creativity. Did it matter that I knew he'd said the same thing countless times before?

He showed me into a room whose walls were covered with tribal masks. He said he'd bought these "diplomats of the sacred" from an artist who'd gone mad. Like his idol Gauguin, the poor fellow had gone to live with a primitive tribe. But unlike Gauguin, he'd discovered that his new friends and family were hunting heads while he lived among them.

Was Picasso unaware that this anecdote was in my friend Lionel's *Make Yourself New*? Had he not read this banned masterpiece that, serialized in *Demain* and other avant-garde magazines, had achieved an underground reputation? I wished Lionel were in Paris, so I could meet him for a drink and report that Picasso was still telling the same story. Though maybe it was fortunate. Lionel's vanity could be easily wounded when he realized that someone—especially someone like Picasso—had never read his work.

What followed was one of those instances for which the master was famous, when it seemed that those blazing-coal eyes read your mind like the Spanish Gypsies from whom, before people found out the truth, Picasso claimed to be descended.

He said, "Let me show you a drawing that was inspired by that American, your writer friend. What was his name? Leon something. Typical American. Naive. Like little children. He was explaining how enlightened and civilized the French are. So I made him this picture"— Picasso led me across his studio until we were standing in front of a framed drawing of a guillotine.

I could hear Lionel ranting about how much he'd wanted the drawing and how Picasso had grinned as he grabbed it. Back in New Jersey, Lionel was probably still wishing he had it, a regret that might haunt him until the day he died.

Picasso gave me a sly smile. He knew that I knew the story.

I said I thought that Lionel Maine was a major talent who would one day be appreciated as the original he was. Picasso looked bored. He said he was sure I was right, but mostly he remembered doing the drawing and my friend thinking he deserved to get it as a gift. Who did he think he was?

I said we'd better get started. I imagined he'd want to be there when I photographed his studio. I warned him not to be alarmed by the small explosions produced by the old-fashioned magnesium flashes

I still used for lighting. I assured him there was no danger that this could start a fire.

Picasso held up his hand. He grinned at me. Then he rocked back on his heels and laughed.

"A terrorist!" Picasso said. "I've always wanted to meet one!"

From the (Unpublished) Memoirs
of Suzanne Dunois Tsenyi
To be destroyed on the occasion of its author's death

IT TOOK THE Germans a while to realize how docile their victims would be. Occasionally one saw struggles, but most people did what they were told. They gathered their possessions, walked to the waiting car or truck. They wanted to live. Who could blame them?

But at first the Germans didn't know that, so they'd send gangs of thugs. Hearing the commotion, Gabor and I would go to the window and look down at the street swarming with woolly gray-green grubs. Potato bugs, we called them.

After I joined the Resistance, I was always sure they'd come for me. I leaned against Gabor, but I couldn't explain why I kept shivering even after I saw which house the police went into. I let Gabor think that my fear was for others. It was safer for him. Often I thought of his photo of me, lying dead on the sidewalk. Would he ever be able to look at that image again if I was shot and fell on the pavement beneath his window?

One rainy night, Gabor and I watched an arrest. At the center of the wriggling potato bugs were a woman and her two teenage sons. The boys were taller than their mother. They locked their arms around her until the soldiers pried them apart.

Gabor and I couldn't speak. We went back to bed. We killed a bottle of bootleg brandy. We said we loved each other and passed out.

Nor did we talk about the mother and her sons the next afternoon, when Gabor got back from Picasso's studio and I returned from the language school, where a German woman told me in broken French that her navy officer husband was going up to the Normandy coast, where they were expecting some action. I told her that the word for *ship* was the street argot term for *urine*. After dinner I would need to fake some illness and go to Ricardo's clinic at the hospital. Our comrades in the north needed to know about the action in Le Havre.

After the war, no one believed that I could have done what I did without Gabor knowing. But it was true. I couldn't put him at risk. He was a foreigner, under suspicion. Every day he wasn't deported was our lucky day.

Each time he left home with his camera represented a decision to choose art over safety. He took pictures of bombed-out houses, of a calico cat living in the rubble of its former apartment. He caught a trio of pretty French girls eyeing a German soldier with such undisguised sexual contempt, that image alone could have gotten him shot. People told him secrets they wanted recorded on film. A priest brought him to see lovely white marble statues of saints, blackened by the coal cellar where they were hidden. I was terrified for weeks after a humorous Resistant posted a broadside on which Gabor's photo of three men in lipstick, mascara, and ermine coats at the Chameleon Club was juxtaposed with a snapshot of Hermann Göring, dressed and made up the same way.

Twice he was required to get new papers. Once he received an official request for a notarized letter stating that Tsenyi wasn't a Jewish name. It made him so angry he wanted to go down to the Gestapo headquarters and say that Tsenyi *was* a Jewish name. Was it hypocritical that I talked him out of the kind of courage I was called upon to show every day, carrying forged documents in my bicycle basket and fake passports on the Métro?

Gabor's love gave me the resolve and strength to help smuggle stranded British soldiers, Resistants, and Jews across the border, to distribute newspapers, to get medical care for the wounded and the Aryan identity cards that people needed in order to work. Meanwhile I was charming my language students into telling me where troops and supplies were being moved.

I knew that Gabor would make a terrible Resistant. He claimed that being Hungarian gave him a talent for keeping secrets. But there was always a chance that he might go to Picasso's studio and have a few glasses of wine, and from pure sociability and genuine fellow feeling, mixed perhaps with the desire to impress the Spanish genius, he would describe the dangerous missions our group was carrying out. Not even Picasso could be trusted with the knowledge that a German officer, practicing his French during a playful language lesson, had given us the information we needed to blow up a munitions train en route to Bordeaux.

I said, "Why make trouble for yourself? Not only are you not Jewish, but Tsenyi isn't even your real name."

Gabor saw the logic in that, though logic wasn't the point. It gave him an excuse *not* to do something that might cost him dearly and would accomplish nothing. He suffered from being cut off without news from his parents. Every so often he wrote them. He told me his letters came back. After his death, I found evidence that these letters were never mailed.

Close as we were, we never discussed the most important things. We never mentioned my contraband radio or the BBC broadcasts. Though it was technically illegal, everyone listened to the nightly half-hour program in French. It wasn't the sort of offense for which you'd get sent to prison, except perhaps in a small town where a cop had a grudge against you or nothing better to do.

For part of every broadcast, the announcer read personal messages. Hello, Mama, I am in a prison camp, but I am safe. Don't worry. Darling, I pray every night for your return from the Front.

Many of these were coded communiqués from de Gaulle's agents in London. I had to listen carefully. Once, for example, I found out that a British aviator had landed in a tree in the woods outside Paris and had to be rescued at once.

Gabor claimed the messages were better than Surrealist poetry. Mama, the fox has gotten into the figs. Dear Cousins, the sunflower wants its coffee. The moon has eaten all the Camembert. The cannibal king is on a diet.

He would repeat them several times. Was he helping me remember them? After the war, he said, Yes, he was. I had been raised to be truthful, but during those years our lives depended on lying. Sometimes I wondered if we would ever get used to telling the truth again.

After the war, Gabor's photo of the Allied troops rumbling into Paris and being welcomed by the exultant crowds became one of the most famous images of that joyous event. Many people knew the story of how Gabor was shot at as he took the picture. A sharp-eyed GI saw the flash and thought he was a sniper.

In the minds of many, this near disaster has become an act of heroism, just as Gabor's documenting the Liberation has been viewed as evidence of his helping to make it happen. Gabor insisted that he had known everything. He used to ask how much *I* knew about what *he* was doing.

I know that he never hesitated to do anything I needed. When I asked if he would mind taking the pictures of friends who had lost their food ration cards, he said he would be glad to. They could come to his studio any time, free of charge. And when I suggested that a steady stream of desperate clients might draw the wrong sort of attention, he said he would take their photos wherever I wanted.

In the same way he'd staged scenarios early in his career, we devised little scenes for him to document. What German, however suspicious, would question a guy photographing two lovely young women in kerchiefs and summer skirts in the Luxembourg Gardens? And who, including Gabor, would suspect that the faces he took for ration cards were being used for forged passports and the Aryan certificates necessary to get a job?

I worked with a counterfeiter known as Cigarette Butt, a moniker he'd had long before the Resistance gave everyone code names. He refused to find another alias. Maybe if he had, his luck would have been better.

Like most counterfeiters, he considered himself an artist. He would have been delighted to know that the portraits he was sticking with pins to fake an official seal had been taken by his fellow artist Gabor Tsenyi. But we couldn't tell him that, no more than I could tell Gabor that his photos were being processed by a guy named Cigarette Butt.

Many of the best pictures my husband took during that time were used on transport visas. Everything he touched turned to art. Except for his book on Picasso, which was work for hire, the images he created during that five-year nightmare reflect his eye, his compositional sense—and the needs of the Resistance.

Once I told him to pretend to be a private investigator snapping a shot of me and my Moroccan boyfriend meeting for coffee (or the foul brew of acorns roasted and served as coffee) in a café. Then we could crop the picture to replace the photo on Ahmed's lost sugar ration card.

Ahmed was a courier from Casablanca. The police were closing in. Subsequent generations have interpreted our transfixed gazes as passion.

Gabor saw his expression for what it was: urgency and terror. But he never said so, and when he printed the picture, he kissed me and said, "Now your other boyfriend can have sugar in his tea."

From *The Devil Drives: The Life of Lou Villars*

BY NATHALIE DUNOIS

Chapter Thirteen: A Shopping Trip

AS A MECHANIC, Lou Villars should have been glad when Bonnet told her he was getting rid of the Mercedes. No client should hang on to a vehicle that was costing him so much time and money. But as a "community liaison worker," Lou was concerned. Would selling the car reduce the ease and frequency of Bonnet's trips to her garage?

Bonnet reassured her. Lou was doing such a good job that he planned to expand her duties. First he wanted to take advantage of her professional expertise. Would she come along when he shopped for an automobile to replace the Mercedes?

What kind of car was he thinking about?

"A Rossignol," said Bonnet.

On the evening before their visit to the Rossignol showroom, Lou drank herself unconscious, then sat up in bed at two in the morning. Wide awake, she replayed her association with the Rossignols, from the night when the baroness stopped by her table at the Chameleon to the evening when the baroness, Didi, and Armand came to inform her that she'd been demoted from champion to mechanic. Lou missed Armand—his patient instruction, his rambling lectures, the candy smell of opium on his clothes and his hair. She knew better than to let herself dwell on the loss of her racing career.

Designed by the modernist architect Alain Park-Joris, the Rossignol showroom's exterior resembled a Babylonian ziggurat or a rocket ship poised for takeoff. Its sophisticated aesthetic was lost on Lou as Bonnet motioned for her to enter first. The showroom contained half a dozen cars, their glossy beauty emphasized by the proportions of the room and the calculated angles at which the high windows scattered coins of sunlight across the glossy exteriors.

Amid all the desirable vehicles, the only one that Lou saw was Armand's green sedan. As she drifted toward it, Didi de Rossignol walked into the room.

Since she'd last seen him, Didi had grown to look more like Armand, as can happen after the death of a loved one. This glimpse of Armand's ghost made Lou want to protect Didi, without yet knowing from what.

Bonnet took out his handkerchief before shaking Didi's hand. Polite to a fault, Didi gave no sign of thinking that this was abnormal.

They chatted a while, then Bonnet glanced at Lou, who beckoned him over to Armand's car. She and Didi knew whose car it had been. They exchanged a freighted look. Didi held Lou's shoulders and kissed her on both cheeks.

He said, "Mademoiselle Lou, allow me to say that you are looking terrific." It was exactly what he'd said the night he'd come to fire her. Then he turned to Bonnet and said, "This is not a new car, as you may have discerned. But I knew its previous owner, and I promise you, it was well taken care of. Cherished, one might say. Thanks to our currently limited access to parts and materials, this sedan, used or not, is far superior to anything we have been able to manufacture since. And the fact that it's not new allows us to offer it to you at a significant discount. . . ."

Lou watched Didi's mouth form words. She prayed, Make him say Armand's name. Make him say that the green car had belonged to his murdered brother. She missed Armand more than she missed Arlette, or Inge, or even Robert. A Bolshevik Jew had killed him. The Israelites deserved their fate. She glared at Didi with something like hatred. Why wouldn't he say *my brother*?

But all that Didi said was, "I'll leave you two to talk it over."

When he left, Bonnet asked Lou what she thought.

She said, "He's right. This is the best. The most beautiful and the best." She would have said anything to drive that car again. It would prove that you could start over, maybe not from the beginning, but at least from a happier moment than the present. This time things would be different, this time—

Bonnet said, "I'll go talk to the salesman." How could Bonnet, who knew everything, not know who Didi de Rossignol was? Or was he pretending for some malicious reason of his own?

Lou kept one hand on Armand's car as Didi and Bonnet reached an agreement. It took almost an hour. Lou was afraid to leave the green sedan for fear she would lose it again. She watched them from across the showroom and several times was sure she saw something like anguish on Didi's face. Why was he selling Armand's car if it was causing him so much pain?

At last the two men shook hands again, Bonnet's handkerchief between them. Bonnet waved Lou over, and she watched them work out the details of how Bonnet would pay for the car and when it would be delivered. Didi wouldn't look at Lou as they said good-bye.

As Bonnet got into his Mercedes, Lou felt the impulse to glance back, together with the certainty that she would regret it. She thought of Lot and his daughters fleeing the Cities of the Plain. Of Orpheus, and Eurydice stranded eternally in hell. Arlette used to sing—very badly—an aria in which Orpheus poured out his grief at having lost his beloved forever.

Lou looked in the window. Didi stood beside the green sedan. Staring fixedly at Lou, Didi spat on his brother's car.

From *A Baroness by Night*

BY LILY DE ROSSIGNOL

ONE EVENING, DIDI came home early from the showroom and filled a wine goblet with whiskey, which by then was hard to obtain, regardless of the fortune one was willing to pay. I asked him what the matter was. He watched himself drink in the mirror.

He said, "Guess who came in today."

I said, "I can't imagine."

He said, "Jean-Claude Bonnet."

I asked what Bonnet wanted. Didi said he was shopping for a car.

"That's too bad," I said.

"Guess who was with him," Didi said.

"Heydrich?" I said. "Göring? Hitler?"

"Very funny," Didi said. "Lou Villars."

"How is dear Lou?" Her name would have upset me even if I weren't hearing it in the context of her having visited the showroom with the minister of information, a well-known toady and mouthpiece for the Nazis.

I felt guilty for having put Lou out to pasture when she was no longer useful to the Rossignols. Later I tried not to feel responsible for the crimes she committed after she worked for us. *After*, not *because*. Not *as a result*. Lou would have done the same things whether or not we'd fired her. Or anyway, that's what I told myself when I learned what she did.

I asked Didi if Lou was working for Bonnet. It seemed unlikely that they would be friends.

"She knows about cars," said Didi. "Bonnet brought her along. She liked Bonnet knowing that she knew the head of the firm, and she liked me knowing that she knew Bonnet."

I asked, "So is Bonnet buying a car?"

Didi mumbled something.

I said, "Tell me you didn't just say that he's buying Armand's sedan."

"We need the money," Didi said. "Anyway, I'm not selling it to Bonnet. I'm selling it to Lou. She loved him."

Minister Survives Fatal Auto Crash
Tours, April 14, 1942

Information Minister Jean-Claude Bonnet was injured yesterday in a one-car accident in which a female companion was killed.

The minister lost control of his Rossignol sedan on a winding road alongside the bank of the Loire. According to eyewitnesses, the car failed to brake at a curve, but sped up, became airborne, and landed in the river. Ejected before the car sank, the minister suffered serious injuries from which he is expected to recover. His companion, the German racing star Inge Wallser, died on her way to the hospital. Mlle. Wallser's funeral service will be held in Berlin.

Given the injured man's position, sabotage cannot be ruled out. The authorities have ordered a thorough investigation.

The yellowed scrap of newsprint still exists among my possessions. It is among the few surviving documents from an era when messages were destroyed as soon as one read them, when the price of sentimental hoarding could be death. Fortunately, that item had been written in the most secret of codes, which is to say the most public: notices in the papers, accident reports, and funeral notices that at that time meant something different to us than they would to someone today. They were the newsprint equivalent of the communiqués coded into the personals on the French-language BBC broadcasts.

Among the encrypted items were the daily reports of the suicides. Death by reaching one's boiling point. Death by one insult too many.

Many people just vanished, leaving nothing but gossip and rumor. The papers also carried announcements of "official" executions. We reread these obsessively, though at that point most of the Resistants shot by the Germans were younger and more left-wing than the people I knew. Later this would change, though by then the aliases by which I'd called the victims were only rarely the names printed in the papers.

Finally, there were the items like the one about Bonnet's accident. Obituaries of a strange sort: notices of deaths that hadn't yet occurred. Didi and I both knew whose death was being announced when I read him the item about the fatal accident involving Inge Wallser.

During the Occupation, we learned to live with fear and humiliation, anger and insults, the witnessing of horrific scenes one could hardly believe were real. We learned to behave as if this were normal life. People still fell in and out of love, made enemies and friends, went to work, slept and woke the next morning to enjoy a few blessed moments of calm before we remembered the world which we were about to reenter.

Rossignol Motors continued to produce luxury sedans long after the other automobile factories had been seized by the Germans or bombed into rubble. I've often wondered why this was so. I've decided that every German boy, every French and British boy, even some American boys had grown up dreaming of driving a Rossignol. They didn't see why this dream should end just because of a war. We were spared for the same reason that Hitler spared Paris. Why would you destroy something that you longed to possess?

Didi was permitted to go on working even after he made it clear that he would not divert his efforts, as so many of his colleagues and competitors had, into producing vehicles for the German war machine. Apparently Didi told quite a few people, though I was not among them, that if his hand were forced, he preferred suicide to treason. Even the half-witted Germans understood and believed him. Let them make their own Rossignols if they wanted to take control of the firm.

Meanwhile they manipulated the currencies until only powerful Germans and celebrity collaborators could afford our cars. The of-

ficial policy of the Reich was that their political and military leaders
were expected to drive a Mercedes. But nothing prevented them from
buying an expensive gift for a girlfriend or boyfriend. They could
spend pleasant weekends driving through the countryside with gasoline coupons unavailable to the French.

Didi hated the Germans more each day. But there was, as I've said,
the problem of our workers. In addition, my husband believed that he
was preserving something French that would survive after the Huns
had departed. When a sale was in progress, I offered to accompany Didi
to the showroom and to use whatever charm or humor I had to lighten
the tension and gloom. He refused to bring me along. He said there was
no telling how these transactions would be viewed after the war.

On the evening that the item about Inge's death appeared in the
paper, Didi and I were at home, reading in front of the fire. This
would have been a rare event before the Occupation, when there were
always parties, and we left the house in different directions. Before
the war Didi had spent his evenings chasing Swedish boys, while I
chased artists. I'd fallen in love—or what I imagined was love—with
some of the most dazzling talents in Paris. The most serious of my
imaginary romances was with Gabor Tsenyi.

But all that had ended. The Swedish boys had gone home, and it had
long since become clear that Gabor and I would never be more than
friends. My husband and I loved each other, as we had from that night
we drove down from the Hollywood Hills. My affair with the driver,
Frank, had been sweet, but he had returned to Italy to wait for the Allies
to invade. Some people swore that the social life had never been more
fun. But it no longer mattered to us. That sort of fun was over.

With the present so full of fears, and the future an abyss, Didi and
I took comfort in talking about the past. *Our* past. It calmed us to
recall that gauzy dream of youth and pleasure, regardless of how the
gauze had been shredded by discord and misunderstanding. We would
say, Remember Hollywood, and it was as if we were watching a film
of a young couple in a sports car on a winding road, leaving a party at
Douglas Fairbanks's mansion. Sometimes we would congratulate ourselves, marveling that a husband and wife could have gone through

as much as we did, stayed together as long as we had, and arrived at a feeling that was love. Pure love. As we reminisced, or just sat there in companionable silence, a new tenderness sprang up between us. We made jokes and laughed. Didi was always funny, but he had stopped trying with me.

I'd tell myself, Enjoy this, Lily. Enjoy it as long as you can. It seemed almost indecent to be finding domestic harmony in the depths of a ferocious war and a heartless Occupation. Money, social position, and beautiful cars had so far spared us the worst. And whom would it have helped if we'd started suffering before we had to? Grief would find us when it wanted, which would be soon enough. For a while, I'm embarrassed to say, the war was good for my marriage.

After I read the newspaper item aloud, Didi said, "What a pity." His dear face, normally so pink, had turned chalky, as if brushed by a killing frost. "Armand's car was in such good condition."

I'd always thought he should never have sold it to Bonnet.

I said, "Poor Little Inge. How we despised her for winning Montverre. All that seems so silly now: *everything* depending on whether a driver, *our* driver, was allowed to compete in a race." Those memories brought us closer. When Didi and I said *we* and *our*, we were including Armand. By then I'd resigned myself to the fact that Didi might never recover from his brother's death.

My husband found despair liberating; it loosened his ties to the world. He enjoyed being with me, but he would have been just as content to give up and join Armand.

I have never known if Bonnet's accident was deliberately engineered by my husband. The possibility might not have occurred to me if I hadn't seen something—a *flicker* of something—on Didi's face when I read him the notice. *Had* there been a problem with the car? Had Didi reached his limit, dealing with the Germans? Was my husband a saboteur, a one-man Resistance cell? It's my opinion that he was, but I will never know. However strong my curiosity, it was better not to ask. It was less risky to keep loved ones in the dark, and Didi and I had plenty of practice, keeping secrets.

When that story appeared in the newspaper, I knew the honeymoon was over. That is, our second honeymoon, happier than the first. I begged Didi to go away with me, to Portugal or Morocco. We had the money and the connections to travel wherever we wanted. But Didi was determined to stay in Paris. His cars were here. His brother was buried here. He would never change his mind.

I am thankful that, so near the end, Didi and I discovered what it meant to have a long and, in our own way, happy marriage. We knew things about each other that no one else could understand. I looked at Didi and saw the total of everything he had been through, the handsome French boy in Hollywood, the heir, the successful manufacturer, the troubled brother of the troubled brother. I knew that this would end badly. But it is a tribute to Didi, to his courage and grace, that I never predicted what the consequences would be until I read about Bonnet's accident. And even then I wasn't sure.

Still, I was constantly worried. When he left the house for work, I'd say, "Have a safe trip!" It must have seemed odd, considering that he was only going a few blocks away. I meant it as a magic spell, an incantation to keep him from harm. But I knew that no prayer of mine, however heartfelt, would save him.

One morning, not long after the newspaper item appeared, Didi left for the showroom.

"Have a safe trip," I said.

Seconds after the door closed, there was a crackle of shots. I ran outside to find Didi bleeding, fallen across our front steps. I told the servants to move him—gently! gently!—inside. It was probably the wrong thing to do. Only when I picked up the phone did I recall that our Jewish physician had been deported. I phoned the American hospital and asked them to send a doctor at once.

My calmness took its toll. Even now, I cannot write about that morning without a torrent of tears.

I knew the doctor from somewhere. He seemed to recognize me too. He was young. Homosexual. Was he one of Didi's friends? He was nicer than Didi's friends. He was tall, handsome, and dark. A regular Rudolph Valentino. Not at all Didi's type.

Eventually I placed him. He was a friend of Suzanne's. We'd met at that party, lifetimes ago, when Suzanne took off her clothes. Gabor had taken his portrait, together with his lover, both of them masked, naked, painted silver, and adorned with peacock feathers. For some reason Gabor had refused to sell me a print.

I thought this when I *could* think again, when I was able to hear distinct, if disconnected, words. The doctor was saying he was sorry. Sorry for my loss. I asked if my moving Didi inside had hastened his death. The doctor said, No, it hadn't. Nothing could have saved him or hurt him more. Then the doctor—Ricardo—lowered his voice and said something I wasn't sure I'd heard. What I *thought* I heard was that I could contact him at the clinic if I wanted to *do something* about my husband's death.

What did he mean by *do something*? I would soon find out. But not before I had gone through the ordeal of burying the dead at a time when even the wood for coffins was rationed and funeral permits had to be purchased with promises and bribes. So many were dying, why should anyone care about a middle-aged auto manufacturer? I had to offer a certain bureaucrat a Rossignol sedan in exchange for a permit, a devil's bargain that history saved me from having to keep.

There will always be those who venerate the rich, people to whom the wealthy are heroes by virtue of having money. Though everyone knew that Didi had been assassinated by the Germans in reprisal for something he may or may not have done to Jean-Claude Bonnet, he was buried with pomp and ceremony in the family vault in Père Lachaise, beside poor Armand, and next to the mother who was lucky not to have lived to see both sons die violent deaths.

I have kept the condolence book with the names of those who paid ceremonial visits. Historians might be interested to see that, on that grim roster, are none of the names of the famous collaborators, the Renaults, the owners of the perfume and champagne firms, the guests who used to come for dinner. By then many of those people were afraid to admit they knew us.

After that, I went mad with grief. I saw Didi everywhere. When I walked into his study and saw him reading in his chair, I almost asked his ghost if it needed more light. Knowing I'd be woken by his voice, I was afraid to fall asleep. I avoided the rooms in which he used to spend time.

Through the closet door, his cashmere-alpaca overcoat whispered to me when I passed, reproving me for being unable to give it away, especially now when, because of the shortages of wool and warm clothes, dozens of people—children!—were freezing to death on the streets. Someone would perish because I couldn't touch, let alone get rid of, Didi's favorite jacket.

A few months after Didi was shot, the doctor returned. I thought he'd come for some kind of official, state-mandated visit to the bereaved. What state did I imagine mandating something like that?

Ricardo sat in the parlor, perched on the edge of the sofa, his expression mournful, as if he really had come to pay a condolence call. He asked if anyone else was in the house. I said the cook was downstairs, but she was a heavy sleeper.

There are only a few reasons why a man asks that question. And I knew this was not about sex or crime. I said, A glass of something expensive?

No, he said. No, thank you. He was on duty.

He asked how I was doing. Physically, I felt fine, but mentally . . . He hadn't come to hear my symptoms. There wasn't time. He told me that the Resistance was in desperate need of money and of a place to shelter and hide refugees in transit.

I heard myself say that I had been waiting for someone to ask me that. Ricardo said he knew. I wondered *how* he knew. I myself hadn't known until I said it. This of course was Ricardo de la Cadiz Blanca, who not only worked as a doctor in a public clinic but was also one of our boldest and bravest Resistance leaders.

Later, when such stories could be told, everyone had a story about the moment they decided to do the right thing. Often these stories involve a silent understanding such as the one that took place between myself and Ricardo.

When he rose to leave, I asked him to wait a minute. I went to Didi's closet and grabbed an armful of clothes. I made sure that Didi's cashmere-alpaca was among the garments I took. I wept as I thrust them at Ricardo and told him to give them to someone in need.

"Thank you," Ricardo said. I could tell that his background had enabled him to appreciate the value of my husband's wardrobe. He couldn't help stroking the cashmere-alpaca, a mannerly calculation of the fortune Didi had spent on a coat he would never wear again.

Around that time, the Germans finally seized Didi's business. They gave me papers to sign and, I must say, a surprisingly decent compensation. Included in our agreement was that I would keep two of our cars for my personal use: Didi's sedan and of course the black Juno-Diane coupe that appears in Gabor Tsenyi's portrait of me at Brooklands.

Maybe they thought I'd see things their way after the war and help them reconstruct what Didi and Armand had built. They said I could hire a lawyer, but they didn't advise it.

I sold the house in Paris. I bought all the art I could from artists who needed my help. I leased a large estate in the country nearby, where I entertained Nazis by night, over basements and under attics where Jews, Resistants, and Allied soldiers were hiding. All this has been commented on, documented, noted, and recorded, and was part of the reason why, in those contentious postwar years, I was never faulted for having been married to someone who sold cars to the Germans.

In fact I was later inducted into the Légion d'Honneur for my generosity and sacrifice during the Occupation. As for those who have criticized me for amassing a priceless art collection so inexpensively, let them search their own hearts and ask themselves what they would have done in my position. I no longer had access to unlimited funds. That art survived because of me. One of my hopes is that the proceeds from this memoir will help me find a way to share that beauty with the world, preferably in an architecturally significant small museum or rural foundation.

From *The Devil Drives:*
The Life of Lou Villars
BY NATHALIE DUNOIS

Chapter Fourteen: Downward

THIS SECTION IS the most demanding of any that I have written so far. It requires a more incisive mind than mine, a more gifted historian, a more talented storyteller—and an experienced forensic psychiatrist—to describe the final stages of Lou's descent from auto champion to espionage agent to torturer for the Gestapo.

Until now I have tried to keep myself out of my work, preferring to let Lou's fascinating career take precedence over my own comparatively humdrum but reasonably virtuous life. But now that I see that I will probably have to at least partly finance the publication of this book with the help of a modest legacy from my bachelor uncle Emile, who owned a small bank in Auxerre, and who kept his sister, my aunt, at home, as a lifelong unpaid servant, I have decided to turn this setback into an advantage, to convert adversity into freedom, beginning with the freedom (which a more conventional publisher might deny me) to reference my own experience in telling Lou's story. And so at the risk of sounding like someone better suited to the mental ward than a teaching position in a well-respected high school, I would like to report a phenomenon that I began to notice whenever I attempted to put words on paper.

For the first and, let us hope, the last time, I experienced what can only be called an aural hallucination. Every time I sat down at my desk, I seemed to hear the hollow plop of a stone falling down a

well—a sound such as one hears in the background of early Kuro-
sawa films. It seemed too perfect, even ridiculous, that my subject was
falling—plummeting, as it were—and that I should *hear* something
falling. Nor did it strike me as the sort of occurrence that ordinarily
happens to writers and scholars like myself, with graduate degrees.

I consulted an ear specialist, then a neurologist, who performed a
battery of tests and found nothing wrong. My friends and colleagues,
the few I trusted enough to confide in, must have assumed that my
work on this book had finally destroyed my already fragile health.

The sound recurred, disturbing and distracting. Paralyzing, to be
honest. In desperation, I consulted a psychiatrist who came highly
recommended. Dr. G. had studied with someone who had studied
with Anna Freud. Best of all, she practiced in Rouen, near the school
where I teach.

At the time I found Dr. G. (who has refused permission to be
quoted by name in this book, even going so far as to threaten legal
action) to be one of those older women who seem to have made their
peace with life—and even manage to find it amusing.

She listened to my symptoms. She asked what I was working on. I
summarized Lou's story. I asked if she thought it was strange, that I
was trying to write about someone who extracted information under
torture, and there I was, in her office, not only telling her every personal secret I could dredge up, but also paying her to listen.

No, she said, it wasn't strange. It was the opposite of strange. She
said that, just as I suspected, what I'd been hearing was the sound of
my subject's soul falling down a well. She said that there was nothing
to be done for it. I might continue hearing the echo until I finished
the book, and then it would disappear on its own.

Meanwhile, I should keep working. She suggested I play music
loud enough to drown out the distracting sound. Given the nature of
my project, she recommended Beethoven's Late Quartets.

Numerous incidents from this period in Lou Villars's life are documented in police reports and files. It is probably unnecessary to de-

scribe how challenging it was to prize this material from the paws of the human watchdogs patrolling libraries and sensitive archives. The dirty little secret of every historian of that era is that we are grateful for the Nazis' diabolical and (to borrow a term from psychoanalysis) anal-retentive passion for keeping meticulous records.

In one such ledger, housed in a section of the Bibliothèque Nationale so off-limits to the general public that even the serious scholar has to sleep with the right curator or bribe the right librarian to gain access, are several neatly handwritten lines on a mildewed page, awaiting conservation. A brief entry notes the presence of Lou Villars at the scene of an auto accident that injured Minister Jean-Claude Bonnet and killed a female passenger listed as—a slight but atypical error—Mlle. Inge Walther.

The least imaginative biographer will find it all too easy to imagine the scene in which Lou Villars was brought to the crash site to give her expert opinion concerning the causes of the accident, a judgment based partly on her career as an auto racer and mechanic, and partly on her extensive knowledge of the Rossignol brand.

On the day after the crash, Lou Villars was driven by the police to the place where the love of her life had just died. The riverbank had already been trampled into a mucky swamp. Lou focused on her white shoes sinking in the mud until she reached the waterlogged green sedan. Heavily armed and exuding menace, French policemen and Gestapo officers patrolled the riverbank.

Lou was so shocked and angry that at first she was almost glad that Inge was dead. Serves the little bitch right! But she soon became very gloomy.

Considering the damage and pain that Lou Villars inflicted, can we even briefly allow ourselves to think, Poor Lou! At what point does a monster cease being human, or human enough to feel the heartbreak that is the unavoidable lot of humankind, human enough for us to feel the compassion we owe the most devilish member of our species?

Ankle-deep in mud, with rain sluicing down her face, Lou recalled those warm nights in Berlin and the trips she had taken with Inge.

Had any of it been real? What did it say about her that she fell in love with women who didn't care about love, but only about power, meaning: men.

However overwhelmed she was by sorrow, confusion, and rage, Lou was still canny enough to wonder: didn't the Germans have their own auto mechanics? Why were they asking *her* to explain why the accident had happened? What could she contribute to a criminal investigation?

She had to crawl under the car with the soldiers and police watching. She liked being covered with sand and mud, even though she was wearing a costly suit. Immersing herself in the puddle of filth felt at once dirty and cleansing. She'd been chosen, singled out, humiliated, and at the same time elevated and set free. Let them watch. She was the one who'd been called on for her expertise.

The car had missed a curve and rolled over. That's what Lou told the police. The report can be found in the archives. The sedan's brakes had failed. The brakes on Rossignols were generally first-rate, so in Lou's opinion foul play couldn't be ruled out. *Don't even trust the mechanics.*

Lou said, "Someone tampered with the brakes."

"Who could that be?" the officers said.

Lou waited a while to answer. Finally she cocked her head like a stout, ungainly bird in a mud-covered, pin-striped suit. "Snitches disgust me. They should all be shot. I'd rather die than be a snitch. But I don't mind saving lives. And if you don't want this sort of thing happening again, I'd say look to the top. You may need to do some . . . pruning. It wouldn't be the worst thing for Rossignol Motors to pass into German hands." She went on to say that a German would never be careless enough to allow a car to leave the shop with brakes like these—brakes that killed a racing champion and almost killed the French official who was probably the target of the attack.

Lou hated to finger Didi de Rossignol. He'd been good to her, or good enough, for as long as it served his purpose. She was simply telling the truth. Someone had frayed the brake line. She remembered how Didi had spit on Armand's car. Deconsecrating it, she understood now.

Didi wasn't to blame for the loss of her athletic license. Nor was it his fault that Chanac and the sports associations had won their case against her. But Didi shouldn't have fired her. They should have found another way.

In the end, things worked out for the best. If the Rossignols hadn't let her go, maybe Inge and the Germans wouldn't have been touched by her story and moved to invite her to the Berlin games. *Had* things worked out? Lou didn't know. Right now she just wanted someone dead. Her former employer would do.

And really, what did it matter? Everything would improve when the Germans beat the Allies and France was a full partner in the New Europe. The hell with Inge, the hell with them all. Lou had no one but herself and nothing but the mission she'd been given by the Führer.

Lou was present not only at the accident scene but also later at a high-level meeting, at which it was ordered that Didi de Rossignol be brought in for questioning. Regrettably, the automaker was shot for resisting arrest.

During the eight weeks that, hospital records show, Bonnet spent recovering from his injuries, Lou confronted the drawbacks of their secret arrangement. Choice bits of information still came her way, but there was no one to report them to, and worse, no one to pay her. Once more she was obliged to depend on the increasingly inadequate income generated by the garage, and, for cigarettes and whiskey, on the boozy charity of the Gasparu-Chanac gang. She had to fire her assistant, Marcel, whom she promised to rehire if her business recovered.

As she sat in her office for hour after idle hour, she had plenty of time to wonder: What *was* the relationship between Inge and Bonnet? Had they known one another when Lou "introduced" them? Did Inge ever love her? Or had Lou been her *assignment*? Had some bureaucrat in Berlin decided to pass Lou along from Inge to Bonnet, from one handler to another?

Perhaps Lou had underestimated Bonnet as a sexual rival, partly because of his terror of germs. Did he use his handkerchief while making love to a woman? And Inge had hardly been the cleanest girl. No one could smoke around Bonnet, and Inge had been such a heavy smoker that Lou, who liked her tobacco, used to worry that Inge's bad habits might shorten her life. Oh, Inge!

Two months after the accident, a cop appeared at the garage and told Lou that a car would come for her tomorrow morning at nine. A chauffeur would give her the keys. She would then drive to the hospital to pick up Minister Bonnet, who was eager to resume their professional association.

Lou considered the offer. Could she go back to work for a man who might have been Inge's lover, and who was partly responsible for her death? Had Lou been driving, she could have saved Inge, even in a car without brakes.

She told the policeman that she would be ready and waiting at nine.

When Bonnet was discharged from the hospital, Lou Villars drove him home. Lou expressed her sympathy for the suffering he had endured. She was glad that he had recovered. Bonnet said his right knee and left elbow still weren't right. Neither of them mentioned Inge.

Only pride kept Lou from asking Bonnet if Inge had ever loved her. Was it true that the Führer had called the French a Negroid, Yiddified nation, and that children like her brother Robert were being killed lest they drain the vital energies of the strong and healthy?

The strain of keeping silent wore down Lou's defenses. It chafed at whatever restraint had prevented her from turning into the ogre that she was about to become.

I realize that the long, convoluted intimacy of the biographical process—the years spent delving into the life of one's subject, exploring the secret corners of another's psyche—should foster understanding, compassion, and even perhaps forgiveness. But how is the most sympathetic biographer supposed to pardon a woman, however mistreated in childhood and thwarted in work and love, for becoming a German spy and a torturer for the Gestapo?

My readers will excuse me if I take a short break because I am hearing that sound again, the splash, the echo, the dying fall of a pebble falling down a well.

From the Gabor Tsenyi Archive

January 12, 1943

My darling son Gabor,
I write in the almost impossible hope of reaching you. Telephone service no longer exists in our forgotten corner of the world. It will be a miracle if this letter finds its way across battlefields and borders. I know of no other way to contact you. Yet I must try, because I have sad news to report.

Mama died last Thursday. It would be awful to think of you going about your day, living your normal life without knowing. I hate to imagine the additional pain, when you finally find out. Though now, as I write this, I ask myself: who really would it hurt for my son to go on believing that his Mama is alive? I just had to stop writing for a moment. Tears filled my eyes when I realized that this is the first time I have used the singular possessive, *my* instead of *our*, to describe you, *my* son.

She was seventy. But we'd recently agreed that seventy didn't seem so ancient. Maybe you would have thought we looked old. So much time had passed since we saw you, so much has happened, perhaps I can be excused for failing to notice the subtle alterations that age and hardship made in Mama's beautiful face. And will it seem strange if I say that, however calmly we talked about death—speculating over which of us might die first, and how the survivor would cope—we both believed in our secret hearts that we would live together forever?

One day, on the way to the market, she sat down in the street. If only she hadn't insisted on shopping! There was never any food to buy. But she would go from habit. I suppose she still met her friends there, though, unluckily, none of them were nearby that day.

I cannot imagine what she went through for the twenty minutes (or so they told me) until they came for me, and I arrived. Sometimes one is lucky not to live in a city like Paris, where no one might have known who Mama was. It could have taken me days to find her.

She was barely conscious, but she knew I was there. She smiled. We brought her home. I moved a bed into the living room and hired a nurse. After that, she failed rapidly, first one thing, then another. Your Uncle Ferenc explained that with the body, it's like falling off a cliff. Once you fall there's no way to climb back up. He made Mama's death sound like a natural process and not a crime that could have been prevented. Though you could say it was one. The constant lack of food and fuel hadn't exactly prolonged her life. I know that resignation would be healthier for me than anger. That's what your mother would have said. I am trying to resign myself. If I were religious, I would say that it was God's will. That it was your Mama's time. There was nothing we could do. But as you know, we were not religious, nor, I gather, are you.

I could fill this letter and a million more with the horrors that ended for her only with her death, and that continue for me without her here to console me. The violence against the Jews was hard for your tenderhearted Mama. There was one incident . . . I'll spare you the details except to say that it involved the kosher butcher you may remember. His shop was just off Karolyi Square. He was forced to butcher a pig and wash down his counters with its blood. Your mother flew into a rage. It was so unlike her! I remember that her speech sounded a tiny bit slurred that evening. Stupidly, I wondered if she might have exceeded her usual sip of sherry before dinner.

Did the assault on the butcher cause Mama's first attack, a warning no one heeded? To think so would make me angrier, but also proud to have spent my life with a woman with such compassion and such a strong moral sense. What was happening made her sick. Literally sick. I only hope you will find a woman as empathetic as she was.

Your Mama and I were blessed to fall in love, doubly blessed to marry and have you. Perhaps your parents were too close. Perhaps we made you feel shut out—an exclusion that led to the long separation that must (and *should*) have been easier for you than for us. Mama and I always understood we would pay a price for our closeness. Would it help either of us if I went on about the shocks I experience now, several times daily? My footsteps echoing through the house, the icy chill of the sheets.

I want to say something about your mother to help you keep her spirit alive, after she is gone. She loved you unconditionally. She thought you were the handsomest, kindest, most gifted boy in the world. Modern thinking suggests there should be more space between a mother and her child. Maybe you thought something like that and insured that distance by staying in Paris. But you never stopped being her darling. She was connected to you in almost supernatural ways.

When insomnia tormented you, she stopped sleeping. Later in life, she'd blamed it on her change, but it had begun long before. I told her your insomnia might be a blessing in disguise. It sent you out into the streets of Paris where so much of your best work was done. It was not a blessing for Mama, in our bedroom at home, where she lay with her eyes wide open, imagining the worst.

The thought of her boy out late, alone, in the dark dangerous Paris streets so terrified her that every time I drifted off to sleep, I heard her sighing and tossing. I told her that, knowing you, you probably weren't alone, besides which Paris was not so dangerous nor (unlike our town) so dark. In the morning she'd go to the pharmacist and buy one money-wasting potion after another. She would experiment on herself and send you the ones that tricked her into sleep.

Since the war began we tried not to talk about you as much as before. It was too painful not to know how you were. But we couldn't help ourselves. We spoke about the past—your work, your book, our visit. We marveled at your generosity and your kindness. How we never once got a letter in which you didn't say how much you missed us and how much you wished you could come home, though it was never clear to us why you couldn't return for a visit.

From your infancy Mama knew you were destined for greatness. Sometimes I would ask why it was taking you so long to find your way. Sometimes it seemed you did nothing but go to cafés, nightclubs, and even, God help us, brothels. She would remind me to have faith in you and your talent.

After your book came out, we talked about what a great artist you were, especially when we woke in the middle of the night, as old people do, both fearing some version of what has now occurred. The thought of you would comfort us, and we would fall back asleep.

Your Mama was right about everything. You should feel only satisfaction at how proud you made her. My only hope, and I know hers would be too, is that you find someone who adores you half as much as we do.

Our love for you has sustained us through the dark hours, and this is the darkest. I pray that I will live to see you again on this earth. But for now I send you hugs, and my undying love,

Your Papa

From *The Devil Drives:*
The Life of Lou Villars
BY NATHALIE DUNOIS

Chapter Fifteen: Nobody's Idiot

ONCE MORE, THE possibility that I may have to finance the publication of this book has proved unexpectedly liberating. I can confess, as another biographer might not, that six months have elapsed—six trying months during which I taught my classes and ended yet another disastrous romantic relationship—since I wrote the last chapter.

This delay is partly a result of my now being compelled to write about a period when Lou Villars's name began to appear on the lists of the interrogators at the headquarters of the French Gestapo—the so-called Active Group Hesse, informally known as La Carlingue. This was the infamous office at 93 rue Lauriston, where French collaborators and their gangster colleagues presided over a kingdom decorated with exotic flowers, gilded Buddhas, and gleaming parquet floors above a freezing, dripping cellar to which prisoners were brought to be beaten by the torturers who would disappear and return, drying their hands, to rejoin the lavish parties upstairs.

In the journals of Jean-Claude Bonnet, a desiccated volume flaking away in a private archive in Tours, are a series of notations, always brief and always the same, in a script with which a graphologist would probably have a field day. On a sheet of onionskin is written again and again: Drive country. As per med orders. Driver: Lou Villars.

Though Bonnet had unlimited access to gasoline, he was understandably wary of getting behind the wheel. Not only had he wrecked his new car and killed a young woman, but he'd also had to order the manufacturer shot. He bought a workhorse Mercedes and hired Lou to drive it. He preferred to ride around at night and to talk—to Lou or to himself—freely, in the darkness.

For Lou it was almost like driving Armand. She loved the sugary opium smell on Bonnet's breath, but unlike Armand, Bonnet gave up drugs when the pain of his injuries subsided. For a while every loud noise reminded him of his accident, and he would begin to tremble. But eventually he got over it and made a full recovery.

The ledgers show Lou receiving a wage that grew incrementally over the period during which she worked for Bonnet. She could re-hire Marcel to run the garage when Bonnet needed her elsewhere. Yet Bonnet no longer seemed quite so interested in the information she provided.

She was grateful for the salary. But more was involved than money. Often Bonnet asked Lou's advice, not only about cars but also about delicate matters at the Ministry of Information. No one had ever consulted Lou about anything important, and Bonnet's trust inspired in her a loyalty and even a love almost as powerful as any she'd felt for Armand or Inge.

Without mentioning Inge, they talked about the Führer. Bonnet knew every detail of that dinner in Berlin. He only wished that the Führer had singled *him* out for such personal attention. Several times he said that if he did get to speak to the Führer in private, he'd tell him about certain weak links at the Paris bureau. He named diplomats and generals, and Lou paid close attention, in case she needed this information later.

Was Bonnet's new chattiness a result of the car wreck? An injury to the brain? Given his position, shouldn't someone know how indiscreet he was when he gossiped? Lou wasn't about to snitch on him—on principle and for practical reasons. Besides, no one would believe her. Sometimes she just listened; sometimes she gave her opinion.

The roads were nearly empty but for bicycles, wagons, and donkeys braying in triumph at having outlasted the cars. As Lou and Bonnet left the city for the countryside they both loved, Bonnet complained bitterly about how the atmosphere at the ministry was changing.

He was surrounded by fanatics obsessed with calibrating how many drops of Jewish blood it took to pollute the French population. He attended meetings at which they discussed who was a secret Israelite. Roosevelt! Churchill! The pope! Hitler had two Jewish grandparents! No rock was too slimy to overturn if a Jewish worm might be lurking beneath it. To be anti-Jewish was to be pro-French. The priests preached love and forgiveness. But in private they said, Don't forget who murdered Our Lord.

Bonnet understood not wanting to socialize with Jews. Even if they weren't naturally greedy, cunning, eager to seduce Christian girls and lower the already low French birthrate by performing abortions, one could hardly tolerate their obnoxious conviction that they were better and smarter than everyone else. Still, didn't it seem counterproductive for French leaders and politicians to spend *every waking moment* thinking about the Jews? Wasn't it a waste of energy to train one's dog, as several colleagues had, to attack Yids on command? What a waste of resources, when cloth was in such short supply, to make them patch their vulgar clothes with ugly yellow stars!

Bonnet could understand the obsession with Jewish money. The Jews owned all the best real estate, the most profitable banks, the priciest art collections. They squandered funds their country needed on their ostentatious weddings and bar mitzvahs. But why confuse a perfectly sensible concern about the Jews with all this occult talk about blood and the Elders of Zion?

At every level of government, it was the only conversation. The Jewish question had to be answered. Send them to Madagascar! They could afford to pay their way. But who, in the middle of a war, could transport several million Jews to an island off the African coast?

Bonnet told Lou about a series of top secret meetings. The committee had reached a dead end, but they'd agreed to find a solution before they met again. They required a special venue, for something like a mass rally. No one knew where to find such a place in Paris. Perhaps Lou could think of a site they'd overlooked.

These meetings were bringing Bonnet into contact with Clovis Chanac. Bonnet found Chanac vulgar and coarse, but helpful, along with his gangster friends, in making the city run smoothly. The Gasparu-Chanac gang had become a private army of enforcers for the Reich and the French Gestapo.

Lou had heard that Arlette had left Chanac and gone back to work for Yvonne. And she worried—needlessly, she told herself—that Chanac might somehow turn Bonnet against her. Clearly, Bonnet liked and trusted her more than Chanac. But still she felt uneasy whenever she knew the two men would be in the same room.

In her anxiety, she encouraged Bonnet to tell her every detail of the secret meetings. And what she heard would likely have been something like this:

The Minutes of a Meeting

Beginning in February 1942, a newly formed emergency advisory committee convened in the Paris office of the minster of the interior. The salon seemed even warmer, more welcoming and brighter when the conferees came in from the wintry chill outside the ministry's bronze doors.

After a few sessions the venue was changed—for reasons having to do with safety, security, and comfort—to the Institute for Study of the Jewish Question, located in the former gallery and home of the Jew Rosenberg, who had made a fortune peddling the work of degenerate artists.

Attending were government officials, politicians, military officers, advisers, economists, engineers, statisticians, as well as experts on the latest genetic and eugenic research. Also present was the police prefect in charge of the Jewish Section of Paris, Vichy dignitaries, the director of the Jewish department, and the deputy director of the Paris bureau, which had the names of every Jew in the city on index cards, color coded by nation of origin. Also certain prominent Parisians, among them the crime boss Clovis Chanac.

In a five-minute speech, after which he had to leave because of commitments elsewhere, Pierre Laval, the head of the French government, exhorted the committee to transcend party politics and personal differences, and, in the spirit of sacrifice, to reach an effective solution to this problem on which, *they must believe him*, their nation's survival depended.

After Laval left, the gentlemen began by transcending their different opinions of Laval. The point was that the head of state had come to address *them* in person. The point was that they were saving France. This was the only way to save it, and they were the only ones who could.

The minister's chief secretary spoke first. Their esteemed German colleagues, Messieurs Heydrich and Eichmann, were insisting that France contribute 865,000 able-bodied worker Jews to the Final Solution of the Jewish Question. This figure was nonnegotiable, though every attempt had been made to reduce this demanding quota.

The committee's task was to decide how this population transfer might be most expeditiously arranged. The urgency of this problem had been highlighted recently when a train left Bordeaux with only a few hundred Jews aboard, an expensive and wasteful trip, consuming precious fuel, leaching time and energy from the Fatherland, all of which so annoyed Eichmann that he'd promised France would pay dearly if anything like that happened again. Apparently Hitler was taking a special interest in the French solution to the Jewish problem.

A statistician performed some calculations, then shook his head. The editor of a far-right paper asked where the Germans imagined they could find a million Jews capable of doing anything besides making money and whining. Chanac asked if the Germans expected them to pull a million Jews out of their asses?

The meeting was called to order. The gentlemen observed the rules of procedure. Their proposals were accepted or voted down and replaced with counterproposals. Only rarely did the temperature rise when, like competitive schoolboys, they vied to come up with the most ingenious plan. Among the first successes, which several committee members later claimed and later still denied, was the decision to call the program Operation Spring Breeze.

Matters of scheduling were discussed. Would they get a credit—that is, a deduction—for the ten thousand Jews deported last year? No, they would not. Besides, ten thousand was a fraction of the figure being named. At the end of the first meeting it was unanimously resolved to table the discussion, pending a report from the census experts and statisticians.

In the interim another meeting was held to rule on acceptable parameters regarding age, gender, health, and so forth. These issues could not be resolved until they heard from the statisticians. Meanwhile the police chiefs from Paris and Vichy began a long dispute about who would assume responsibility for tactical operations that might be awkward for the French cops.

The original guidelines specified males between sixteen and fifty, 90 percent able-bodied. This seemed reasonable and passed on the first vote, with the proviso that the statisticians and census experts could adjust down to age fifteen and up to fifty-five if it would make a significant difference in meeting the quota. It was respectfully pointed out that the color coding of the index cards was no longer relevant, since the distinction between French Jews and foreign Jews, a division about which Vichy felt strongly, was from a numerical standpoint impractical and would have to be abandoned.

But the cards would still be useful. Don't throw them away! Everyone laughed, which lightened the mood a bit.

Things appeared to be going well, especially when it turned out that the Germans were not really so inflexible about deadlines and numbers. In fact they were open to negotiation, especially when several ministers admitted that the original figures had given a somewhat alarmist picture of the Jewish threat to France.

The committee applauded when it was announced that the Germans had cut the number of Jews to be deported from Paris to 32,000. Unfortunately, this was followed by bad news from the statisticians, who said that many Jews, tipped off in advance, had already left, and the original estimates of the Jewish population had been *wildly*, perhaps intentionally inflated. Someone asked if anyone knew who might have done this and why, but the question was ignored. Someone else suggested adding

Jews married to Aryans, a group originally exempted. There were quite a few thousand of these, so that would be a help.

How would it change the equation if they included women between the ages of twenty and forty-five? And why not throw in the critically ill, who would die anyway if they were left behind? The children would be entrusted to Jewish social services. A Jewish social service agent reported that the Jews had been taxed to pay for emergency clothing for several thousand children. Everyone agreed that this plan was thoughtful, humane, and showed admirable foresight.

That spring there were several tedious meetings to decide what to do with the Jews' house keys. Who would guard their possessions? What about their fat juicy pets? asked a general who thought his question funnier than his colleagues did. Someone muttered that the pets could be handed over to the concierges, and the general asked: were the concierges allowed to eat them? The Jews could bring one suitcase apiece. This passed without debate, with a show of hands, especially since it was understood that this was German policy. It was more sensible to safeguard the Jews' property in situ rather than to risk it getting lost in transit.

Several meetings were spent on the question of how the Jews would be transported. The police insisted on unanimous assurance that a fleet of late-model buses with sealed windows would be outfitted and ready to roll for Operation Spring Breeze.

Meeting attendance slacked off until word got out that a new deadline had been set. Eichmann wanted all the Jews, or a high percentage, out of France by late July. Otherwise there would be drastic repercussions. No one wanted to speculate about what these punitive measures might be. *They* would be held responsible. Meanwhile the experts kept downgrading their estimates of able-bodied Jewish adults. Another deadlock ensued when the Vichy government was still reluctant to deport the French-born Jews along with the rest.

Late in June, the committee heard that Eichmann was coming to Paris to look into the logjam and speed up the process. The delegates might have been excited if it hadn't been represented as the equivalent of the principal coming to chastise the class.

Even so, they were disappointed when Monsieur Eichmann decided not to meet with the entire assembly but only with a select few. They reported back that Eichmann had given permission to let 11,000 children travel along with their families as a humanitarian gesture. Consequently, the minimum age for male deportees was lowered to two, with the acknowledgment that in the upset unavoidable during the transfer, it might be hard for officials to determine the precise age of babes in arms, and younger children might be sent by mistake, of course along with their parents. Or should the families be separated? This was tabled for future discussion.

Though the decision to include children elicited mixed feelings, the motion passed without debate, partly because it solved a lot of problems. Mainly, the problem of how the Jewish social services were supposed to take care of the children when there were no more Jews? The French couldn't feed their own kids, let alone hungry Jewish mouths.

Eichmann had suggested July 14 as the target date. But he saw the logic when it was pointed out that Bastille Day might be a tactically unwise occasion for the roundup. A sizable fraction of the non-Jewish population might be in a restive state due to the celebrations.

By now the Paris police and the military were asking the civilian committee members if they had *any idea* how big a job this was. The propaganda department argued that it would be traumatic for the average Parisian if the city center was the scene of heart-wrenching dramas, terrified children torn from the arms of desperate parents.

One council member suggested that the populace might not be all that upset to see their Jewish neighbors disappear. One major real estate investor said they shouldn't underestimate the effect on the average citizen (especially the lower classes) of all those nice, newly vacant apartments going on the market at reasonable rents.

After that they discussed a plan to separate families with children from childless Jews, so the families could stay together at least temporarily, thus sparing the average Parisian more tragedy than was necessary to witness. The French police spoke up for the occupying army to be more visibly involved; with their natural gift for classification, the Germans would be better equipped to determine which Jews should go to which detention centers, the childless Jews straight to Drancy, the families elsewhere, to be determined.

For the first time since the committee's inception, everyone talked at once. Until the mayor's voice rose above the noise, asking where the hell they planned to *warehouse* thirty thousand Jews until they could start moving them out?

After all the discussion, after the hammering out of fine points, more than 13,000 Jews were rounded up by the French police in the early morning of July 16, 1942. The unmarried and the childless were sent directly to Drancy and from there to Auschwitz. The others were brought to the Vélodrome d'Hiver. In the heat of July, the glass-covered greenhouse (its ceiling painted blue for camouflage in case of a bombing raid) sheltered the Jews, among them 4,000 children.

Unlike the committee members, many of the Jews had heard the BBC broadcast on which it was explained what had already happened to 700,000 Jews in Poland. The parents and older children knew they were going to die.

The stadium lights shone round the clock, and there were frequent loud broadcasts of German military songs interrupted by public service announcements informing the transit-camp residents of medical symptoms that warranted immediate attention.

The field and the track were off-limits except to the very sick. There was a great deal of illness: scarlet fever, measles, diphtheria, hemorrhages, appendicitis, gangrene. Families lived in the bleachers, diapering their babies and putting their kids to sleep, and the little ones urinated on the heads of the children sleeping below. The parents took turns sleeping or trying to sleep. No one slept much, except for the narcoleptics, who slept all the time. No water, no sanitation, terror, childbirth, despair, disease, suicides, infanticides. There were screaming fights for the watery soup ladled directly into people's hands by the Quakers and the Red Cross.

Neighbors who lived near the Vélodrome reported not sleeping for nights. And these were people who had learned to sleep through motorcycle races, circus music, the cheering of sports fans. These more normal, soothing noises would resume several weeks after the removal of the Jews and the necessary sanitation department cleanup.

By then the Jews had been shipped to transit camps in France, and from there to the east. For most of them this meant Auschwitz. According to the orders handed down by the Vichy government, the children were to be taken from their parents, by force if necessary, and sent off on separate convoys.

Fewer than 200 adults and none of the children returned. The survivors belonged to the small group of 2,500 who came home—a fraction of the 76,000 French Jews who had been deported.

Do we know that Lou Villars suggested the Vélodrome d'Hiver? We do know that Bonnet was present at the meetings during the time when the committee was stalled over where to "warehouse" the prisoners. We know that Lou Villars was working as Bonnet's driver, that he told her about the problem and asked her advice, and that she'd given athletic demonstrations in the Vélodrome. Since then, she'd gone to the stadium for boxing matches, bicycle races, hockey games, the circus, and political rallies. So the Vélodrome would have occurred to Lou more readily than to Bonnet, who had no interest in sports and avoided germ-ridden crowds.

There were many reasons why Lou Villars might have thought of the stadium where she'd appeared at the start of her failed career. What welling up of anger would those memories have caused, what resurgence of the resentment inspired and intensified by every time she'd been cheated, lied to, betrayed by those she'd trusted?

Why not tell her boss that she knew about a space where thousands could be housed? Why not seem savvy and smart? And why hadn't anyone else thought of the Vélodrome? Why did they need *her* to suggest it? Didn't they like sports? Had the French patriots forgotten the massive rally that had been held at the stadium to celebrate the release from prison—to which he had been unjustly sent for writing and printing the truth—of the national hero Charles Maurras, the first to prove that Christ was not a Jew and to alert his fellow patriots to the Jewish lies spread by Hollywood films like *Ben Hur.*

Do we know that Lou Villars *didn't* do it? Surely there will be readers who will say: Didn't this woman do enough? Wasn't it enough to tell the Germans where the Maginot Line ended? Must she also be responsible for the suffering at the Vélodrome d'Hiver?

What would Lou have said? She would have said that if she didn't do it, someone else would have—and gotten all the credit. Someone else would have suggested the Vélodrome or somewhere smaller and darker, much worse for the families in transit.

Was she responsible for their deaths? Did she pick up a gun and kill even one Jew? All she'd done was mention a place with a large capacity. And it was just a suggestion. What they did with it wasn't her fault.

I have already written about the explosive combustion that can occur when two damaged or incomplete individuals combine to form an entity more dangerous than either one alone. We have seen how, with Lou and Inge, this demonic partnership resulted in the breach of our country's defenses. And now Lou's growing closeness to Jean-Claude Bonnet, a charged intimacy she hadn't had with a male since Armand de Rossignol's death, drew her ever more deeply into a world of terror and pain.

On Christmas Eve, Lou drove through a snowstorm until dawn as Bonnet raved about a priest who'd pinned a Jewish star to the blanket swaddling the baby Jesus in his church's Nativity crèche. Let his Jesus save him from the firing squad! Let his pervert pope get out of bed with the Führer long enough to intercede for some pedophile monk in Montmartre.

Bonnet said, "I didn't just say what you may imagine you heard me say."

Lou took a sharp corner and headed toward the Canal St. Martin. "What did you say?" she asked.

Angry at himself for having revealed too much and eager to shift the blame onto his listener, Bonnet said, "You know, you're very good at getting people to say more than they mean to."

Was Bonnet praising or criticizing her?

"Thank you," Lou said uncertainly.

Then he said, "I have another job I think you would be good at."

On the nights when her services weren't required by the Gestapo, Lou lay awake in her room and watched the endangered innocents reaching out to her for help. Dressed in white robes, a solemn procession of imperiled souls marched across the darkness. She saw the children who would be killed if the fanatical Resistants blew up a train because a German official was on it. She saw the farm families who would starve if the Communists stole their land, as they had in the Soviet Union; the hardworking French people enslaved by the greedy Jews; French mothers and infants torn apart and sold.

Finally she saw the Resistants themselves, those deceived and deluded girls and boys. She was saving them as well, from themselves and each other.

She didn't want to hurt them just because they imagined they could keep their secrets from her. She got no pleasure from the harsh tactics it often took to extract vital information. Nor did it please her to hear about the Resistants executed by firing squads or shot, in cold blood, in their homes or hiding places. She mourned these unfortunate French youths who had been tricked and lied to, and who didn't deserve to die.

Late one night, at a bar, a French cop suggested that Lou got a sexual thrill out of bloodying the pretty girls. Lou landed two punches, blackening both of his eyes, until his pals pulled her off him.

But when Lou worked with the prisoners, she was never angry, nor did she think that her methods were gratuitously violent. She had a system she followed closely, rules for what she would and wouldn't do. She never once got carried away or did more harm than she'd intended.

She didn't have to nearly kill the prisoners in order to make them talk. She only had to persuade them that they no longer had any control, that their lives and their loved ones' lives depended completely on her. Fighting the temptation to compete against herself, to see if she could crack a prisoner faster than she had the night before, she never once forgot that this holy work was not to be taken lightly: her prisoners were human beings who felt pain, just as she did. She often thought of Joan of Arc, and it made her proud that the power had been taken back from those who had tormented and burned the Maid of Orléans.

Was it wrong to make one person suffer to prevent harm to many? When Lou pondered that, which she tried not to, it gave her a headache. She'd leave those questions to the philosophers and do what she did best.

She was surprised by how much trouble it took to get prisoners to reveal things they once would have told her and Inge for two glasses of hard cider. But it made sense. Time had passed. Positions had hardened. You had to sacrifice for your country. A war was being fought, inside and beyond the border. No one could pretend not to be affected. The Resistance was blowing up bridges and assassinating citizens on busy streets, even on the Métro, where passengers should feel safe.

No one was asking Lou to put on a uniform and put herself in harm's way. She never once killed anyone. At least no deaths are on record.

Her bosses relied on her to help make sure that the right side won and innocent people weren't hurt. Lou did one thing, and she did it well. She could make prisoners talk. She had no interest in what some of her colleagues enjoyed: the detective work and arrests. She disliked the interrogation methods—the dental extractions, the ice baths, the skull crushing, the application of electrodes—that required specialized techniques or more than one technician.

Thanks to the rigorous documentation kept by the French office of the SS, only some of which was burned before the Allies liberated Paris, we know exactly when Lou showed up at the headquarters on the rue Lauriston, how many hours she worked—occasionally through the night—and how much (decently, but not generously) she was paid.

Books have been written about the culture of La Carlingue, where the torture chambers employed a receptionist who combined the duties of a doctor's nurse with those of the madam of a brothel. It was her job to avoid traffic snarls, to make sure that all the rooms were occupied and no space was wasted. We know there was a physician on call, a descendant of Madame Tussaud, of the wax museum Tussauds. The joke was that the wax-museum guy was called in to rule on whether a prisoner was living or dead. Music was played to drown out the prisoners' screams. The German officers and the French police once got into a fistfight about whether to play Wagner or Piaf.

Among Lou's new coworkers were many old pals from the Gasparu-Chanac gang. Every so often Clovis Chanac dropped by, though mostly he preferred watching to dirtying his tailored suits with the bloody punching and kicking.

As the Occupation dragged on, the gangsters thrived. They were among the few Parisians smiling on the street. Who would have dreamed they'd be paid by the state to do what they'd done for fun when it was illegal? But now that they had to work harder to exceed the limits of acceptable gangster behavior, the criminals grew competitive about their reputations for senseless violence. Crazy Pierrot Gasparu became famous for carrying the heads of executed Resistance agents in a leather briefcase specially designed for him by Coco Chanel.

Several studies of the Gasparu-Chanac organization have been published, moderately informative histories that for some reason fail to mention Lou Villars, whose career paralleled that of the gang, but on a higher level. Lou was the only woman on the staff at rue Lauriston. Everyone knew that her gender was partly why she'd been hired. It was believed that the prisoners would crack sooner when they suffered the shock and shame of pain inflicted by a female, especially when that woman dressed—and was as strong—as a man.

There were only two victims, both now dead, who wrote accounts of being interrogated and tortured by Lou Villars. Both agreed that Lou dispensed with the savage beatings that her colleagues favored. Nor, they noted, was Lou a fan of the near-drownings and pretend hangings popular among the jailers who liked staging dramas in teams.

Lou was known for using her cigarette lighter to get information and for working slowly, partly because (again the records show) she was getting paid by the hour. All her life she'd hated snitches, so it was unsurprising that she respected the prisoners who refused to talk. When they confessed and implicated their friends, she had no problem turning them over to her colleagues.

Lou's lighter became notorious. Prisoners dreaded the moment when it appeared from her pocket. This was the elegant love token she'd received from Inge, the first present she ever got. The fury and the sense of betrayal that it inspired now so transfixed her that she seemed spellbound as she applied its flame to the skin and hair of the male and female prisoners.

The lighter was engraved with Lou's initials, *LV.* A popular joke— the letters stood for *laide et violente*, ugly and violent—was typical Resistance gallows humor.

Lou's voice would grow more threatening. Then she would begin inflicting a series of burns, mild as mosquito bites. Suddenly, Lou flicked her lighter close to her victims' eyes, asking if she should bring the flame closer. Sometimes the smell of singed eyelashes caused the prisoners to faint, and Lou would douse them with water, a process she called—her joke—putting out the fire. This technique nearly always got results. Lou rarely had to call anyone's bluff, not even the hard-core fanatics.

Using this method, Lou Villars prevented a hijacked munitions convoy from reaching Clermont-Ferrand. She found six Jewish boys hiding in a convent and a British agent on his way to a meeting place where he was captured along with the Resistants smuggling him out of the country. It never failed to amaze Lou how many lives could be saved, how much destruction could be averted, how much good she could do with the minimal energy required to light one cigarette.

Yvonne

BEFORE THE OCCUPATION, the Chameleon Club did well, particularly with a revue called "Madame la Marquise." The show featured a series of variations on a popular song about a marquise who keeps phoning home to learn she has lost everything, her estate has burned, her husband has killed himself. And the servants keep reassuring her that everything is fine.

A dozen groups performed the same number. Singers in chefs' hats acted out the lyrics while cooking up a poisonous witches' brew. An actor crooned into a microphone wearing only a Nazi helmet and ladies' panties. Everything is fine, Madame la Marquise. The audience admired the creativity lavished on a familiar tune with its obvious comment about the razor's edge they were walking.

After the invasion, no more jokes about Germans. They told German jokes at some clubs, but Yvonne wasn't taking chances. And no more humor about everything being all right, dear Madame la Marquise. The Jewish singers were gone, and Yvonne had to scramble when the saxophone player fled to Lisbon. The black musicians had vanished too. Rarely did one see a dark face on the street. Josephine Baker had taken refuge in her château, where, according to rumor, she was aiding the Resistance.

Yvonne did what she could with the talent left in Paris, but some spice, or spirit, was missing. The choices had narrowed, unless one had a fortune to spend on reviews like the ones in Montmartre, shows whose titles were their price tags. "Two Million." "Three-Point Five."

After Pavel was forced to emigrate to Buenos Aires, Yvonne choreographed the dances herself, though that was not her strong suit.

Against her better judgment, she hired a poodle act with a trainer named Pedro who dressed as Marie Antoinette. Desperate, she took on a girl named Suki, who shimmied in a nightie and never got out of bed, and a couple of tango dancers, Zolpi and Lora, a Romanian brother and sister costumed as Gypsies of the opposite sex. They doubled as fortune-tellers. Zolpi had a cousin from Yvonne's hometown. For years the couple had been dancing at the club, begging Yvonne for a job.

In theory, the Chameleon should have been closed when the Germans took Paris. Its counterparts in Berlin had been shuttered for years, though a few nightspots survived, thanks to their influential patrons and investors. The Chameleon Club owed its existence to the fact that it was listed in the Officers' Edition of the military tourist guide *Paris Once*, published for the German soldiers who'd believed the Nazi recruiting promise: *Paris for Everyone Once.*

The book described the Chameleon as a snake pit of French vice, the moral equivalent of those medical museums where visitors can study birth defects and the damage poisons do to one's organs. In this case the sexual organs; the poison was being French. To the Germans, being French meant having lots of sex. Germans flocked to the club and spread the word: the Chameleon was good clean fun!

It was a miracle that the club was still open, that Yvonne's clients had a place to go and halfway decent entertainment. The floor show no longer mattered so much. The audience entertained itself. The Germans and the regulars came to look at one another. But how long could that last? People got tired of seeing the same people in the same clothes, be it a Gestapo uniform or the top half of a tuxedo.

The club's homosexual clientele knew how the Germans were treating their brothers across the border. The more principled stayed away, but others enjoyed the thrill of proximity to danger. It took their minds off their problems to sit near a table of German soldiers and watch a Norwegian who called himself Lady Sinbad (whom Yvonne soon fired for onstage drunkenness) do the Dance of the Seven Veils.

The band learned to play "Lili Marlene" and other German songs when the drinking slowed down. These sentimental favorites got the crowd singing until they were thirsty.

Yvonne had prided herself on knowing everything that went on in her club. But for the first time, there were certain things she chose not to see or hear.

Fat Bernard confided in Yvonne: her real name was Berthe Klein. Yvonne said she hadn't known that. In fact she'd already forgotten. Yvonne mentioned two forgers who frequented the Chameleon. A counterfeiter named Cigarette Butt and an elderly Hungarian with an eye patch whom Cigarette Butt called Maestro, and for whom Yvonne had great respect. Yvonne told Bernard to let them drink for free. They could provide her with Aryan papers. Bernard said she'd already asked, and they already had.

A few weeks later German soldiers barged into the kitchen and asked to see the papers of Yvonne's entire staff. It gave Yvonne great pleasure to watch them approve the identity card that Cigarette Butt had made for Fat Bernard.

Despite the hardships and shortages, Yvonne raised the staff's salaries. After all, she was paying her dishwashers to wash German spit from the glasses. She insisted the club remain a haven for runaways and strays. She took in dozens of Jewish kids and lent them money to leave the country.

One night a British guy stayed on after everyone else had gone. He said his name was Ducky and that he was a singer, stranded in Paris. He asked for a top hat and tails, a cane and green face paint. He did his Pinocchio act for Yvonne. He played Jiminy Cricket and sang "When You Wish Upon a Star" from the Disney film, in English with a fake but convincing French accent.

The crowd adored Ducky. They were touched by his song, and they forgave him for forgetting his lines and improvising nonsensical lyrics. Certain patterns in Ducky's gibberish made Yvonne suspect that he was sending coded messages to someone in the room.

Eventually Ducky didn't show up for work. Fat Bernard passed Yvonne a note that said, The cricket has flown its cage.

One rainy night, after hours, Arlette showed up at the Chameleon. Drenched, in a wet fur coat, she looked like a street dog. One eye was mottled purple. The corner of her mouth oozed blood. "Police, open up," she said. She was crying. Bernard brought her back to the office. Yvonne lent Arlette a warm sweater and ordered a pot of tea and whiskey.

Arlette said she was leaving Chanac. He'd hit her once too often. Yvonne wanted to ask why she'd been with him in the first place. But she knew the answer, which Arlette would never admit. Yvonne had never liked Arlette and her loathsome mermaid song. But compared to the present, those nights when Arlette and Lou reigned over the club seemed idyllic, a vanished paradise, lost forever.

Arlette said, "I've got a new song. I'll direct the whole production. The dances. The music. Everything. Give me a month."

"A month," said Yvonne. "No longer. It's good to have you back."

"Mes Souvenirs" was the runaway hit of 1943. More talented singers recorded it, but their versions weren't half so successful. What made the song so popular weren't the lyrics or the tune, but Arlette's performance.

Arlette regained a few pounds and her cute Little Mermaid body. She still looked sweet, not in a fish tail this time, but in costumes and wigs she changed throughout her routine. Though the title, "My Memories," may have suggested a bittersweet reflection on happy times gone by, a sad tribute to loved ones lost in battle, *memory* was Arlette's euphemism for sex and having babies.

My memories, my memories, Arlette sang, dressed in a short ruffled skirt, turning her back to the audience, bending over and shaking her ass to the drumbeat on each syllable of *sou-ve-nir*.

First came her memories of the soldier who stayed for one night and shipped out in the morning. Arlette ran offstage and reappeared with two identically plump, blond baby dolls. With a cute little twitch she bent to kiss each infant forehead.

The next verse recalled the handsome farmer who kept a cow that gave her the milk she needed to nurse twin babies. The audience giggled as Arlette skipped offstage and pranced back with four dolls this time, two in tiny farmers' berets.

Her memories, boom boom boom, her memories, boom boom boom. And now the memory family grew to include two new baby memories of the mayor, who took pity on a poor French girl, a single mother with four children, and set up a private nursery school, paid for with all the new taxes. Arlette's fans could laugh at the new taxes and laugh even harder when she reappeared, arms akimbo, struggling under the weight of six squirming doll babies, three in the crook of each elbow.

Then, lest anyone take this in the wrong spirit, lest anyone imagine that Arlette was impugning the morals of French women, a male dancer in a French army uniform and a Maréchal Pétain mask marched onstage. He presented Arlette with a medal and pronounced her Mother of the Year for having borne the most children for the glory of the French nation.

French and Germans, soldiers and performers, transvestites and artists of all ages were happy to laugh together. Part of the fun was that everyone thought the joke was on everyone else. Everyone could have a few drinks and enjoy a song that briefly convinced them that sex and war were funny.

One night Bernard knocked on Yvonne's office door and said she'd better come out front. They had special guests: Jean-Claude Bonnet. Clovis Chanac. Pierre Gasparu. Two Germans.

Oh, and Lou Villars.

There wasn't one of them whom Yvonne wanted in her club. There wasn't one of them whom she wanted *thinking* about the Chameleon. She often thought about Lou. It was uncomfortable to know that a woman she'd banned from the premises was a driver for Jean-Claude Bonnet and a torturer for the Gestapo. Also it was upsetting that the star of her show was the former girlfriend of the torturer *and* of one of the city's most powerful gangsters.

At first, after Arlette returned, Yvonne had expected Chanac every night, despite Arlette's assurances that she had too much dirt on him

for him to show his face. And when he didn't appear, Yvonne had begun to assume that he wouldn't.

The club was crowded. Every table was full. The show had gotten
off to a good start. Everyone was laughing. A poodle had run under
Pedro's (Marie Antoinette's) skirt.

Lou and her friends weren't laughing. They stood near the doorway, glowering. Soon no one was laughing.

When Yvonne went over to welcome them, Lou stepped forward.
She shook Yvonne's hand, embraced her in a stiff hug, then kissed
her sloppily on both cheeks and said, "We'd like a table for six." Lou's
breath smelled of whiskey and cigarettes.

Lou's hair was cut short and slicked back. It hurt Yvonne's heart
to see that Lou was slightly balding with a peak in front, like a man.
So much time had passed, so much had been broken and could never
be fixed since Lou had appeared at the door with blood on her white
flannel trousers. What a sad confused girl she had been, and how age
and time and bad luck had transformed her into the bully who blocked
Yvonne's path.

Lou ranked below the others. But she used to work here. The Chameleon was her territory. This was her party.

Lou said, "In fact I'd like my old table."

Yvonne turned to see who was sitting there. An older woman and
a younger one, both in white tuxedos. Florencia and Lola had been
coming here for years. They'd seen Yvonne talking to Lou. They recognized Bonnet and Chanac. They knew that their table used to be
Lou's. Both women got up to leave. Yvonne reminded herself to tell
Fat Bernard to let them drink for free, forever.

As the busboys whisked away the dirty dishes and brought out a
new tablecloth and coasters, Lou told Yvonne, "My friends have just
come from a stressful meeting. They need to relax."

Though it took only minutes to set the table, Yvonne apologized
for the delay and told Lou that the first round was on the house. All
the rounds would be on the house. It was the cost of doing business.
The bartenders were alerted to water Chanac's drinks. Only when

those small but all-important details were arranged could Yvonne consider the potentially volatile situation: Chanac and Lou had come to see their mutual former girlfriend.

Arlette always went on last, after Marie Antoinette and Zolpi and Lora. But now Yvonne made a quick decision. Let Arlette perform before Lou's party had any more alcohol and time to figure out what to do when she sang.

Arlette wasn't happy about the change, but neither was she pleased to hear that two angry former lovers were in the house. She was a professional. She realized that it would be wise to tone down the shaking of her ass. Tonight's crowd would have to make do with a lot less boom boom boom.

Arlette was still singing the first verse, telling the story of the sailor on his one-night shore leave, when a male voice shouted hoarsely, "Abyssinia!"

Abyssinia? The music stopped. Arlette's jaw went slack, her arms hung down, her fat little hands paddled the air like flippers. How could a woman who made her living from striking sexy poses let herself freeze in such an unflattering attitude?

"Abyssinia," repeated Chanac. "Show them Abyssinia." Then, still shouting, he informed the crowd that Arlette had a birthmark on her ass the shape and size of Abyssinia.

Lou half rose and made a fist, as if to punch Chanac. Bonnet placed a restraining hand on Lou's arm. Chanac watched, so enjoying the drama he'd set in motion that he lost interest in Arlette, who skipped ahead to the final verse, which she sang in a quavering version of her normally wobbly voice while the musicians struggled to figure out what key she was in.

Yvonne had always prided herself on the calm, hospitable grace with which she'd soothed the ruffled feathers of her peacock clientele. For decades, she'd dealt so firmly but politely with those who'd overindulged that they felt free to return the next night, impeccably behaved.

But now all the emotions she'd held in check, anger and irritation, contempt and disgust, grief over the loss of her voice, the nights she'd stayed up worrying about the club, the mornings she'd woken in fear of being deported, every insult and anxiety, every petty criminal, cop, government official, and German soldier who'd purposely or accidentally offended her or her customers, every ass she'd had to kiss, everything that Lou and her friends represented, all of it swirled together and stirred up something inside Yvonne, something present but so dormant she'd hardly suspected its existence.

Yvonne heard herself order Lou Villars and Clovis Chanac to get out and never come back.

"Why me?" said Lou. "It wasn't my fault. You're blaming me for the shit this guy does?"

"You too," said Yvonne. "Go."

Everyone in the club was watching. Yvonne could feel the force of the crowd's desire to protect her, to turn back time to the minute before she'd insulted Lou Villars, the Minister of Information, two Germans, and the leaders of the Gasparu-Chanac gang. But Yvonne had already moved far beyond the audience's power to help her.

Bonnet glared at Yvonne and then at Chanac, blinking exaggeratedly, like a turtle. He focused on one, then the other, exuding quiet threat. Meanwhile their German friends were visibly irritated about how the evening was turning out. They'd come to see Arlette shake her ass. My memories. Boom boom boom. My memories. Boom boom boom. This was not the memory they'd imagined taking back to their hotel rooms.

Fat Bernard signaled the band to play. "Sweeter than sweet," she sang. But nobody was paying attention to anything but the surly, slow-motion exit of Lou and her friends. No one sat at that table all night.

Lora and Zolpi tangoed frantically, then sashayed through the room. No one wanted their fortunes told. Marie Antoinette swept back onstage, but her poodles, sensing something, barked and refused to jump through hoops. Luckily, Marie-Pedro was a seasoned veteran who turned the stage fright of his "lambs" into a comic variation on his regular act.

Somehow they got through the evening. But moments after closing, Vilma, the coat check girl, asked to speak to Yvonne in private.

In Yvonne's office, where she had never been, and where she struggled to memorize every detail in case she never saw it again, Vilma
told Yvonne that, on his way out, Bonnet asked her to inform Yvonne
that he would send his men around tomorrow afternoon to escort her
to his office. Together they would make sure that misunderstandings
like tonight's would never occur again.

Yvonne asked Vilma to repeat what Bonnet said. This time the girl
closed her eyes so as to more accurately channel the minister's voice.
This time she placed more emphasis, *his* emphasis, on *never.*

From the (Unpublished) Memoirs
of Suzanne Dunois Tsenyi
To be destroyed on the occasion of its author's death

FOR ONCE, THE movies got it right. We *were* an army of shadows, a band of friends and comrades who would have been safer as strangers. We were like students at a secret school at which failure could mean death.

My own work involved rescue rather than violence and revenge. But I would be lying if I pretended I wasn't delighted when the right target was blown up, the right evil bastard murdered. The crucial thing was to stay alive and not betray or endanger others.

After the war, things got more complex, as they always do. Cliques and factions formed. There were resentments, publicity grabs, inflated claims of personal heroism when in fact we'd all been brave. Otherwise we couldn't have done it.

On the night when Yvonne threw Lou Villars and her friends out of the Chameleon, Ricardo met me at a café where we would not be noticed. Pretending to be lovers, we exchanged a passionate kiss.

He whispered that there was a woman who needed to leave France at once.

"France?" I said. "Not just Paris?"

"France," Ricardo said.

When I think back on that night, on the events that would cause so much pain en route to such costly triumph, I can still smell disinfectant spiced with ether, Ricardo's signature cologne. He had just come from performing a surgical operation. I knew better than to ask: had he been resetting some Nazi thug's broken nose or removing a bullet from a wounded Resistant?

You could say that our work was good training for being a human being. We cared about one another but were careful not to be nosy. Ricardo and I never discussed the fact that he had fallen in love with a man named William "Ducky" Curtis, a downed British pilot (and singer) who'd performed at the Chameleon until a German general, a regular customer, figured out that he was sending messages in code. Now Ricardo was hiding him in the hospital, claiming that Ducky was in a coma, his face completely bandaged, until the Resistance decided what to do next.

Ricardo and Ducky survived. It is one of the happier stories to have come out of that painful era. They now divide their time between London and Buenos Aires.

Ricardo and I ordered wine. *Salud.* We clinked glasses. Each of us drank a sip. Then Ricardo told me what had just happened at the Chameleon and that the woman who needed to leave was Yvonne.

As far as I know, Yvonne never officially joined the Resistance, but connections were made at her club and communications exchanged. For months, as a singing cricket, Ducky had signaled the British secret service.

When you wish upon a star, a parachute will fall from the sky near Strasbourg. When you wish upon a star, a transport will land near Caen.

There was also a poodle act in which the little dogs done up as lambs would bring messages scrawled on napkins to undercover Resistants drinking at the bar. I'm not sure that Yvonne was aware of that, though formerly she'd insisted on knowing everything that happened in the Chameleon.

We convinced ourselves that certain people, like Yvonne, would always be safe. Mostly this turned out to be wrong. It was always shocking to be reminded that nothing and no one (except Picasso, I suppose) was immune to the dangers the rest of us faced.

By midnight Ricardo and I were with Yvonne, in her office. Yvonne didn't need to know that I had already smuggled, or arranged to smuggle, forty people out of France. Forty, more or less. I didn't keep count. Counting was unlucky. It was something the Germans did.

Yvonne needed a new passport and papers. She knew several counterfeiters she trusted, but lately for some reason they'd stopped coming to the club. Ricardo and I couldn't look at each other. Yvonne didn't need to know that Cigarette Butt had been deported to Germany, where, we'd heard, he was being forced to work for the other side.

Gabor's portrait of Yvonne on the eve of her escape is among the most moving and controversial of his career. He has been criticized, as if there were something morally wrong about photographing a woman in such obvious distress. What else should he have done? There was no way to comfort her. Could he have forbidden Yvonne to think of all that had happened during the years since that first night she refused to let him take her picture?

Gabor knew what he was getting on film. Only after he got the shot did he embrace Yvonne, dry her tears with his handkerchief, and tell her in Hungarian and then in French to trust him, everything would be fine.

Gabor shot the passport-style picture that we used for the documents. Unlike the more artful portrait, this official snapshot was lost, probably after Yvonne moved to Buenos Aires, where she and Pavel opened a chic transvestite club that thrived until Péron came to power. After that she retired to Miami, where she died, decades later.

So we had Yvonne's image. But how would we get the fake papers with Cigarette Butt gone?

I gave Yvonne a warning look: say nothing in front of Gabor.

Gabor said he knew a counterfeiter.

Ricardo frowned at me. I shrugged. Don't blame me. I didn't tell him.

Two hours later Gabor returned to the club with an ancient Hungarian who looked like a shriveled root vegetable with an eye patch. Up close, one could see the striking figure he'd been. Was this the person we were entrusting with Yvonne's life? It was Gabor I trusted, and he loved Yvonne.

"Maestro!" Yvonne said.

"You two know each other," said Gabor.

Yvonne said, "Cigarette Butt used to bring him to the club."

Thirty-six hours later, the old man delivered the passport of a Hungarian-born Swiss citizen who looked exactly like Yvonne, an inspired work of art that would fool the most suspicious Nazi.

Whenever I heard about how this or that artist took a stance, or didn't, during the Occupation, I wanted to tell the story of how Gabor saved Yvonne. But I never have. Perhaps some part of me changed in those years and cannot be changed back from a woman who believes: the less you say the better. The less you say about the *other people*. Let them tell their own stories. Interviewed about myself, I've had no trouble talking. Let others talk about themselves. They are entitled to privacy, even after death, another reason why I want these pages destroyed after mine.

By the time Yvonne's documents were ready, it was no longer safe for her to travel by train. So I persuaded the baroness Lily de Rossignol to drive her across the border.

Seeing them off, I envied them. What an adventure they would have! Had I known what awaited me, I might have begged them to take me along. In fact I nearly did. Some impulse or premonition almost overcame me as I watched Yvonne and the baroness drive away from her château. Watching them leave was wrenching, though I knew that I needed to stay in Paris.

That night, Gabor and I were awoken by someone banging on the door. How ironic that after all those nights when Gabor tossed and turned until we got up and went for a walk, all those nights when we'd stayed awake watching the cops round up our neighbors, we were sleeping the dreamless sleep of the innocent when they came for me.

From *The Devil Drives:*
The Life of Lou Villars

BY NATHALIE DUNOIS

Chapter Sixteen: A Chance Meeting

AFTER THE INCIDENT at the Chameleon Club, my great-aunt Suzanne was arrested on suspicion of having aided the escape of the club's owner, Yvonne. In the reeking archives of the offices in the rue Lauriston, it is recorded that on the night of February 23, 1943, Lou Villars spent the hours between midnight and 3:00 A.M. interrogating a Mlle. Suzanne Dunois. Jean-Claude Bonnet and another guard had interviewed her earlier, so we can assume that by the time Lou arrived, my aunt had already suffered considerable violence.

How ironic that Lou's portrait graced the cover of the book that launched the distinguished and lucrative career of my aunt's future husband! How upsetting to find that you are at the mercy of someone who lost a legal case partly because of a photo your lover took. Someone who may blame *you* for having been present when she learned that her brother was dead. Suzanne must have assumed that her goose was cooked, that Lou had plenty of reasons beyond the professional to torture her—and enjoy it.

But though their paths had crossed at critical points, let me suggest that Suzanne Dunois didn't know Lou as well as I do. My aunt could hardly have been aware of the battles raging inside the woman who walked into the room in the man's white shirt, khaki trousers, and, ominously, a rubberized fishmonger's apron.

Suzanne could not have known that, as she entered the cell, Lou recalled a vision she'd had as a girl: a blond woman in pain, her head thrown back, her pretty face streaked with blood. When had she imagined that? At the convent school. The strangeness of seeing her fantasy realized was so unnerving that it took Lou a while to identify the woman with the rabbity teeth as a bloodied version of the Hungarian photographer's girlfriend.

Lately Lou had been feeling an almost maternal tenderness for the victims and for the almost childlike trust with which they entrusted themselves to her. It had come to seem so intimate, the work they did together, this ritual transaction of denial and surrender, almost like a religious ceremony, a series of sacraments culminating in confession and absolution. It wasn't hatred Lou felt but love for the souls she was saving.

The fact that she knew Suzanne Dunois made this an unusual case. Her heart went out to the attractive Frenchwoman who'd been led astray by her foreign friends. Suzanne's connection with the past gave Lou's compassion a special luster. She pitied not only her victim, but also herself. She mourned the innocent she'd been when she'd worked at the cabaret for the arrogant Hungarian tramp who humiliated her in front of Bonnet and his friends, men whose good opinion she valued. The Hungarian whore who had shamed her in front of Chanac, whom she despised, which made the shame even worse.

But it wasn't Suzanne's fault. Suzanne was French, like her. The sooner Suzanne told Lou how they'd smuggled Yvonne out of Paris, the better their chances of catching the Hungarian brothel madam.

Lou interrogated Suzanne all night and into the following day. This time she departed from her usual practice. This time blood was shed before the lighter appeared. My great-aunt Suzanne was a stylish woman, but she always wore long sleeves. Everyone knew that this was to hide the scars she'd gotten during the Occupation. Who else but Lou could have inflicted those marks?

At one point Lou stepped back to study her victim's ravaged face, which looked exactly as it had when Lou had imagined this scene, as a girl. She'd mistaken it for a glimpse of Joan of Arc, but now she understood that it was a vision of an enemy of the state.

Lou was the judge, the jury, the guardian, the fierce and holy angel with the flaming sword. She took out her cigarette lighter.

She flicked it once and then again, nearer Suzanne.

She said, "Should I bring it closer?"

Often it has seemed clear to me, what Lou was thinking or feeling. But now as I try to imagine what exactly moved her to spare my great-aunt, I realize how little I understand. Was she moved by enduring love for the dead or sympathy for the living? Some vestige of humanity, suppressed compassion, or perhaps nostalgia for the lost happiness of the past? Was that what made Lou suspend her interrogation without getting what she wanted? I would like to think that it was Lou who persuaded her bosses to let Suzanne go, even though she hadn't told them how they'd smuggled Yvonne out of Paris.

The whites of Suzanne's eyes were scarlet. Her arms were a map of sores. But she hadn't been blinded. And someone had let her live. Her courageous refusal to disclose any information gave Yvonne the time she needed to reach Spain, then Lisbon, from where she sailed for Buenos Aires.

From *A Baroness by Night*

BY LILY DE ROSSIGNOL

THE PHONE ONLY worked intermittently and was probably tapped. For the first time since I'd left Hollywood, people arrived unannounced. Before the Occupation no civilized French person would do that. It was such a social taboo, I can recall the exceptions: once, drunk at midnight, Gabor Tsenyi and Lionel Maine threw pebbles at my window—and were turned away. And then there was that evening when I visited Gabor, and he gave me my portrait, and we had our little misunderstanding.

But during the war, at all hours and in every sort of weather, people knocked and were admitted. I never asked how they got there or how they planned to get home, though the house in which I was living was a twenty-minute drive from Paris.

Late one night, Suzanne Dunois showed up at my door.

She was active, as was I, in the anti-Nazi cause. I would never have imagined that Gabor's little friend would become one of my most trusted contacts. I'd thought of her as a silly girl with a pretty body. I'd never wanted to know what she thought of me: a bossy, rich, older woman with designs on her boyfriend. But by then, the fact that two comrades in arms had once been in love with the same man, and that one of them had won—all that was too insignificant to consider. Our history had been wiped clean, or almost clean, by the history around us.

Suzanne told me she knew a woman who needed to leave the country. It was already too late to risk the usual escape routes. They needed me to drive her across the Spanish border.

I asked who it was. Suzanne couldn't say. Did I know her? The maddening girl couldn't tell me that, either. But fine, yes, she could say that much. Yes, she thought I knew her. I offered Suzanne a glass of wine. Perhaps a drop of brandy? She said, Just water, please. Since we'd come back from the south, she'd had so little alcohol that one sip would go straight to her head.

That was typical of what still annoyed me about Suzanne, regardless of how much the war had done to change my opinion. A certain self-righteous quality, earnest, even pious. Holier than thou. But that too was the sort of thing which was no longer supposed to matter.

"One sip?" I said. "Remarkable. I envy you, I do."

Suzanne said, "Gabor sends his regards."

Later Gabor would claim that he too aided the Resistance. But as far as I knew then, he was mostly spending his time with Picasso and other celebrity artists, photographing their studios in Paris and in the provinces, where they waited out the war. The images he made during those years were not his best work, though there are some first-rate portraits he took in the process of shooting photos that were used for fake documents and passports.

Had Suzanne meant to hurt me by mentioning him? I hadn't seen Gabor in a while. I asked how he was doing. Suzanne said he was fine, though he was worried about a friend. I said, Gabor is always worried. Suzanne pouted, like a child. She said he had reason to worry. There had been an "incident" at the Chameleon Club, earlier that evening. That was how I knew that Yvonne was the woman who needed to be driven across the border.

I said, "It's a good thing I like to drive."

I'd always admired Yvonne. Some of my most amusing evenings had been spent at her club. Sentiment overcame me, a longing for the days when Gabor and I scanned the dance floor for clues to the mystery of sex and for photographic subjects. I'd been disappointed when Yvonne let Arlette perform her repulsive routines. But they had helped save the club, where a lot of good was done, in secret, for our cause.

I would have done anything for Yvonne. I adored the idea of rescuing her, regardless of the risk. I didn't adore the idea of being caught and taken prisoner. But I had cyanide capsules. And except for the awfulness of knowing that one's corpse will turn that vile unflattering blue, poison wasn't the worst way to go. That was how I'd been thinking ever since Didi's death. Unhappiness was a great advantage in my Resistance work. Nothing fuels bravery more than the lack of the will to live. I'd come to understand why Didi, mourning Armand, had sabotaged Bonnet's brakes.

Yvonne and I were instructed to travel as many hours a day as we could, respecting local curfews. Suzanne gave us convincingly authentic coupons for gas, which I hadn't been able to get since Didi's death. Given the danger and the seriousness of the mission, I had to repress a shiver of pleasure when I realized I could once again fill up the Juno-Diane and take it on out for a spin.

If I got tired, we were to pull over and hide the car as best we could and sleep by the side of the road. Hotels might have Yvonne's picture. If we were stopped, we should say that Yvonne was a naturalized Swiss citizen of Brazilian-Hungarian descent. Her mother was dying in Rio. She was booked on a boat from Lisbon. She had the necessary papers, including one stamped with the seal of a German admiral who had once been a personal friend.

Suzanne gave me a bottle of pills. She said they were for courage. Nazi drugs the Luftwaffe pilots took to stay awake. For years we'd been hearing about these drugs. They were legendary in our circle. I didn't ask where they'd come from. I assumed from Ricardo.

Later, when I learned that Suzanne was arrested on the night we left, I felt not only guilty but *morally unclean* to think that, while she was being tortured, Yvonne and I were having the time of our lives! I do remember noticing that Suzanne looked stricken as she watched us drive off. For a moment, I considered turning around and asking her to come with us. Though it would have been crowded in the Juno-Diane.

For the first half hour Yvonne kept her eyes closed. I thought, *This* could be a long ride. But after I persuaded her to take one of the pills, she became much friendlier and eventually quite chatty.

We had plenty to talk about. We talked about everything, really.

Yvonne's childhood, raising ducks, delivering babies. The grateful new father who paid her way to Paris because she'd saved his child. Anecdotes from the early days of the Chameleon Club. How she'd wanted to be *interesting*, wearing red and keeping pet lizards.

I told her all about Didi, how we met and how he died. She said she was sorry. She'd known some but not all of the story. Her opinion was that Didi had meant to kill Bonnet, which made him a hero. After decades at the Chameleon, Yvonne didn't have to be convinced that Didi and I loved one another as much as any "ordinary" married couple.

I'm not sure why we avoided the subject of our mutual friend Gabor. Nor did I feel I could ask Yvonne why she'd let Arlette sing those wicked songs. Didi had done business with Germans. None of us were clean. I believed, or chose to believe, that not one Jew had been killed because of a luxury sedan, or a song-and-dance routine performed by a lesbian couple dressed as a sailor and a mermaid.

Neither Yvonne nor I had forgotten what had happened to the millions of innocent people who'd been less lucky than we were. We were nervous but fatalistic. We would see what happened. The pills gave us stamina, courage, and hope, which (along with luck) was all we needed.

We flirted and giggled our way through the roadblocks and checkpoints. The guards believed our story. Two attractive middle-aged women, a dying mother, a boat waiting to take the grieving daughter home to Brazil. When she had to, Yvonne looked devastated, which was probably how she felt.

Several times they made us get out so they could admire the car. They walked around it gingerly, as if it were a bomb that might explode. I understand what sort of men they were, these German oppressors, these traitors to the French people. But it is a testament to human decency and civilization that none of them acted on the impulse to shoot us and steal the car.

The weather was good, the road empty except for the convoys of soldiers who honked their horns and whistled at us, or the car, as we passed.

The car ran like a dream. Thank you, Didi. Thank you, Armand.

We stayed awake the whole time. The curfews didn't seem to apply to us. No one stopped us for driving at night. The gods were on our side.

This is what I'd been missing! A friend and a bottle of Nazi bomber pills. If only Yvonne and I could have been friends before. I realized those were different times, and we were different people.

Yvonne described the scene with Lou, Bonnet, Arlette, and Chanac in the club. The story went back so far and had so many subplots that it got us all the way to Limoges. There a garage staffed by Resistants checked out the car, gave us food, and even collected a few of our phony petrol coupons.

One night, in a pensive mood, Yvonne said she hated thinking she'd lost her club and might die because of a birthmark on the ass of a tone-deaf, gold-digging slut. I told Yvonne she wasn't going to die. Not now. That was the point. Yvonne said she hoped not. A giant rabbit hopped into the road, caught my headlights, and froze. I swerved and missed it. We laughed until I could hardly see to drive.

We talked about the war. About the scenes we'd witnessed and couldn't get out of our minds. I told Yvonne how much I admired her for kicking Lou out of her club. Lou Villars was the devil, and so were all her friends. By then all Paris knew what Lou was doing for the Gestapo. But more time would have to pass before historians confirmed the rumor connecting her with the breach of the Maginot Line.

Yvonne said, What a coincidence that Lou had worked for us both! She wondered what had poisoned the heart and mind of that poor girl who only wanted to dress like a boy and find someone to love her. Neither of us blamed ourselves. Why should we? It wasn't our fault.

I wish our conversation could have been recorded. I found it intensely interesting: the jabbering of two women high on Nazi amphetamines and the prospect of freedom. But maybe it would have sounded like those tedious postwar novels about beatnik road trips through the American West.

We talked about Adam and Eve and the Serpent. About the possibility of counting the stars in the sky. About what Jesus meant when he said the poor would always be with us. About politics, economics, love and sex, about the afterlife.

Sometimes we'd be struck silent by the sight of a bombed-out farmhouse. Then one of us would say, The Allies are going to win. The other would say she hoped so. Until the sunshine and the fresh country air, together with the pills, convinced us that the Allies were on their way to save us. We just had to get out of France for a while. We'd soon be back in Paris.

I asked Yvonne if she still sang. She said, No. Never. Not for years. Not even when she was alone. She'd traded her voice for a cigarette, a drink, for anything that promised to help her feel less alone and worry less about the club. It would hurt to hear how she sounded now. The pain of it would kill her.

I said, "Fine. Take another pill and think about it again."

Outside Bordeaux, she turned away from me, turned her face toward the window. At first I thought she might be crying. But then she began to sing.

Her voice was throatier than when she'd sung in the club. Rougher and sadder, but beautiful. More beautiful, in a way.

I was afraid that she would stop. How strange that this should scare me more than the chance that we might be captured and shot.

She sang, *I salted the waves with my tears. I begged the captain to let me sail with them until I found him beneath the water. None of them could make me believe I would never see him again, never feel the weight of his body or his arms around me. All night I heard the waves. We know where he is, they said. He is sleeping with us. Not with you.*

Of course I thought of Gabor. Of being with him in the club. And all the time, all the days and years between now and then seemed not just lost but wasted. With one verse, Yvonne's ballad had dimmed the dazzle of the pills. Dark, unwelcome emotions began to creep back in.

Never again, she sang. *You will never see him again*. She held the note. *Again.*

I knew I would never hear that song again, never sung that way again. I would never return to this moment. The grief I felt was unbearable. The pills were wearing off.

I said, "If I weren't driving I would give you a standing ovation."

She said, "Thank you. That wasn't so bad. Now's the part where I welcome you to the Chameleon Club."

"What happened to the baby?" I said.

"What baby?"

"The one you delivered, the infant whose father paid your way to Paris. The one you just told me about."

Yvonne said, "Just told you? That was yesterday. These pills must be very strong."

We each took a swig from the bottle of wine I'd grabbed from the remains of Didi's cellar.

"I have no idea," said Yvonne. "What happened to the baby."

Every so often we'd circle back to the subject of Lou. Yvonne said that when she'd been younger and fond of all that drama with her fortune-telling lizards and so forth, her chameleon predicted that Lou Villars would die a violent early death.

Yvonne said, "Let's hope so."

We were laughing about that when I said, "See those mountains on the horizon? I think that's the Spanish border."

Yvonne reached inside her purse.

Did she really mean to pay me? What did she think I was? Her hired chauffeur? I thought, She is Hungarian. Who understands them, really?

She handed me the bill. She said, "Look at it. Look at the face."

I looked at it for as long as I could without driving off the road. I slowed down and looked harder. I said, "Who's the old guy with the eye patch and the long white hair?"

Yvonne said, "The guy who minted the money. It's my lucky charm. It's what got me this far. I have two of them, fifty-franc notes. And I want you to have one."

I still have that bill among my possessions along with such cherished totems as the newspaper item about Bonnet's accident and the first print of Gabor Tsenyi's portrait of Lou and Arlette.

From *The Devil Drives:*
The Life of Lou Villars

BY NATHALIE DUNOIS

Chapter Seventeen: *La Commedia è Finita*

WAS IT COINCIDENTAL that last night, still suffering from a case of writer's block involving weeks of silence, insomnia, cartons of cigarettes, gallons of black coffee, waves of self-loathing and doubt, I turned on my geriatric television and found myself watching, through a pebbly curtain of static, a documentary made by—who else?—an American woman. It was expertly, even slickly produced, featuring lots of archival footage and interviews with surviving heroines of the French Resistance.

There was the baroness Lily de Rossignol, in whom age had not dimmed one microcarat of beauty, charm, or magisterial entitlement as she strolled through the gardens of her château in Provence. There was my great-aunt Suzanne Dunois. Though she is quite elderly now, one can still see the pretty girl with rabbity teeth whom Gabor Tsenyi fell in love with. And that is just to mention the two who play major roles in my book. There were other heroines from elsewhere in the country.

The documentary was being shown to honor the memory of the baroness de Rossignol, who had died in a one-car auto wreck, driving a vintage Rossignol, her classic Juno-Diane coupe, not long before the film was aired. What the women in the film had in common—besides personal charisma and that smoldering volcano zest that makes certain older (French) actresses so inspirationally sexy—was that they

were all filmed in gardens, at dinner tables with intelligent talkative
friends, or in book-lined studies. All possessed the enviable cheekbones and the unblemished skin that younger women diet for and coax
with costly ointments. If only one could market the cosmetic wonders
that an unimpeachable moral conscience can do for one's face!

Of course I thought of Lou Villars. What would she look like, if
she had lived? She was already getting fat. Or so the last photographs
show. Not that it mattered. Regardless of the prejudice against grown
women who aren't sticks, no one would want to interview her. Nor
would she agree to tell a TV audience what she did during the Occupation. Perhaps some famous male documentarian, a Marcel Ophüls
or a Claude Lanzmann, would have tracked her down and filmed an
obese troll of indeterminate gender slamming her front door in the
faces of the camera crew.

What normal person wouldn't rather hear about the daring rescues, the heroic sacrifices and near escapes? What masochistic impulse made *me* want to tell *Lou's* story? Is it any wonder that this
manuscript was turned down by the same editors who have profitably
published the memoirs of several women in the film?

But when you start to write a person's life, it is like signing a contract. You are morally obliged to stay with it until the final chapter.

I followed Dr. G.'s advice and purchased a recording of Beethoven's
Late Quartets, which I played when I worked, loud enough to drown
out the stone falling down the well. I hope my readers will understand
that this was not a metaphor but a medical symptom.

At first the doctor's suggestion seemed not to be working, or rather
to be working in an unhelpful way. I stopped hearing the stone and
did nothing for several weeks but listen to the quartets.

When I try to analyze, if only for myself, why they move me so
deeply, why I thought them the most beautiful music ever composed,
my powers of description fail me, and the anguish that I feel over my
limitations, the mediocrity of talent and intelligence that I will never
in this lifetime transcend—well, all that became impossible for me to
distinguish from the music itself, from the lamentations of the violins
and the cello. Never before have I heard such an urgent outpouring of

emotion, the dark clouds of frantic anguish scattered by bright rain, buoyant balloons of playful hope shot down by arrows of despair. The surprises! Dear God, the surprises! And those *big dynamic beautiful chords!*

I cannot explain why I became so obsessed by a piece of music, or why it seemed like the perfect background for the life of Lou Villars, or why I felt and still feel such gratitude to the doctor (whose wish for anonymity I am legally compelled to respect) who suggested that I listen to it while I worked, because it would humble and encourage me, at once. Which it has, even as I throw myself, again and again, against the brick walls imprisoning a lycée instructor writing a biography of a female Nazi war criminal, working on it during her frustratingly brief school-vacation breaks!

I have tried not to mention it, but I can't help pointing out what strength of character has been required for me not to muddy Lou's story by bringing in the daily mortifications I experienced at the school where I teach. How could I describe the awfulness of the 1980s and the 1990s, when one couldn't say anything, or the present, when I am older and have less patience for students secretly texting each other while I am teaching them to read: a little Racine, a little Camus. Who wouldn't want to escape that for another place and time, even the tragic and violent era in which Lou Villars lived?

In the winter of 1944, German intelligence began hearing that the Allies were planning an invasion across the English Channel. Everyone with any information-gathering experience was pulled off their regular jobs and sent to work on the coast. You could throw a stone into any café in Normandy and hit a German or Allied spy with only the flimsiest excuse for being there.

Historians have proposed countless explanations for why the Germans were so far away when the Allies landed on the Normandy beaches they gave Native American names. The Germans had been led to believe that the landing would take place at Pas-de-Calais. Even after the invasion began, double agents reassured them that all this was a diversion to distract them from the real action, farther north.

When I say I believe that Lou Villars thought (or at least claimed) that she could have changed all that, that she knew where the Allies were really landing, that she had information that would prevent the Allied Liberation of Europe, I can imagine—no, I can *hear*—my readers saying: *Was there no horrendous historic crime that Lou Villars wasn't involved in?* Wasn't it enough to tell the Germans where the Maginot Line ended? Wasn't it sufficient to tell the leaders of Occupied Paris where to warehouse the Jews? Did she also threaten to reveal where the Allies were landing on D-Day?

But don't my readers agree that each event makes each subsequent one more likely? Once you have betrayed your country and been partly responsible for the deportation of thousands of Jews, why *not* foil the Allies' attempts to rescue Europe from people like you? If history proves anything, it proves that Lou would have been able to do it—she had the means, the motive, the opportunity. She had done it before.

Even as I write this, I am painfully aware of my failure to keep a promise I made at the start of my book, a lure that may have persuaded my readers to wade deeper into the swamp of Lou's psyche. I wrote that I hoped her story might contribute something to the literature exploring the mystery of evil. *What did I imagine that contribution would be?* Am I any closer to understanding Lou than I was on page one?

Bonnet told Lou that, whenever she liked, she could take time off from the Paris office and travel along the coast. Her cover would be her former hobby, which she was urged to resume, lecturing regional athletes who'd held out through the Occupation. They were lucky that sports, along with the state, was a permitted religion. It helped the faithful get through life, as the banned faiths once did.

Ledgers show that these trips were approved by the office of Jean-Claude Bonnet, and that in the months before the Normandy invasion, Lou spoke to the athletic associations which, against all odds, had continued to meet in Calais, Caen, Cherbourg, and other coastal towns.

Too bad there is no record of the conversation during which Bonnet asked Lou if she still had contacts at the sports clubs. Neither referred to her travels with Inge. Neither addressed the important questions. It was the perfect (unspoken) conversation to have at an interview for a job for which a talent for secrecy, lying, and conceal-ment was the major qualification. Lou's whole life until then had been preparation and practice.

How glad the Rouen Swimming Club was to have Lou back! They'd survived. She was alive. They'd all made it. So far.

Even as the women welcomed Lou, she watched them register Inge's absence. They didn't ask where Inge was. They were French. *C'est l'amour.*

Someone found a few beers they passed around the parish hall above the basement to which they advised Lou to go at once, if sirens sounded. Just last night there was a firefight directly above the airfield. Two British planes were shot down.

No sirens sounded during Lou's lecture. Once more, a voice spoke through her, this time about the importance of every woman being mentally and physically capable of taking care of herself. The athletes had reached that conclusion; it confirmed them to hear Lou say it. She still talked about the glory of France, so she hadn't lost her patriotic fervor despite everything that had happened to their ravaged country. The women applauded and emptied their purses to improve on the prearranged fee.

The problem was that she left with nothing to tell Bonnet. Paris already knew about the aborted air raid, and that the downed British pilots had escaped. No one had seen anything suspicious. Or no one was telling Lou. In the cafés, she saw more agents than local people. It was a party for spies.

Lou apologized to Bonnet. He said not to worry. Sooner or later she'd see or hear something interesting, as she had so often before.

One rainy morning, the postman brought Lou a letter from a woman named Hélène Michaux, inviting Lou to speak to a meeting of the Calais women's tennis club.

Bonnet said that Calais was exactly where they should be looking, in the ruins of the port the Germans had bombed in 1940, on their way into France.

The road north from Paris passes near the house where Lou grew up, and, if one makes a long detour, past her convent school. As Lou set out on a chilly late winter morning, let us suppose that she drove past these sentimental landmarks.

How often in the grip of some crisis do we find ourselves drawn to a beloved childhood place, as if by revisiting it we could erase the intervening disappointments and begin life anew? In one such despairing moment, I returned to my family home, walking the distance from the high school where I teach. My parents had long since retired to Portugal, to a gated community of expatriates, from where they send me an annual postcard: always the same fishing boat bobbing in a harbor, reminding me of my birthday and by extension of their (biological) role in my existence. Standing on the sidewalk across from the beauty shop above which we lived, I wept so hard and for so long that some "thoughtful" resident called the police.

There was so much I wanted to tell the handsome young gendarme who asked if he could help. But I couldn't speak. I dried my eyes on my sleeve. I imitated a sane person and calmly walked away.

Why should we suppose that Lou was anything but cheerful as she headed north? She was looking forward to giving her speech, which she rehearsed as she drove. The mission with which she'd been entrusted by Bonnet was as critical as any assignment she'd shared with Inge.

Bonnet had given her gas coupons. All her expenses were being paid. Her car, which she'd tuned up herself, was humming. She passed her old house, now deserted, and the convent school, where she paused to listen to the silence that had replaced the voices of girls at play. How far she'd exceeded the low expectations of her governess and her teachers!

There wasn't much traffic, but even so the trip took nine hours, and Lou was tired by the time she found the café where Hélène had arranged to meet. The sight of the women waving to her across the bar perked her up. There were seven, all young and attractive. Hélène was blond and extremely pretty.

Later it would be revealed that these women comprised the all-female Resistance network, code named She-Wolf, which operated throughout Brittany and Normandy and across the Channel. Led by the half-French, half-Scottish Hélène Michaux, who later settled in Great Britain and became a celebrated sculptor under her real name, Eileen Mitchell, the agents of She-Wolf were trained to kill, but only in emergencies or in self-defense.

A half dozen academic colleagues have written about this group. Each of these scholarly monographs, all with a feminist slant (what male academic would risk his career studying women, however courageous?) offers a slightly different take on the cadre's objectives, its achievements, and its uniquely nonhierarchical power structure.

The women had been informed about Lou when their contacts in Paris noted her long absences from the torture chambers and heard that she'd been sighted on the coast, asking questions. They put these facts together with the following nugget of information:

In a bar near the docks, a woman named Elise Becker used to sit alone at a table and talk to herself, or to anyone who would buy her a beer. She'd ramble about how it was her fault that the Germans breached the Maginot Line.

At that time she'd been living in the northeast with her husband, who dug ditches, poured cement, and finally left her for a prostitute younger than their daughter. He beat Elise when his government contract for additional work was canceled. Elise had complained about him, in detail, to a French woman who dressed like a man and her German girlfriend.

When the Germans invaded, Elise couldn't shake the feeling that she was to blame, despite the fact that her husband always accused her of having delusions of grandeur. She'd told the two women, the German and the French one, where the line ended. Her husband said the fortifications stopped where they stopped. A blind man could have found the gap.

No one paid attention to Elise. But one night a member of the She-Wolf group was at the next table, eavesdropping on a pair of suspected German agents, when she overheard Elise's story and recalled something about a female collaborator, a torturer and a spy who wore men's clothes and had been seen in the area.

Though Lou never knew it, she was famous again. The survivors of her brutal interrogations, Suzanne Dunois among others, had spread the word about who she was and what she was doing, giving speeches to right-wing bodybuilders and asking if anyone suspected the neighbors of harboring Jews or Brits, if any submarines had been seen off the coast, if anyone had noticed an enemy parachute landing.

Hélène Michaux had arrived in Calais a year before, claiming to have fled a Nazi official who'd tried to rape her in Saumur. She was pretty, so people believed her. She'd rented a house on the beach outside the ruined city. She ran on the sand and played tennis. The women in the tennis club urged her to invite Lou to speak, as did Hélène's comrades in She-Wolf and her other contacts in the Resistance.

Over drinks at the café, Hélène flirted with Lou and gazed at her throughout Lou's impassioned speech. Afterward, Hélène invited Lou to her seaside villa. She told Lou that she was an heiress, but in fact the house was paid for by the Resistance and used to shelter agents en route to join de Gaulle in London. Lou was charmed by the feminine decor. Even the bathtub was pink.

Lou extended her visit for two extra days. Hesitant to bother Bonnet, she decided to stay without his permission and return with information that would make him glad he'd sent her.

The Resistance wanted to be sure about Lou before taking action. One night, as Hélène and Lou gazed out at the ocean from Hélène's bedroom window, Hélène mentioned that some friends had seen boats landing on a beach down the coast. Hélène described the cove. Did Lou think they were smugglers? Probably, Lou told her, and kissed Hélène again.

They stayed awake making love and talking, exchanging stories from their lives—Lou's partial truths and whatever fictions Hélène invented. When Lou left, she promised to return when she could.

Two days later, the "smugglers' cove" was swarming with German soldiers. The British secret service was surprised that Lou hadn't been more circumspect.

Lou made several trips to Calais, each time submitting a list of expenses to Bonnet's office. Always she billed her employers for her hotel room, though she stayed at Hélène's.

So we see Lou embarking on one final ill-fated romance, a new love that, as new love often does, follows an old, self-destructive pattern. Once again Lou found herself involved with someone who was using her, deceiving her—and convincing her that she was loved.

Which of us has not fallen for a heartless automaton pretending to be a human? Normally, we condemn these liars, these two-faced cheaters. We despise it when, like Arlette, they sacrifice a trusting soul on the altar of greed and ambition, or when, like Inge, they play Mata Hari, faking infatuation to further some evil agenda.

But do we feel differently when we see Lou betrayed by someone on the side of the *good*, Lou tricked by a heroine trying to prevent Lou from harming innocent people? To prevent Lou from interfering with the Allies' plan to liberate Europe? Are we less upset when someone bends the rules if we agree with the person doing the bending?

Perhaps these speculations should be tabled for another time— ideally, for when *The Devil Drives* is discussed on one of the lively book shows so popular now on French TV.

Lou Villars was assassinated in early 1944, two months before D-Day. No one has ever taken credit or blame for her death. It seems almost certain who ordered her killing, though this information appears only in a Resistance memoir that has recently been called into question, and that for legal reasons I will not cite by author or title.

She was tried in absentia by the Raisin Noir network, a Resistance group based in Paris. It is assumed that Suzanne Dunois testified, though obviously no records were kept. An order of execution was issued, and several cells in Brittany, including the She-Wolf unit, were enlisted to arrange for the sentence to be carried out.

It has been a challenge to reconstruct the chain of events that led from Lou being a person whom the Resistance was monitoring to her being considered a serious threat, a bomb that had to be defused before she got back to Paris.

With D-Day so soon approaching, the Resistance must have had other concerns. It is possible they believed poor Elise Becker, whose story military historians would later find evidence to support. If so, the operatives might have welcomed the chance to take justice into their own hands and punish the traitor who'd not only delivered their country to the Germans but also worked for the Gestapo. If they waited until the war ended, she might escape, as many did, or she might have been tried and acquitted, as many were. There are those who deny that revenge, vigilantism, and assassination occurred on either side. But such is human nature.

My own theory, which readers will not find in any other study of the period, is that something convinced the Resistance that Lou must be neutralized at once. Knowing Lou's nature as I do, having allowed her—invited her!—to take up residence in my psyche, I can easily imagine the scene in which Lou, whose instincts were always sharper than her intellect, sensed that her passion for Hélène wasn't returned. Attuned by sad experience to any slackening of attention, Lou may have tried, as she often had, to rekindle her lover's interest by inventing boastful fantasies about her own importance.

She insisted she had secret information about the Allies' planned invasion. She told Hélène why she'd been sent to the coast, to collect the information Bonnet wanted.

We will never know if she was pretending, or if she really knew, exactly when and where the Allied invasion would occur.

It was not where the Germans thought! She'd obtained copies of secret maps. No, she hadn't brought them along! Did Hélène think she was stupid? She'd committed them to memory and would report back to her bosses. She cared too much about Hélène's safety to tell her what she'd learned.

Had Lou somehow intuited the truth about Hélène? In which case were Lou's extravagant claims an ingenious method of sealing her own doom, an elaborate form of suicide, of ending a life that had become too hopeless and sad?

Whether or not Lou sensed that Hélène was eager to contact her Resistance comrades, she couldn't help noticing that her friend seemed impatient for her to leave. Mulish with hurt and resentment, Lou rambled on about how, acting on classified information, she could still win the war for the Germans.

If only she'd kept her mouth shut! But it was already too late.

By the time Lou had driven a short distance from Hélène's house, calls had been made. Lou's route home, which clever Hélène thought to ask, had been mapped and transmitted.

It thrilled Lou to imagine that Hélène's curiosity about what roads she was planning to take was a sign that her lover wanted to keep her in mind, to imagine her on her journey, to know where she would be, and when. To keep her close at all times.

Hélène had said that she wanted to visualize Lou, every step of the way. She wanted to see her in her mind, as if they were still together.

And Hélène *did* think of Lou constantly, from then on, and for days. She saw her on the road, as we do, driving faster than she should have because a storm was brewing. Lou slowed down when it began to rain and she felt the road slip under her threadbare tires. Hélène pictured her driving through every drenched village and past the dark canals into which willows dipped their mustard-colored fronds.

Had the weather been balmier, might she have driven quickly enough to be out of the area before the sharpshooters had time to assemble? Would she have gone a different way? Or did she stick to her plan because it was the route she was traveling in Hélène's imagination.

I can say with some assurance that I know more than anyone alive about the career of Lou Villars. Yet despite everything I have learned in my research, despite my personal views about crime and punishment, justice and retribution, despite my knowledge of the carnage for which Lou was to blame, why does some part of me still hope that Lou enjoyed that final drive?

She had reason to be cheerful. She was in love. She was hoping this new romance might last. She liked her work, and more important, she was carrying out the Führer's will. When the Germans won and a new order was established, when the Reich gave France back to the French, she would be decorated with the honors she'd once expected to share with Inge.

Lou drove between rows of sycamore trees. A fine aerosol of rain moistened the earth and thickened the iridescent pinfeathers of early spring grass. What a long distance she had traveled since that trip with Papa to the convent! How far she had driven—a woman, alone, supporting herself, living and dressing the way she wished. She had so much to be proud of! Her best drives might still be ahead of her. There was no telling what might happen.

Lou was buoyant as she drove the winding stretch between Le Tronchet and Châteauneuf, a route that is still marked green—for its scenic beauty—on the Michelin road map. There was no reason to hurry. Soon she would be back in Paris, coping with the stresses of her job.

Not far from Abbeville, Lou stopped for a flock of sheep. Warm steam rose off their fragrant wool as they bleated and jostled one another. Normally impatient, Lou watched the sheep with affection, happy to see them so fat. Good French people would be eating lamb stew, French children drinking milk. She thought of a story Armand had told—how long ago that seemed!—about a driver hitting a flock of sheep and losing a race and dying.

Just as the last sheep crossed the road, Lou heard Armand's voice. Drive like you're driving the wounded over a muddy battleground pitted by bullets and shells. Each wasted instant, each idle second means that a soldier will die.

Lou stomped on the gas and took off.

Is it a sign of how drastically my work on this book has unhinged me that I seem to see her looking reproachfully at me, in her rearview mirror?

Half an hour beyond Rouen, two hay wagons were stuck, crisscrossed, blocking the road. Cursing, Lou swung out of the driver's seat and approached the carts. Their owners were nowhere in evidence. Perhaps they'd gone to get help.

Three sharpshooters stepped out of the woods and strafed Lou with bullets. Her killers kept shooting long after her riddled body lay still. Glossy pools of thick blood beaded the wet, black highway. Luckily for Lou's killers, the rain had gotten heavier, washing away the evidence even as it was created. They dragged her bleeding corpse over to her car, heaved her into the backseat, and moved the wagons off the road. Two of the assassins drove Lou's sedan to a secluded spot where they burned her beloved Rossignol with her body inside. No one would be the wiser. A war was going on.

It took Jean-Claude Bonnet a week to notice that Lou hadn't returned. A perfunctory investigation uncovered no evidence. It was conceivable that some harm might have befallen her, but it was equally likely that she had deserted and was waiting for the end of the war in some obscure town, under an assumed name. It hardly seemed worth the trouble to take local hostages and threaten to shoot them unless someone came forward with information about a cross-dressing lesbian torturer-spy whom the Nazis never acknowledged as having worked for them in the first place.

The Allies were about to invade. No one had time to think about Lou. No one missed her. No one mourned her. No one, until now.

Good-bye, poor Lou. Farewell cursed and lonely soul, sinning and sinned against. If there is a merciful God, perhaps your afterlife will be less painful than your tormented sojourn on earth.

Lou's bones lie unclaimed in an unmarked grave not far from where a superhighway scars the countryside. It is possible that her remains were moved to a landfill when the new road was constructed.

The Slaughterhouse, A Coda

I can easily imagine a publisher summoning me to his office to suggest that I cut most, if not all, of the preceding chapter. The only cut I would agree to (and which I have preemptively made) has been to remove the superfluous details of how I learned that Lou's last lover, Eileen Mitchell, was alive and well, an artist still working in her Sussex cottage.

I wrote Eileen Mitchell a friendly letter. My English, I should say,

is excellent. But I received no reply. By that point I was used to my in-
quiries going unanswered.

Eileen had to be at least eighty. I had no time to lose.

The trip cost more than I could afford. I decided to use Uncle
Emile's money. I could always claim it as a business expense in the
event my book made a profit.

It was my first time in the Chunnel. As we hurtled under the water, my jaw began to throb, a common reaction, I've heard. I rented a
car and, though I am not a confident driver—especially on the wrong
side of the road!—I found my way, without incident, to the famous
sculptor's "cottage." Perhaps I picked up, by osmosis, some of Lou's
self-assurance behind the wheel.

A young black woman greeted me, wearing a paint-speckled shirt
and jeans, and a bright green, red, and yellow ribbon tying back her
dreads. She was pretty but not very friendly, even slightly hostile.

I had forgotten to plan what I would say when I arrived. I suppose I
intended to tell the truth. I'm writing a book about Lou Villars. Could
I interview Miss Mitchell about her memories of Lou?

Would this girl even know who Lou *was*?

"May I help you?" she said. Clearly, she was in charge. Eileen's
young lover, I thought. Or was she her caretaker? My contacts had
been uncertain about the state of Eileen's health. I explained that I
was writing a book about women who had worked undercover for the
Allies in France.

The young woman seemed to be on the point of saying something,
then shrugged and motioned for me to follow her toward a barn behind the rather grand main house, definitely not a "cottage." I asked if
the barn was Eileen's studio.

I had seen a snapshot, taken years before, of the sculptor posed with
her work, enormous bronze castings of forest and jungle creatures,
powerful statues that were photographed and used in the fund-raising
campaigns of several international wildlife preservation foundations.

My guide shrugged again and kept walking.

It was indeed Eileen's studio. Her art was what I saw first. The barn looked like a slaughterhouse, crammed full of monumental sculptures in various mediums, all depicting the battered corpses of horses and cows. Some were whole, some hacked to pieces. There were stacks of equine heads, bovine offal, ropelike coils of oxtails.

"Isn't it lovely?" the young woman said.

Lovely was hardly the word that came to mind. But what word would have been better? I had suddenly lost all my English.

"Formidable," I said.

The young woman pointed at something. It took me a while to see Eileen sitting in the midst of the studio, on a low wooden stool. She didn't turn or rise to greet us, though she must have heard us come in. Was she thinking about her work? I was sorry to have disturbed her.

I said I could come back later, in an hour or two. My guide waved me on. She told me to walk around Eileen and stand very close, in front.

Eileen looked up but didn't appear to see me. Fragile as a songbird, she wore a lab technician's white coat. Her shell pink scalp was visible beneath her thin, uncombed hair. Her ruddy face was deeply creased. A ray of sun shining through a gap in the roof beams backlit a fringe of fur around her chin. Was this the beauty who had stolen Lou's heart—and arranged her execution?

Her blue eyes were milky as beach glass. Sad and sweetly apologetic, her gaze had turned inward, away from a world reduced to a source of confusion, embarrassment, and regret. Her smile was wobbly, uncertain. Did she recognize me from somewhere? The young woman said I was writing a book. Eileen nodded and smiled again.

What had I wanted to ask her? What was Lou really like? Did she talk about her life? What secrets did she tell you? Did she explain why she did what she did? Was any of your "love" real? That was the question Lou would have asked. Was I channeling my subject?

I knew that this was the end of my book. That my search for the causes of evil would end in this studio, confronted by the husk of a woman who had spent the end of her life making animal body parts.

I reached out and took Eileen's hands in mine. She seemed willing to allow this. I could feel her bones, her veins, her trembling fingers. And it gave me some comfort—encouragement, one might say—to know that I was holding the hands that had held the hands that Lou Villars had dipped so often in blood.

Lycée Jeanne d'Arc
Rouen, 2010

Paris
July 12, 2011

To the editors of *Libération*,

I can imagine you smiling as you pass around this letter and ask your colleagues at the newspaper, How often does *this* happen? How often does a little old lady write us to complain that a recent book review wasn't harsh *enough*? But given the passions still excited by the history of our nation's collaboration during World War II, perhaps I won't be the only reader to object to your June 10 review of *The Devil Drives: The Life of Lou Villars*, by Nathalie Dunois.

Perhaps my letter will be one of many addressing this travesty plucked from the garbage dump of our soulless, America-worshiping culture. Surely others will share my surprise that your long established, highly respected book section chose to review a volume that is, to begin with, self published by one of those new companies that will print anything its author has the euros to pay for.

The brief length at which the review was assigned indicates how seriously (not very) your editors took this distortion of a history that should not be exploited and degraded by the sexual fantasies and sloppy research of a "writer" who claims to be related to a surviving heroine of the Resistance. Is this what one gets for surviving?

Among the "facts" and theories your reviewer fails to challenge is the suggestion that my late husband, the world-famous photographer Gabor Tsenyi, *owed* Lou Villars a print of her portrait, the double portrait taken with her girlfriend at the time—his iconic "Lovers at the Chameleon Club, Paris 1932." And the "biographer" hints that his reluctance to hand over this valuable work of art was a sign of the self-involvement she imagines typical of male artists.

Possibly your reviewer said enough about the dithering '68er feminist mentality of seeking some psychoanalytical *theory* that might explain or even excuse the crimes that Lou Villars committed against France and the French people, before and during the war. And your critic should be commended for citing the *errors of fact* that are alone enough to discredit this abysmal book. Will your coverage increase the interest in this compendium of lies, and perhaps also its sales? I would never have heard of it, if not for your review.

Let me backtrack and state that the author, Nathalie Dunois, who purports to be my grand-niece, is not related to me. At all.

A few lines into her preface, I became alarmed when she described an apartment where she claims to have visited me, and which has no resemblance to anyplace I have ever lived. I never owned a "modernist" chair that children were forbidden to sit on. Are there no fact checkers left? That she calls my home "enviable" might have set off alarms.

The laziest photo researcher could have tracked down pictures of me and seen that I often wore sleeveless dresses, well into old age. Thanks to good luck and good heredity, my arms remained shapely and were never scarred during the sadomasochistic orgy the author describes taking place in the torture chambers where Lou inflicted so much pain on my Resistance comrades.

But not, as it happened, on me.

The mad biographer's claims could easily have been disproved by a publisher less interested in profiting from a salacious history of a cross-dressing Nazi lesbian spy, capitalizing on a name (mine) still remembered by a few as the heroine of a time that no one will discuss. The author's references to the secrecy that still surrounds this shameful era are the only points on which we agree.

To his credit, your critic mentions the "ill winds that continue to swirl around this vexed period in our history." I would have said "unceremoniously buried like a vampire that refuses to stay dead." Or "distorted in the carnival mirror of convenient lies and willful forgetting." But that is what *I* would have said. Let that pass. I have left instructions to insure that my own journals and written reflections on that time and these subjects will be destroyed when I die.

As I began the book, its author's remarks on this topic led me—
briefly!—to think I might find *some* of her work congenial. Though
I suppose my suspicions and yours should have been aroused by her
admission that she felt free to "embroider a bit, fill in gaps, invent dialogue, and make an occasional imaginative leap or informed guess
about what (her) subject would have thought and felt." One can only
speculate about the motives that inspired her to write a book that so
randomly mingles fact and fiction.

Judging from the personal evidence and the many distracting personal confessions, this Mlle. "Nathalie Dunois" was obviously trying
to add some drama, substance, and meaning to an otherwise lonely,
unfulfilled, and disappointing life as a provincial schoolteacher. She
admits this in her sad, if disingenuous, preface.

Perhaps it will demonstrate the purity of my intentions when I say
that, against the advice of friends and legal counsel, I have decided not
to press charges against my alleged "niece." That she has invented a
family connection should tell readers all they need to know about the
authenticity of her book. Is Dunois her real name? Has anyone looked
into that? I cannot think what she means when she says I refused to
help her write her "biography," since, until I read your review, I was
unaware that it existed.

But that is not why I am writing, or not entirely. I want to correct
two specific mistakes your reviewer cites as facts. Repeated enough,
they will *become* facts.

Mlle. Dunois writes that I accompanied Lou Villars in her search
for her mentally handicapped brother in a Paris asylum for children.
The writer admits there is no evidence of this unpleasant outing.

That is because it never happened. I never went with Lou Villars
to a mental hospital where she learned that her brother had died of
"powerful seizures." I would remember if I had. I cannot imagine why
any sane person would invent a story like that.

The second major error occurs in the chapter about Lou Villars's
work for the Gestapo.

Mlle. Dunois notes correctly that I was arrested after an incident at the notorious Chameleon Club and the escape of its owner,

Eva "Yvonne" Nagy. She notes that Lou Villars and I knew each other from before. Less correctly, she claims that Lou tortured me for hours.

As much as I would like to take credit for holding out long enough to give Yvonne Nagy time to reach the Spanish border, I must inform your readers that it wasn't like that.

I did know several heroic Resistants who *were* beaten and burned with a cigarette lighter by Lou, which was part of the terror I felt when she entered the interrogation chamber, dressed (as the author describes) in a white shirt, khaki pants, and a rubberized apron.

But when Lou looked at me, was she really seeing a vision from childhood, as the author suggests? My impression—but what do I know?—was that she recognized me at once.

She closed the door behind her.

Only someone who has been in my position can understand what I felt when a grin spread across Lou's face. She slapped me on the back, shook my hand, and said something like, Well, hadn't we gotten ourselves into a pickle? She asked how Gabor was. I said he was fine. Considering that his girlfriend had just been arrested.

Lou looked puzzled. Did she think I was making fun of her?

"Me," I explained, infusing the word with all the false friendliness I could muster.

Lou asked me to tell Gabor she'd acquired a print from a private collector, a Jew. At a reasonable price. One of Gabor's photos of her at the track, inspecting an engine before a race. She liked the picture very much! Better times, and so forth.

I remarked that life seemed to be agreeing with her. She hesitated, as if to make sure that she hadn't missed another insult.

She told me that now she was going to punch me in the nose. The blow would not be especially painful but would produce a lot of blood.

She struck me with her open palm. It stung, but not that much. Then she told me to yell as loud as I could. She said, "Scream, but don't ham it up. Someone is always listening."

No one who has not faced a nearly certain, protracted, and agonizing death can know what it is like to have one's life given back. With a snap of the fingers. Like that. Having since recovered from several serious illnesses, I can say that what happened to me that night in the rue Lauriston was something like, though not the same as, hearing goods news from a doctor. The killer changes his mind, drops the gun. The pistol doesn't go off.

Through the walls, I heard screaming. I listened and learned and did what my suffering comrades did, while Lou sat there and read the newspaper on which there were photos of Hitler and Maréchal Pétain. It took her ages to finish. Then she used the paper to mop up my blood and smear it all over my face. She crumpled the paper into a ball and tossed it in the corner.

Lou Villars left the room and returned with two German officers. She told them she had tried everything, but I wouldn't talk. They didn't think I looked messed-up enough, but they didn't care. This was about an incident in a nightclub. Somebody's pride had been hurt. I was glad they seemed to assume that having helped Yvonne escape was the extent of my work for the Resistance.

Perhaps Lou told them what to assume. They knew Lou had her reasons. They trusted her. Anyway, what was at stake? A Hungarian woman who ran a nightclub for cross-dressing male and female perverts?

One of Lou's bosses said that if Lou couldn't get me to talk, no one could. And then they let me go. More than a half century later, I still cannot believe it.

Though I am opposed to violence, I believe that Lou Villars deserved her fate, by which I mean her execution by the agents of the Resistance. Not only for the crimes she committed during the war but for facilitating the invasion. My blood too was on her hands, but no more than I needed to shed.

What I do know, and why I am writing to you, is what didn't happen. And those are the lies (I assume only two of many) that this Nathalie Dunois has written about me in her mendacious book with its cheap romance-novel title.

> Yours respectfully,
> Mme. Suzanne Tsenyi (born Dunois)

Postscript to the
Sixtieth Anniversary Edition
of Lionel Maine's *Make Yourself New*

BY ALTHEA MAINE

IN THE LOVELY sun-splashed house, high above the Oregon coast, where my grandfather spent his final years surrounded by beautiful young women, I became obsessed with taking his pulse. He suffered from a heart arrhythmia, and I'd been instructed to call his cardiologist if (to be honest, I was never quite sure what this meant) his heartbeat changed from its normal trippy staccato.

I was supposed to check his pulse in the morning and again in the evening. But every few hours I found myself reaching for his frail wrist and pressing my fingers into the sinewy hollow between the bones. My grandfather allowed this, extruding his arm from under the bedclothes with a look of beatific forbearance.

I waited for a signal, the flutter of blood, a hiccup, another bump, two faint beats, then several strong throbs in succession. Was there something sexual, even incestuous, about this intimate communication, my fingers probing for the secrets of his heart? Grandpa's "interns" seemed to think so, and they raised their perfect eyebrows. How could I have explained that when I took my grandfather's pulse, I imagined that I was feeling the pulse of a generation, the rhythm of his prose style, the syncopated jitterbug of his salad days in Paris?

By that point, Grandpa Lionel had some bizarre fixations. He was obsessed with *Carrie*, the horror film based on the Stephen King novel about the innocent, awkward teenager whom the bullying popular kids turn into a knife-wielding, flame-throwing engine of gory vengeance. In fact he was only interested in the final scene: Carrie is dead, but her bloodied arm rises up out of the ground, terrifying the penitent girl who has come to lay flowers on Carrie's grave.

This was in the old days of clunky VHS tapes. My grandfather used to say, "Rewind it. Play it again." No please, no thank you. Not Grandpa. There was always a young beauty nearby who was thrilled to do what he said. The honey girls, we called them, as they posed around the house, pretending to read Grandpa's books. He liked girls with long, shiny, straight hair: easy to find in those years.

It was no longer even faintly alarming when Carrie's arm punched its way out of the ground. It was much scarier to watch the tape rewind so her arm was sucked back under.

The grandchildren—myself, the daughter of the son Grandpa called little Walt in his books, along with my three stepsiblings, Rain, Jeremiah, and Max, the offspring of the kids he fathered in the 1960s and 1970s, with Alison and then with Lauren—thought Grandpa's mind could have stayed more focused if he'd been encouraged to do something more demanding than watching the end of a horror film.

But our cousin Alan argued that, given Grandpa's age (well into his nineties) and uncertain health, maybe it wasn't so bad if the guy wanted to watch someone coming back from the dead. Alan is a therapist, so the rest of us tended to listen, though later we had reason to wonder if he was any saner than anyone else. My theory is that we all inherited some rogue gene from Grandpa.

Anyway, we never argued with our grandfather, who loved us, I still believe. But he was first and finally his own creation and the center of that creation: the irrepressible, eccentric, reprobate bad-boy genius. We knew that he would rip us apart if we got on his bad side. If, for example, we so much as *mentioned* another writer besides Lionel Maine and possibly Rimbaud.

When we asked about his Paris years, he'd growl and say, "Who wants to hear those old stories?"

He did like telling a story about an evening he spent with Picasso, who, for reasons that became murkier over time, drew a sketch of a guillotine. Grandpa desperately wanted the drawing. But Picasso, that stingy bastard, wouldn't give it away.

We looked at each other and shook our heads. The guy had hung out with Picasso!

There was another story he liked to tell. It took place after the war. Apparently, he and some friends attended a reunion at the baroness Lily de Rossignol's château in the south of France, where some of them had taken refuge after Grandpa left Paris.

People still marveled about the champagnes they drank at that château. No one but the baroness could have procured those vintages during the war. Grandpa always said that one of the things he regretted about leaving France when he did was that he'd missed sipping those legendary champagnes right under the Nazis' noses.

By the time of their reunion, most of the guests were middle-aged. Some were older. Grandpa, for example. The oldest was Professor Tsenyi, the father of Grandpa's photographer friend Gabor. Gabor's ancient Papa had traveled to Provence from his home in Vienna, where he'd escaped from Hungary after the war. He still had a grin for his hostess and a wink for the sexy French girls.

Grandpa and Gabor went for a walk, mostly to get away from the baroness, who, after her wartime heroism, had reverted to her old habits of making scenes and bossing people around. At least that's how Grandpa told it. His books make it plain that he didn't like the baroness much.

Grandpa's former girlfriend Suzanne, who had recently married Gabor, distracted the baroness with conversation while the two men made their escape. According to Grandpa, that was the least of the sacrifices Suzanne made for her lucky husband.

The two old friends were strolling in the garden when Gabor grabbed Grandpa and whispered, Don't move! He pointed to a shadowy space between some lavender bushes.

In the gravel was a dragon with a bright green frog's head and a striped serpent's tail. It was alive and breathing. Its black eyes met theirs—and blinked.

Grandpa and Gabor hunkered down. It took them a while to

crouch because their knees were stiff. They had a good laugh about that. How old and creaky they'd grown. How had they managed to live so long? That was something they'd never expected.

The dragon turned out to be a snake that had swallowed a frog. *Half* swallowed a frog. The frog's head and front legs and the front of its body protruded from the snake's unhinged jaws. The snake couldn't finish digesting the frog, which was so fat that the snake couldn't move. So it was a standoff. Gabor and my grandpa could have watched forever, if they'd wanted.

It was too late to rescue the frog.

Gabor had his camera. He took a picture. A great one. According to Grandpa, it was always that way: truth and beauty flinging themselves in front of Gabor's lens.

Gabor told Grandpa, Take a look. You think only humans are cruel?

Grandpa knew that nature could be brutal. He also thought, but didn't say, that a snake swallowing a frog was not the same as what Gabor and Suzanne and the rest of Europe went through during the war—which Gabor seemed to be implying, in his cryptic Hungarian way. But who was Grandpa to tell Gabor what Europe had been through?

Grandpa didn't need to say anything. The two friends understood one another. In the hearts still beating beneath the wrinkles and frangible bones, they were still the two *young* (as Grandpa realized only then; at the time he'd felt old) guys who'd finished each other's sentences as they'd knocked around Paris looking for someone to buy them a drink.

Sitting up in his king-size bed, high above the Oregon shore, Grandpa asked one of the honey girls to bring him the massive volume of Gabor's photographs.

Like a litter of puppies, we jostled for position around the photo of a snake eating a frog.

I couldn't look at it very long. Grandpa picked up the remote.

Gabor was dead. They all were. Grandpa, the oldest, had outlived them all, except for Gabor's widow, Suzanne.

My grandfather loved her, all his life. Even when he was old, his eyes misted whenever he mentioned her name. But he made fun of her, quite cruelly, for the ferocity with which she guarded Gabor's estate.

In that glowing golden room, high above the Pacific Coast, the girls looked at the snake and the frog while Grandpa's attention drifted, and he watched and rewatched the end of his film.

One afternoon, while Grandpa napped, I played the tape all the way through. I had to keep the sound low, but I could follow the plot. I was curious as to why my grandfather was interested in the story of a pubescent girl so betrayed and humiliated by her classmates that she turns into a killer. It was an odd choice for Grandpa, who by that point mostly preferred romantic comedies, Katharine Hepburn and Spencer Tracy.

I rewound the tape and stopped it just before the only slightly romantic scene, the calm before the bloodbath. Carrie and her blond Adonis prom date are flirting at the school dance.

The next time Grandpa waved imperiously for me to turn on the VCR, I restarted the tape from that point. Carrie and the boyfriend flickered onto the screen.

Grandpa bellowed with animal rage. I practically vaulted across the room. I didn't dare to admit I'd done it.

I fast-forwarded to the end. Grandpa nodded and settled back in bed. I surrendered the remote. Grandpa played the tape backward and forward, making what I suppose you could call his own experimental movie.

Years later, I can still close my eyes and see Grandpa's harem gathered around his bed, poring over a photograph of a snake eating a frog, while my grandfather watched a bloody arm rise again and again from the grave, just when we in the audience are thinking that the murderous girl is dead and that the danger is over.

About the author

About the book

Insights,
Interviews
& More . . .

Read on

Meet Francine Prose

About the author

FRANCINE PROSE is the author of twenty works of fiction; her latest novel, *Lovers at the Chameleon Club, Paris 1932*, was a *New York Times* Bestseller. *A Changed Man* won the Dayton Literary Peace Prize, and *Blue Angel* was a finalist for the National Book Award. Her most recent works of nonfiction include the highly acclaimed *Anne Frank: The Book, The Life, The Afterlife* and the bestselling *Reading Like a Writer*. The recipient of numerous grants and honors, including a Guggenheim and a Fulbright, and a Director's Fellow at the Dorothy and Lewis B. Cullman Center for Scholars and Writers at the New York Public Library, Prose is a former president of PEN American Center and a member of the American Academy of Arts and Letters and the American Academy of Arts and Sciences. She lives in New York City. ∾

Author photograph © by Stephanie Berger

Behind the Book

Lovers at the Chameleon Club, Paris 1932 began with a Brassaï photograph I saw at a museum show in Washington. I was familiar with the photo, "Lesbian Couple at Le Monocle, 1932": a portrait of two women sitting at a table in a bar, one in a sparkly evening gown, the other in drag with short hair and a tuxedo. But the wall text said something I hadn't known, which was that the woman in the tuxedo, a professional athlete named Violette Morris, had worked for the Gestapo during the German occupation of Paris and had later been assassinated by the French Resistance.

A little research turned up an even more interesting story. Morris was an Olympic hopeful and a professional auto racer. When her license to compete as an athlete was revoked by the French government as punishment for being a public cross-dresser, Hitler somehow got wind of it and invited Morris to be his special guest at the 1936 Berlin Olympics. By the time she got back to France, she was not only spying for the Germans, but she was the person who told them where the Maginot Line ended—where they could breach the French defenses. During the occupation, she did indeed work for the Nazis and was killed by the resistance in 1944.

It was such an amazing story that I considered writing it as nonfiction, but I soon decided that I would have more liberty, and that my readers and I would have a lot more fun, if I wrote it as a ▶

3

novel. As the process went on, the novel became less linear, and about all sorts of things besides Violette Morris (in the novel named Lou Villars). Moving back twenty years from the date of her death, I found myself writing about Paris in the 1920s, and using several different voices. Gabor, the photographer, is writing letters home to his parents in Hungary, as did Brassai. An American, Lionel Maine, is writing a novel/memoir about expatriate life, a little like Henry Miller. There are several other faux-memoirs, some "published," some not, one by a baroness, one by Gabor's wife. And Lou's story comes to us in the form of a life history by her "biographer," Nathalie Dunois, a teacher at a regional high school, who cannot seem to separate her own life and her own problems from her subject's. Hitler and Picasso make cameo appearances.

Each person has his or her version of the truth about the bright and glorious days of Paris in the 1920s, the theatrical spectacle and intrigue of Berlin in the 1930s, and the darker era that began when those two worlds came together. As always, the novel ended in a very different place from that in which it began. I started off writing about a woman in a tuxedo and wound up writing about art, love, evil, money, auto racing, espionage, insomnia, seduction, and betrayal—and the way that history changes, depending on who tells it. ∾

A Conversation with Francine Prose

Original interview done with Stephenie Harrison and published on Bookpage.com in somewhat different form. Reprinted with permission from BookPage.

One thing that makes this novel so compelling is the masterful way you blend fact with fiction—it's not always clear exactly how much of the story is real and how much you have made up.

To be perfectly honest, by the time I got through writing the novel—five years—I was no longer precisely sure how much was "real" and how much I'd made up. Yes, history is a narrative, like fiction, but the one thing I wanted to avoid was what I mostly dislike about the sort of "historical fiction" that puts so much emphasis on period details that it detracts from the characters—who, I hope, are central in this novel. I see the book as a contemporary novel that happens to be set in the past.

From the title alone, it's made clear that sex and romance will play a large part in this story, but one of the really exciting things about this novel is its straightforward (and some might feel, quite modern) approach to sexuality and gender politics. Can you talk about where your inspiration for the Chameleon Club and its little coterie of outcasts and lovers came from? ▶

The inspiration came from a photo by the great Hungarian-French photographer Brassai and then a series of photos. Brassai took a lot of pictures at a club called Le Monocle in Paris. Most of its customers were cross-dressers, mostly women. Just lately, I was reading a biography of Jane Bowles, and I found out that during a trip to Paris she'd hung out at Le Monocle. That was very exciting to me: I hadn't known.

Villain or not, Lou Villars is really the star—she's complicated, confused, the antithesis of boring, and definitely an enigma. Perhaps most striking, in a book filled with so many voices, she's also the one main character who doesn't get to speak for herself. What was the motivation behind that decision?

Lou was by far the hardest character to write, and I tried writing her sections many different ways—first person, second person, in letters, etc., etc. And nothing quite worked. It wasn't until I hit upon the device of the "biography" that I was able to do it, partly because I was able to pass my problems along: my problems with, and confusions about, such a deeply conflicted and complex character became the biographer's problems. And her understanding of Lou helped me understand her.

As any book about World War II must, yours takes on the character of Hitler. What was it like to tackle such a prominent, infamous figure within the scope of fiction?

I can't tell you how much fun it was to write a dinner party scene that included Hitler, and to capture something about the way people describe being in his presence. There's a book called *Hitler's Table Talk*—a transcription of his dinner table monologues—that was very helpful. Hannah Arendt created an enduring controversy when she wrote about the banality of evil, but Hitler was a living example: profoundly evil, shockingly banal.

One particularly lovely passage is when Gabor, a photographer, talks about how he has cultivated his eye for detail by pounding

6

the pavement and increasing his likelihood of observing the miraculous. Is there a writer's corollary for those who attempt to capture the world through words rather than pictures?

Same process: pounding the pavement. You just keep looking at the world, overhearing, watching, and trying to figure things out.

There's something about the 1920s and 1930s—and definitely about Paris—that people today find endlessly romantic, even with the knowledge of what will historically follow. Why do you think that is?

So much was happening then—in art, in music, in writing. Just to list the artists at work during that period in Paris is stunning. People were finally freeing themselves from the restraints of the nineteenth century and trying to lead lives that were creative, interesting, adventurous, and rewarding.

If you could travel back in time to spend one decade in one city, when and where would you go and why?

Obviously, I'd like to have been in Paris in the 1920s and 1930s—that's partly why I had to write a novel in which I could imagine myself back there.

At one point in the novel, a character posits that each of us leads a double life. If this is indeed true, what two lives do you lead?

I'm a writer (being a novelist implies a certain amount of control) and a total slave to my beloved granddaughters.

What resources did you draw upon to write this book? For readers who are interested in learning more about Paris leading up to and during World War II, are there any books you would recommend?

I read a great deal and then forgot almost all of it. There are many fascinating memoirs of the period such as John Glassco's ▶

A Conversation with Francine Prose
(continued)

Memoirs of Montparnasse, as well as history books, especially about Paris between the wars and during the occupation. Many heroes and heroines of French Resistance have written memoirs. I watched Leni Riefenstahl's *Olympiad* for its footage of the Berlin Olympics and Marcel Ophuls's *The Sorrow and the Pity* for its marvelous portrayal of France during the war: the collaborationists and the resistance. Two of the most helpful books were *And the Show Went On* by Alan Riding and *Bad Faith* by Carmen Callil.

What are you currently working on?

I'm beginning to think about a new novel—and also writing a brief biography of Peggy Guggenheim, who knew many of the historical figures in my novel; I'm obviously not ready to let go of that time. ∽

Have You Read?
More by Francine Prose

MY NEW AMERICAN LIFE

Lula, a twenty-six-year-old Albanian woman living surreptitiously in New York City on an expiring tourist visa, hopes to make a better life for herself in America. When she lands a job caring for a rebellious high schooler in wealthy, suburban New Jersey, it seems that the American dream may finally be within reach. But things take a sinister turn when Lula's Albanian "brothers" show up in a black SUV to remind her that all Albanians are family—and that Lula's family has a very serious favor to ask.

Set in the aftermath of 9/11, *My New American Life* offers a biting and darkly humorous portrait of an era when dreams and ideals began to give way to cynicism, fear, and still-resonating questions about what it means to be an American.

ANNE FRANK:
THE BOOK, THE LIFE, THE AFTERLIFE

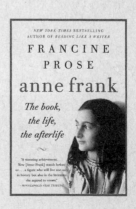

In June 1942, Anne Frank received a red-and-white-checked diary for her thirteenth birthday and began writing one of modern history's most compelling documents. Now, with the understanding one great writer has for another, Francine Prose deftly parses the artistry, ambition, and enduring influence of *The Diary of a Young Girl*.

Through close reading, Prose first

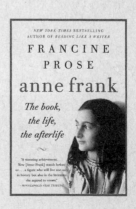

marvels at Frank's rare talent and careful editorial choices. Prose then investigates the diary's afterlife: the obstacles Otto Frank faced in publishing his daughter's words; the controversy surrounding its Broadway and film adaptations; the claims of conspiracy theorists who have cried fraud; and the rewards and challenges of teaching one of the world's most read—and banned—books.

GOLDENGROVE

At the center of Francine Prose's profoundly moving novel is a young girl facing the consequences of sudden loss after the death of her sister. As her parents drift toward their own risky consolations, thirteen-year-old Nico is left alone to grope toward understanding and clarity—and to fall into a seductive, dangerous relationship with her sister's enigmatic boyfriend.

Over one haunted summer, Nico must face that life-changing moment when children realize their parents can no longer help them. But for all the darkness at the novel's heart, the narrative itself is radiant with the lightness of summer, charged by the restless sexual tension of teenage life.

READING LIKE A WRITER

Long before there were creative-writing workshops and degrees, how did aspiring writers learn to write? By reading the work of their predecessors and contemporaries, says Francine Prose.

In *Reading Like a Writer*, Prose invites you to take a guided tour of the tools and the tricks of the masters. She reads the work of the very best writers—Dostoyevsky, Flaubert, Kafka, Austen, Dickens, Woolf, Chekhov—and discovers why these writers endure. She looks to John Le Carré for a lesson in how to advance plot through dialogue, to Flannery O'Connor for the cunning use of the telling detail, and to James Joyce and Katherine Mansfield who offer clever examples of how to employ gesture to create character. She cautions readers to slow down and pay attention to words, the raw material out of which literature is crafted. Written with passion, humor, and wisdom, *Reading Like a Writer* will inspire readers to return to literature with a fresh eye and an eager heart.

A CHANGED MAN

What is charismatic Holocaust survivor Meyer Maslow to think when a rough-looking young neo-Nazi named Vincent Nolan walks into the Manhattan office of Maslow's human rights foundation and declares that he wants to "save guys like me from becoming guys like me"? As Vincent gradually turns into the sort of person who might actually be able to do this, he also transforms those around him: Meyer Maslow, who fears heroism has become a desk job; the foundation's dedicated fund-raiser, Bonnie Kalen, an appealingly vulnerable divorced single mother; and even Bonnie's teenage son.

Francine Prose's *A Changed Man* is a darkly comic and masterfully inventive novel that poses essential questions about human nature, morality, and the capacity for personal reinvention.

BLUE ANGEL

It has been years since Swenson, a professor in a New England creative-writing program, has published a novel. It's been even longer since any of his students have shown promise. Enter Angela Argo, a pierced, tattooed student with a rare talent for writing. Angela is just the thing Swenson needs. And, better yet, she wants his help. But, as we all know, the road to hell is paved with good intentions . . .

Deliciously risqué, *Blue Angel* is a withering take on today's academic mores and a scathing tale that vividly shows what can happen when academic politics collides with political correctness.

CARAVAGGIO: PAINTER OF MIRACLES

In *Caravaggio*, Francine Prose offers an enthralling account of the life and work of one of the greatest painters of all time. Called "racy, intensely imagined, and highly readable" by the *New York Times Book Review*, *Caravaggio* includes eight pages of color illustrations and is sure to appeal to art enthusiasts interested in one of history's true innovators. *Caravaggio* is another engaging entry in the HarperCollins's "Eminent Lives"

series of biographies by distinguished
authors on canonical figures.

THE LIVES OF THE MUSES:
NINE WOMEN AND THE ARTISTS
THEY INSPIRED

All loved, and were loved by, their artists,
and inspired them with an intensity of
emotion akin to Eros. In this brilliant,
wry, and provocative book, Francine
Prose explores the complex relationship
between the artist and his muse. In
so doing, she illuminates with great
sensitivity and intelligence the elusive
emotional wellsprings of the creative
process.

THE GLORIOUS ONES: A NOVEL

The Glorious Ones travel the length and
breadth of seventeenth-century Italy,
playing commedia dell'arte in the streets
and palaces with equal vigor. Founded
by the ingenious madman Flamino
Scala, the small company of players
endures kidnappings and passionate
affairs, cabals, riots, disgrace—all
manner of triumph and hardship.
Pantalone the miser, sunny Armanda
the dwarf, gossip-loving Columbina,
and evil-minded Brighella view their
myriad shared adventures through
markedly different eyes. Yet not one
of them is prepared for the strange
twisting of the road brought about
by the mysterious arrival of Isabella
Andreini, who has come to direct the
wayward troupe.

Discover great authors,
exclusive offers, and more
at hc.com.